TRITAN EVOLUTION

A TRITAN EVOLUTION COLLECTION, BOOKS 1-3

MYRA DANVERS

RAVENOUS INNOCENCE

TRITAN EVOLUTION, BOOK I

FOREWORD

Make sure you sign up for Myra's Newsletter so you never miss sexy NSFW art, free things, exclusive deals, and loads of other cool shit you do not want to miss...

Sign up for Myra's Newsletter today!

https://myradanvers.com/mailing-list/

*For my dickbag family members who've never let me finish a
single effin' sentence in my whole life.
Here's a whole book full of 'em, ya turds!
(I wouldn't change a single one of you.)*

*And to Addison Cain, without whom I would still be in
revision hell. Thank you, oh Alpha my Alpha.*

A note from the Author

This is book one in the series, *Tritan Evolution*. It is not to be confused with the series called *The Last Tritan*, though it was previously named that. There's an explanation coming, and I'm going to try to make it as straightforward as I can. For a little more clarity, flip back once to see a breakdown of my books in their respective series.

I cut my authorling teeth in a weird little corner of the internet called Literotica, where free dirty stories go to flourish or die, based on the reception from what can be accurately and fairly called a snake pit of anonymous readers. Brutal honesty, in exchange for free stories.

The Last Tritan—in its original form—dominated the top ten of the top fifteen spots in Literotica's Hall of Fame for the category I was listed in. Which is absolutely a humble brag, but I also worked really hard to get there and I'll never forget how I got my start. I had ambition that went beyond publishing free stories, and it wasn't long before I took the whole thing down and rewrote it.

The resulting story (which begins with <u>this</u> book, *Ravenous Innocence: Tritan Evolution, book I*) is a thing I am deeply proud of. I learned so much from rewriting Tritan, and I don't regret the time I took to make sure I knew my craft.

But...

For the people who read the first, raw version of Mila and Asher... there was something bitter sweet about losing the bulk of the original story to the editing bin. I've been dodging requests to release the original for years, until one day... I realized that the two versions of Tritan are so different from each other that they can exist on the same bookshelf without one smothering the other.

So this is it. The edited version of Tritan. More mature, same character names and places, but utterly different than its predecessor, *Flame to Frost, The Last Tritan, Book I.*

They can be read separately, as they are essentially very different stories that merely share similar elements.

Thank you, and enjoy!

I wasn't supposed to be here.

Wasn't allowed to walk amongst my fellow citizens, enjoying the beautiful, sunny day. I'd been forbidden to stroll through the over-crowded market, unattended and unprotected. To do as I wished without the express permission of my father—and the accompanying escort —was to invite dire, world-altering consequences.

It wasn't safe.

I smiled, soaking up the sun and watched a jewelry merchant hawk his wares. Watched as he snared the attention of a tall, willowy woman, seizing her elbow before she could pass his display. Tugging, he pulled her into the shade beneath his tent and the flapping azure awning, thumb stroking the pale skin of her upper arm. Directing her gaze to follow a trinket with his free hand, he bedazzled her with glittering stones and polished silver that danced in the shadowed half-light.

I pressed my palm to the pendant perched on my breastbone, torn. As of yet, I hadn't actually done anything deserving of consequences. Had, in fact, done nothing but watch, enthralled by the market's chaos. Thrilled by the colors and scents of the Tritan people, I watched from the sidelines. Pretending I was just another face in a sea of silver-blonde, Tritan heads, to whom words like 'consequences' and 'unsafe' did not apply.

But I wasn't one of them, blood or not.

My fingers tightened around my pendant, considering as the precious, ugly stone glittered in the sun, tossing distinct shades of blue, green, and purple onto the street before me. Simply being here was a risk to everything my father and I had sacrificed over the years, surrounded by the crush of unsuspecting masses, each more sightless than the last. Most unable to sense the ki burning thick and sweet in the air. That such a power could go unnoticed by so many was a blessed curse from the Goddess herself, drowning me in the temptation to reach out and touch them... to blend in. To taste the living flames of their ki and know *normal*. To *be* normal, if only for a few stolen moments.

I clenched my fist, letting the tarnished family heirloom bite the meat of my palm. At once concealing the scatter of blues, greens, and purples before they were recognized, and letting the stone drink deep of my life force. It feasted with greedy abandon, starving for ki willingly given. Storing my excess in its stony, cold heart in return for blessed, numbing calm.

A service only the Glaith could provide to one such as me.

I shuddered, drained, for now, but conflicted. There wouldn't be another chance as perfect as this, what with my father occupied by some important State Senate meeting and my target already marked. In fact, everyone who might take an interest in my actions was in that meeting. The rest, the Priestesses with their keen ki-sense, were locked away, deep in the heart of the temple.

No one would recognize me here. None could sense what I really was beneath the Glaith.

And yet, I hesitated, eyes fixed to the merchant conducting his business. Fingers tight about my pendant, keeping myself firmly in check. My father had given *everything* to keep me free. Free to live and make mistakes. It was a debt I could never even begin to repay, and yet, in this, he was *wrong*. The man was blinded by his need to protect and coddle. Couldn't see the raw potential simmering in my veins... desperate to be set loose...

I grinned.

If it were possible to harness my birthright, I alone would decide how it would be used. Not my beloved father. Not a faceless, tyrannical High Priestess, moored in tradition and secrets, who would claim me for the temple simply because of what I was.

Me.

Alone.

And if I failed? Consequences were only for those foolish or weak enough to get caught.

Finished with his sale, the merchant kissed his customer's wrist and tucked a handful of coins into his purse, setting pale eyes to scan for his next conquest before he'd finished with the last.

This was it, then. My moment. I let the pendant fall. Let it settle above my shift, separating its numbing influence from my skin and leaving myself vulnerable—for in its absence, the rest washed in.

Ki.

My accursed birthright.

Awareness burst inside my skull. The ki of every man and woman in the market—of Tritan blood or otherwise—called to me, whispering their secrets all at once. Begging me to reach out and touch, to drink until I'd filled the bottomless, ravenous void. There was no bracing for it. No way to prepare for the kiss of the Divine. And here, in an overcrowded market separate from the Glaith for the first time in four years, I swayed, staggering under the weight of their ki. Knuckles white and jaw slack, suffering an endless, blazing inferno writhing just out of reach, I struggled to master it before it swallowed me whole.

The stone in my pendant was warm now, working to consume the flames I'd fed it, to store the ki I couldn't contain alone. I could feel the heat through my shift, knew it would need time to cool before I could feed it again, lest it overheat and sear my skin. Four years, my pendant of Glaith had protected me, shielding me from any consequences my existence might provoke. Numbing.

Too long.

Knuckles white, I forced the whispers back, straining to bank the flames of their ki without reaching for the Glaith. And then, taking even, measured steps, I merged with the busy foot-traffic, letting my country-folk carry me toward the jewelry merchant. On my lips, a practiced smile. Careful to evade skin-to-skin contact with the press of the crowd, I focused on the pendant swinging between my breasts. Glaith was the only guard and escort I needed. A safety net giving me permission to meet the merchant's eye and dance with a viper.

"Goddess be with us," the merchant trilled, stepping into my path. "Such a beautiful young lady! My dear, you simply glow with *youth!* Come," he said, butter-soft fingers finding purchase on my elbow, guiding and hustling me into his shaded tent. "I have just the thing to complement those striking eyes."

I blinked, straining *not* to look at his fingers upon my skin. Swallowing a groan as his ki blazed through me, my focus narrowed to him and little else. Both a relief from the roar of the crowd and a painful, intimate burden, but I allowed him to lead me into the shadows. Listening to his ki whisper tales of false smiles and sharp instincts as that thumb traced a trusted pattern on my skin.

"It's a pleasure to make your acquaintance, miss..."

Insincerity oozed through my skin, and I knew he didn't care. Knew it was a tactic to lure me into a false trust so he could relieve me of more coin. But my first name held no power, gave him nothing that could bring my father into this or lead the merchant to realize who I was, if my efforts here went sideways. So I smiled, and said, "Mila," tapping two fingers to my temple. My tone light. Carefree.

"Mila," he breathed, returning the gesture of respect. "Beautiful name for a beautiful girl, but"—he hooked a single, slender finger beneath the pendant's chain, *tsking*—"oh, no. No no *no!* This simply won't do. I cannot bear such an outdated, battered piece distracting from your radiance, my dearest Mila."

"It—" I cleared my throat, taking a tiny conservative sip of his ki. Looking for deception, only to find genuine distaste for an outdated, battered piece worth more than everything else in his shop combined. "It was my mother's," I said, letting him taste old sorrows.

The grip on my elbow tightened, light eyes widening. "Ah. Well. The Goddess can be cruel, for all her wisdom. I'm so sorry for your loss, child. Come," he said, fluttering bejeweled fingers. "Sit. I have the perfect piece to soothe such pain. Why don't you take your dear mother's pendant off, and I'll have it cleaned? Perhaps we can replace the jewel in the center. How about a nice sapphire to match your eyes, hmm? I happen to have a selection of loose stones for just such an occasion."

Pushing my ki through the pad of his dewy thumb, I trapped his hand on my elbow and directed his attention away from my pendant. Toward the case I'd seen a week prior while perusing the markets with my father, for I'd already chosen what I'd be leaving with today. "You are too kind, sir, but I couldn't. I haven't enough coin to—"

"Nonsense," he breathed, pulling me deeper into the

tent. Something akin to fatherly instinct lit up my senses when he dropped the hyper-cheerful sales pitch and said, "Everything is negotiable, darling. *Everything*. Remember that lesson, and you'll do well in life."

A tentative, fragile smile spread across my lips, no less effective for all that I'd rehearsed. "Thank you."

"I won't hear it," he said, patting the back of my hand. Each pat landed with a burst of ki behind my eyelids. Dazzling. Enthralling. "Now let's find the piece with 'Mila' written on it."

I smothered the grin begging to be set free, allowing him to guide me around the tiny shop, hand in hand. Flitting from one display to the next, the merchant remained unaware as I slid beneath his skin. Drinking just a little *deeper* to learn him from the inside out, while he filled my every cell with power and confidence.

I'd been *right*.

This was right, this Divinity thick in my blood was *mine*.

The light shifted, signaling the arrival of another patron, but I didn't spare the newcomer a glance, instead driving my merchant to stop before a display of brooches. It took little more than a tiny *push* to make it his idea to open the case.

"Oh, darling, *yes*. This is it." He lifted the brooch, letting it catch the gloomy half-light. "It's far from the most valuable piece in my collection, but it was made for you. I feel it deep in my bones."

Did he now? The Glaith hung heavy about my neck, the most innocent expression I'd rehearsed fixed to my lips. "It's beautiful," I whispered, inspecting the savage likeness of a snarling wildcat with tiny amber eyes.

"Isn't it? But I'm selfish." He winked. "I simply

cannot go another minute without seeing it against your skin, my dear."

I returned his smile, tilting my chin back as he pinned it to my shift. And yet, my fingers lingered upon his skin, maintaining the connection with that which had become mine. "Thank you," I breathed, meeting his eye. Watching his pupils dilate. "It's beautiful. It must also be... expensive?"

The merchant blinked, pulse pounding at the base of his throat, unable to tear his eyes from mine. Unwilling, for he too, could taste the Divine. Through me. "Ex-Expensive, yes. Yes. But for you," he said, licking lips gone dry, "I'm happy to see it go."

What would it hurt to take just a little... *more?* To drink just a little deeper from my merchant and celebrate this tiny victory? My fingers tightened on his wrist, mouth watering, hungering for his ki. He wouldn't notice the absence, not really. How could he miss what he couldn't sense? What he'd *never* sense, for he was not of the Blood.

"A fine choice," came a voice from behind, making me jump. "Not sure it's worth the risk, but a fine choice, nonetheless."

Heat rushed to my cheeks, fingers jerking free of the merchant on a startled gasp. Fist crackling with stolen ki, I spun to face the fool who dared disturb me.

He caught my wrist, standing too close, fingers rough and warm—but utterly devoid of ki.

I blinked.

Blinked again, turning the full strength of my senses upon him. Nothing. Not a lick or whisper of ki. "Impossible," I breathed, meeting eyes darker than pitch, trying to wrap my head around the contradiction standing before me. Every living thing had ki to some degree, for without it we were nothing but fuel for the next generation. And yet this man, obviously so full of life, possessed nothing of the sort. Unless...

My eyes dropped to his neck, absent a chain that might have swung with a pendant like mine. Dressed in formal black and gold, dark hair cropped close and kept neat, the man had the gall to smirk at me. Clean, sharp jaw framing a handsome face, his were *not* the features I was accustomed to seeing. Too dark, build too big to be of Tritan blood. My gaze dropped further still, to the hand on my wrist—and the chunky, masculine ring sitting proud on his pinky finger.

Glaith.

I knew without seeing those distinct blue, green, and purple shadows scattering the light. Knew what the ugly stone set in a foreign family crest meant. But... "Impossible," I said again, though this time it was a dry squeak. This time, I pulled away, for he *couldn't* be what I thought he was. The Glaith was coveted by Tritan's *Priestesses* for its responsive reactions to ki. This *man* couldn't possibly know what his ring was truly worth.

It was a coincidence, nothing more.

Trying to step back, I tucked my pendant beneath my shift, reuniting the warm stone with my skin, just in case. When the Glaith touched my breastbone, it pushed everything else out, deadening my forbidden senses once more. Turning my knees to water as it swallowed the Divine.

"The brooch," he said, ignoring my attempt to free myself from his grasp, though those dark eyes tracked my every movement. Tracing the pendant beneath my shirt. "How much?"

The merchant blinked, still under my sway even without my touch on his skin or my ki thick in his veins. "F-For the lady, nothing. A gift, sir."

"Take your hand off—"

"Nonsense," the intruder returned, fingers tightening on my wrist. Near to bruising with the unspoken warning. "You have a living to make. To earn nothing from an item of such fine quality is a crime where I come from."

I bristled with the implication, spluttering, the reprimand plain enough.

"Well," the merchant breathed, each passing moment pulling him further from my influence. "If you insist—"

"I do." The intruder dropped a few foreign coins into the merchant's outstretched hand. "Besides," he continued, full lips twitching when he met my bewildered scowl once more, "it's my pleasure to part with the coin if it'll buy me a few moments of the lady's time."

I wrenched my wrist free at last, pressing a trembling hand to my throat. "Do I look like a commodity?"

He turned those obsidian eyes down at me, invading my space with a single step. "You'll have to excuse the presumption, but I rather think you'd prefer if I *didn't* say what I think you are."

"And I think *you'll* excuse my rudeness, but I don't care what you think I am—"

"Asher. Captain Asher Rawlings of His Majesty's Imperial Army."

A Caledonian.

The heat rushed from my cheeks, taking my breath with it.

A Caledonian. Goddess, with all my power, how could I have been so bloody stupid? So blind?

I swallowed the bubble rising at the back of my throat, and said, "Right. Well, Captain Asher Rawlings of His Majesty's Imperial Army, I don't care what you think I am. Because whatever it is, I can assure you, you're wrong."

Asher hummed, low at the back of his throat. Inky eyes glittering with something I couldn't name.

And then, without speaking another word or breaking eye contact, he removed his ring.

2

———

An Elite.

Not just a ranking Imperial soldier, but a full-blooded, Caledonian Elite. It wasn't the formal black and gold uniform, the dark hair and eyes, or the tanned, bronze skin that gave it away. No. It was his ki.

Brilliant. Blinding. *Beautiful.*

So much *more* than anything I'd ever felt before. Next to him, the merchant was nothing. A blip of empty space, forgotten as soon as my gaze moved away. This man, this Elite was impossible and wrong, for I'd heard tales of the Imperial ki-wielders, but nothing in working memory could match the fire burning through my veins. My blood. More powerful than anything I'd ever sensed, his ki breezed past the Glaith's protection. Stunning me into complete stillness with nothing more than his touch.

My head fell back as a set of large, calloused hands landed on the bare skin of my shoulders. Steadying me.

Goddess, his touch! His was *not* a secret whisper

beckoning me closer, but a primal demand that sent power surging through my veins, pendant be damned.

"H-How?" I breathed.

He shook his head, lips tight, eyes fixed to my face as he jerked his chin toward the exit. "A word? In private?"

The breath leaked from my lungs in a single, slow exhale. "A... word?" I returned, blinking, ensnared by his foreign, inky gaze. Such power! It called to me, even through the Glaith, setting my skin ablaze. Urging me to toss years of caution into the flames. So *beautiful...*

"Come," he said, and—point made—returned the ring to his smallest finger.

A tiny, fractured sound burst from my lips at the loss and the ensuing wash of numbing cold, and I stumbled forward, reaching. "Wait—"

The intruder turned without answer, pulling me from the tent as if he had any right to touch me, let alone direct where I went. But... I didn't fight like I might have. Like I *should* have. Didn't resist his touch on my skin.

I *relished* it.

"Thank you, sir," the merchant trilled. "It's been a pleasure to do business with one of the Empire's finest." He waved, baring a golden tooth and glossy smile, his pockets heavy with Caledonian gold. So far removed from my influence that his fatherly instincts didn't seem to mind me being pulled from the tent by a man who thought he could buy my time.

Without a backward glance, the captain steered me through the crowd of my country-folk with a rough hand on my upper arm. Dark eyes flicking from face to face. Ceaseless. Vigilant.

Sweat bloomed along my hairline as Tritans made

way for the dark-haired foreigner, giving me a moment to inspect the broad cut of his shoulders. Long, lean legs that screamed of strength and health. Deaf and blind to the sweltering masses going about their business. My every available sense fixed to *him* and the ki I could no longer feel.

And yet, that sweet taste lingered upon my skin.

More.

I *needed* more.

If I could just reach out and touch it again... Goddess, what would it feel like *without* the Glaith between us? Skin to skin.

"Do you have any idea how lucky you are?" the captain hissed, hustling me into some dark little corner between two buildings. He shook his head, fingers tightening on my bicep. "If one of the others had found you first..."

I blinked, left hand moving to the pendant of Glaith about my neck, eyes never leaving his face.

"To risk revealing yourself for the sake of a trinket," he snorted, dark eyes flicking over my shoulder, watching a shadow pass the mouth of the alley. "Stupid. So bloody stupid."

The insult prickled my skin, but I took a step toward him and thumbed the clasp securing the pendant around my neck. So... savage... so *raw*. I just wanted to touch it...

"You're lucky I'm the only one who can sense you," he continued, uttering a breathless laugh, turning dark eyes down once more. Pinning my soul to the back of my spine.

Skin to skin...

The Glaith slipped from lax fingers, clinking and

clattering on the cobbled street. Well and truly separate for the first time in four years, my ki-sense unfurled great dark wings behind my ribs.

"*What is wrong with you?*" he hissed, stooping to recover my pendant. Going to his knees in the cramped alley.

Eyes fixed to the crown of dark hair bowed before me, the entire population of the market made itself known. Men and women, each with varying degrees of health, emotional spectrums, and available ki. So much information. Flooding my senses with the brilliant pulse of ki, burning me from the inside out.

But I swallowed it down, for next to him, they were worthless. Utterly eclipsed by the mere memory of the only one I *couldn't* sense. Somehow, *incredibly,* blocking my efforts to break through his Glaith and drink until I couldn't.

"Did you hear me? You are a beacon without this pendant, girl." The stone atop his finger caught a beam of sunlight between the passing shadows of the Tritan civilians outside the mouth of the alley, throwing off the Glaith's trinity of colors as he knelt before me.

My eyes fell, landing on his ring.

Skin to skin...

I smiled.

"I felt it the instant you took it off." He jangled my pendant, making it dance. "Felt you clear across the market." He stood, towering above me once more. "Even now, your ki is..."

Meeting that dark gaze, I placed my palm on his chest. Fingers splayed. Trying to turn his heat into fire before I withered in the cold without it.

"What..." He shook his head. "What are you?"

"Take off your ring and find out."

Eyes narrowed, he lifted his finger, letting my pendant dangle in the tight space between us. "No."

But I would *not* be denied. "Have you ever sensed another like me?" I pushed him back, holding him with the weight of my palm. "Can you imagine what it would feel like? Without the Glaith?"

Skin to skin...

He shook his head, brows furrowed.

"You have ki I've never tasted before, Captain Rawlings," I breathed, heart pounding in my ears, close enough to see the darker ring of his pupil. To watch it dilate as he stared down at me. Shadows from the street flicking over us both. "I just want to touch it. Just for a moment."

Silent, he said nothing. Did nothing but breathe. Watching me.

And because silence wasn't a 'no', I reached for his hand, thumb tracing the stony edge of his ring. Feeling the distant sparkle of numbness laced with something... wild. Something burning just out of sight. Trembling, I tugged, and for a moment his fist refused me. Kept the ring secure.

"Please? Just for a moment."

He exhaled, nostrils flared. Pupils blown out. Allowing the ring to slide off his finger for the second time before the sun had risen to its full height. Swinging from my index finger, the Glaith lost its power over us.

With no warning, awareness of him exploded behind my eyes, ki searing everything it touched.

Back arched, a scream died in my throat as I tried to deal with the surge. Tried to cope with my skin touching his, and nothing between us. Every muscle tight with effort, blind to everything but the ki ravaging me from within.

He was hiding an impossible secret—I knew it the moment he faltered, echoing my shock, lips parting on a silent gasp. I knew it even before his nostrils flared, eyes wide. I knew it before his ki-sense whirled through my system and the link between us took root, twitching with a living power all its own.

I knew it, because I *felt* him.

Blood to Blood.

A young man in the prime of his life. Powerful. Elite. Raw and savage, yet braced by an iron fist of control I simply did not possess. Blood surged through his veins as his ki whipped through me. Touching, learning me in the same way I now knew him.

"What—" He cursed, strong fingers flexing, crushing me to his chest. "What *are* you?"

My knees wobbled, but I didn't give voice to the answer he already knew. Head spinning with molten waves of stone and wind, reducing me to a gasping, wide-eyed fool.

Too much! Goddess, it was too much!

I couldn't contain this! I needed—

I reached for my Glaith and came up short, fingernails scraping my breastbone, desperate for somewhere to dump the excess before I forgot why I should care. Needing something to distract from this impossible Caledonian Elite. And when I could not speak, lost as I was, he pulled me closer.

Impossibly strong, inside and out.

"What are you?"

I bared my teeth, refusing to be outdone. "You're..." I swallowed the sopping wet ashes powdering the back of my tongue, unsure if they existed outside of my over-wrought brain or not. "You're Elite. Such power—it's reserved for the Goddess' chosen few..." A tremor rippled through me... his eyes... so dark. Begging me to tip forward. To fall into their depths and drink from the Void itself. "You shouldn't..." Lifting trembling hand, I traced the stubble on his chin with my forefinger, gasping at the ki that sparkled between us. "Impossible."

A low groan rumbled in his throat, and he swallowed, catching my wrist in a much larger hand. For a long moment, he simply stared down at me, but when my tongue darted out to wet lips dried by searing winds of ki and living shadows, something in him snapped. I felt it happen. Even before he pressed his lips to mine, I felt it.

Warm and soft, his kiss spoke of the forbidden. The impossible. Making my core clench with unnatural speed and fervor as ki whirled between us. Sending blood surging in delicate tissue. All around us. Invisible to the hoards of sightless mundane going about their business a scant few feet away, where only their shades could see us. The scrape of a day-old beard dragged a splintered groan from my chest, and, hands slipping down my back, he seized the taut globes of my bottom. Spreading me.

Pulling me closer.

Would that he could drag me inside his skin, where I could drink him dry and soothe this blessed, painful ache.

His teeth traced my lower lip, filling my lungs with breath and heated ki, pressing a thick bulge against my belly.

I gasped, drinking him in, demanding more. Gorging until my every cell was filled to bursting. Drawing on him as heavily as I drew upon his lips. *Needing* it. More. There would never be enough.

A puff of breath warmed my cheek when he twisted, breaking away from my lips with a curse, his fingers bunching the fabric of my shift. Inching it indecently high. But he drew back, setting his forehead against mine. Petting my hair back with calloused hands. Obsidian eyes concealed behind scrunched eyelids, labored breath leaving my skin damp. "God, the taste of you, girl." He released my bottom and cupped the back of my neck, forcing me to still. "What are you?"

"I'm—" my voice cracked, and I cleared my throat, blinking as the world settled around us. Dazed, I squinted up at the man, admiring the rugged, handsome features so different to my own. Alien. Bronzed skin, muscular frame, dark hair and darker eyes— everything I wasn't.

A *Caledonian*.

Kissing a Caledonian Elite in public? Had I lost my damned mind? My father would...

Nothing.

My father wasn't here. And I hadn't had enough. Not now. Not ever.

I buried my fist in his hair, pulling him back. Driven by instinct I didn't recognize as my own. By a needy itch below the skin, the likes of which I'd never felt before. Before *him*.

"Wait—" he gasped against my lips, capturing my wrist. And then, marshaling every last drop of willpower *either* of us possessed, he folded my fingers about his ring. Pressing his Glaith into the palm of my hand.

A squeal tore free of my lungs as the Glaith stole it. Stole everything I'd never known I needed, slapping me with a wash of freezing numb I hadn't the skills to bypass. Hissing, I broke away, trying to fling the offensive shard of blistering cold into the street.

"Stop," he choked, pulling me with him as he sank to the ground. Back thumping against brick, hands wrapped about mine. Keeping the Glaith secure between us as my pendant dangled from his wrist. Pooling in his lap. "We have to stop before—"

"No!" I snarled, trying to jerk free, to reclaim that inferno and inject it beneath my skin once more. "Who are *you* to deny *me*?"

Hot and hard, his hand found purchase on my nape, pressing his forehead to mine. Dark gaze forcing compliance. "Your *equal*. Now stop—Stop!" he snarled, teeth bared, sweat peppering his skin. "You need to learn control before you lose it and get yourself killed. Or worse. You have no idea the kind of danger you're in, girl."

I shook my head, fingers of my free hand burrowing beneath his collar, thin skin of my knees imprinting on the cobbles between his spread thighs.

But he pressed on before I could utter a word of denial. "I'll teach you that control." His fingers flexed, knotting the fine hairs at the back of my skull, his voice a breathy whisper loud enough for only my ears. "No one knows better than me what you're hiding. What you are."

One hand braced above his heart, the other forced to clutch a ring of Glaith with a foreign family crest, it was my turn to be silent as I tried to think through the haze clouding my brain.

Releasing my neck, he gentled, setting a thumb to my bottom lip. "What's your name?"

"Mm, yes." A dainty cough made us flinch as one, for there, standing at the mouth of the alley were two Tritan ladies, their long, silver-blonde hair tied in elegant knots. Both wearing the silver mantle of a Priestess. "That's what *I'd* rather like to know."

3

———————

"Priestesses," I breathed, blinking into the shaded half-light. Clutching at the collar of Asher's crisp uniform with one hand, thick Elite fingers with the other.

Cursing, Asher shifted, dark eyes fixed to the women standing sentinel at the mouth of the alley. In one fluid movement, he stuffed my pendant into his pocket and drew me to stand. Lacing his fingers with mine, our palms surrounding his ring, we shielded our secrets from their senses. Only then did we face them, presenting a united front to the powerful women bearing down upon us.

Cheeks blazing, I glanced at the sharp Caledonian profile of an impossible Elite who'd promised to teach me control.

Mine.

He squeezed my fingers. "Good morning, ladies."

The younger woman cleared her throat. "You have the divine pleasure of speaking to the High Priestess of the Tritan faith, sir."

My knees wobbled, any flush of color in my cheeks fled, leaving me dizzy and quite sober. *The* High Priestess? Goddess above, my father wasn't going to kill me for being so stupid and selfish—he was going to flay me alive and scatter the remains of my hide over the entire city. For if the High Priestess had sensed me, if she knew my secret, it was all over. Everything we'd worked to conceal so I could remain free of the temple?

Gone.

All of it, gone.

I clutched the ring of Glaith so hard, it threatened to crack beneath my sweaty fingers. Tried to cloak myself in confidence and power once more, for *surely* I was caught. Why else would one of such power and honor come *here?* Now? And if, by some miracle, this was a coincidence...

One touch. That's all it would take. A single moment of contact with my skin, and she'd know.

Elegance in the flesh, the High Priestess stepped into the darkness, watching me down the length of her pin-straight nose. But it wasn't until her eyes skimmed over our joined hands that something akin to fury cracked through that beautiful mask. "You shouldn't be here."

Pressing against a wall of Elite strength, I watched her every movement with the eyes of a cornered animal. Reaching for confidence that was not mine by rights. "I'm sorry, Mistress, I—"

"Not you, girl." She turned her gaze upon Asher. "Him. What are you doing here, so far from the Senate and that ridiculous royal entourage choking up the courtyard? Haven't you a duty to attend, soldier?"

Asher inclined his head, slipping his free hand into

his pocket. Twice shielded as he toyed with my pendant out of sight. "Just enjoying the day, Your Grace. I had to see for myself if the tales of Tritan's markets were true."

"And?"

"They've far exceeded my expectations."

The High Priestess hummed, taking a single step, piercing blue eyes returning to my face. "That doesn't explain what you are doing with a young Tritan lady, in a dark alley no less."

Asher shrugged—the high flush and swollen lips answer enough. "I can assure you she's quite safe with me."

With a sniff, the High Priestess said, "My, what a comfort *that* is," and came to a halt a scant few paces away. Wary, yet confident, if the stiff set to her shoulders was any indication.

"Please accept my apologies," Asher said, pressing two fingers to his temple as if he were born Tritan. "Impropriety was not my intention."

Although she didn't bother to acknowledge the gesture of respect, a tiny, forgiving smile touched the corner of her lips. "Of course not."

"If you're on your way to the Senate meeting," Asher said, thumb stroking the back of my wrist, "I'd be happy to escort the lady wherever she'd like to go. I'd hate for you to be late on my account."

A single, perfect brow rose as her gaze flicked back to his face. "I have no illusions about what you'd be happy to do, but I'm quite sure we can handle it from here. That will be all, soldier," she said, dismissing him without the courtesy of her full attention.

She didn't know.

She *couldn't*. For if she had any suspicions whatsoever about the man standing at my side, she'd never behave with such disrespect. No, if she could sense the power we possessed behind the Glaith, she'd bend the knee and *beg* forgiveness...

Smothering a grin, I straightened my spine, holding ground as the Priestesses closed the gap. "I don't require an escort, thank you. I'm staying."

The High Priestess said nothing. Merely pressed forward with eyes narrowed, cornering us in the dark.

But I hadn't finished here. Hadn't had my fill of the impossible Elite ki singing at the back of my mind... On my lips...

No one—not even *she*—would take what belonged to me. Not without a fight.

Asher pulled his fingers from mine, taking the Glaith with him. Ki pulsed through my veins once more, enough to stop the High Priestess in her tracks. Enough to know there was a secret in my blood, but Asher's Glaith-laced hand settled on my elbow before that spike of ki overflowed. The weight of his ring dropped into my right pocket, out of sight. Glaith the only backup plan I'd ever trusted. His fingers found purchase on my nape a moment later, keeping me hidden. Ready for whatever came next.

I smiled, slow and sure. Skin flushing with a fresh surge of ki.

Mirroring me, the High Priestess gathered herself, pulling strength from the afternoon breeze—I could smell it. Could feel it thickening the air all around us. Waiting for her call.

The fool.

"This is your only warning," the High Priestess murmured, shaking her hands loose at her sides. Her frosty gaze fixed to mine, and mine alone. "Send your toy away before it gets broken."

Hands flying to her lips, wide blue eyes snapping between us, the second Priestess stepped back. "Mistress..."

I sneered. Thought she could take what was mine, did she? Thought she could break him so easily? That I'd *let* her?

No. Alone, I might've had cause to cower before her. But now? With him? Knees flexed, I braced, held back by Asher's hand on my nape. Buoyed by the Elite arsenal waiting just out of sight, in the shadows at my back.

With cold fire blazing in her eyes, the High Priestess pressed closer, still. Lips set in a tight, thin line, she extended her hand, palm up. "Come, child. Don't make things worse for yourself."

Saying nothing, I watched her fingers. Watched as she closed the gap, walking blind and arrogant into my Elite trap. Only a few millimeters left, before the might of the High Priestess herself was *mine*...

I reached for my ki mixed with his, trying to push through the Glaith and immerse myself in that bottomless well of strength and power.

But an instant before the cool weight of her palm settled on my forearm, he stepped back. Giving me a tiny push toward certain doom in the High Priestess' arms, he left me without the protection of his Glaith, the aid of his strength, or the confidence inspired by his control.

Head snapping to the side as I stumbled, I gaped. *"What—"*

The High Priestess' gasp cut me short, her grip tightening with strength enough to bruise as my secret was revealed once more. As the market lit up around me and my entire life burned away in a single puff of tri-colored smoke, she mastered me. Swallowing the defiant flames beneath my skin with teeth bared, she hardly bothered to break a sweat. Taking everything and nothing. All of it gone, leashed and buried beneath a delicate wisp of probing ki-sense wielded by a *true* master of the art.

This was no fledgling, impossible Elite toying with power he shouldn't have and didn't understand, but the head of the Tritan faith. A fully trained Priestess of the highest order, touched by the Goddess herself! Her power outstripped my own by several orders of magnitude—and her control?

Absolute.

She needed no such crutch as the Glaith, for *she* was the most powerful Priestess in living memory.

A Trila-Glís.

And me?

Nothing. Nothing but a cursed idiot of the worst kind.

I blinked, ceding the battle of wills before it had even begun. Crumpling to the cobbles, ready to press my forehead to the stone and beg until my voice gave out and the ground swallowed me whole. "Y-Your Grace, I—"

A cool, pale hand settled on the back of my neck, washing me with a ki so pure and true, it hurt to be near it. "Be still, my little rogue. All is well."

Goddess, her voice! How had I failed to note its beauty? How had I mistaken such hypnotic serenity for malice?

"Annabelle, darling. Go on ahead," the High Priestess murmured, petting sweat-damp hair back from my face. Her perfect, sacred knees marked by the alley's filth as she soothed me. "We'll be along shortly."

"Yes, Mistress," the other said, though I didn't see her depart. Could see nothing but the purity radiating from deep within her mistress. And with each frantic beat of my heart, that same perfection eased the hurt of rejection. Urging me to forget one Captain Asher Rawlings, the betrayer who had nothing to say for himself, for in his place? Where he once stood at my back, spinning a web of lies?

Nothing but shadows.

He was gone.

4

"So."

I didn't lift my cheek from her thigh. Couldn't bear to meet her eyes or wipe the scalding tears from my own.

Cool, gentle fingers threaded through my hair. "What's your name, child?"

"Mila." I cleared the torment from my throat. "My name is Mila, Your Grace."

She snorted, smoothing an imaginary wrinkle in her silver skirts. "And your surname?"

Eyes squeezed shut around the burning, salty ache, I shook my head. To reveal such a thing was... it was... I couldn't...

Stroking my hair, the High Priestess hummed under her breath, sending ki pulsing through me... so soothing... "Your name?"

I blinked. "Tannovic."

"Ah." She patted my back, laying a twisted length of my hair over my shoulder, then moved to stand.

Breaking away, she took her ki with her. "A senator's daughter. I should have known."

The blood rushed from my face so fast, my head spun. Leaving me gaping up at her, sprawled on the cobblestones. "Goddess, what—*how* did you—"

"So you *have* heard of the Goddess, then?" Her laugh echoed through the hollow space in my chest. "I shall have to commend your father on his exemplary parenting skills."

"P-Please, Mistress, you can't—"

"What I cannot do, my little rogue, is leave you *here* after what you almost did to that Caledonian soldier." She cast a glare over her shoulder, at the path he must have taken, and so missed my shocked flinch. "And neither can I miss this meeting, much as I wish I could. No, our prime minister would enjoy *that* entirely too much." She pursed her lips and with a sigh, clapped the commoner's grime from her hands, then reached for me. "It's far from ideal, but you'll have to come with me."

I scrambled to my feet, unbalanced. Overwrought. "Go to the Senate with you? I can't possibly—" I shook my head, retreating until my back bumped the wall, scrubbing the tears from my cheeks.

"Come now. You can't get into any more trouble than you're already in," she said, matching my retreat with a cheeky smirk. "And I'll do everything in my considerable power to cut this meeting as short as I can."

"You don't understand!" Heart trying to punch through solid bone, I reached for my pendant and came up empty. Scarcely managing to contain the scream clawing the back of my throat bloody, I said, "My Glaith. It's... I must have dropped it."

"Oh, the Glaith cannot save you from what you are, girl. Not for long, anyway. You were already breaking through, though I wasn't certain until I tasted your ki myself." She smirked, collecting my hands in a touch laced with false serenity. "We're lucky I sensed you when I did. I shudder to think what would have happened to that young man had I been too far away to intervene."

And there it was. He'd managed to play the victim and escape with his secret intact—with my pendant, no less, the stinking, evil Elite bastard. Teeth clenched hard enough to make my gums squeal, I tried again, enforcing the captain's lie, if only so *I* could be the one to tear it down and watch it burn. "Mistress, *please*. My father said there would be Elites at that meeting. I can't—"

"Of course you can, and you will," she returned, spinning on her heel in a swirl of silver skirts, the strength of her grip belying that delicate frame.

"But the Glaith—"

"Glaith dependency is not something I tolerate in my Priestesses, Mila. It fosters weak and lazy Priestesses at a time when trust in the temple and the divine arts are at an all-time low." Pausing at the threshold between dark and light, private alley and crowded market, she straightened my simple tunic, and said, "I will shield you from the worst of your... affliction. And then we shall have a little chat with your father about his duties as a Tritan citizen and a parent. Come, Miss Tannovic. The Caledonians await."

I flinched, unable to refuse as the High Priestess herself marched me to the Senate.

Where my father waited.

5

———

"**M**ila, what in the world are you doing here —*High Priestess?*" My father stood, the scrape of his chair against the tiled floor drawing the attention of the senators and aides alike. And, eyes threatening to burst from his head and set me ablaze right there in the middle of the chamber room, my father's jaw snapped shut. Pulse pounding above his collarbone. Fists clenched.

"Ah. Senator *Tannovic.*" The High Priestess cast an icy glare across the room, sizing my father up before I could utter a word of apology. "Just the man I was hoping to see. I apologize for the delay," she continued, addressing the rest of the Senate. "I came across a situation in the market that required my immediate intervention."

My father's pale skin blanched, but he gestured for her to take a seat at the head of the table. Avoiding my eye. "In the market, you say?"

A tall man at my father's side cleared his throat. "I hope nothing is out of sorts? Wouldn't want to give the

Caledonians cause to revoke their trade deals on the eve of signing, would we?"

Propelling me toward the far end of the table, where the second Priestess from the alley stood beside a plush chair, the High Priestess sighed. "No need to worry, Mister Prime Minister. I have everything quite in hand, though I'll be having a word with Senator Tannovic after this farce of a meeting."

Dabbing at his forehead, my father pinned me with *the look*, then tucked his handkerchief into his breast pocket. "Of course, Mistress."

"Your Grace, *please*," the prime minister said, spreading his fingers on the desk before him. "Don't start this again. Trade with Caledonia is good for Tritan's economy. They are here to offer peaceful terms—"

"Indeed," the High Priestess replied, taking her seat and wrapping her ki around me as she continued to address the men and women of the Tritan Senate. "And yet, these so-called peaceful terms come with a full royal battalion. I can't imagine why."

My father cleared his throat, though when he tried to speak, his voice crackled. "It's a"—he coughed—"battalion in name only, I'm told. They're officers in an honor guard. Not soldiers and not a functioning military unit."

"There, you see?" the prime minister said, shuffling a stack of papers, eyes downcast. "A perfectly reasonable explanation. No need to judge them before they've even arrived. But I see *you've* felt it prudent to bring a pair of Priestesses along," he said, lacing his fingers atop the desk as he looked to me and the other woman from the alley. "I thought we agreed *not* to bother with a show of force?"

The High Priestess flicked her wrist at me, shaking her head. "The girl has shown some surprising, completely unexpected aptitude, though I wouldn't go so far as to call her Priestess, Mister Prime Minister. I merely thought she'd enjoy learning the ins and outs of a political arena. Perhaps one day I'll be able to convince her to attend in my stead," she concluded, to the chuckles of several senators—save one.

My father's knuckles threatened to split at the seams, the veins in his forehead pulsing with ire, though *still*, he wouldn't look at me.

But something in my chest pulsed, tugging my attention toward the door opposite to the one we'd come through, drowning out the squabbling of my elders and the twisty, awful feeling writhing in my stomach. In spite of the High Priestess' aid, I turned, drawn to what approached from the hall beyond. Ki—it could be nothing else. But...

I swallowed, taking a half-step toward a tsunami so bright, so vibrant, all I could do was stare with sightless eyes as it rushed toward us.

Jerking me back, the High Priestess redoubled her effort to tether me. Manufactured serenity coursed through my veins, urging me toward peace though her fingers had sunk into the meat of my forearm. "It seems our guests will be here in a moment," she said, regardless of the crease between her brows and the unseen battle of wills. "If anyone would like to spare themselves this drudgery, now is the time."

"*Honestly*, Your Grace," the prime minister snapped, but was interrupted by a firm, three-tiered knock.

As one, the Tritan Senate stood, all eyes turned toward the door I couldn't look away from.

Several tall brawny men with dark hair and golden skin filed into the room, each dressed in identical crisp uniforms of Imperial black and gold. Dark eyes restless in stoic faces. They took no notice of the seating prepared for the dignitaries and made no effort to introduce themselves. Upon each of their hips, concealed beneath the lapels of formal jackets, were instruments containing the Glaith. I could feel it, could sense the ki stored within as if it were attached to six tiny blazing suns.

Sweat trickled down the back of my neck, agitating the fine hairs standing on end as I stood there, torn.

These men were Blood, each and every one. Six Caledonian Elites, to be precise, all standing much too close, regardless of the High Priestess' efforts to restrain me. It would take five, maybe six steps to close the distance... Less to taste their ki firsthand and compare it to the betrayer's leavings still festering behind my ribs. Whispering of impossible things.

I expelled a shaky breath, reaching for the pendant that wasn't there, then latched onto the High Priestess' light, refreshing ki to try to lose myself in the might of *true* power. To forget the sting of deception and everything that had come before it.

"Ladies and gentlemen of Tritan," said a tall, thin Caledonian man. "It is my profound honor to announce the council members of the Caledonian Empire and the imperial guard." The herald straightened his jacket, inclining his head as the first imperial stepped through the door. "I give you the esteemed Unus Gladius, Master Curator to Emperor Octus Clavius, the first and youngest Elite Emperor in thirteen generations. The Master Curator speaks with the full authority of his imperial sibling, and as such, his word carries the weight of the Empire itself."

He was of middle age, this Caledonian Curator. Wisps of gray winged back from his temples, fine lines marking a distinguished face—handsome, but as far as I could tell, *not* of the Blood.

One of the imperial guards stepped forward, readying a chair directly opposite the prime minister before the herald spoke again.

"General Harper Tilcot, Elite commander of the Northern wing of the Caledonian Armed Forces."

I shivered. Elite. And this one oozing a smug surety that had me turning away with fists clenched. At once trying to refresh my palate, and reaching for the Glaith that wasn't there. Rubbing my breastbone raw and warm.

Oblivious, the herald continued. "Lieutenant General Killion Hastings, second in command of the Northern forces."

The High Priestess squeezed my wrist and caught my eye, filling her lungs with a deep, slow breath. Nodding when I did the same—but it was of no use.

"Colonel Conrad Viridian, and Captain Asher Rawlings, who represent the Caledonian infantry and special forces for the North, respectively."

Colonel Viridian was a stockier build than his superiors, but no less intimidating for his Elite status, his additional presence in the room making it all the harder for me to draw breath. But he was not the one whose pleasant smile and polite nod made the cesspit in my chest flutter and kick.

It was him.

Blood to Blood.

He was the one who had me sweating, unable to move for the adrenaline pumping through my veins. And there, about his neck, was a length of silver chain disappearing beneath a shirt rumpled by *my fingers.*

My pendant.

I took a step, teeth squealing against each other. If I could just... touch him, if I could run my hands over that tanned skin, his ki would fill me as it had in the alley. Impure Caledonian filth, yes, but...

My mouth watered, and I took another step. I could gorge on his ki for an eternity and never exhaust him. I could inflict endless misery, make him beg forgiveness. He'd weep for relief, and *still,* I wouldn't drink him dry.

A dull jerk in my left shoulder stopped me short, and with lips curled back, I spun.

The High Priestess' knuckles were white upon my forearm, though her face held no hint of the effort she expended. No signs of the concern lacing her ki as she doused the fire burning beneath my skin, *or* that she recognized the man from the alley I'd victimized.

As for Captain Asher Rawlings? He hadn't even bothered to acknowledge me as he took his seat. And me, ready to toss everything I'd ever known to the wind.

Scowling, I stuffed my hands in my pockets—and found a warm iron topped with Glaith.

His ring.

6

———

Scarcely avoiding a startled shriek, I jerked my hand free of that poisoned Glaith, instead turning to watch the prime minister stand. Trembling with cold sweat.

"It's wonderful to play host to such an illustrious group, and welcome," the prime minister said. "Welcome all. I hope your stay in our humble city finds all of your needs met. Now, allow me the honor of introducing Sasha Calypsil, esteemed Trila-Glís and High Priestess of the Tritan faith."

Inclining her head, the High Priestess remained seated as the prime minister continued to ramble off the names and titles of the men and women in the Tritan Senate. She appeared unaware of the treasure I'd stumbled across, or indeed that the man sitting across the table from her was the very man she'd seen as victim to my loss of control. But when Elite ki spiked through my mind, probing all the dark unseen corners with brisk efficiency, I lost interest in the sonorous voice of the prime minister. Forgot the coming storm that was my father's retribution as my attention glided toward the captain once more.

Fingers poking through the buttons of his shirt, he traced my pendant out of sight. One dark brow raised in challenge. Pulling at my ki from across the table... Tasting. Taking no more than a tiny sip, yet there all the same. Such a thing I hadn't thought possible. Unless...

The Glaith. My pendant was brimming with years worth of *my* ki, now in the hands of an impossible Elite with power and arrogance enough to try such a reckless maneuver beneath the very nose of the High Priestess.

I almost smiled, letting my fingers inch toward my pocket. In spite of the danger, or because of it, I answered his challenge, for he was not the only one capable of such things.

His ring held heat, warming the tip of my index finger with unseen presence of stored ki. The history of a life lived in hiding—familiar and alien all at once. And worst of all, completely open to no other but me. A secret bridge built for two.

Smirking, he lured me back, letting me slide behind that iron-clad control that had kept him safe from the High Priestess' senses in the alley. Letting me taste what no other knew was real or possible. Letting me see everything that he was, without so much as a blink or blush. No remorse. Not a moment of regret for all the trouble he'd *pushed* me into, the dirty, cheating parasite that he was.

I seized the ring, pressing the Glaith into the heart of my palm—and flung his ki, everything he offered as *equal,* back in his stupid, handsome face.

The captain lurched, inky eyes going wide, and for

the space of a dozen heartbeats, he stared at me, face void of all expression.

And then he smiled, raising a single finger to his lips.

He needn't have worried. I'd keep his secret, though he hadn't done the same for me. Oh yes... That impossible Elite was *mine* to play with.

"With introductions out of the way," the prime minister said, spreading his hands in welcome, "shall we begin?"

General Tilcot stood, smiling down at my country-folk, though his eyes lingered on the High Priestess. "Thank you for the most hospitable welcome, Lords and Ladies of Tritan. To be blunt, we come seeking an alliance. We seek the union of the two greatest nations of our time in a marriage of trade and good faith. Our people are both of the Blood, and though we sit on opposing sides, it is the same coin. Priestesses keep what *we* use. Store what Elites expel." He inclined his head, a lock of thick, dark hair shifting across his brow as his gaze swept over the High Priestess. "Yet Caledonia's history is steeped in Elite blood. In violence. For generations, Elites were locked away, hidden from the gentry in dank, filthy cages where we could not pose a threat to the populace. Little more than savages destined to die young. Berserkers."

Straightening, he unbuttoned his left sleeve, and continued. "Our gifts are not of peace and healing, as that of your Priestesses, but of war. Of death. A single Elite, ki-mad with bloodlust, can wipe out an entire enemy battalion in moments." He paused then, seeming to enjoy the shocked murmur rippling through the Tritan Senate, rolling his sleeve back to reveal the glitter of tarnished gold set against his skin. "But such power comes with the highest price. An attack of this magnitude has, without exception, always come at the cost of Elite life. Until now."

"Glaith, I presume," the High Priestess drawled, tapping out a lazy, left-handed rhythm on the polished tabletop, containing me with the other.

"It's a simple technology, and yet, it allows an Elite the freedom to live among the regular populace. This is but a prototype," he continued, addressing the High Priestess directly. "It does not contain pure Glaith ore, but an alloy. As you can imagine, we've had to be frugal with what little we could procure. But for the first time in our lengthy, blood-soaked history, an Elite can focus his power. Channel it toward anything of his choosing without the risk of certain death. No longer are we caged beasts, doomed from birth to die with the screams of our enemies chasing us into the Void." Slipping the manacle off his wrist, he tossed it into the center of the table, letting it spin a lazy circle.

"From my understanding," the High Priestess said, "you've had your Elites relying upon the Glaith for several generations already. This is nothing new."

"Quite right you are," the general returned, stepping closer. "We've become dependent on the stuff. But this?" he said, pointing toward the manacle gleaming between two countries, "This simple bracelet represents a monumental leap forward in Glaith technology. What we lack, is the one thing we need to live free. Glaith ore is as precious as it is rare—"

"And Tritan is your closest neighbor with mining rights," she finished, crossing her arms, releasing me in her fit of temper. "And what, Goddess willing, do we get in return for giving you the Glaith?"

"Protection, of course!" the general said, spreading his arms to encompass the Elites all around him.

Ki licked the back of my neck, drawing a splintered gasp from my throat while obsidian eyes twinkled. The smug prick. If only I could wipe the smile from his lips...

"With our alloy, and *our* technology, your Priestesses will experience an ease they've never known before. They will no longer have cause to fear, and neither will they *be* feared by their fellow citizens. Why"—the general turned to the curator, placing a massive hand on the royal sibling's shoulder—"our very own Lord Curator has designed the next generation of these simple gauntlets using our Glaith alloy. This is what we offer you. A permanent solution against the ravages of our birthright. Priestess and Elite, both."

"Permanent?" the High Priestess breathed, standing, fingers splayed on the table before her. "You seek to bind the Glaith to your own people?"

"Now, Your Grace," the prime minister began.

But she ignored him, icy glare fixed to the general's face. "Such action would enslave your people, and *mine*." She laughed, low and unamused. "And who will hold their tether, I wonder?"

"Madam, I insist you control yourself!" the prime minister hissed. "There is no call to be rude, especially in a situation that does not concern—"

The High Priestess slapped both hands on the table, thunderclouds building behind her light eyes. "Does not concern me? You seek an alliance with a nation who would enslave *my* Priestesses, sir. Everything to do with this disappointment is my business."

Free to turn my attention elsewhere, my eyes went to the one place they *shouldn't.*

"Do I need to remind you that temple and Senate are not ruled by the same governing body in this country?"

A shocked expletive burst from the prime minister's lips. "How *dare* you."

I stepped toward that inky stare, reaching again for a ring brimming with impossible ki. Tuning out everything but the urge to chew the smug clear off his lips.

Tilting his jaw toward me, the captain laced his fingers atop the table. Showing off his skill without touching my pendant, even as he tugged me closer. Flooding the bridge built for two... blurring the lines...

"Go ahead," the High Priestess snapped, taking three massive steps to block my path. "Make your alliance with these warmongers. It has no bearing on me or mine. But *my* girls will not be enslaved by these Caledonian manacles—" she slipped her hand in mine, cramming her ki down my throat until my eyes glazed over, and I was too bloated on ethereal fumes to take another step. "No matter how pretty the package."

"Enslave them? Oh, come now." The general crossed thick arms over his chest, brows climbing toward his hairline as he leered. "Just like a woman to be so dramatic. We offer a viable solution to an age-old problem. We've all heard the myths of Priestesses going ki-mad, Your Grace. It's not just an Elite problem, if the legends are to be believed."

She whirled on him, fingers near to crushing mine. "My Priestesses don't need the Glaith, General Tilcot.

They spend their lives learning to control their Goddess-given power, and I will not see them succumb to something as despicably *weak* as Glaith dependency."

"Weak?" A vein in the general's neck began to pulse, drawing my eye. "Your lot are nothing more than trumped up healers! We are *soldiers*. Weakness? Bah!" His countenance savage, dark eyes glittering, the general continued to glare, forehead dewy. "Tell me, do I look weak, you foolish woman?"

"It's High Priestess, to you, sir," she returned. "And my girls have no need of a substance to control their power. They are strong without it."

"And yet, you toil away in your labs beneath the temple," the general said, swiping a bead of sweat from his eyes. "Experimenting with the Glaith. That's rather hypocritical, don't you think?"

With an eerie stillness, the High Priestess' fury became mine, leeching into my blood. Replacing the manufactured calm with unquenchable flames. And as one, we turned to the prime minister. "You've already sold us out."

"Now, Sasha, please," the prime minister said, flashing his palms. "Let's all take a breath and—"

"No. We're done here. As for your offer," she added, turning once more to the Caledonians, "allow me to counter. You may send any number of Elites to me for training, so they might know the true freedom of mastering the power they were born to wield. I will free you from your dependency on dirty Glaith alloy, no questions asked."

The general threw back his head, and laughed. "The Elites are strong *because* of the Glaith, *High Priestess*. You would deny them from experiencing their true potential? Is your ego really so—"

"That's enough, General." All eyes shifted to the curator. "We come to you with a generous offer to trade technology, and this is the treatment we receive? I have never been so thoroughly disrespected in all my years." His lip curled, revealing strong, white teeth. "And by a woman, no less."

The prime minster snapped his fingers, gesturing at a pair of young women to begin distributing refreshments. "My deepest apologies, Master Curator. You must understand it was never our intention to include the High Priestess in matters of State. Rest assured, she and I will be having words after this meeting has concluded. Nothing is more important to this Senate than organizing a fair trade agreement between our great nations." He laughed, dabbing at the sweat soaking his hairline. "The things we could do by combining our resources are limitless."

"Ah," the High Priestess breathed, gliding to the back of my father's chair. Placing her free hand on his shoulder, she continued, "And here lies the crux of the matter. What are you hoping to gain by selling off Tritan's Glaith technology?"

"A trade agreement is hardly selling the nation's secrets, madam." Sweeping a hand through his pale silver hair, cheeks stained a deep, embarrassing crimson the prime minister cleared his throat. "You're being utterly ridiculous."

Humming, the High Priestess shrugged. "Agree to disagree, but you'll remind me to give thanks to the Goddess for ensuring those labs remain under my control, won't you?"

Pinching the bridge of his nose, the prime minister tried one last time. "Trade keeps our economy growing. Surely you, of anyone present, can understand just how many lives could benefit from the ground-breaking prototypes Tritan's scientists are producing in your basement?"

A smile flicked across her face. "I'm intimately aware of the good those products shall bring when they've moved beyond the prototype stage. I am also," she continued, squeezing my father's shoulder, "well aware of just how dangerous that technology has the potential to be in the wrong hands."

The curator tented his fingers, leaning back in his chair. "I'm not sure I like what you're suggesting, madam."

With a snort, the High Priestess turned to leave. "Then I'll leave you to nurse your wounded feelings. Come along, girls. Senator Tannovic?" she pressed, snapping her fingers. "A word?"

Clearing his throat, my father shuffled the papers before him and got to his feet, watched by the shocked faces of his coworkers and insulted guests alike. "Very well, then. If you'll excuse me, ladies. Gentlemen."

But without err, my eyes returned to the captain's. To that infuriating smirk and the stolen chain glimmering about his neck.

Lips tilting, he rubbed the bare spot on his right pinky finger. Taunting me to indulge, just once more...

A hand landed upon my shoulder—fingers biting deep enough to haul me from those inky depths. Jaw flexing, my father propelled me through the door after the High Priestess, neither speaking nor meeting my eye.

The instant the door whispered shut behind us, the High Priestess whirled. "Have you lost your bloody mind, Senator?"

"I beg your pardon?"

"Annabelle. We need a moment, if you could..."

"Of course, Your Grace. I'll return to the temple at once," she said, curtsying. And without a single word or backward glance, fled her mistress' wrath, earning the jealousy of everyone she left behind.

The High Priestess stepped up to my father, undeterred by his height advantage, her eyes and ki blazing with ice-cold fury. "Are you aware of my station?"

"Well yes, of course. But I don't—"

"Then you are aware there are consequences in place for those who would seek to keep a Priestess from the temple?"

"Now hold on just a moment, Your Grace. I—"

Pressing closer, her voice dropped several octaves. "Are you aware, Senator Tannovic, just how close to the edge your daughter is? She very nearly lost herself in the market today. Very nearly caused an international incident and could have started a bloody *war,* if I hadn't been close enough to stop her from draining a Caledonian soldier dry."

Swallowing, his breath coming in shallow pants, my father persisted. "I'm quite sure I don't—Mila wouldn't—"

"The time for deception has long passed, you arrogant fool. We are *lucky* I sensed what she is before any harm was done. And I don't care if I have to use force to do it, Senator," the High Priestess hissed, seizing my elbow. "But this girl is coming with me."

7

———

"Going with *you*?" my father spluttered, matching the High Priestess' determined stride toward the exit. "To the temple?"

Fingers tight on my elbow, she snorted. "That is generally where I conduct my business with the Priestesses, yes."

Goddess. The temple. Where my secrets would no longer be mine, and I'd be forced into a life of servitude to a deity I had no faith in—my fault. All of it. For succumbing to the temptation to stretch my dark wings, and allowing myself to be manipulated by one Captain Asher Rawlings of his Majesty's Imperial Army. Thieving betrayer.

"I presume," my father said, wrapping his hand around my free elbow, "we're not being given a choice in the matter."

"That you presume my invitation extends to *you* is remarkably forward, Senator."

For a moment, as they flanked me through the

narrow hall, he said nothing—though his grip tightened and his cheeks flushed with so casual an insult.

"Oh, relax," the High Priestess drawled, eyes twinkling. "I'm teasing. How about a private tour of the temple and all her many wonders, hmm? So you might see for yourselves we Priestesses are not hiding nefarious evil behind our walls."

"And here I was, under the impression the temple was off limits to those not counted among your ranks."

I averted my gaze, for I did not need my gifts to know he'd relent, unable to resist the chance to see the temple for himself.

Neither, it seemed, did the High Priestess. "Information is a valuable commodity, Senator, and one I'm unwilling to risk exposing. Especially in this particular political climate."

Valuable indeed, or so the secret weight in my right pocket would have me believe.

"A sentiment we share, Your Grace," my father replied, and opened the courtyard door, flooding the hall in bright, afternoon sunlight. "And though the notion of a private tour of your facilities—by *you*, no less—is tempting, I would be remiss in failing to note the convenience of it all. You'll have my daughter on temple grounds, where *you* hold all the power."

Well... not *all* of it. Something defiant fluttered in my chest, setting my fingertips tingling with the memory of that wild, impossible ki.

"We could just as easily meet at my estate. Or on neutral ground," he continued, arms crossed over his chest, blocking the exit. "But then you wouldn't be able to figure out how you're going to use Mila to your advantage."

The High Priestess smirked, showing teeth. "Much as you'd like to think otherwise, my intention is not to steal her from you. But neither can I allow her to go untrained after what I saw in that alley. What I sensed."

I scowled at the floor, at my feet perched on the edge of light and dark. How, with all her Goddess-given power and control, could she be so blind? That he had managed to evade her at all was ridiculous. The most powerful living Trila-Glís duped into naming *me* predator and swaddling the poor, mistreated Captain Rawlings in a victim's cloak? Absurd.

"For now, she'll be tested for Priestess aptitude."

Stepping back, I clutched at the ring through a fistful of bunched skirts. "Tested?"

"Nothing painful or barbaric, I assure you." She squeezed my shoulder, her ki pulsing through my blood, urging calm I couldn't begin to understand, let alone feel in light of what I stood to lose. "Every Priestess who has come before you has taken this test. It's a marker of our truest nature and scope of potential, nothing more."

I swallowed, hitching a practiced smile to my lips as sweat dampened my nape, laboring not to reach for the Glaith hanging heavy in my pocket and flee before this test took what I was unwilling to give.

And yet, it came as no surprise when my father adjusted his collar and said, "Very well. We accept your offer. On one condition."

A single, fine brow rose. "Oh?"

"We're taking my coach."

"Whatever for?" she asked, free hand planted on her hip. "The temple is little more than a ten-minute walk from here."

"You spoke of valuable information, Your Grace," my father said, whistling for the attention of his personal aid on the street below. "Even went so far as to conceal Mila from that other Priestess and the senate until you know how you can use her. So yes, we'll accept your offer of a guided tour of the temple. We'll even submit to your little test, though I imagine it's something of a formality at this point. But until today"—he shot me a cutting glance—"there were two people who knew our secret."

Lips pursed, the High Priestess hummed. "And now there are three."

"I intend to keep it that way," he agreed, and turned, descending the steps of the Senate in a swirl of blue robes. "Nothing more will be left to chance. Not if I can help it, Your Grace. Come along."

Kneading my thigh with balled fist, I followed, unable to bring myself to correct my father's assumption. Unable to tell him that until today, there had been only *one* who knew what was truly hidden beneath the Glaith.

And now there were two.

"Oh, you *can't* be serious," the High Priestess said, hand on hip, though she reluctantly followed in his footsteps. "That vehicle is positively garish."

The coach glided to a halt before us, Glaith engine powering down with naught but a slight hum. All four rails of the elegant, *garish* coach touched the ground as one, and before we could take a step, the pilot exited his chair and opened the double doors with a flourish. His Eloran accent rolling over his greeting. "Your coach, Senator."

"Thank you, Josh. Ladies." Pressing two fingers to his temple, my father held the door. "After you."

With a huff, the High Priestess gathered her skirts and accepted Josh's hand, settling herself on the forward-facing bench. But I avoided my father's man. Bunching my skirt around the secret weight in my pocket, I settled at the High Priestess' side, once more wearing the skin of a demure senator's daughter.

Obedient. Poised.

Sweating through my shift, I held the bundle of fabric and forbidden secrets balled tight in my fist.

Taking the spot directly opposite, my father said, "To the temple, Josh. The High Priestess and I have business."

Josh made a strange sound as his eyes landed on the High Priestess' face, cheeks flushing a charming rouge. "H-High Priestess? Oh, aye. At once, sir. Your Grace," he stammered, then hurled his lanky body into the pilot's chair without another word, dropping the privacy partition between pilot and honored guest.

As the coach lifted off the ground, my father steeled himself. Spine straight, jaw set. "Mila is free of her curse with the Glaith. What the Caledonians offer can—"

"What the Caledonians can, or cannot do is no concern of mine," the High Priestess replied, and released my forearm, allowing me a moment to breathe clear of her influence. "If the girl is indeed what I suspect, it's nothing short of a miracle that she's managed to cope so long without help." Tinkling laughter filled the cabin, and she reclaimed my wrist. "Even now, it's taking everything I've got to stop her from marching back into that chamber room and unleashing unimaginable destruction upon every ki-wielder and citizen unlucky enough to stand in her path."

I jerked my hand away from the ring, shaking my head. "No. I wouldn't—"

But the High Priestess raised her palm. "You cannot deny it. Not from me. The Caledonians and their dirty Glaith are no match for you, girl."

Dirty Glaith? Again, I shook my head, for the ring in my pocket was pure. Tainted with the lingering heat from *his* skin and bursting with a power that shouldn't be, but in all other ways, no different from my stolen pendant. Pure Glaith ore, pretending to be an ugly stone.

A stone I was unwilling to lose, no matter the foul, Caledonian taint sending whispered lies through my skin. Without it, I had nothing to bargain with. No leverage to reclaim my pendant and show Captain Asher Rawlings what power looked like when it was truly free. When it was unbound by his precious control.

Right hand dipping into my pocket, I toyed with the inert band, tracing the foreign family crest.

No. I couldn't allow it to be discovered. That the High Priestess hadn't *already* sensed it was the only convincing argument for Divine interference I'd ever encountered. Though why She hadn't seen fit to inter-fere *before* I'd landed myself in this situation was beyond me. Unless...

Unless there was something at the temple She intended for me to have.

And if the Goddess herself wished to keep it from her chosen... who was I to decide otherwise? Why shouldn't the ring remain here, hidden in my father's coach? All I had to do was... drop it. Let it roll out of sight until I could reclaim what was mine.

My father cleared his throat, meeting my eye for the first time since I'd been escorted into the chamber room. The flush creeping up his neck waxed long and poetic of all the trouble I'd earned, though his voice splintered when he said, "She's my daughter."

The High Priestess' tone was gentle, her words firm. "She's a daughter of the Goddess, whether you wish to admit it or not."

"Even so."

I dragged a ragged breath through my teeth, ring poised to drop.

"Much as it might appear otherwise," she said, gazing out the window as we glided onto the temple's long, narrow drive, "I have no intention of making another enemy in the senate." She turned her eyes upon my father, an elegant coil of hair shifting to fall over her shoulder. "But the best place for Mila, the *safest* place, is the temple. And you know it. I am the *only* one capable of guiding her through this without a tragedy."

My father snorted. "So long as she wears the Glaith, Mila doesn't need—" his eyes landed on my throat, flushed skin blanching pale in seconds. "Where is your pendant?"

I flinched, stuffing the ring back into my pocket— and in doing so, the Glaith bit my palm.

Ki arced through my blood, straightening my spine in spite of the High Priestess' touch upon my skin.

His ki. It tugged and pulled, kissing fragile nerves with breathy amusement, coiling about my finger. Winding up my wrist in a lazy twist, he took his time. Tasting. Unconcerned with getting caught, for *he* was not the one sitting beside the High Priestess. *He* hadn't been promised control and the wild unknown, only to be tossed aside.

No.

He'd taken what he wanted and pushed me to ruin.

Teeth grit, I forced the ring from my finger, denying the luxury of so much Elite ki *and* his insufferable, disembodied amusement. The smarmy prick. Goddess, what I wouldn't give for one minute alone and unfettered—

"Damnit, Mila!" my father hissed, snapping his fingers before my face. "Where is your pendant? What have you done with it?"

"I..." Now was the time. To give it up, to clip the dark wings begging to taste freedom and distance myself from Captain Asher Rawlings for good. Time to chase the hurt and anger from my father's face and accept the punishment I'd worked so hard to earn.

I glanced at the High Priestess. Eyes dropping to the hand still wrapped tight about my wrist. Noting the serene tilt to her head and the patient smile as she awaited my answer.

Utterly void of suspicion.

"I..." I swallowed, for it wasn't possible that she could have missed *that* amount of ki flaring hot and wild *right in front of her.* This must be the test she spoke of. She had to be waiting for me to admit what I had. Unless...

"Damnit, Mila. Where—"

"I dropped it," I whispered, and slid the ring onto my middle finger, holding the surge of Elite ki at bay with little more than pure stubborn determination.

Finding ease in repeated exposure, my eyes never wavering from the High Priestess' profile.

"For the love of the Goddess," my father snapped. "How the bloody—it belonged to your *mother*, Mila! How could you lose it?"

Nothing. The High Priestess didn't know of the foreign power I possessed. Couldn't sense it.

"I know where it is," I whispered, and let the ring return to the depths of my pocket—where it was safest. "I'll get it back, I just need—"

The High Priestess patted my forearm, an easy smile tracing her lips. "I startled her, Senator. If she's lost her Glaith, I'm to blame. Besides," she continued, "she no longer has any need of it. Mila will be taught to harness her gifts."

"And the other Priestesses?" my father asked, clutching at a bronzed safety bar at his hip. "Without the Glaith, they'll be able to sense her."

"Hers is a secret that cannot be kept forever." Lips pursed, the High Priestess paused, collecting both of my hands in hers. "But until I know for certain what the Goddess has given this girl," she said, "I will keep her hidden myself. You have my word."

"Thank you, Your Grace," I murmured, and turned, gazing out the window as the temple grounds flicked by.

Only the trees saw my smile for what it was.

8

Josh brought the coach to a graceful halt, setting it down before the temple's front step. And, jaw slack, I followed the High Priestess from the vehicle, breathing deep of the fresh, fragrant breeze whispering through the trees. Impeccably kept, we stood in a lush garden of such impressive abundance, I hadn't a hope of naming everything if I spent a lifetime trying. And yet, it wasn't the exotic flowers that caught my attention, or the elegant, sweeping architecture of the Temple itself, but three gnarled, ancient trees.

All three flowering, in spite of the late season.

"Do they bear fruit?" I asked, taking a step toward the closest, the one with tiny blue flowers and a deep craggy silver trunk.

Chin tilting to the specimen in question, the High Priestess smiled, slow and easy. "Not anymore, I'm afraid. They're too old to care for young. We call them the Sentinels. And this is Blue."

I flicked a smirk in her direction, unable to tear my

gaze from the ancient giant, for I could sense something simmering beneath the surface. Something wild, speaking in a language I hadn't the tools to understand. "How old is too old?"

"At least as old as the temple itself," she replied. "They were the first to be planted here. It's said they have a heart of Glaith"—she shrugged, joining me— "though I'm not sure how much truth there is to that particular myth."

It wasn't a myth. I could hear the Sentinels whispering, could feel the specter of a thousand Priestesses humming beneath their skin, beckoning me closer to the ki stored in those mighty trunks. Their Glaith hearts eased the urge to reach into my pocket and taste the captain's ki... replacing it with the desire to blend with the embodiment of calm serenity... "Beautiful... They're... *beautiful.*"

"That they are," she agreed, setting her palm against Blue's mighty trunk. "And they bloom year-round."

The Sentinel seemed to sigh, leaves and petals shivering beneath her touch as the ki of a Trila-Glís filled its heart.

"We maintain them," she continued, patting the thick skin. "I'd wager they're more Priestess than I am, at this point."

Clearing his throat, my father joined us. "It's a... fascinating old tree. Really... uh... big."

Nostrils flared, I shot him a look, but turned away from the Sentinels and their whispers of power. There'd be time enough to drink from that ancient tap.

"My apologies, Senator." With a secret little smile, the High Priestess met his eye. "I don't get many chances to show off all the wonders we house here—and I'm in the mood to brag."

Inclining his head, my father clasped my shoulder. "You have our undivided attention."

"Then come," she said. "We've got a lot to talk about."

"And lots t'see, I hope," Josh said, wringing his hands as he stepped down from the coach, face lit with hope and eager expectation.

Lips pursed, the High Priestess nodded. "Oh, why not? Join us. I'll have someone take the coach to the back lot."

"You've my thanks, Your Holiness." Grinning, he fell into step at my side, his honey-brown Eloran eyes flicking over everything in sight. "Tell me, lass," he whispered. "Just how'd your father manage this, eh? A private tour of the temple? *The* temple?" He shook his head, laughing under his breath. "I canna believe we actually get t'see it."

While I had no answer for him, I couldn't condemn his enthusiasm. Not really, for this was an honor bestowed upon so few. And the temple itself *was* incredible. Benches seemed to grow straight from the earth, living roots twisted and exposed to the elements, yet thick and sturdy. Inviting, even. Goddess, the very path we walked on was a lattice of interwoven branches, roots, and moss, complete with tiny twigs and leaves reaching for the sun. Where there was stone, something living had grown through and around it, incorporating it into the very architecture of the building.

So it came as something of a surprise when intricate, handmade carvings caught my eye. Standing out amongst a collage of organic design, feathers had been hewn into ashen wood. Each as wide as my torso, they reached for the earth, cradling the front entrance in a downy embrace. Wings, poised to either draw a visitor to a feathery bosom, or sink savage talons into an intruder and take flight. But what species had the temple chosen for a mascot? "An owl?"

"What else?" the High Priestess asked and took my hand in hers, tethering my ki once more. "An owl is the Goddess' chosen form."

Great wooden eyes stared down at me, unblinking over a fierce hooked beak—and I smiled. Flight *and* deadly predatory skills? As chosen forms went, I certainly understood the appeal.

"Welcome to the Temple of Milithia," the High Priestess said, and released her grip on my shoulder, reaching to open the great doors of the temple. They moved easily on well-oiled hinges, a feat which—given their size—seemed an impossible thing for the slight figure of the High Priestess to accomplish on her own. But she managed, motioning for us to follow. "Ah, Annabelle," she said, upon spotting the lesser Priestess who'd been at the senate meeting. "If you wouldn't mind, there's a gargantuan Glaith coach parked out front. Could you take it to the back lot?"

"At once, Your Grace."

"I hate to ask," Josh said, "but... will the lassy be alright piloting a vehicle of that size?"

The High Priestess snorted. "Quite. You might say Annabelle's qualifications are... extensive. And I'd expect nothing less," she added, smirking. "The Glaith engine was conceived here, in the temple labs. That lassy, as you say, is the very reason you have a coach to pilot at all."

Eyes tracing the outline of her retreating back, Josh hummed. "Really now?"

"Keep it together, Master Trapper," my father murmured, smirking as he tugged Josh's arm.

With a tiny smile of my own, I nudged him with my elbow, watching a flush of color stain his cheeks. And then, trying to take in as much of the magnificent architecture as I could, I followed along in their wake. Ignoring the weight in my pocket and the subtle whispers of forbidden ki in favor of what was before me.

Everything within sight, from the slight, upward slope of the floor, to the earthy scent in the air, was organic. Twisting and turning it was a mimicry of the straight lines and strict, harsh edges I was accustomed to seeing in the nation's traditional buildings. Here, wood wrapped around stone, as if commanded to do so by the Goddess herself.

Curiosity piqued, I pressed my palm to the wall, sending a tendril of ki into the wood. "It's alive," I gasped, then laughed. Breathless and awestruck. "The entire temple it's... alive!"

"It's *what*—" Josh stopped short, glancing around with wide eyes.

The High Priestess' teeth gleamed in the half-light. "Very good, Mila. I'm impressed. It takes most Priestesses several years to put that together." She leaned in, her tone dropping low. "It's something of a poorly kept secret among those of us who've been here the longest. We hold bets each year to see which of the initiates will figure it out first."

"But—" I pressed harder, trying to communicate with the tiny spark in living wood. "How? How is this done?"

Her reply was nothing but a coy smile, and one I should have expected. This was the Priestess' haven, after all. Here, the paltry rules of nature did not apply. Not to them... Not to... *me*...

Placing her palm on a stone tablet embedded in the wall, the High Priestess unleashed her ki. The tile lit up, sparkling with the Glaith's trademark blue, green, and purple before fading, once more a lackluster gray. After a moment, something tumbled deep inside the walls, clicking and turning. And then, to my open-mouthed shock, a door swung back, revealing an airy, open office. The entire back wall was glass, overlooking a courtyard filled with yet more exotic flowers and trees.

Josh cleared his throat. "Might I ask just how *you* know the walls are live, lass?"

"Simple deduction," I replied at the same time my father said, "No."

Cheeks flushed, Josh stepped back, palms raised. "Apologies, sir. I'll just... uh... wait out here. With the living walls."

Ushering me into her office, the High Priestess said, "We won't be long, Master Trapper," and let the door swing shut on silent hinges.

"Goddess," I breathed, trying to take it all in. "I hadn't realized we'd come up this high. How—"

"There are no stairs here, Mila. Aside from the front steps, of course. Easier on the knees."

Nodding, I drifted toward the windows. "What are *those?*"

She peered over my shoulder, following my finger to a flock of truly massive birds fanning their wings in an elegant dance. Birds who would have stood taller than me, but for my elevated vantage point. "Ah, the planeth.

Impressive, aren't they? A gift from across the ocean. Extinct now, but for a few scattered flocks in sanctuaries like ours."

My father hummed. "Do they fly?"

"Goddess, no." She laughed, the tinkle sending a wave of shivers cascading down my back. "They're much too large for flight, thankfully, but they do jump."

"Do I want to know how far?" I asked, eying their thick, muscular legs and foot-long beaks.

"Only if you intend to spend any time with them. They look positively savage, but we keep ours nice and fat. Haven't had a serious injury in almost a decade. Do you see that one? The big colorful one standing just there, fanning himself?"

I nodded.

"That's the flock leader. He protects the others, and it's him you have to impress if you wish to stand on flock territory." She stepped behind a desk laden with flowers and plants, and flicked her fingers at the pair of chairs set before her. "Please, have a seat."

The captain's ring bumped my hip, affording me a confidence I hadn't earned, but I dropped into a plush white chair as she bade. Tracing the seams in so fine a leather with my forefinger as the High Priestess watched me.

It was my father who hesitated. "Is your office... private?"

Her icy blue eyes didn't waver. "Quite. We are free to speak at will." And then, with a sigh, she pulled a strange, spiked little plant front and center. Composed of muted brown and greens, it sat in a tight bundle atop a bed of dry earth in a plain clay pot. Nothing at all like the incredible variety blooming all around us.

Nose wrinkled, my father asked, "What is that?"

"Do *you* know, Mila?"

I shook my head, yet couldn't tear my eyes from its unappealing brown flesh. There was... something about it. A hint of spice lurking beneath the surface. A whisper of something... *other*.

"This," she said, giving the pot a quarter turn, "is the Lotus Regula. It is the only living example of its kind, and is the most valuable of all the many wonders and priceless things housed here at the temple."

I straightened, turning the full weight of my attention upon this so-called lotus.

"It's... ah... beautiful?" my father said, taking his seat.

She laughed. "It certainly isn't. But go on," she said, and placed the lotus in his hands. "Tell me, what do you feel?"

"It's a bit... crunchy," my father replied. "I think you need to water it more often."

Head tilted, I frowned, for I could hear more than mere whispers now that I was really listening. The lotus was hiding a tiny fire—a spark hidden within an ugly, desiccated shell.

"It's lifeless in your hands, Senator. Nothing but a dried out relic, but at the touch of a Priestess?" She reclaimed the pot and wrapped both hands around it, closing her eyes. A tiny crease formed between her brows as she concentrated, pouring a delicate stream of ki directly into the roots. As I watched, the horrible little thing unfurled, dried leaves pulsing with new life, growing three new sprouts before my eyes. And from the center, a single, massive silver flower blossomed, emitting the sweetest fragrance I'd ever encountered.

Releasing her grip, the High Priestess pushed it toward me, reclining in her seat with hands folded across her belly. "It takes a Priestess to give the lotus life."

"Goddess, it—" It was singing! I could hear it, could see the ki surging thick in the glossy petals. My fingers traced the spot where my pendant wasn't, and without an aid to ease my burden, I leaned forward, drawn to the casual show of Priestess strength. "Incredible."

"The lotus can be traced back to the old country, Mila. It has been passed from one High Priestess to the next, from Trila-Glís to her successor, for thousands of years. All the way back to the same generation in which the Goddess blessed our blood."

"A fascinating parlor trick, to be sure," my father said, inspecting the lotus with creased brow. Touching one delicate silver petal with his forefinger. "But what purpose does it serve?"

The High Priestess collected her lotus, banishing the ki and returning it to its original state—sleepy hibernation. "A parlor trick to you, Senator Tannovic, but to your daughter? Tell me, little rogue, can you feel it? Is it *nothing* to you?"

My breath came hard, lungs tight as my eyes followed the lotus, unable to look away. How was it possible that my father felt *nothing*? Could hear *nothing* of the ethereal hymn raising gooseflesh on my skin? Even now, while dormant, I could hear it calling. Louder than the forbidden Glaith in my pocket, the Sentinels trees, and the High Priestess combined. Louder even, than the captain's impossible ki nipping at my fragile restraint, for the lotus remembered *every* Priestess who'd ever laid hands upon its withered flesh. I knew before the High Priestess confirmed it... for it was *their* song crawling through my bones. Thousands upon thousands of Priestesses. All cherished. Each adding their own unique lyric to the song of my people.

"The lotus has but one purpose in this life," the High Priestess said. "To reveal the true nature of the Priestess who feeds it. To rank her as either Triloth or Trila-Glís. This is your test, Mila," the High Priestess whispered. "Take the lotus in your hands and make it sing for us. Let it into your heart so we may see your Truth."

Sweat bloomed on my nape. My upper lip. Tracing the length of my spine—for *this* is why I'd been sent here. I could feel it, could hear it in the lotus' song.

The lotus was mine.

My Goddess-given birthright.

With hands that trembled, I claimed the ancient thing. Careful, for a moment, not to touch flesh imbued with such power. Savoring the moment, in spite of how I'd managed to find myself here.

"What's going to happen?" my father asked, leaning forward in his chair. Otherwise, still.

"No Flourishing is the same," the High Priestess returned, her voice growing more distant with each beat of my heart, with each new verse playing in my head. "Most cannot make it flower, and as such, are named Triloth. Priestesses in their own right, yes, but not contenders for *my* seat. Only a Trila-Glís—"

The tips of my fingers brushed the dried bundle— and that was it. With a single touch, I was lost, swaying to a music meant for my ears alone. Enthralled as it rose in pitch, with force enough to drown the voices of those standing closest to me.

Goddess, *this.*

Blind, I clasped the lotus in both hands, covering as much of the wrinkled skin as I could—but this time, I was *not* the one starving for a taste.

The lotus reached for me, sending tendrils of ki through my skin, reaching for the truth that lay hidden in my core. Starving for that which only the Blood could provide. It needed ki to survive, to propagate new life, and in return, held the memory of a thousand Priestesses. A tether between this world and the Void, the lotus bound them all.

"*... Feed it, Mila,*" the High Priestess whispered, her voice echoing beyond the limit of physical hearing. "*... allow the lotus to feast and claim your place among us, child...*"

Submit? As I had for the captain? I bared my teeth, fingers bloodless in my effort to deny them all. Refusing to bow, I screamed in the face of those trying to take from me.

"*... Don't fight it, girl... let the lotus see your Truth, and forget your fear. There is no persecution here...*"

Lies.

Lies that chilled, urging the dark wings trapped behind my ribs to unfurl. To beat back the waves of sedation and fight for dominance, refusing to be swallowed up by the many. With a snarl, I met the lotus halfway. Clashing with the shades of my people, with thousands of forgotten sisters and the tiny handful who still walked among the living. Their ki struck with force enough to stagger, laced with pure knowledge and millennia upon millennia of combined experience. All of it bound up in the lotus' song. Singing with a single voice, they demanded I bend.

So... hungry. Denied *so* long...

That was the lotus' truth. Perpetual denial. None had been able to quench its thirst. All those women, all that *power*, and not a single Priestess had been equal to the challenge.

Creeping... reaching through my very skin, the lotus wriggled closer. Its hunger eclipsed all but my own, desperate for more. Determined to take what I had been born to wield.

"... That's it, Mila... let the lotus in and show us what the Goddess gave you..."

She wanted to see, did she? The great and powerful High Priestess needed a flower to show her what I wasn't hiding?

Fine.

Lips peeled back, I turned on the lotus, seizing the delicate tendrils of ki before they could sink into me. Before they could take at will.

Let them see. Let them *all* see.

I forced the lotus to drink, and drink deep, baring myself to generations past. Exposing myself to judge and jury of my peers long taken by the Void, and yet, I did not kneel. Where the lotus begged for ki, I gave it. Forced the ancient thing to feast on my excess until it was ripe and heavy in my palms. Deaf to all but the song playing an endless loop, I forced it beyond satiation. Pushed until the lotus could take no more and the High Priestess' voice could be heard above those of my people—her words meaningless in the moment.

And still, I gave. Filling that desiccated flesh with everything I had, and in return? Their song... their knowledge... all that ancestral wisdom would be mine...

When I was finished, the lotus would sing a symphony to its savior, and no other.

With no choice but to accept, my essence rushed through tissue long left to ruin. I gave the lotus what it wanted—gave until the excess spilled over my clenched fingers and coiled about my wrists.

"... Mila! That's enough! Stop! Mila stop!"

Enough? Oh, but I'd hardly begun! Hadn't claimed payment for the gift I'd given so freely. Had yet to reach into the Void and seize what I was owed.

"Mila!"

Ice seared the back of my neck, shattering the delicate wisps of ki connecting me to the lotus in an instant. Lips parting on a silent scream, I was pulled from the edge by the Glaith. Forced to return to consciousness with a callous jerk, utterly drained. Denied. A debt left unfulfilled by the High Priestess herself.

"Breathe, girl," she whispered, pushing damp hair back from my face with trembling fingers. "Come back to us. That's it. Breathe."

I wanted to snarl and rage. Wanted to unleash the pain of denial she'd etched upon my every bone with a pen of Glaith, wanted to scream until until I couldn't and *she* knelt in supplication, begging for mercy.

But I couldn't.

I could do little more than what she commanded, dragging oxygen into lungs tight with agony. Blinking away tears.

So close! I'd been scant seconds from touching the Divine and all that came with it.

"Goddess," my father whispered, his familiar voice chasing away the last of the fog clouding my vision. "What does it mean?"

But the High Priestess had nothing to say. She merely stared at what had become of her most precious belonging, keeping a chunk of Glaith pressed to the back of my neck.

Without the strength to swat her away, I gazed at my Truth.

The lotus had indeed been transformed. It clung to my wrists, fuzzy runner vines holding it secure. And from my hands? *Dozens* of midnight flowers. They spilled over my fingers, some tiny, others capable of competing with that of the High Priestess for size and girth. No two were the same, and yet, each and every bud shared an enchanting mix of black and silver—the most prominent among them, a matched pair the size of my palm, glimmering with lingering ki.

On the right, a silver blossom with a black heart— its twin boasting black petals streaked with moonlight.

Petals stained by my Truth, and yet, I remained unrepentant.

After all, *they'd* wanted to see.

9

For long moments, no one spoke. There was nothing but the distant buzz of the temple's daily activities, and the ringing in my ears that only came when the Glaith touched my skin. Worse still, this particular bit of Glaith had never tasted ki, was unlike the ring or my pendant in its stark absence, for virgin Glaith was *hungry*. And the High Priestess had chosen me to feed it.

"What now?" my father asked, pale eyes fixed to the mess I'd made of my Flourishing.

The High Priestess cleared her throat. "Now," she murmured, shifting, one hand keeping the virgin Glaith pressed to my nape, the other reaching for the lotus intertwined about my fingers and snaking up my wrists. "Now we have a hard conversation."

"Just what does this mean?" my father hissed, helping her untangle the vines from my clenched fists.

But the High Priestess didn't respond, instead redoubling her one-handed effort to free the lotus from my clenched fingers. Under their manipulations the pot fell away, for the lotus had outgrown that dusty prison at my command, showering my lap in dirt and shards of clay. Both of us left poised on the cusp of true fulfillment, robbed before completion.

When she succeeded, and the lotus was torn from my hands, the High Priestess replaced it with that hateful ore. "Keep that close. Understand? No matter how uncomfortable, you're *not* to be separated from the Glaith until I say otherwise. Until I've had a moment to think."

I nodded, without the energy to speak or tear my eyes from the dark, moonlit petals of my Truth. From the debt owed and the song of my people now hidden from my ears. I could do little more than watch as she placed my lotus in the center of her desk, her veins standing out on skin gone utterly bloodless.

At length, the High Priestess reclaimed her seat, hands folded atop her desk doing little to hide a tremor that hadn't been before. "You heard that foul Caledonian general accuse Priestesses of going ki-mad, yes?" When I nodded, she leaned forward, cupping the lotus between both hands. "The general has his facts right, I'm afraid. Our history depicts a tragic tale of the very first Trila-Glís and her twin sister, from the time before the Blood split and men and women *shared* the worship of the Goddess. The sisters were identical in all areas, but one. The firstborn was Trila-Glís, destined to wield the might of the Divine and become our first High Priestess. Her sister, however, was Triloth, powerful in her own right, yes, but not the match of her elder sibling."

"The difference being?" my father asked, collecting my cold, limp fingers.

"With a single touch, a Triloth Priestess can sense everything about their subject. Down to the most subtle of emotional motivations, or lurking illness. But they are limited. They cannot manipulate ki, yet they are vessels for it. The Triloth contain ki in a manner similar to that of the Glaith itself." She paused, laying her palms flat, eyes tracing dark petals. "It takes a Trila-Glís to do both. It is our burden to *use* what the Goddess gave us."

Nodding, my father said, "The Trila-Glís are what bind them together?"

"That's right," she said, lips twitching. "And so it's been since the very first. In spite of the vast difference in their ki, those twin sisters of long ago were devoted to one another. They created the foundation on which the faith was built."

The High Priestess stood, pacing toward the panoramic glass wall overlooking the Planeth and the courtyard beyond. "The eldest, Glísel, was said to be able to commune with the Goddess herself, and at Milithia's behest she began to gather the Blood, scattered as they were across the continent. But neither sibling was prepared to deal with the ki of so many gathered in one place. It eventually drove Glísel mad." The High Priestess stroked the shining silver petals of the flower before her. "When Glísel met one such as herself—those named the Trila-Glís in her memory— the powerful ki was enough to break her mind. She was overcome with an insatiable hunger, and slaughtered more than half of Milithia's children in a single night."

I swallowed, tearing my gaze from the lotus sprawled out before me... reaching... "That's awful."

"Yes, I rather imagine it was. But the tale does not

end there, my dear. Glísel's Triloth sister, whose name has been lost to time, sacrificed herself to stop her sibling from destroying everything they'd built. She used their bond, and when Glísel attacked her own blood in a blind rage, they were both swept away in an instant, ferried into the Void on Milithia's great, silent wings. It was the link between them, you see. Built over a lifetime, it was enough to destroy even the might of a ki-mad Trila-Glís such as her.

"When the dust settled, the Blood who remained rose from the rubble, and among them was the young Trila-Glís challenger who had unintentionally triggered the catastrophe. Shaken, but alive, she plucked this very flower from the ashes and, in returning it to hibernation, showed herself worthy to claim Glísel's throne. But she knew in her heart there would come a time when she would face another such as herself. Another Trila-Glís who would challenge for the throne. And since that day," the High Priestess continued, once more gathering the lotus, "the Priestesses have trained. We use our power to heal. To *restore* life. To change it to our whim —" she grimaced, then commanded my Truth to retreat back into its shriveled brown shell. Muting the music calling out to my heart. "But that doesn't mean we're immune to failure."

My father's fingers tightened on mine. "How so?"

The High Priestess cleared her throat then turned toward the overlarge bookshelf behind her. In the center, set behind thick glass, was an ancient book cracked open to a blank page. "This book contains the account of every High Priestess to rule the Blood over the centuries. It contains the history of our people, recorded through the eyes of the women who saw it happen. In this book," she continued, returning her attention to us, "are tales of triumph—of which there have been many—and the tragic stories of those powerful Trila-Glís like Glísel who lost their way."

Hardly daring to breathe, I did nothing, said nothing... terrified for what came next. For her to damn me.

"Without the proper training, a Trila-Glís will slip into madness, Mila. They become Empaths. Ki-hungry, mindless creatures of impulse. They are drawn to the ki of any living thing, and will kill without discrimination or remorse, trying to fill a bottomless void. They are doomed."

I blinked, pulling my fingers from my father's grasp, for without the flames of vengeance bubbling in my gut, I could *see*.

She was right. The only viable option was to stay, to learn from the best of my people, or become the worst. But how was I to forget the whisper soft rasp of bearded cheeks—or the betrayal of rough hands turning on me? Pushing me to a life absent the freedom he'd claimed for himself?

"Not once," the High Priestess continued, reclaiming her seat, "in all those pages, is there mention of *two* challengers for my throne."

"There isn't now," I whispered, meeting her eye. "I have no interest in—"

"Yet here you sit, five years *after* the emergence of my challenger, a young Trila-Glís named Carly. My protégé."

"One must wonder," my father said, straightening his robes with a snap, "if this Carly of yours can compare to Mila."

I flinched. "Dad, *no.* I don't—"

"You saw what she did to that flower. Can Carly do the same? Is there any competition?"

"The difference, Senator Tannovic, is that I don't worry for the safety of those closest to Carly."

"Nor do I. With the Glaith—"

The High Priestess threw back her head, and laughed. "All the bloody Glaith has done is allowed your daughter to come into her power, unchecked. It's made her weak. A creature of impulse *you* created, and the only cage that might be capable of containing her should I fail, is made of the dirty Glaith your precious Caledonians seek to force upon the Blood. Does that surprise you, Senator?" she asked, brow raised. "That I've seen the dirty Glaith you've staked your daughter's life on? Goddess, we created it *long before* the Caledonians did. It's an alloy made with iron. Cheap production," she said with a sniff and flick of her fingers, cheeks flushed with passion, "but capable of rendering a ki-wielder utterly senseless. A slave. Is that what you want for your only daughter?"

"Of course not!"

"Then to have such *perfect* conviction, you must've spent a lifetime studying the Blood, the Glaith, and how they compliment or hurt one another?"

"Again," my father said, though his tone had quieted, "of course I haven't."

"Then you'll be happy to know I *have*," the High Priestess snapped, eyes returning to mine. "I don't know why the Goddess has sent a second challenger for my seat, but I don't much care. I won't see you descend and neither will I see you enslaved. Not if I can help it."

Shifting, my father crossed left ankle over right, but said no more.

"I'm prepared to offer you a unique position here at the temple, Mila. No one need ever know what you are."

Swallowing, I flexed my fist around the Glaith. "What does that life look like, Mistress?"

She pressed her palms flat to the table and took a breath, offering a fleeting smile. "You'll learn to control your power under my personal tutelage, but will be ranked as Triloth of moderate ability."

Unfolding, my father sat forward once more. "A convenient lie that keeps her under your thumb."

No, it was freedom. I wouldn't have to accept the trade of pendant for ring and allow the captain to go unpunished. I could bridle those dark wings begging for freedom, learn to train them before I flew.

And when the captain and I next met...

"These grounds are the home of more than just the religious center of our faith. Mine is an offer of sanctuary. You may pursue your intellectual interests, become an artist, or enter the faith. It doesn't matter to me as long as *you* are safe, Mila."

"And as long as she's never recognized as a challenger for your seat," my father returned, scowling. "You'd keep her hidden away. Your secret weapon."

The High Priestess stood, rounded her desk, and moved for the door. "Join me," she said. "Allow me to show you this place is no prison, but a home for rare and dangerous things."

I watched her go, barely able to contain my smile.

My father stood, shoulders stiff as he drew me to his side. "As you say, Your Grace. But I'd like a moment alone with my daughter, if you don't mind."

"Then I shall join young Josh and protect him from the living walls. Don't linger."

When the door whispered shut behind her, my father wrapped me in an all consuming hug. "Goddess, Mila. I've been sick with worry. Are you alright?"

I nodded against his chest, taking a moment to absorb his strength before I pulled away, and whispered, "I'm sorry."

He squeezed me, unaware that his embrace no longer felt like home for a rare and dangerous thing.

10

───────

"Where we goin', Your Grace?" Josh asked, tight on the High Priestess' heels as she led the way through twisting halls.

"I thought our newest Triloth Priestess might like to see the seat of worship here at the temple."

"Your newest"—Josh whipped around, wide, honey-brown eyes finding mine in the half-light—"Miss Tannovic, you're... you're..."

"A Triloth Priestess of moderate ability," the High Priestess said, patting his shoulder with a smile.

Gaping at me, he shook his head. "But how's such a thing possible?"

I shrugged, grinding the virgin Glaith into my palm. "Late bloomer, I guess."

"These things happen," the High Priestess agreed, breezily dismissive. "It's not overly common, but they happen."

My father squeezed my shoulder, and my chin dipped once in acknowledgment. We could do this. It was an easy lie built from the dregs of popular expectation. Nothing more than what they all wanted to hear and see, for of course, both Trila-Glís were already living and accounted for. No one was looking for a third. A rogue. For that matter, no one was looking *outside* of the Tritan women of faith for a *fourth...* and this one absent Tritan blood altogether.

Grinning now, Josh pressed two fingers to his temple. "Then you've my congratulations, Miss Tannovic." Shaking his head, his smile softened, and he said, "A Priestess," under his breath, seemingly awestruck by the revelation.

"These," the High Priestess said, turning left and saving me from his glassy-eyed admiration, "are the salt caves. They existed long before Milithia's followers settled here, but have magnificent benefits for those of us who wield ki."

Stepping farther into the caves, I gasped. "It's so... *quiet* in here."

"It's the salt." Hands sweeping out, encompassing everything from the torch-lit walls to vaulted ceilings, she inhaled. "Nothing can grow down here. The silence you're experiencing is the near complete lack of biological life. That ever-present scratching at your ki-sense is muted within these walls." She gestured at row upon row of ornate wooden benches. "This is where we come to meditate, to learn control over our Goddess given power, for here, we are free from its influence." She sent me a pointed look, glancing at my left hand buried in my pocket. "Here, *none* of us need the Glaith."

Hearing her unspoken permission, I released the virgin Glaith, allowing my senses to unfurl. For the first time since my gifts had made an appearance, there was... peace without pain. Silence that welcomed, except for the vibrant lives of those standing next to me.

"Rather cold and dank down here, if you ask me," my father said, squinting at the furthest wall. "And where is the second exit? Seems unsafe to house the most powerful women in the country without the necessary safety measures."

Ki licking quietly at my edges, I smirked, for I was my own safety measure. But... he had a point.

The High Priestess laughed, eyes crinkling. "If nothing else, Senator, I appreciate your attention to detail. There is a door at the other end of this hall."

"And where does it go?"

Silver robes swirling about her hips, she crooked a finger, and said, "To the courtyard."

But my father was not to be dissuaded. "Would that be the same courtyard housing the flock of gigantic planeth?"

"As emergency exits go," she said, smoothing her skirts, "it's not ideal, for one should never take a planeth unaware unless they are feeling particularly light on their feet, but it was the only option available to us. We've plans to make third exit through this side"—she pointed to the opposite wall—"next spring."

"As long as there are plans, I suppose," my father allowed, watching Josh stroll past the wooden benches as he went deeper into the caves, toward the far end of the room where an altar glowed under the light of several tiny candles.

Behind the altar, standing tall and silent, lurked a series of seven statues, and, head craned back, Josh asked, "What're those?"

The High Priestess' smile was sad as she too, tilted

her chin back, gaze fixed upon a twenty-foot statue of a beautiful woman with waist-length hair. "Salt carvings depicting Milithia's early history."

"I thought the Goddess' chosen form was an owl?" I said, joining them, my pockets laden with Glaith. With my ki and *his.*

The High Priestess nodded. "She was a woman, once. Like us."

"Wha' happened?"

Gesturing at the second statue in line, of the same woman with a massive frilled snake coiled around her shoulders and a contented smile etched upon her frozen lips, the High Priestess took a breath. "She was murdered by the serpent who consumes the world, by the betrayer she welcomed into her heart and into her domain."

I flinched, right hand clenching around the ring hanging heavy in my pocket, kept separate by little more than fabric and willpower.

"But Milithia is the Divine," she continued, "and for her, true death is impossible. The serpent came from the sea, and though he ruled the waves, he had never known one such as her. Milithia owned the land and the air, the sun and the moon, and everything in between—and the serpent coveted her power."

She moved toward the third statue, this one showing Milithia brought to her knees, the serpent's fangs embedded deep in the flesh above her breast. "She was caught unaware, poisoned by the betrayer, and to preserve herself she shifted her form, taking on the savage beak and wicked talons of an owl. But even the Divine can err."

We moved down the line, to an owl bound by the

slick coils of the serpent. "In her chosen form, Milithia was master of the air—brutality and grace wrapped in one heartbreaking package. But the serpent was clever. He'd watched her from afar, knew the awe-inspiring power she possessed, *and* had discovered a possible weakness."

"Flight."

"Yes, Miss Tannovic. An owl is master of the sky, but trapped on the ground by the weight of the serpent's coils, Milithia was vulnerable for the first time in her existence. She could not spread her great wings," she added, a sad little smile tugging at the corner of her lips —and one I understood all too well.

"Don't tell me the serpent *ate* her," Josh asked, already standing before the fifth statue.

"He did. And in doing so, he absorbed the power of the Divine." Here the High Priestess paused, giving us time to take in the image of a satiated serpent, his belly thick and full. "Trapped, and losing ki, Milithia did the only thing she could." She gestured at the sixth statue, a carving of the serpent consumed in flames. "She gave up her power over the sun and burned him from the inside out, destroying them both."

"She died?"

"In a way, yes." We turned to face the seventh, and final statue—an owl rising from the flames, great wings spread wide, the serpent clutched in mighty talons. "But they were both changed forever. The serpent was kissed by the Divine, and he too, was exempt from death. The flames burned away everything they were, remaking them as something new. He became master of the land and sea, for when he was reborn, he possessed a fierce set of clawed feet."

"An owl's feet."

She nodded. "In destroying him with the power of the sun, Milithia bequeathed the serpent with dominion over daylight and doomed herself to the night. But he did not inherit the fire with which she defeated him, for he could not contain it. The serpent is a creature of the sea, and the fire would not go to him."

I toyed with the band of iron hidden in my pocket. "So he became a god?"

"Yes. And his first act as the newly Divine was to banish Milithia from her homeland, for it was an island."

"Land an' sea," Josh breathed, his dark eyes glittering in the half light of the caves.

"Heartsick and full of rage, Milithia tried to shift back, to become the woman she'd been so she could crush the serpent beneath her heel and reclaim her power—but that too was forbidden to her. She was trapped in the form of an owl, for that was the form she'd taken upon her death, and was, therefore, the only one left to her upon rebirth. Left with nothing but fire and wind in her belly, Milithia took wing, seizing the serpent in her mighty talons. The men among her followers saw her intention to exact vengeance upon the serpent, and where Milithia saw a cheat and a thief, the men saw ingenuity and a fierce determination to win, whatever the cost. They were besotted with the serpent, and for her love of them, Milithia could not do it. She could not take something that inspired such love and devotion. No matter the great personal cost. So she fled, and the Priestesses with her."

I rubbed at my throat, abandoning the ring, arms crossed over my ribs. "That's so sad."

The High Priestess touched my elbow, shaking her head. "Hers is a story of perseverance, Mila. Of forgiveness and rebirth."

"What happened to th' serpent?"

"He still rules the land and the sea, of course."

Josh made a sound at the back of his throat. "Fire an' wind are a better combination anyway."

"I'm glad you think so. Now. Time is wasting. Let's move along to the labs. There are a few things down there I think you'll enjoy."

Josh straightened, head snapping to the side. "Glaith prototypes, Your Grace?"

A sly smile stretched across her lips. "Possibly."

He rubbed his hands together, grinning. "Ah, now you're speakin' my language, Your Grace."

Lips pursed, the High Priestess returned his smile, and guided us from the caves. "Do you know much about the Glaith, Josh?"

"Aye," Josh replied, falling into step beside her. "My father owns a share in th' mines, and my brothers support their families on mine wages."

"Then I expect you'll enjoy this most of all. Now you can see the sum of all their hard work and what we've managed to do with it. Ah, here we are." With practiced ease, she pressed her palm to a Glaith panel, stepping back as a set of double glass doors parted before her. Inside, I counted a dozen Tritan and Eloran heads bent over workstations, all focused on strange looking devices, wrapped up in conversation, or mixing colorful chemicals in delicate tubes. "Please don't touch anything unless I tell you otherwise."

Josh flashed his palms. "Count on it."

The High Priestess caught my eye. "Thank you, Josh, but I'm afraid I wasn't speaking to you."

I averted my eyes, left hand dipping back into my pocket—but nothing would ever be able to prepare me for the shock of touching the virgin Glaith, no matter how many times I did it.

Nodding, the High Priestess turned to a large bronze cylinder. "This is something I know you're already familiar with, though you may not have seen it like this."

Josh didn't hesitate. "Oh, aye. I recognize it. And seein' as I pilot one most days, I *should.* Glaith engine, yeah?"

The High Priestess clapped him on the shoulder. "Indeed it is, Josh. Well done."

It was his turn to blush. "Aye, well..." He cleared his throat, scrubbing at the back of his neck. "Da always said t'know your vehicle. I couldna stand not knowing how it worked. 'Course, that doesn't mean I figured it out."

The High Priestess winked. "Good. Must keep *something* for propriety's sake, hmm? And don't worry, Senator," she added, smirking. "It won't be long now before we're ready to reveal the next line of Glaith engines for you to stick in a ridiculously over-priced coach."

"More efficient and capable of greater speeds than the last?"

"Naturally," she replied, then waved at a tall Tritan man. "Ancaster?"

He dropped what he was doing, and said, "Your Grace?"

"This is Mila," she said, pulling me front and center, her fingers tight on my shoulders.

"Have we a new Priestess?" Ancaster asked, scrubbing at his cropped silver-blond hair.

"Triloth of moderate ability," I said, tapping my temple.

"Welcome, little Triloth. Most Priestesses aren't a danger down here," he said, returning my gesture. "Don't have the power to do any real harm to the prototypes. Just keep your hands to yourself and there shouldn't be a problem."

The Glaith dug into my palm as the High Priestess' fingertips bit into my shoulders in silent warning. "I will, sir."

Eyes crinkling, he rubbed his hands together. "Right. The grand tour! As you've heard, my name is Ancaster, and with the High Priestess' aid, I run these labs."

"They're impressive, sir."

"Then let's start with the most impressive thing we have to offer," he said, sweeping his hands over two delicate circlets of silver—one finger-sized, the other much larger—connected by a fragile chain of the same precious metal. "These are the Dosmui Circlets." Fingers splayed over his heart, he winked. "Named for their brilliant creator, of course."

A slender Eloran woman across the bench snorted.

"Not a word from you, Alicia," Ancaster huffed, plucking the silver Dosmui Circlets from their case.

Alicia made a sound at the back of her throat, and though a smile twitched her lips, she did not look up from her work.

"Anyway. These circlets are worn like so—" The largest circlet swung open on a tiny hinge, and with his free hand, Ancaster snapped it shut around his wrist.

Then, careful of the thin silver chain, he slipped the ring over the middle finger of the same hand, pausing only when it stuck over the knuckle. "At their core, the circlets are pure Glaith. Unlike our esteemed Trila-Glís here," he said with a nod at the High Priestess, "a Triloth Priestess hasn't the strength to do more than a few minor healings a day, if any. But with *my* circlets, they'll be able to draw upon ki stored within the Glaith itself, for the longer it is worn by a ki-wielder, the more powerful the circlet. It will greatly improve their capacity to heal."

"That's incredible!" my father breathed, eyes fixed upon the silver chains.

"You hear that, Alicia? *Incredible.* And I haven't even showed them the most impressive part!" Ancaster stooped toward us, voice lowered to a theatrical whisper. "I'm not of the Blood, you see, but I carry the gene. *All* Tritans do. This design allows those of us who merely carry the Blood to access ki stored within the Glaith. And with the proper training, they'll grant any regular old citizen the power to heal as the Priestesses do."

My jaw slackened.

"Ah ha! You see Alicia? Shock and awe."

"Careful, wee Triloth," Alicia said, her voice light and airy, vibrant green eyes glittering. "You'll not want to give him too much praise. His head won't fit in the room."

"But that *is* incredible!" Josh returned. "Such a thing will save thousands of lives."

Ancaster nodded. "You're quite right, lad." He tapped a workbench beside the case for the silver circlets, picking up a half-finished, golden set of the same make and design. "We're still testing the benefits of several different metals for optimal conductivity, you see, but we're hoping to be in production by the end of next year."

"Promises, promises," Alicia said, approaching. "You canna' say that until you've figured out the charging issue. You canna' expect the Priestesses to be responsible for charging a nation's worth of circlets, now can you?"

Ancaster tapped the side of his nose. "Don't you worry, my dearest Alicia. I've already got that figured out."

She made that sound at the back of her throat. "Right. Well, come this way if you'd like t'see a final product."

My father nodded. "Please."

"This 'ere is a shield," she said, and it was only when she turned that I realized just how young she was. "Powered by the Glaith, o'course. Go on, wee Triloth," she said, sparkling green eyes meeting mine before she jerked her chin toward her project. "Touch it. It's stable enough."

The High Priestess laid a hand on my shoulder. "Allow me," she said, and stepped forward, placing the tip of her index finger against a smooth Glaith panel. Infused with her powerful ki, it lit up, making the Glaith sparkle and dance.

"Just'a little more, Your Grace. Ah. There. That's enough. Hands off, if you please." Alicia flicked a switch when the High Priestess broke away, adjusted two round silver dishes, then said, "You'll want t'step back. Testing shield!"

A rippling blue field flickered into view between the

two silver dishes. Tiny hairs all over my body stood on end, raised by the crackle of static, the scent of burning ozone thick in the air. "Goddess, but that's pretty."

"Aye, but dangerous, wee Triloth." With a gleeful smirk, Alicia picked up a little ball of paper and tossed it at the shield. It promptly burst into flame. "I don't recommend touchin' it, yeah?"

My father tapped his chin, pale blue eyes gleaming. "Can ordinary citizens use this, as they can the Dosmui Circlets?"

Alicia ribbed her boss, grinning. "Just as soon as Ancaster gets his *incredible* technology t'work, sure. Don't see why it couldna be adapted t'fit anything with the Glaith at its core."

"I can't even imagine the potential this has—" Before I could finish, the shield flickered twice, then died, leaving an afterimage burning in my eyes. "Wh-What happened?"

"I didn't give it much power, Mila," the High Priestess said.

Alicia shrugged. "I'm afraid t'admit, the shield is limited by the strength of the Priestess who wields it. You're Triloth, girl, and you'd likely need a few friends t'make the shield last more than a few minutes. Now, with the Trila-Glís activating it, we've a different story. Would you like t'see—"

An explosion rocked the ceiling above us, setting off a chorus of screams and rattling dirt loose from the rafters.

My father's hand wrapped around my elbow as he pulled me tight to his chest. "Goddess be damned, what in the world was *that*?"

"I—" The High Priestess gasped as another, lesser

explosion popped above us. "I don't know! Just a moment! Let me—"

I released the virgin Glaith just in time to feel her senses whip out around us, touching every living thing within the temple grounds. When she came back to herself, eyes wide, pupils dilated, I knew what she'd say before the words crossed her lips. For I had felt it too.

"Goddess. We're under attack."

11

———

Something above us crashed to the floor, igniting another round of terrified screams as a poof of dust was shaken free of the rafters. I glanced toward the ceiling, rolling the virgin Glaith between thumb and forefinger as a chorus of questions circled around the room. Spoken so quickly and by so many people, I couldn't begin to put names to faces.

"What's happening up there?"

"Who would dare attack us here? We're a peaceful nation, for the love of the Goddess!"

The foundations of the building shook with the next explosion, rattling test tubes and setting the scientists off once more.

"Can you hear that?"

"Are those *screams*?"

Seizing my forearm, the High Priestess motioned for silence, but it was my father who said, "It's the Glaith. They must be here for the Glaith."

"Who?" Ancaster asked. "Who's here for the Glaith?"

For the space of three breaths, the room was silent. And then, "The Caledonians." It was an answer spoken by my father and the High Priestess as one, for they both knew. She with her otherworldly senses, he because of the countless hours spent negotiating trade deals with the very warmongers currently hammering those beautiful carved front doors to bits.

"But they're our allies!" Ancaster said, spluttering.

"That doesn't change the fact that there's an army of Elites on our front steps," the High Priestess snapped, glancing at my father. "The Priestesses cannot hold them. Do you understand me, Senator?"

My father nodded, swallowing. "They'll be here for the prototypes and raw materials, I'd wager. Bet they'd *love* to get their traitorous hands on technology that allows unblooded citizens to wield ki, too."

Ancaster cursed, clenching his fists as he spoke above the terrified mutterings of his colleagues. "We will not sit idle and let those bloody warmongers take what we worked so hard to create! What are your orders, Your Grace?"

The High Priestess shook her head. "There's no time. Goddess, they're already at the gate." She shook off her anxiety, summoning a young woman in a white coat. "Send word to the others that I'll be up in a moment. They must hold the line for as long as they can, do you hear me? We're evacuating these labs."

"Y-Yes, Your Grace."

The High Priestess nodded, pushing a trembling hand through her silver-blonde hair. "Good. Hurry now. We haven't a moment to spare. I'll be right behind you."

Stepping forward, Josh cleared his throat. "Have you any weapons? We could fight—"

Ancaster cut him off with a humorless bark of laughter, thunderclouds gathering behind his pale Tritan eyes as he flung his hand toward the ceiling. "None I'm willing to test right now, son. They're more likely to backfire and kill us all than do any predictable good."

I knew the feeling well.

"Then we flee." My father released me, stepping up to stand beside the High Priestess. "My estate is neutral ground. We'll go there."

Ancaster snorted. "Senator, do you think neutral ground will matter to those willing to attack a bloody *temple*?"

"Perhaps not," the High Priestess allowed, "but we cannot stay *here*." She clapped her hands. "Now. I want each of you to pack up a sample of your work—the best you've got. You will destroy the rest. And then..." She trailed off, pressing her hand to the hollow at the base of her throat. "And then you will flee."

"But this is our home!"

She flinched when a crash was followed by a series of terrified screams from the floor above. "Not anymore, it isn't. Quickly now. The Priestesses can't hold the line for much longer."

Scrambling to do as their mistress bade, the men and women of Tritan's research program began to dismantle their experiments.

Tears shining unshed in her eyes, the High Priestess squeezed my arm. "Mila, come. Help me with this."

Wrenching my eyes away from the organized chaos, I moved to her side. With trembling hands, she pulled a chunk of virgin Glaith from the bin, pressing it between her hands.

"What are you doing?"

"Glaith absorbs ki, Mila. Its limit to store ki over time have not yet been reached, even here in the temple labs. Just a moment—" She raised her voice, shouting above the din of destruction. "Place anything you want destroyed on this bench, please!" After several shouts of affirmation, she turned back to me. "You and I are going to dump as much ki into this Glaith as we can, my little rogue. Between us, we shall incinerate everything the Tritan science department has worked for over the last five years. Now," she said, putting the last shard in place and completing the circle, "give your Glaith to your father and take my hands."

I did as she bade—though the captain's ring remained in my possession even as the ki of a Trila-Glís flooded my every cell. With each new item added to the pile, I winced, heart beating at the base of my throat. Every distant scream and unexplained *bang* pushed my heart rate higher, until sweat beaded along my brow and my breath came in uneven bursts.

"Relax, Mila. It's going to be okay."

Lost to the seductive whisper in the air, I turned sightless eyes upon her, tasting the lie. "No. It won't."

The High Priestess cursed, cupping my cheeks in her palms. Forcing calm. "You must promise you'll keep the Glaith on your person at all times, Mila. I know it won't be enough to contain you forever, and I wish I had time to build a proper wall around your power, but for now a promise must suffice."

"Y-yes, Your Grace. I promise."

She nodded. "Good. I wish—"

"That's the last of it," Ancaster said, clapping the dust off his hands. "They can take whatever else they find but it'll be of little use to them without one of us to decipher it."

"Good. Now flee! Through the salt caves." The High Priestess squeezed my hands. "Are you ready?" At my nod, she offered a weak smile, then said, "Good. Then give me everything you've got—"

Something above us shattered, striking the floor with enough force to buckle my knees.

But I didn't flinch, for my mind had been flooded with another, wilder ki. The Elites had broken the line. I could feel it. Without the Glaith to deaden my senses, I couldn't *stop* feeling it. "They're coming," I whispered, voice lifeless in the face of so *much*.

"I know. Are you with me, Mila?"

The Elites... they were so... wild... so *powerful*...

"Are you with me, girl?"

The captain. Standing directly above... he was... coming. For me... I could feel those rough fingers on *my* pendant... caressing... so hungry...

With a snarl, the High Priestess pulled me to her, seizing my mind in an unbreakable grip. Too late, three young Priestesses barreled into the room, their faces streaked with soot and blood. But the High Priestess would not be distracted. She forced me to dump the excess ki storming through my system into the Glaith clenched between our hands, commanding my ki as if it were her own to use. Exhausting us both.

"Just a little more, Mila. That's it. Get back! All of you, back!" But for all her power, all her mastery of ki, her hands trembled in mine. I felt it when she swayed, nearly at her limit—but I hadn't had *my* chance. I shifted her grip, my hands on top as I reached deeper, pulling everything I could reach to the fore. Forcing her to take *everything*, as I had with the lotus.

And then, just as the blackness began to creep in, the High Priestess tossed the Glaith into the pile of Tritan research and incomplete technology. It ignited in a flash of blinding white, incinerating everything within reach and searing the exposed skin on my cheeks and chest. A scream tore free of my throat, and I collapsed, trying to shield myself from the heat.

Hands, rough and familiar pulled me free, running over my exposed skin.

I groaned, trying to avoid the stimulation—it was too much! Too soon... my ki-sense was bleeding and raw. And my skin... "Don't. Goddess, *don't!* The High Priestess... help... help *her*. Leave me be."

"Don't you worry, Miss Tannovic." Josh. Hands too familiar on my shoulders. Neck. Face. Propping me up against his hip. "Ancaster got her free o'the blast. Now up you get. I know it hurts, lass, but we've got t'move." He hoisted me over his shoulder, one arm wrapped around my waist as he sprinted from the room, squeezing the breath from my lungs with every step.

After a few more seconds of contact with his vibrant, Eloran ki, however, I began to squirm. "J-Josh. Put me down." I dug my nails into his lower back, trying to get his attention.

"Just relax, Miss Tannovic. I've got you."

"I-I'm going to be sick..."

"Right." He skidded to a halt, swinging me down from his shoulder just in time for me to expel the contents of my stomach all over the floor. "Alright, miss?"

I nodded, pressing my forehead to the wall.

"Step back, Josh. Allow me." Ki—brilliant and fierce —brushed over raw nerves as the High Priestess pressed her hands to my face. "Thank you, Mila," she whispered, commanding the burned skin on my face and chest to cool, to knit and become whole. Effortless. "That was quite the show, my darling."

When she finished, I sighed, head falling back, watching with hooded eyes. How? How had the High Priestess recovered so quickly, when I was too weak to do more than simply *be*? Too drained, even, to reach into my pocket and drink from a well of Elite strength.

She smoothed my hair off my face, smiling as she said, "Here. Your Glaith."

With a nod, I honored my promise. Grinding my teeth against the wash of icy cold nothing.

"Good girl. Now, go with your father and the others. I'll be right behind you."

"But—"

"I cannot leave my Priestesses behind. Go. I'll follow."

My father's hands settled on my shoulder. "Up you get, Mila. Can you run?"

"I can carry her if you'd like, sir?"

"N-No," I breathed, letting my father pull me up, dragging me behind him. "We can't leave her—"

A streak of brilliant green light whooshed past my head, freezing a scream in my throat as the wall behind us collapsed in a puff of hot glass and bits of stone. The rubble spattered over me, and my father grunted, taking the brunt of it. Staggering and disoriented, I coughed, scrubbing at the grit covering my face. "Daddy! Goddess, are you alright?"

He groaned, a trembling hand finding mine as the

dust settled all around us. "Yes"—he coughed—"I'm fine."

Heavy boots crunched on broken glass. "Ah, there you are." And through the haze of debris, I could see who'd spoken. Could see General Tilcot himself filling the ruined doorway. A smirk fixed to his lips. "We'd like a word."

"A *word?*" the High Priestess snarled, her fury punching me through the Glaith. "General Tilcot, you've broken more treaties than I can count! How *dare* you attack us here!" One hand pressed to the wall, she shoved filthy hair back from her face. "Get out of my house before I remove you."

"Well, you see," the General replied, stepping aside to reveal several more dark shadows at his back, "we weren't the first to break treaties today, Your Grace. Your people are traitorous cowards, or hadn't you heard? Caledonia was bombed this morning. By Tritan religious extremists. *Your* people."

"What—that's absurd!" the High Priestess exclaimed. "Worship of the Goddess is *peaceful—*"

"I'm not interested in your pathetic excuses, woman. You, and any other Priestesses you're hiding in this little treehouse paradise, are coming with me. You shall be interrogated under the suspicion of terrorism against the Empire. Everything in these labs, including the rats cowering behind your skirts, are now property of the Empire of Caledonia."

The High Priestess squawked, reeling back from the accusation. "Terrorism? Are you *insane?* We are a peaceful nation, sir. We've hardly any military to speak of, and certainly none residing here at the bloody *temple!* We are your allies, for the love of the Goddess—"

"Not after this morning, woman. What will it be? Will you demonstrate the ethics of your so-called peaceful nation, or are we in for another showing of your true colors?"

"Our true—General *Tilcot*. You will not lay a single finger on my people."

"Oh, I assure you, woman. I'll be doing *much* more than that."

The High Priestess slid her right foot back, summoning her ki in a whirlwind around her. "Senator Tannovic, you know where to go and you know what I expect of you. Now flee. I will take care of these pests."

Face ashen, my father merely nodded, placing a trembling hand on my elbow as he tried to force me to move.

An evil grin twisted General Tilcot's handsome face. "I thought so."

"Mila. Let's go, lass," Josh hissed, joining my father in his attempt.

I swatted at their hands, lips pulled back as I glared at the general. "I stand with the High Priestess."

"No, lass, you won't. She's a powerful woman. She can handle this. Now come, girl. Don' make me throw you over m'shoulder."

General Tilcot took another step, shifting a heavy looking weapon off his shoulder. At his touch, it began to glow a vibrant, poisonous green. "Fan out, Elites. I want every one of these Tritan scum hogtied at my feet in the next five minutes. My boots are in need of a good cleaning."

With a laugh as savage as that of her rising ki, the

High Priestess shook out her hands. "Do you plan to shoot me, General Tilcot? Because that's the only way you can move beyond this room. I've taken your measure, Elite. You cannot hope to match my power."

"I guess we'll have to see about that, now won't we?"

I stepped clear of the rubble, gathering my ki about me as the High Priestess had. It wouldn't take much. Just a single touch... and I'd blend my ki with that of the general's. I'd feast on his essence until there was nothing left, and then? The dark shadows all around him were next. It would be over before it had even begun.

"M-Mila, no." Hand outstretched to stop me, my father elbowed past Josh—just as a familiar face stepped clear of the general's shadow.

I froze.

Captain Rawlings.

He too was armed, and though his weapon was smaller, it glowed with thrice the brilliance of the gargantuan thing clasped in the general's large hands. And when his eyes found mine—which they did without fault—his lips curved in a dark smile. Lips I had touched only this morning. Hands that had cradled were now encased in fine black leather, wrapped around a thing meant to kill.

I stumbled back, left shoulder bumping against my father's, right pressed against Josh's chest. "Goddess, *no*." His pendant—*my* pendant—winked at me, concealing him from the High Priestess' senses. A power she was unprepared to face, because I had not warned her!

"I've got her, Senator!" Josh wrapped his hand in the fabric at my lower back, hauling me away. "Let's *go*, Miss Tannovic."

"Get your hands off me! I have to—"

"You're not going anywhere with that little Priestess, Eloran," General Tilcot said, tipping his head to one side, then the other, cracking his thick neck as he drew a dainty set of golden chains from his pocket. Letting them dangle on a thick index finger. "She's *mine*."

Trembling and gray, my father stepped in front of me. "You'll not lay a hand on my daughter."

The captain took a step, inky gaze blazing defiance.

"A senator's daughter, hmm?" the general said, inspecting my soot-caked clothes and skin. "I'll make you an offer, Senator. Bring her here, and I will consider making her my personal slave. If for no other reason than I enjoy breaking spoiled brats." He laughed, baring perfect, white teeth. "You can resist, of course, but she will be detained either way. And I won't be feeling so lenient then, you see. I'll make her a garrison whore before she's sold to the highest bidder."

"How *dare* you make such vile—"

The general grinned and raised two fingers. A mockery of the Tritan salute, for a moment later those fingers fell, and he said, "Attack."

Four Elites rushed forward, large bodies dwarfing the slight form of the High Priestess. But she did not falter. She waited, even as they washed over her, letting them damn themselves.

One by one, they fell, dropping to the floor, boneless and without the ki they had come to rely upon—a lenient punishment for those who dared touch Milithia's chosen without consent. For though it would be laughably easy to do so, she did not kill the would-be usurpers. Not a single one.

She flicked her now-sloppy braid over her shoulder,

stepping over a crumpled Elite. "Is that all you've got, General Tilcot? I must say, I'm rather disappointed. I thought you came prepared for a fight."

He snarled, chains in hand as he lunged for her. But general or no, he too fell at her feet. Unconscious and alive, though I screamed, "Kill him, mistress! Please!" Begging to watch a man die, and all but shouting that there was something corrupt within my breast.

Sending me a cutting glance that demanded my silence, the High Priestess ignored me, for the general was but a minor irritant in the face of the power possessed by a fully trained Trila-Glís.

"Bloody hell," Josh breathed at my back, entranced, as I was, by the beauty of the High Priestess in action.

She took a step toward the only Elite still on his feet. "What of you, boy?" she asked, hair beginning to stand on end with the static of stolen Elite ki. "Do you dare challenge me in my own house?"

Cold dread swept through me when he didn't reply, and I shook Josh's hands off, rushing to the High Priestess' side. "High Priestess, please! Be careful—"

"Did I not tell you to leave?" she snarled, head snapping toward me, pupils so dilated, black had swallowed the blue.

Captain Rawlings chose that moment to strike—but the High Priestess was ready. She caught him about the throat, her slender fingers curved into savage claws as she latched on, stripping him of his life force without hesitation or remorse.

A grunt burst from his lips, but the young, impossible captain was more than he appeared. He had the strength to spare and used it wisely, pulling his left glove off with his teeth, he flung it to the floor and seized my pendant.

"No!"

It was too late. The High Priestess cried out, over-whelmed, back arching as she tried to contain the ki of *two* rare and dangerous creatures. And though his knees had begun to buckle and perspiration beaded along his brow, a smile spread across his lips. For his gaze had found mine once more.

I sunk an elbow into Josh's middle—over and over and *over*—letting the virgin Glaith clatter to the floor when he released me. Swelling in answer to the betray-er's challenge, I bellowed, surged toward them with great, dark wings beating at my ribs.

Grunting, the captain broke the chain from which my pendant hung, engulfing her forearm. And with gloved hand, dug into his trouser pocket, withdrawing a bracelet of matte black.

Dirty Glaith. I knew the instant I saw it—felt a cold like no other spilling from the combination of iron and Glaith. "Your Grace!"

Recovered, Josh's arm looped about my waist, and I lashed out—only to feel the bite of my promise at the back of my neck. As the High Priestess had done, Josh pressed the Glaith to the back of my neck. Cutting me off from the whirlwind of chaos of two clashing super-powers, I was helpless to do *anything* but watch as Captain Asher Rawlings completed his attack. With a tiny, audible *click* that echoed through my every cell, I watched the Mistress of the Temple crumple before him.

"Time t'go, Miss Tannovic."

"You bastard," I rasped, grunting when he set his

shoulder to my ribs. "Put me down! You don't understand!"

"Hate me all you want, lass, but you're *my* charge. I'll not lose you t'likes of *him*."

As Josh began to sprint, ferrying me away from the scene of my greatest sin, I watched Captain Rawlings shake his head, recovering as he rose to a full stand. It was not the threat of violence, nor the alarming lack of ki where the High Priestess had once been, that bought my compliance.

No. The terror that seized my heart was inspired by the *promise* glittering in those inky depths.

12

"How could you?"

Josh brushed a sodden lock of hair from his eyes, glaring as he set me down on a wooden bench in the salt caves. "And what exactly would you have had me *do*, Miss Tannovic? Challenge him to a brawl? He took the High Priestess down as if it were *nothing*." He glanced over his shoulder. "You're a Triloth Priestess. You couldna stand against something like that, even if—"

"Shut your mouth," I snarled, virgin Glaith cutting into my palm. "You have no idea what I am capable of."

"I've known you since you were *twelve*, Miss Tannovic." He laughed, then seemed to think better of it, throwing up his hands with a disgusted snort. "Get that bloody door open, Ancaster. We've got a ki-mad Elite hot on our tails, and it'll not take him long t're-cover. What good is a fuckin' emergency door tha' won't open?"

"It's jammed!" Ancaster shouted, his face red and

glistening. "The damned thing hasn't been opened in years."

Tapping the pins holding the door in place, my father scrubbed at his forehead with the back of his wrist. "We'll take it off the hinges, lads."

For a moment, I watched them work, crushing the Glaith between trembling fingers. Fighting not to dissolve into a blubbering puddle of tears. I should have warned the High Priestess the first chance I'd had! Maybe then she wouldn't have been taken unaware. Maybe then, she'd be here to guide us from this place. To guide me...

"Is she gone? Is the High Priestess really gone?"

The question drew my attention to the three young Priestesses we'd acquired in the labs. Huddled together, they clung to each other in the semi-dark.

I swallowed, averting my eyes. "She's alive. That's what matters."

"And what of the Elect? She must be taken too. I can't sense either one of them. What will we do without the Trila-Glís to guide us? And—and the others. Goddess."

"Hush," the tallest of the group breathed, tilting her face toward me, and I recognized her as the willowy young Priestess who'd parked my father's coach in the back lot. Annabelle. "When can you sense anything but yourself in these caves? We know nothing for certain, sister. Don't borrow trouble."

I made a sound at the back of my throat, for they did not know what I'd seen. How easily the High Priestess had fallen at his hands. They did not know what I'd done.

"It's Mila, right?"

My eyes flicked to her face, and I nodded once, jaw clenched too tight to speak.

"Belle—" she inclined her head, pressing two fingers to her temple. "Call me Belle. Are you alright?"

A startled bark of laughter burst from my lips. "No!" Throat aching and vision blurred, I shook my head. "I just watched the High Priestess—and now we have to leave her here. With *him*. Because I didn't—"

"Shh," she soothed, and reached for me.

I leapt back, swiping at my eyes with the back of my hand. "I'm-I'm sorry. You can't… don't touch me."

"Apologies, sister." She showed me her palms. "I only meant to ease your pain."

"Th-Thank you but I don't need—"

"That's it!" Ancaster shouted. "We've got it open. Quickly now. Through the courtyard."

Hair damp with sweat, blue robes snapping about his ankles, my father claimed my elbow, but I shook him off, glaring at Belle. "How? How can I leave her behind? How can *you*?"

"Because she sacrificed herself for us, Mila." Belle smiled, tears spilling over her lashes. "The Goddess will protect her, but we cannot fight this army as we are. I was there. I watched the Elites break the line like we weren't standing there trying to hold it. They have… their weapons are… I don't know. The power…" she shivered. "We can't fight them. Not now. We don't have the resources. But what we're doing in the labs is too important to fall into the wrong hands. Into Caledonian hands. They'll corrupt any good we were trying to do here. Those people," she continued, pointing to the dark tunnel swallowing the ragged line of filthy refugees, "are the vehicle of our vengeance. Right now, those men and women of science are what's important. We must get them to safety, where they can be protected, and *then* we will plan our counterstrike."

Smoothing damp palms on my skirt, I nodded, clutching the High Priestess' Glaith. She was right. If a true Trila-Glís could fall so easily, what hope did I have, weakened and with no training to speak of?

"We'll sort it out later, girls. Quickly now," my father said, shepherding Belle into the dark. When it was just the two of us, he held his hand out to me, beckoning.

I filled my lungs with a deep, steadying breath and reached for him. "Daddy—"

Captain Rawlings skidded to a halt at the end of the hall, weapon spitting green flames at the floor, *my* pendant clutched in his free, gloveless hand. Inky eyes darting from me, to my father, and back.

My father shouted, hands outstretched. "Come to me, girl!"

Captain Rawlings swung his weapon toward my father. "Don't take another step, Senator."

An uncharacteristic sneer spread across my father's face and he pressed forward, daring the man to shoot.

The captain grimaced and shifted his aim to my face. "I said, don't."

"You'd shoot an unarmed girl, Elite?"

"Are you willing to bet that I won't?"

Blood screamed in my ears.

"I thought not," the captain continued, taking another step into the caves. "Now, kindly stand back, Senator. That's it. All the way into that dark little hole."

"Daddy—"

The captain's ki whipped at me through virgin Glaith. Whispering... urging... "Come to me."

"Don't you dare," my father hissed, fists clenched at his sides.

The captain raised his palms, letting his weapon dangle by the trigger from his middle finger. And he took another step, this one to the side. "I'll be good to you," he purred and swept his thumb over my pendant, caressing, making me feel it on my lower lip. His ki surged into my mind, hammering at me with a soothing promise, abusing the link he'd left behind with a kiss. "You'll never want for anything."

"You're not a slave!" my father shouted, voice cracking. "You're a senator's daughter! *My* daughter! Come on, baby girl. Come here. To me."

Hands trembling, I tried to turn, tried to focus on my father above all else... Trying *not* to feel the promise tugging at me... teasing my senses...

The captain smiled. "It won't be a bad life. I know you can feel whatever this is—" he gestured at the twenty or so paces separating us, shortening the gap with another step.

"Don't let him do this to you, baby. Please!"

The captain tilted his head to the side, glancing back toward the direction he'd come, ignoring my father. "The others are coming, little Priestess. Trust me when I say you don't want one of them to realize what you are—"

"*You* don't know what she is!"

With a throaty laugh, the captain's dark eyes flicked over my shoulder. "Of course I do." He took another step, letting my pendant—my *mother's* pendant—catch the dim light and my father's eye. "We're the same, she and I."

But he was steady. "Hardly, my daughter is a thousand times your superior."

"I know it doesn't make sense right now, Priestess," the captain continued, slipping a little closer, "but I'm trying to help you. You don't want one of the others as your master."

"Her master? Ha! She would never—"

The captain flung everything he had at me, swamping my mind with want... desperate need. "Come to me, little Priestess..."

I blinked, taking a step forward. Scratching at the back of my mind, my father's voice continued to needle me. But... I could no longer hear individual words. Could hear nothing but the purr vibrating through the air between us, super heating my skin and thoughts.

"That's it. Good girl... Only a few more steps."

My knee struck a wooden bench, and I frowned, blinking down at the offending object.

"Baby please!" my father shouted, stepping into my peripheral vision. "Come here. Come to me, baby girl."

Ki whipped at me, and I turned back to Captain Rawlings as he took another step. "Look, I know it's not ideal, and I certainly never thought—" he swept his hand through thick, dark hair, pendant swinging wildly beside the sharp line of his jaw. "I didn't want—"

He didn't *want*? Had he not made that clear in our alley? When he'd pushed me into the arms of the one woman I'd spent years trying to avoid? A woman *I'd* betrayed in turn. My throat constricted, but I wrenched my eyes from his handsome face and stuffed my hand into right pocket. No. I wouldn't be taken by sweet, soft words and enticing ki. Not again. This was *all* his doing.

Lies.

When his ring slipped onto my middle finger, Glaith biting deep, his eyes lit up. "Can you feel it?"

I could. A perfect match made of deceit.

But I had seen my Truth. I had watched the High Priestess' face blanch white in the shadow of dark wings begging for freedom. I *alone* knew what lurked behind the Glaith.

"I can give you *everything,*" he whispered beneath my skin. *Come...*

Wanted everything, did he?

Lips pulled back, I snarled, spinning the ring until the Glaith sat in my palm, trying to crush the foreign family crest into dust. Letting my Truth fill a precious stone already brimming with Elite ki. It reacted faster than the virgin Glaith the High Priestess and I had used in the labs, heating up against my skin. Burning the flesh of my palm—but I persisted, ignoring the searing pain.

The captain's eyes went wide. "What are you doing? Stop!"

"I—" my fist began to smoke, "—am not—" flames of blue and purple ignited my skin, "—a slave!"

But I didn't stop. In spite of the agony, I watched it burn, pushing until the pain faded and the world began to spin.

Although his lips were moving, I could no longer hear the young captain... the betrayer. Could only see the alarm spreading across his features as he began to sprint toward me. But the Glaith was too hot, and with the last of my strength, I peeled the ring free from twisted flesh, and tossed it toward the wooden benches. Sending a prayer to the Goddess that my aim be true— that this is why she'd sent me here.

To stop *him.*

For a moment, as it bounced on the wood, nothing happened. The captain's feet pounding against the cold, salty floor eclipsed the silent dance of metal on wood, and when his ring disappeared from sight, I knew all was lost.

I had truly failed.

My knees wobbled and I sank to the floor in a boneless heap, watching with disinterest as the captain continued to close the gap. It wouldn't be long now.

A flash of white seared my retinas, but I was without the strength to shield my eyes before it all went black.

13

"Mila!"

Seized with bone cracking coughs, I gasped for breath, smothered by heavy smoke filling my lungs.

Fire.

I peeled my lids open, unable to see anything but a hazy, orange glow.

Fire. The salt caves were on *fire*.

Struggling to bring the world into focus, I planted both hands on the still-cool floor—and screamed.

My entire being exploded with agony, and I gasped, trying to locate the source in my inebriated state. As soon as I did, however, I wished I hadn't. My right palm was burned black and raw, an oozing wound consuming most of what had once been recognizable. Rendering it useless.

The ring. I'd overloaded the captain's ring.

Captain Rawlings.

He wasn't dead—I could feel him even now...

Using my undamaged hand, I pushed myself up,

teeth clenched so hard I was sure they'd crack under the pressure. I could see his tall figure through the flames, pacing at the edge of an uncrossable barrier.

"Mila! Oh, thank the Goddess, sister, I thought you were dead! Josh! Over here! she's alive!"

I squinted, trying to make out the blurry faces of Belle and Josh hovering above me.

"Miss Tannovic! Can you move, lass?"

My head swiveled around as my father dropped to his knees at my side. "Goddess, Mila. I thought I'd lost you."

A funny little sound crawled up the back of my throat. Something halfway between a groan and a laugh. Hadn't they? Wasn't I dead?

"You have to stand up. Come on now. The fire won't keep him back for long."

I turned bleary eyes to the flames. Captain Rawlings had stopped moving, was simply standing as close as he could bear, eyes fixed upon me. Making me feel every last drop of seething fury. His denial.

"Come *on*, lass!" Josh stooped, sweeping his arms beneath my legs. "I've got you. Just wrap your hands around my neck—Gods, your *hand!*"

A hysterical giggle burst through my lips and I flexed my right fingers, snorting when the skin crackled and flaked. "That's pretty gross, isn't it? I can't even feel it..."

My father captured my charred fingers in his, hiding them away from sight. "Don't do that, Mila. It'll be okay, baby girl."

"You haven't called me that in ages, daddy." Cold all over, I closed my eyes and went limp, unable to feel anything at all. So... *so* tired...

"Mila, wake up!" A chilly finger forced my eyelids open as Priestess ki kissed my senses. "She's in shock. I don't have the strength for a healing of this magnitude, but—"

"You won't have anything t'heal if we wait much longer, Miss Belle," Josh said, pressing me closer to his chest.

"Yes," my father added, gasping for breath. "We haven't got much time before they're on us again."

"This way," Belle replied, her voice distorted through the fog filling my ears. "You must run straight through the planeth or they *will* defend their territory. They'll already be agitated by the others running through their flock."

An explosion rocked the tunnel, making Josh curse on a stumble, cracking his elbow on the stone wall. To his credit, he tried to protect my head, but the shock rippled through me anyway, dragging a ragged yelp from my raw throat, vision stuttering. Squeezing me closer, Josh pushed through, murmuring a litany of soothing gibberish under his breath as he went.

He needn't have bothered, for I was long past the point of caring. What was another bump or scrape? Just add it to the list, because Goddess knew I couldn't tell the difference between them anymore. I squinted, trying to focus on the blackened mess my right hand had become. But... there were two burned dead things dancing before my eyes. Had I ruined both hands and forgotten?

Our ragged group burst into the courtyard, sunlight forcing me to bury my face against Josh's chest.

And for a moment, it seemed as if everything might fall into place. That is, until a two-toned squawk reverberated through my ears, followed by a hollow *thonk, thonk, thonk!*

"Don't stop moving!" Belle shouted over her shoulder, sprinting just ahead of us, the flash of her silver skirts flicking in my peripherals.

The planeth.

Great colorful wings spread wide, one of the massive, flightless birds threw his head back, snapping his lower beak in quick succession of three—a warning which was quickly picked up by the rest of the flock. As my father, Josh, and Belle continued to sprint through planeth territory, the flock-leader crouched low, his great feathered frill puffing wide for a moment before it flattened against his skull.

And then he jumped, launching his weight toward Josh from across the courtyard, screaming in that strange two-toned squawk. Separating us from my father and Belle, he landed on the path in front of us, stomping his feet and spreading his wings as he pulled in a great, rumbling breath, rising to full height. Neck coiled.

Josh skidded to a halt, dropping me to my feet and throwing me behind his back. "Easy, you big fuckin—"

Too late, Belle tried to repeat her warning. "Josh, *no!*"

Without the strength to do more than cling to his shirt, I watched with detached fascination as the planeth charged, stopped, then charged again, spreading his wings and stomping with every bluff.

"Don't move," Belle whispered, her face pale as ice beneath the flush of exertion. "He's testing you. Don't move."

Josh made a sound at the back of his throat, fingers

so tight on my wrist I could feel the bones grinding together. "Easy for you t'say, Belle."

"Hey!" my father shouted, clapping hands. "To me, bird! To me!"

The flock-leader tilted his head, glancing over his shoulder.

"Keep pushing!" came a shout from the tunnel. "They cannot be allowed to escape!"

When the Caledonians spilled into the courtyard, it sent the entire flock into a new wave of two-toned screams. Screams that convinced the flock-leader the time for bluffing had passed. His beak snapped shut a few meager inches above Josh's left shoulder—hardly a hair's breadth from the tip of my nose—and it happened so fast, I hadn't the time to blink, let alone think of ducking clear.

In the next seconds, three things happened all at once. The flock-leader screamed his rage as he readied himself for a second strike, great, orange eyes fixed upon my face.

My father charged forward with a battle cry worthy of either the very desperate, or exceedingly foolish.

And then, in a rush of static-wind, a blast of brilliant green plasma soared over our heads, striking the flock-leader in the center of his chest. Without another sound, he dropped dead in a puff of smoke and feathers, rendering the whole flock still.

Eyes wide, I glanced over my shoulder.

Captain Rawlings. On one knee at the mouth of the tunnel, weapon braced over left wrist. When our eyes met, he lowered his weapon and struggled to recover his feet, the link pulsing in my chest deplete. Even from this distance, I could see the sweat fresh on his brow.

Before I could process any of it, however, Josh swept me off my feet and tossed me over his shoulder without so much as a single word of warning. "Up, Belle. *Up!* Quickly now, while we've the chance."

Hand pressed to her throat, eyes fixed upon the corpse of the flock-leader, Belle didn't move from her knees in the dirt until my father stooped and wrapped a hand around her bicep.

"Up, Priestess! We've got to go!"

"Don't take another step!" General Tilcot hollered in his deep, booming voice. "You're under arrest by the order of the Emperor—"

"Shoot, and you'll kill two Priestesses with one strike!" Josh roared, halfway to hysterical. Dragging Belle behind him, he pressed forward, sprinting flat-out.

Twisting as much as I could, I raised my head. Watching a dozen Elites file out of the tunnel, weapons raised, swarming around a deflated Captain Rawlings as he was forced to sit there and watch us go, hand planted against a tree. Dark eyes burning into mine, panting with the exertion required to save my life.

General Tilcot snarled, raising his weapon. Taking aim.

"This way!" Belle cried, barreling through a wrought-iron gate at the end of the courtyard, tugging my father through, her slender hand clasped in his. "The parking lot isn't much further!"

The now-familiar sickly glow of green ki lit up the general's weapon and I screamed a warning too late.

A burst of hot wind sailed over our heads, sucking the breath from my lungs. It struck my father square between the shoulder blades, tearing a ragged hole in flesh, muscle, and sinew as it passed through his chest.

He collapsed without a sound in a tangle of twisted limbs, face down in the dirt. Eyes wide and staring at nothing.

Nothing at all.

My heart stopped beating as his ki was torn from my mind, taking with it the only link I'd known since birth in a torrent of anguish.

The last thing I heard before—again—losing the battle with the darkness, was the echo of my own broken screams.

14

———

"Watch her head!"

"Get in the fuckin' coach, Belle!"

I landed with a thump on carpet, the familiar scent of my father's coach filling my nostrils.

"We're in! Drive!"

Josh engaged the Glaith, piloting the coach forward before the engine had finished whirling awake. A green flash of light announced an explosion behind us, and I groaned when my whole world shifted to the right, damaged hand striking something hard.

"Goddess, is that a road block? We won't be able to get to the senator's house. Not through that."

"It doesna matter, Belle. The senator's house isn't safe. Not anymore. Don't you understand? We need t'get outta the city, and on the road to Elora. Tritan has fallen."

"Then we'll have to stay off the roads—There!" Belle shouted. "Turn there! To the forest!"

A moment later, the whole coach swung to the left and I slid forward, striking my forehead on something hard that smelled strongly of feet. "Ughh." Trying to shift was too much effort, and I collapsed back to the floor, suffering the foul odor until the coach shifted again, this time in the opposite direction.

"Arrgh! We've got company and we're too fuckin' heavy! Brace for impa—"

Another flash of brilliant green preceded the tinkle of breaking glass, though I couldn't feel the sharp rain for the blinding heat kissing the left side of my face. I didn't feel the impact until my lower back connected with a set of knobbly knees. The breath whooshed from my lungs, forcing silence when I might have screamed my agony. And when we came to a stop, the resulting crash continued to ring in my ears long after the world had stopped quaking.

"If you can move, get out right now!" Josh hollered, wrenching the door off the hinges before I'd even managed to open both eyes. "Come 'ere, Miss Tannovic. That's it. Don't look behind you, lass."

"W-Why?" I croaked, unable to do so much as lift my head.

Josh hauled me from the wreckage, ignoring the broken glass and my involuntary squeal of pain as he dragged me behind him at a run. "I know you're not right at the moment, Miss Tannovic, but you have t'run now, girl."

"Where's—" I swallowed, throat too dry. "Where's my father?"

His fingers tightened around mine.

"Where, Josh? Where is he? Why can't I feel—"

An explosion rocked the earth, close enough to feel the shock behind my eyes as I stumbled along behind my Eloran friend.

"By the order of the Empire of Caledonia, *stop where you are!*"

Josh cursed, then hollered over his shoulder. "Get t'the trees! That's our only hope!"

But we were not the only ones fleeing the advancing Caledonian soldiers. Dozens upon dozens of my silver-haired kith fled alongside us, their screams leaving deep, ragged scars upon the fabric of my soul. Tritan's scientists ran single file through the madness, pressing closer to the looming dark of twisted, ancient trees. Dodging debris and people alike.

When we reached relative safety in the arms of the forest, Josh flung his hand out, motioning for silence. "Get down! Let them lose us in the chaos!"

I tugged on his sleeve, throat tight and achy. "Josh? Where's my father?" When his only answer was to flex his jaw and cling to silence, I reached for my father's ki.

But there was nothing there. The link to the vibrant, loving man I'd known all my life was gone.

The soft sounds of countless dozens filtering through the woods hardly registered as I tried again, turning blank eyes back in the direction in which we'd come.

Gone.

Simply *gone*.

"No!" A strange, broken sound burst from my lips, and I reeled back, flinging my ki as far as I could. *Nothing.* The link was dead. I screamed, slamming both palms to the ground, trying to force life into an empty shell already well beyond my reach. Heedless of the charred mess my right hand had become. Numb to the pain. "Daddy, *no!*" The tattered remains of my ki pulsed through the soil as I reached for him, touching every living thing I could and discarding them just as quickly —even when the tiny things in the soil reached back, drawn to my ki in a way I'd never experienced before.

But it was all for nothing. He was gone.

"Shit," Josh hissed against my ear, throwing himself over me. His weight pressed me to the forest floor. Fingers sealing the anguish behind my lips. "I'm so sorry, lass. So sorry, but you canna make a sound. *Please.*"

A terrible quiet settled over my mind and I stilled beneath him, going limp. Lost in pain and the fluttery ki of the flora beneath my skin.

"Mila? I'm going t'move my hand now, lass. I need you to be quiet, you hear me?"

I blinked.

"Mila?" He peeled his hand away from my lips, peering into my eyes. "Shit. *Shit.* We have t'go," he hissed at the others. "You must be silent or it's all over. I know it's horrible, but you canna let yourselves be captured. The scientists an' their technology canna fall into Caledonian hands. Can you stand, Miss Tannovic?"

My answer was a wild sound I'd never heard before.

"Shh, girl. I know. Come 'ere." He hefted me off the ground, wrapping me in his embrace and breaking my connection with the heartbeat of the forest. "Arms 'round my neck. That's it," he whispered when I didn't comply. "I've got you." And for the second time that day, Josh swept me away, squeezing me tight enough to stop my soul from shattering as he fled through the forest.

When the shaking started, it preceded a wave of

bone-crushing sobs I could not contain—but we were far enough away from the Elites that he didn't bother to hush me.

15

"Can you hear me, Priestess?"

"Hold her up." Hands slipped beneath my back, pushing me forward. "That's it, little Triloth. Easy." Ancaster. I recognized his voice as he slid in behind me, long legs braced on either side of my hips. "Just rest now," he continued, guiding my head to his shoulder. "We'll get you all fixed up in a moment."

"Mmph..." I cradled my ravaged hand. Keening low at the back of my throat.

"Shh, honey," Belle whispered, smoothing my hair back. "Shh. We're going to try to fix your hand, sister. It's —" she cleared her throat. "It's the worst of your injuries. The rest are superficial."

I flexed my fingers, not bothering to open my eyes. "Doesn't hurt."

"Nerve damage, then. Can you feel this?"

My arm moved of its own accord, and I begrudgingly cracked an eye open. A filthy Belle was holding my charred right hand in her lap, prodding the meat of my palm, twisting it to and fro, inspecting the extent of the damage. And I felt nothing.

With a half-hearted sigh, I grunted. "No."

"I rather expect that's a blessing at this point. Now" —she gestured for the other two Priestesses among our number to come to her side—"I'm nothing compared to a Trila-Glís when it comes to the healing arts, but it'll have to be enough." She took a deep breath. "Are you ready?"

I lifted one shoulder. Careless. Despondent.

"Right." Avoiding my eyes, she slipped the Dosmui Circlets on, fidgeting with the positioning.

"It's just a way to channel your power, Priestess. That's all," Ancaster soothed, and pushed the hair back from my face. "You've been with the Trila-Glís for healings. It's the same thing, but of course, you'll be the one to do the work. And you'll have Clara and Gina at your side."

"I understand." Belle took another deep breath, her exhale hot and damp against my cheek. "You'll have to hold her, Ancaster. Once I've repaired the damage to the nerves in her hand, I expect she won't be so docile."

"On with it, Priestess. I've got her."

Without further hesitation, light Triloth ki spread through me. At first, I could scarcely feel it. Her touch was so gentle, so careful as she brushed against me, that my mind drifted back toward the darkness. What was the point? What did it matter if my right hand remained useless for the rest of my days? But then... something ignited in my right middle finger. I twitched in Ancaster's hold. It didn't hurt... but... I sucked in a breath, eyes snapping open as I tried to yank my hand free. "Goddess, what're you doing? Stop. Belle, stop!"

She turned wide, blank eyes upon Ancaster. "Hold her."

"Here, wee Priestess, bite down on this, lass." Another Eloran face—Alicia—swam into view and she pressed a bit of leather against my lips. "It's the shoulder strap of my satchel, girl. You canna do it any damage. Bite hard as you can. It'll all be over in a few short minutes."

I took her offering, if only to muffle a scream as Belle redoubled her efforts, waking more nerves in my ruined fingertips. "Ugh," I groaned, whimpering around the leather. Gooseflesh erupted all over my skin and I shook, flushed and sweating. "Hurts..."

"Shh," Ancaster murmured, squeezing me. "It looks much better already, Triloth. You're through the worst of it."

"M'not Tri—" My eyes rolled back in my head, hand burning with Priestess ki and renewed function. With a strangled scream, I writhed against Ancaster, chanting, "Please, please, please," through clenched teeth.

He shushed me, refusing to let me pull my hand away from the fire in Belle's grasp. "Almost there, Triloth. Almost there."

On a snarl, I spat out the leather, glaring up at him. "Let me go, you sadist! It—Goddess—it's on fire!"

"It just feels that way. You're lucky you didn't lose your hand. The pain will ease, just breathe with me, girl. Breathe."

With a sob, I did as he asked, pressing my face into his shirt, letting him control the flow of oxygen into my lungs.

"That's it, with me now, Triloth. Deep breath in— good—and out. That's it. Almost done."

Belle released me with a gasp, taking her demon-ki with her. "That's it. That's all I can do for now."

I snatched my hand back, clutching it to my chest when Ancaster, too, released me. Flexing, I watched tight pink skin move over fragile bones, wishing for a place to lick my wounds in private.

Josh cleared his throat. "Alright, Miss Tannovic?"

My chin dipped once, though I shivered in the light breeze.

And in spite of the ashen, gray pallor staining her cheeks, Belle smiled at me. "I'll be able to do more after I've recovered some. And I'll see what I can do about that scarring, Mila, but at least the worst is over. How does it feel?"

I flexed it, grinding my teeth against the lingering tingle in my fingertips. "It's functional. Where are we?"

"Somewhere between Elora an' Tritan. In the forest," Josh said, bumping my shoulder as he took a seat beside me. "It's a few days to the Eloran border. Maybe less."

"You know," Ancaster said, sidling up to us. "I rather think that's what they'll be expecting. And if the Caledonians take the road, they're sure to beat us there, especially if they've commandeered any of the Glaith vehicles."

"What're you thinkin' then, man? Go somewhere else?"

"Yes. And with so many other refugees in the wood, we'll be able to make our escape, largely unnoticed. We should go straight to the Glaith mines in the mountains. It's a bit farther..."

"Aye, it's at least a week's hike. Maybe more."

"Yes, it is that, but—" Ancaster took Belle's hand,

tapping the Dosmui Circlets still wrapped around her slender wrist and middle finger, then dropped to his knees in the dirt, scrambling for a stick. "But we'll be exactly where we need to be, where we can continue our research. It's exactly where the Empire doesn't want us to go. We have four Priestesses at our disposal, which means we can set up Alicia's shield here"—he sketched a few jagged lines in the dirt—"and unless they're willing to risk scaling the Canodill Pass, they won't get through to the mines beyond. At least not until we've figured out some sort of defense. A turret, perhaps."

Alicia nodded, pretty green eyes narrowed. "Aye. Four Triloth Priestesses should be more'n enough to keep the shield burning at full strength. I mean, it's not th'same as having one o'the Trila-Glís at our beck an' call, but these four will do just fine. It'll work. We've done it with less power before."

Josh scrubbed at the stubble on his chin. "It won't be an easy trek."

"No. But it's the only way we can honor the sacrifices made to keep us out of the Empire's clutches." Ancaster stood, brushing dirt from his hands. "These prototypes and the people who created them must remain free. To fight another day. For Tritan."

A quiet chorus of "For Tritan," rang through the small clearing. The only voice that remained silent, was my own.

"So that's it, then?" Josh asked, making eye contact with every member of our ragged little group. "We're agreed? To the Canodill Pass and the Glaith Mines beyond?"

Silence reigned as Tritan's refugees looked to one another, questions burning in their eyes. A distant explosion, followed by several dozen voices raised in terror settled it.

"To the Canodill Pass," Belle said, turning toward the commotion. "And we must hurry."

"Right. Pack up. We're headed that way!" Josh pointed, assuming the air of an experienced leader. "And I want you t'walk in single file. Make it as hard as possible for those bastards to follow. Keep a firm eye on the person ahead, and if you're havin' trouble keeping up, speak up. I'll na' leave a single one of you behind."

In the ensuing scramble, I simply stood there, watching the panic flicker across each face, flexing my newly scarred right hand.

Numb.

I'd done this. I'd kissed him, and in doing so, had created a bond with an impossible Elite—a bond he would use to hunt me down. Blood to Blood. I could feel him, even now. Our link lived alongside the space that had belonged to my father... until... until...

I shivered, aching with the burn of tears, but in spite of the dreadful hollow space in my chest, they would not come—not with the threat of the Caledonian army at our backs. Trembling, I glanced over my shoulder. His comrades might have other objectives, but the captain was coming for *me*. I could feel it. *Him.* Could I allow the others to pay for my mistakes, for the curse of my Blood? What if I were to just... slip away? What if my going to him would give the others a chance to be free, even as it gave me the chance to claim vengeance for everything lost?

Josh rushed to my side, cheeks pale. "Come on, lass. Get your wee ass movin'."

I sucked a breath through clenched teeth, shaking my head. "I think—I think you should leave me here."

"Are you out o'your fuckin' mind?"

"No, you don't understand. I think... It's my fault that—"

"No. I'll not hear a word of that talk, Miss Tannovic. Your father—" He coughed. "Your father was a great man. A *great* man. You know he'd have been devastated to hear you talkin' like that. Above all else, Mila, he wanted you to be free, and I'll see that dream accomplished if it's the last thing I do."

I shook my head but couldn't force the denial past the ache in my throat.

"Now take my hand, girl, and run with me."

"No—"

He tangled his fingers with mine, ki flooding my senses the instant we touched, filling my cells with a rejuvenating warmth. I gasped, head spinning with the rush. I could replace what I'd lost in the salt caves. I could take it *all*...

I wrenched free of his grip, ki singing in my blood as I spun away. Goddess, it would be so easy... and I was *so* hungry for it...

"Alright, Mila?"

"I-I'm fine." And I *was*. My head snapped toward the trail of my fellow refugees as they disappeared into the gloom, following the call of their ki. If taking such a tiny sip from Josh could fill me with such *vigor*, surely the others could afford to donate a little? And then there were the Priestesses... with their pure white ki. So beautiful...

"Mila?"

I stopped short, standing just a few uncomfortable

inches behind Belle with no recollection of how I'd come to be there.

She smiled. "Goodness, you're looking better. How are you feeling?"

"I'm—" I took a step back, feeling something thump against my upper thigh with the movement, and without further thought, dipped my hand into my pocket.

Virgin Glaith pulsed in my grip, absorbing the ki and subsequent dark urges whirling inside me at the slightest touch. But, *how*? I'd destroyed his ring and all the Elite ki stored within that Glaith—my savaged right hand was proof enough of that. So where... "The High Priestess..." But of *course*. My promise to keep it on my person at *all* times. Tears blurred my vision as I squeezed the Glaith until my knuckles went white and the thin new skin on my right hand split and bled. Staining the inside of my pocket with a crimson smear.

"Don't worry, sister. We'll free her someday soon. Are you ready?"

I scrubbed at the dampness in my eyes and set my jaw. "Lead on."

16

"We need a break, man," Ancaster panted, staggering to a halt, hands planted on his knees. "We're not—" he gasped, pushing sweaty hair away from his face. "We're people of intellect. I'm afraid we're not used to this level of physical activity."

"That's alright." Josh pressed his hands on his lower back, stretching toward the canopy above. "I'll see if I canna find us some water, if one o' the Priestesses could check our flanks. Don' want an Elite crawlin' up our asses while we rest."

"That's not how it works, unfortunately," Belle said, hands on her knees. "We are Triloth, and need the touch of a living thing to know it inside and out." She cursed, pretty face twisting. "Damn. If only we had one of the Trila-Glís—"

"You'd what?" I asked, thumbing the Glaith with the puffy, distorted fingers of my burned hand.

"The Trila-Glís have no need of physical touch," she said. "It sharpens their insight, sure, but if we had one of them, we wouldn't be running blind—and that's only a start."

"That's a right pile, seein' as now those pricks have *both* o'the Trila-Glís," Josh said, turning to Ancaster. "Have you anything that'll magnify a Triloth's senses? As the Dosmui Circlets do for their ki?"

Ancaster shook his head. "Nothing that's moved beyond the drawing phase, I'm afraid. We'll have to rely on our wit and righteous determination."

"And what of the other refugees?" I whispered, though no one heard me, for I had turned my gaze back toward the waking nightmare I'd once called home. I could feel him. Captain Rawlings. Even through the Glaith clutched tight in my twisted fingers, I could feel him lodged deep within me.

Belle sighed, shaking out her mane of long silver hair. Running her fingers through the sweat-soaked snarls, she said, "A sip of water would be nice. The scientists aren't the only ones unused to this level of exercise. I don't know if I can keep this up much longer without something to eat."

"I've got berries, here," Ancaster called, falling to his knees before a squat little bush dotted with red fruit.

Josh made a sound at the back of his throat. "Careful, man. That stuff is best left for the birds."

Ancaster shrugged. "A little indigestion is worth it at this point. Oh," he said, stuffing his face with a handful of berries, leaves, and tiny twigs, "and if you see any birds, feel free to send them my way."

"Up t'you, then."

Belle drifted to my side as Ancaster plucked the bush bare, setting her hand on my elbow. "You're good at this, Josh. Surviving in the woods?"

"Oh, aye. Grew up in the north. My brothers and I made a game of it when we were kids."

A fat black squirrel darted past my foot, chittering at the top of its lungs even through a mouth stuffed full of a strange, bruise-green fruit twice the size of its head. Tail twitching, it scrambled up the trunk of a tree, squalling the whole way as it cast baleful glares over a furry shoulder.

"Right noisy little pest, that," Josh said, watching as the squirrel yipped once more, then disappeared into the foliage, darting over a network of branches that carried it out of sight in seconds. "Won't be so chipper if I can get you on a plate, will you?"

"Would anyone like some of these?" Ancaster asked, holding a fistful of red berries aloft. "They're quite tart, but not so bad once you get past it."

Glaith clutched tight in my fist, I pulled away from Belle. "I'm just... going to close my eyes for a moment."

"Try to get some rest, Miss Tannovic. We're stopping here for the night anyway. I'll just be off t'set some traps. Hopefully we'll wake on the morrow to something o' substance."

"Come sit by me, sister," Belle said, tugging me toward the edge of the group. "Let's get some rest while we can, yes?"

How could I sleep with the space my father had occupied nothing more than a blank, numb void? How could I rest knowing the man who'd slaughtered him lived? Or that the captain had *known* why his army was parked in our courtyard, but had said nothing to warn me. That he'd tried to take me for himself, instead, knowing exactly what it would mean.

But I followed without a word, Glaith biting my

palm as I settled down beside her, wide awake even as the others began to nod off. I sat there, watching through the night, listening to the forest whisper.

Tiny woodland creatures foraging through the underbrush became the footfalls of a thousand Elites, tireless in their pursuit of Tritan's refugees. The song of the night-beasts waking for the hunt sent my pulse pounding at the hollow of my throat, and I would have dropped the Glaith, would have lost myself in the seductive promise of Elite ki, if it weren't for the captain. For the fear that doing so would unmask my ki, and draw him to me.

When a nameless, winged shadow floated overhead, however, I jumped, doing just that. The Glaith tumbled from my sweaty palm as I sank my teeth into the back of my wrist to avoid screaming at the top of my lungs. The shadow landed in the trees above our pitiful little camp, great luminous eyes the only visible feature as it watched over us, unblinking. I almost laughed. A night-bird of some sort, and hardly the terrifying thing of nightmares. If he were here, my father would know what it was.

But of course, he wasn't. Not anymore.

A ragged breath burst from my chest, carrying with it a tiny sob as I reclaimed the Glaith and stood, slipping away from the group. It was too much! This pain—it eclipsed *everything*. I stumbled through the brush, blind to my surroundings for the tears burning my eyes.

Ancaster groaned from somewhere off to my right. "In other news," he said, hunched at the edge of the clearing, "it should be noted that those red berries are, in fact, not fit for human consumption."

I coughed, nails scoring my palms. "Are you ill?"

"Quite," he said, punctuating his admission with an intense round of dry heaving, veins bulging on his sweaty, flushed forehead.

"Belle will help you. Go to her," I said and abandoned my countryman in his hour of need, for I knew nothing of curing a poisoning. Knew nothing but the all-consuming pain beating a savage rhythm against my ribs. Knowing it was fruitless and reckless, but unable to stop myself, I dropped the Glaith into my pocket and reached for him. Reached for the space he'd occupied since I'd first tasted ki all those years ago.

Gone! Teeth clenched so hard I could feel them shifting in my gums, I slammed my fists to the earth, burying my fingers in the soil. Goddess, but it *hurt*! He was gone. There was nothing left—nothing but that accursed link with the captain lurking somewhere in my heart, roused by my use of ki.

But it didn't matter. I sobbed, trying to force the poisonous ki from my heart before the Void consumed my blackened soul—and why shouldn't I let it? Why shouldn't I leave this tattered group of my people before they too saw my Truth? Why shouldn't I turn and face the Caledonians head on, offer myself as distraction? Why shouldn't I simply unleash this pain that *they* had caused? Why should I be the one to suffer for their sins?

Ki spiked free from my hands, bursting into the soil and the tiny root fragments hidden beneath the earth.

Awareness exploded in my mind as I purged the anguish from my heart. The secret heartbeat of the forest was at my fingertips—a massive oak tree standing tall and proud in the middle of this great wood. The largest being in this forest by far, and although it was several days away by foot, its roots spanned many times the circumference of the canopy above. The majestic giant snared my attention, leaves shivering as my ki pulsed through it. Thick bark-armor groaned as sap began to run out of season, and a dozen tiny feet prickled my mind—the mammals and birds who called the great grandmother home. I reached for them too, my ki whipping through each little body as I searched them, familiarizing myself with their patterns.

Without making conscious decision, I expanded my search, stumbling across the refugees, for they too filled the forest, dotting the edge of my awareness. Families trying to flee the tattered, burning carcass of everything they'd ever known. Each making the pilgrimage north, to Elora, pursued by the Caledonian forces. Just as we were.

Lips curled back, I fed from the forest, gorging on that ancient power in exchange for the sorrow burning my heart. Pure, wild ki filled me, restoring all I had lost in the interaction with the captain, though it wasn't enough to break free of him. The betrayer fought my attempt, curbing my efforts with *my* pendant clutched tight in his fist.

Filled with primal, elemental fury, I snarled and felt him recoil.

But the captain was a man apart. An Elite with impossible strength, and he knew how to use it. Power surged between us, striking me with a terrible force, flooding my system with a seduction as sweet as it was laced with shadowy intent.

I could go to him... It would be *so* easy to slip away... he'd be good to me...

My father hadn't raised a slave.

Eyes unseeing, I seized every life force around me,

sipping at hundreds—thousands—harming none even as I hurled their collective energies toward him. The animals of the forest screamed with me, disturbing the evening quiet with their alarm. And still, it was not enough to break the link we shared, though for now, the captain conceded defeat. Forced to withdraw from my might.

With a gasp, I wrenched my hands from the dirt, falling back. "Goddess," I breathed, staring at my filthy palms, gooseflesh rising up all over my body. Before my very eyes, the angry red flesh of my scarred right hand began to fade, reducing the swollen, puffy skin to something that might have resembled normal in the right light. "Such power." I laughed, voice high and thin. Why should I flee? When the forest was filled with the screams of my people and the footfalls of the army who'd made us all homeless? We'd lost everything thanks to those filthy, traitorous Caledonians. Goddess be damned if I'd make it easy for them now by running. Why should I flee with this new power pulsing through my veins? Not even Captain Rawlings could hope to match me. Not now.

Trembling, I caressed the earth. "Beautiful..."

There, hiding in the dark beneath my feet, was so much potential. All it needed was a little... nudge. Careful this time, I blended with the forest, feeding the earth my poison. My pain. For a moment, nothing happened but the exchange of energy and incomprehensible information. And then, as I stood witness, little green shoots sprang up through the detritus, reaching for the sky as they grew with unnatural, ki-fed speed.

With roots plunged deep into the earth, they were connected. To everything. And with my hands buried in the earth, I drew upon the forest's bounty, guiding it. Letting it take root in my raw and bleeding heart. I did not have to continue living with the Void where my father had once been. Did not have to suffer the agony of his absence, for the forest was a willing recipient of my torment. The trees did not speak in the language of emotion. They were the seasons and the elements. They took what I had to offer without judgment, and in return, fed me the secrets of their wild magic.

Seeds buried beneath the soil sprouted at my command, eating the footprints we'd left behind as they flourished, disguising our tracks. Already established saplings pulsed with new life, shivering without a breeze, their roots swelling with ki as their thin trunks thickened—the growth too insignificant to be seen by the naked eye, but there all the same. Vines—dormant for the late hour of the season—coiled around the trees, glossy green leaves bursting with new life.

Yet all, each and every one touched by my senses, were stained by my Truth.

Moonlight petals streaked with shadows.

Dozens of little mammals scurried in earthen tunnels, hidden from my senses until they brushed against a root intersecting their underground highways. I watched from above as they went about their business, leery of disturbing them as they gathered food, mated, slept. Oblivious.

A slightly larger mammal hopped into my mind, paws brushing a plump vine as it chewed at the bark of a thin sapling. Tiny, fluttering heart. Ribs expanding several times a second with quick, short breaths. A herbivore. A rodent, perhaps. Startling at every sound, muscles tensed to flee.

Fascinated, I aimed the bulk of my attention there, focusing on the tiny creature. Was that—I pressed a single, delicate tendril of ki toward it—was that new life quickening in its womb? In spite of it all, a smile bloomed across my face. Pregnant. The little rodent was newly pregnant and eating for a litter of at least six.

Something made it flinch, its whole body pulsing with adrenaline an instant before it was airborne, separate from my senses until all four paws touched the earth once more. It continued to bounce through the forest with such speed that I almost couldn't follow, zipping through the underbrush in an erratic pattern. When it came to a stop, tucked under a fruit-bearing bush, it stilled, hardly daring to breathe—and I with it.

Was she being pursued? Or had the soon-to-be mother found safety?

I turned blank eyes in her direction, blending more of myself with her—just as my link to the little mother went black in a single, blinding instant of pain. A scream tore free of my throat as the heels of my palms flew to my temples. Gone! Little Mother was gone! She was dead!

The Void yawned before me once more, beckoning me to fall into its limitless depths. I staggered to my feet, swimming against the flow with everything I had. And it was not enough! She was gone, and with the passing, oxygen starved seconds, her young went with her. Each new lost life pulled at me, until the weight of all seven, tiny still hearts was too heavy a burden to carry. They were dragging me into the Void. Even the ki of the forest was not enough. I was lost—

Elite strength washed through me, anchoring me to the correct side of this existence. Calling me back from the edge, he threw himself in front of the Void as I clawed my way back to the light.

That noble, selfish, parasitic *bastard*.

"Mila!" Belle's pale face swam into view.

Blinking away the urge to fling myself into the nothingness, I seized the Glaith with shaking hands, but... allowed the captain to linger, even as the remaining strength left my body in a great rush. The forest would keep him back, but for now... I allowed the comfort of simply feeling him there.

"Goddess, Mila, what's happened? Are you alright?"

A tremor shook me. "She's-She's—"

"Breathe, Mila. Breathe with me. That's it," Belle whispered, stroking my face. "What happened?"

"It-I was connected to her ki and—"

"What's all the screamin' now?"

My breath stilled in my chest, for there stood Josh, handsome in the evening light, a dead rabbit dangling from his left hand. Its fluffy brown fur was ruffled, sticking out at odd angles, and its neck... "No..."

"Everything all right, Miss Tannovic?" He whirled around, fists raised, flinging his macabre prize to and fro. "Is it the Caledonians? Are we under attack?"

"You-You—" I choked on a sob, trembling so hard my teeth rattled together inside my head. "She's dead."

"What!" Josh's gaze flew around the sleepy camp, eyes flicking over the pale faces of the refugees. "Who's dead?"

I pointed. "She was preg-pregnant, and you... you *murdered* her!"

Bewildered, Josh raised the limp body in his hand. "Are you talkin' about the wee cony, lass? Good gods, Mila, are you fuckin' kidding? Why would you do that?"

Pressing his free hand to his chest, Josh said, "I think I just had a heart attack."

A terrible sound crackled from my throat, and without further evidence of my imminent breakdown, Belle draped her arm around my shoulders and ferried me away from the group. "That's it. We're okay. Come with me. That's it."

I dropped to my knees, shaking all over. "Dead... Goddess... they're all dead..."

"Hush..." Belle's hand brushed over my tangled mane as she wrapped her arms around me, pressing my cheek to her chest. "You're okay, Mila. You're okay."

I wailed against her, clinging to her skirts as ugly, hiccupping sobs stuttered forth from the center of my being. So much death... I buried my face against her shoulder, dumping every spare ounce of ki I had into the High Priestess' Glaith, pressing until it began to burn in my palm once again. Overtaxed. Too hot.

And in the distance, the captain watched with fingers wrapped around my pendant, sampling the flames of chaos licking at my edges, but doing little more. A silent observer of my deepest grief. A rock-steady shadow in my periphery I could not banish, for there, in the rays of early morning sun, was his mark. Perched on my right middle finger, sat the ghost of *his* ring. A backward 'AR' seared into my twisted skin.

His initials.

Branding me, inside and out.

Belle squeezed me, running a soothing hand down my back. "Let it out, Mila. That's it. It's okay."

Pushing my specter away, I did as she asked, bawling until my throat was raw and the Glaith glowed with unnatural light—and still, the tears continued to fall with no sign of stopping. When my breath came in staggered gasps, blackness dotting the edges of my vision, Belle called for the other Priestesses.

"We're going to help you rest, Mila. We're going to take the pain away."

Lips curled back, I pulled away. "N-No. Feeling this" —I stabbed at my chest—"is the only thing that makes sense. I was with her wh-when, when he..." I staggered crumpling beneath a fresh wave of tears. "I couldn't—I couldn't *do* anything! He's dead! They're a-all dead."

"Sleep now, Mila," she said, placing a gentle hand on the side of my face, great luminous eyes filled with sympathetic tears. "Let me take some of the hurt."

Beautifully soft Priestess ki silenced any further argument.

17

I woke with heat moving beneath my skin. Crawling through sinew, kissing aching, tired muscles with fresh strength. Renewing all that was depleted, and leaving behind the purest vitality that forced lucidity upon me before I'd completely left my foggy nightmares behind.

Asher.

I knew before my eyes flicked open. Before alien amusement teased at groggy edges and called me to continue our battle. Didn't bother to hide the sinister, hungry twist pulling me awake.

Sweating, I let my senses flare out, expecting to find a battalion of soldiers lurking in the gloom. I tried to banish the Elite ki seething in my blood, to replace it with the ancient might of the forest before I succumbed to temptation.

To him.

But the wood was still. Silent, except for the night things going about their business.

Heavy.

Flushed with unnatural heat, I gathered myself, adjusting my tunic as I staggered into alertness. And for the first time since my ki had begun to flourish, I didn't trust the story whispering through my blood.

He was here. Manipulating me from the shadows. Glutting himself on my power—feeding my pendant with Elite ki. Toying with the bond he'd left etched on my very bones, he helped himself. Drank deep of my every flitting, terrified emotion. Leaving nothing untouched.

Absolutely *nothing*.

I could feel the scratching sweep of calloused palms. Knew the strength of his hands, and the surety of his touch. That confidence found the peaks of my breasts and lingered there. Making the little nubs tighten and swell with something forbidden I'd only ever dared to explore when the hour was darkest. Something hot and sinful and *not meant for him*.

But still, he took. Paying for it with a glimpse of that very same *something* writhing in him. Though it was hotter. Darker. More demanding and hungry than anything I'd ever known before.

Like molten steel. Somehow hard and hot and aching all at once.

I gasped, sweating freely in spite of the damp chill in the night breeze. Back arching against sticks and leaves, I unintentionally sent his hunger lurching south when I pressed my knees together and drew his attention to what was building between my thighs.

Ravenous. Starving to corrupt and take and claim.

To possess.

Clawing at the spot where my pendant had been, I tried to deny it. To deny *him*. Rolled to hands and knees, then forced my eyes to open and see what was real, for Captain Asher Rawlings wasn't the only one who'd found a new source of strength.

And mine was *willing.* Goddess, the forest was *eager* for the exchange of primordial ambrosia for my paltry, Elite-tainted ki.

Hissing, I buried my fists in the rich loam that had been my pillow, connecting with the limitless network of root fibers and creatures thriving all around us.

The captain made no effort to hide. Turning toward the attention of so ancient a being, he dared to smile, as if to say, *come on then, little Priestess. Let's play.*

And then I felt it.

My pendant. Pressed to the soil only half a night's walk from the very spot where I knelt, the arrogant sadist!

He thought himself above me? Thought his precious control and Elite training could surpass what the forest had given me? I laughed, clapping the rich earth from my palms and took what the grandmother freely offered, using it to fuel my flight and reclaim what he'd stolen.

"Good evening, Triloth," came a voice from the shadows—and I scrambled back with a barely contained scream. "Beautiful night, isn't it—"

Startled, I acted on purest instinct, wrapped his ankles in woody young vines and dragged the ki from his body before I realized who it was. Before I heard the note of camaraderie in a voice I knew, I'd drained the man of his ki before he could utter another polite word.

Ancaster collapsed in a boneless heap at my feet. Eyes showing white, lips slack, a drop of drool hung stringy and wet from his chin.

"Goddess, *no*," I breathed, coming back to myself with a horrific jolt. And, hands beginning to tremble, I knelt. Desperate to feel the flutter of life, horrified that it might be... absent. That I'd killed without a thought. Or worse... for the pleasure of vengeance, without a single instant of hesitation.

Ancaster's chest rattled, laboring to draw breath, but alive.

Shaken, I exhaled a sob, returned what I'd stolen, then fled into the night. Feet flying over fallen logs, leaping quiet streams, and darting between trees both old and young. I didn't stop until sweat had soaked through my tunic and my sorrow fermented and went sour, replaced by bubbling rage.

He had done this, not me. Infecting me with his Elite corruption. Endangering the lives of the only people I had left.

It ended tonight.

Giving my heart a moment to settle and slow, I knelt by the edge of a stream. Splashing my face. The back of my neck. Trying to cool my heated skin and brace for the coming battle.

The captain was close, for in my blind flight, I'd run straight toward the source of comforting lies, hunting the return of my pendant and the frosty nothingness that came with it. It wouldn't take long to find where he waited, but I'd come plenty far enough.

Whatever trap he'd set for me would have to be abandoned if he desired another encounter. Another chance to enslave me.

So I settled in to wait, letting the night breeze dry my tunic and the sweat-soaked hair plastered to my nape. I glutted myself with the forest's bounty, so the captain would have nothing to cling to when he finally appeared. No more taunting, perplexing heat could slip beneath my defenses if the vessel was already stuffed to overflowing, now could it?

I didn't waste that time with girlish hesitation, but neither did I set a trap—the only backup I needed was the forest herself. The only thing I did in preparation, was remove my sandals and bury my feet in the forest's strength. That way, all he had to do was touch a living thing connected to the great-grandmother oak, and I'd have my way. I'd have my pendant, and be finished with the betrayer and his lies forever.

Long before the underbrush crunched, I felt him. Couldn't help *but* know where he was. Could hardly sense anything *but* the Captain of Special Forces and all his hypnotic, blinding power. And with the Trila-Glís captured, why should he bother to hide? I was the only one left who knew his secret. The only one who could sense the coming hurricane and hope to see what lurked inside that storm.

There was no ceremony that accompanied his arrival. And for several long minutes, neither of us spoke. Separated by a chattering stream that might as well have been a bottomless chasm, I was afforded the luxury of sizing him up without the risk of falling prey. Trying to see everything *but* the hard lines of so handsome a face. The broad shoulders hidden beneath a uniform that fit too well, and showed no signs of hard travel as my own simple tunic did. The gleam of gold on his shoulders that denoted his rank as a Caledonian Captain. On his hip, a belt weighted down with a weapon and several pouches of various things that didn't concern me.

And around his neck, a hint of silver, for my pendant lay safe. Next to his polluted heart.

"I'm sorry," he said at length, taking a step closer. Voice petting and soothing, a breathy whisper I strained not to hear. "Your father—"

"Don't." I shook my head, trembling inside and out. Not ready to look directly at the wound that had yet to fester. It was too soon to lance it.

He swallowed, offering a tiny frown that positively *reeked* of sincerity. Real regret. "Ah. Well. I *am* sorry. That"—he clenched his jaw, making the muscle twitch —"his death was never my intention."

"And yet."

"And yet," he agreed, inky eyes reflecting the moonlight for an instant before that light was swallowed up.

I extended my right hand, palm up. Letting him see the scars without seeing the brand. *His* brand. "I want my pendant."

Wickedness replaced the sorrow. "Then give me back my ring."

"You know I can't."

He shrugged, tugging my pendant out. Letting the Glaith catch the silver light. His thumb passing over the stone. Slowly. Black gaze fixed to my face, making sure I felt it in all the most secret places. "I'll settle for your name, little Priestess."

But I refused to be baited. "If you were really sorry," I hissed, shivering, "then you'd have come offering General Tilcot's head."

Asher exhaled a breathy laugh. "Not so innocent after all, but a bloodthirsty warrior. You impress me more with every passing moment."

Cheeks burning, it was my turn to laugh, though it

held none of his cool restraint. "Watching everything you love burn before your eyes can have that effect on a girl. Why don't you come here and find out just how serious I am?"

He took another step, though this time, he had the courtesy to let the smile slip away. "It doesn't have to be this way. Come with me, warrior Priestess, and I'll help you kill the general myself."

Lies. Tempting lies cloaked in a beautiful package, but lies all the same. I shook my head, clenching the shiny scars twisting my right hand. "Don't take another step, traitor."

Full lips flicked in amusement. "Or what?" he drawled, daring me to follow through.

Instead of words, I began to gather ki. Pulled it from the rich soil beneath my feet, and wove it about my shoulders. Dipped my hands in it. Readied myself for a fight I wasn't entirely sure I intended to survive.

Asher nodded, letting my pendant fall. Stripping off his uniform coat. Exposing muscled arms, narrow waist, and a broad chest that did... *something* to my insides. Made them flip and dance and squirm, no matter that he was preparing for battle.

"Give me my pendant," I said, "and I will allow you to leave here tonight. Unscathed."

At this, he simply spread his hands, smiling through his teeth. Inviting me to take the first strike, as if I would be fool enough to attack a man easily twice my size. As if I would so much as approach a bloody *soldier*—a man trained to see beauty in war—if he weren't bound and restrained.

A smile creased my lips, and it wasn't the delicate mask of a Senator's daughter.

That girl was dead.

And *I* didn't have to move a muscle to attack the captain.

Much as I wanted to throw myself at him, to scream and rage until I tore him down, I held myself utterly still. Thought of all those who had fallen so that I might go on. Those who had been captured or died. For me. For the refugees of science upon whom their hopes for rescue were laid.

Of the Tritan people, it was my father's face that burned the brightest. But he was not alone—flashes of poisonous green light had seared their terrified faces into my brain forever. Whether I'd been there to watch them fall or if they'd been alone when the Caledonians came, I saw them.

The High Priestess, enslaved or dead.

Even the Goddess herself. Milithia, whose name had inspired my own. Whose temple now lay in smoldering ruins.

All of them taken by the Empire.

Burned and begging for retribution. Vengeance.

Justice.

The Glaith hung heavy in my pocket, but I ignored it. Turned everything I was, took every facet of my Truth, and sent it down into the soil rich with life, and fed the grandmother the anguish of a nation destroyed.

Pain and fury and seething, black hatred exploded from my very being. Ripening roots and sending seedlings into mature growth in seconds.

And with a scream that echoed through the ages, I threw it all in Asher's face without taking a single step. Watched him buckle, folding to his knees as he was ensnared. He, the betrayer who dared to offer protection for the price of everything I'd ever known or loved. Burying me in a landslide of anguish, choking me with grief so thick, it was a wonder I could draw breath without drowning on muck.

Goddess, but I did so much *more* than simply breathe.

Roots and branches descended upon him, capturing him in their unyielding arms. Restraining wrists, ankles, even wrapping around the base of his throat. Thorns stabbing into golden flesh, shock lashing at the tainted spot in my heart where he lurked.

But still, as he was swallowed up, bit by bit, he didn't have the decency to beg for mercy. That accursed sinister smile still fixed to his lips growing all the more wicked.

Hungry.

Fists clenched, I ordered his tomb sealed. Air-tight, but for a tiny gap above his heart where a chain of silver gleamed, yearning to be returned to its place on *my* breast.

Only when bark grew gnarled with false age, and silence fell on the wood once more, did I dare to cross that babbling creek. At first, taking tiny, mincing steps. Pausing to test his restraints with every breath. Braced for a counterstrike.

He didn't fight.

I laughed. And how could he? Even *I* was leery of the thing I had called into being. A great cocoon of living wood, thicker than I was tall. Stained black, and in the right light, streaked through with silver.

My ugly Truth made manifest.

Hysterical, I bounded forward. Drunk on ki, for now, with Asher's imminent demise, there was nothing they could do to stop what was coming. Nothing *any* of them could do to clip the dark wings snapping at their brittle cage.

Disregarding caution, I plunged my scarred right hand into the captain's prison and hooked that silver chain with the crook of my index finger. Pulled, until it was freed.

But the pendant caught on something that refused to yield.

I pulled harder, setting my feet. Grinding my teeth. Giving the delicate chain every pound of effort I could without breaking it.

A splash of sickly green stained my left peripheral, followed by a voice that said, "Gonna have to ask you to stand down, little lady."

18

———

"I've been assured you *probably* won't kill me," the soldier said, a sardonic little twist to his lips. Lit cigarette bouncing with every spoken word, he continued, "But you'll forgive me if I'm not keen to take any chances after that impressive display, eh?" He jiggled his weapon, keeping it trained on my face, and though it paled in comparison to the brilliance of the piece Asher had held, it was more than capable to turning me into a shocked puddle of goo.

Gaping, I blinked. "How—" *How* had this man, this mundane soldier, managed to stand there all this time without my knowing it?

From inside his woody prison, the captain jerked the chain back inside the hole.

I yelped, trying to scramble back before his grip set —before his ki—

Strong fingers wrapped around my wrist, threatening to either break bone, or drag me inside with him. And with a gasp, my knees turned to water. My heart stuttered and spit, trying to cope. Failing to manage the wave of orderly Elite strength. All that control...

Goddess... his ki! It sang and raged, screaming of conquest. Of triumphant possession. All his careful planning—the risks and the lies—had paid off.

This man was no equal of mine! He was order to my chaos, a soothing balm to the firestorm of hurt tearing me to shreds, and if I'd just *let* him ease that pain...

Sobbing, a tattered plea escaped my lips. "*Please...*" For through the living wood, I could feel another sort of heat. One that *burned* and unmade. Scorching the ties I held to the tomb I'd called into being. That which should have been a final resting place for a man I hated, had become a trap of my own making. With gilded bars and enough to sustain even my endless hunger.

Putting the other soldier to shame, the captain's weapon blasted through the right side of the cocoon, expending enough ki to turn the night to day and blind my every sense. Freeing his torso and allowing him to draw a ragged breath that ended in a laugh. "You didn't think it'd be that easy, did you?" the captain said, grinning. And though he was still trapped, still restrained and held, it wouldn't be for much longer. Not long until he possessed everything he'd come for, and so much more... "Have to admit," he added, infecting me with his touch, his ki. "You've impressed me, yet again, my little warrior. Wasn't expecting your trick with the plants, ineffective as it might have been."

The soldier nodded, solemn, ashing his smoke, yet keeping me in his sights. "Never saw anything like it. You sure can pick 'em, old man."

With a shrug, the captain said, "To be fair, Marco, I *do* have something of an unfair advantage."

This so-called Marco snorted, inching closer. Weapon never leaving my face. "My momma always said to use whatcha got. Nothin' unfair about that."

"Quite right," the captain replied, pulling me closer.

And in that moment, through the fog of too much, I knew two things with *absolute* clarity.

The Captain of Special Forces had baited me using the one thing he knew I wouldn't be able to resist.

And I had been *unforgivably* arrogant. Had run straight into this trap—*his* trap—with eyes wide open. Blind to everything except the surety that I couldn't fail. That this was a mission given to me by the Divine.

By a Goddess I *knew* to be dead, for I had seen Her burn.

A sob escaped my lips, but no matter how I struggled, I could not break his grip. Could not turn away from the hated beauty of his ki, and with every breath, the reason *why* faded away...

"Hush now," he whispered, thumb brushing over twisted skin marking the back of my wrist. Sending a chill racing through my muscles. Over my skin. "It's over now, pet," the captain breathed, struggling one-handed to escape the last of my flimsy prison. "You'll want for nothing—" he kicked at the inside of his cage, crumbling wood both charred and burnt. "And I'll see that you get justice for your father. I promise you that, girl."

Tears ran hot and painful down my cheeks. In moments, he would be free, and I... I would not.

"Don't cry, Priestess," Asher whispered, and with his free hand, pulled a set of golden bracelets from a hidden pocket in the shadows. Glaith. Not the dirty stuff he'd used on the High Priestess. Pure Glaith ore wrapped in gold.

I wasn't threat enough to warrant extreme measure.

"Hurry it up, will you?" the soldier hissed, shifting his grip. Turning the muzzle of his weapon away for the first time since he'd made his presence known. Confident in Asher's ability to hold me, he watched the trees, crushing the burning ember of his smoke, but remained vigilant. "Bind the girl, and let's get the fuck outta here before someone realizes we've gone. I've got a lumpy cot and a bottle of the good stuff waiting for me."

"That wouldn't be *my* bottle you're referring to, would it? I've a mind to celebrate tonight," Asher drawled, bold enough to let his thumb pass over my lower lip. Flooding me with strength and a sense of forced-calm that did nothing to ease the pain chewing my heart into bloody strips. Plucking the feathers from my wings, one by one.

I should have fought—I knew it. Knew just how much I'd hate myself for being taken without spilling so much as a single drop of Caledonian blood.

But it was hopeless.

He had seen the very best I had to offer, and he had weathered it with a laugh. Goddess, he might as well have called me cute and ruffled my hair for all the terror I'd been able to inspire. Knees buckling, I sobbed in earnest, my wrist still caught in a grip I didn't even try to break. Fingertips held fast to his chest spread of their own accord. Luxuriating in his endless strength.

Stepping free of my ruined cocoon, the captain tucked my pendant beneath his shirt and knelt at my side. "None of that, girl. Warriors don't cry, hmm? Besides," he said, tipping my face back. Capturing every drop of my attention in a gaze so black, the Void itself would have been jealous. "You did *well*. With you at my side," he continued, breath sweet and warm against my lips, "none will be able to touch me."

But I would be a slave. My father would look on from the Goddess' side and weep tears of shame for all of eternity.

Catching my lips, Asher kissed me. Giddy with the proof of his success, he let the golden chains dangle. Forgotten as he swallowed my anguish with a breathy groan. Replaced it with ravenous heat and a sense of scarcely contained *victory*.

He'd won, and it had been easy. *I* had made it easy in coming here. In answering his call after Belle and Josh had warned me of the consequences. That I wasn't ready to fight an army by myself—let alone a single impossibly powerful Elite, my equal or not—was now abundantly clear.

But it was too late.

Hiccupping, I succumbed. Kissed him back and allowed his ki to infect and spread, yielding to that glorious heat, no matter its corruption. No matter that it wasn't my choice or that it meant passing the burden of my people's freedom to a handful of Triloth Priestesses. To the scientists and their incredible technology that wouldn't be *nearly* enough to stop an Empire helmed by Captain Asher Rawlings.

The last of the rare and dangerous things.

I let him deepen that kiss because for one instant, he made me forget. For the love of the dead Goddess, I *mewled*. Reached for him with both hands. And when his tongue slipped past my lips, I melted in his arms. Keening against him, I indulged a beast with hunger enough to swallow me whole. Wet and desperate and aching for an end to all of it.

"M'kay," Marco said. "When I said hurry it up, I meant put the fuckin' chains on her, mate. But if you're keen to put on a show..." he trailed off, waggling his brows, grinning at my heated, tear-stained cheeks.

"Shut it," the captain drawled, suckling at my lower lip. Crushing me tight against his chest, he pressed himself against my belly. A secret brand of pulsing need that made me ache, breath hitching. "Let me enjoy this," he said, fingers cradling the base of my skull. "Just for a moment longer..."

Let him savor the victory he'd wrought from my flesh, before he bound the Glaith in the hollow bits he'd left in his wake. Before he tied me to him for the rest of time, feeding from the chaotic strength in *my* blood?

Clarity sparkled behind wet lashes, giving me a moment—just a single instant—to draw a breath that wasn't laced with Elite ki.

Fingers tightening, ki strangling me, the captain braced, for he could feel it rising in me.

Defiance.

But I had already attacked the man who'd claimed to be my equal, and for my efforts? Humiliating defeat.

So I plunged my free hand into my pocket, caught the High Priestess' Glaith, then turned my attention to Marco, the man I *probably* wouldn't kill. Their friendship was the only weakness the captain had shown me since we'd met this morning. Calling on the dead Goddess, this last time, I dragged Her power through the earth. Wrapped it around Marco's ankles and tied him to myself.

Embracing the chaos—the truth of my birthright—I took his paltry ki. Draining him unconscious in an instant, I took everything he was and stored it in the

Glaith. Clinging to my promise before I unleashed a darkness that could compete with the captain's hideous order.

"Priestess—"

"*Release me*," I hissed, holding a life the captain cared about in my ruined palm. Not bothering to voice the threat he could feel in my blood. The rising horror.

Asher braced, gathering himself. Prepared to contain me and save his friend, as if the necessity were no more than a minor, irritating delay.

Feeling something rip, I stopped the other's heart. Let dark wings spread at long last, and took a life.

19

S narling, the captain tried to box me in. Tried to wrap me in heavy layers of ki and smother the fires of retribution before his precious Marco suffered brain damage.

I laughed, utterly taken by the power oozing thick as syrup through my blood.

And when he tried to fashion walls around me, I flew through the open ceiling with wings made of purest darkness. Soaring above him, then turning down. Falling on him with force enough to crack bone, if this weren't a battle fought using the unseen. When he built a roof of ki, I oozed through the earth. Poisoning the soil beneath our feet. Only to pop up and sink my teeth into his calves and drink his ki straight from the vein.

Over, under, around, or through, there was *always* a flaw in the order. Always a way for me to slip his leash. I just had to find it.

Or *make* it.

My smile grew sinister.

Hungering for the moment that he finally figured out how to contain me, if only so I might explode and kill us both.

"Are you not impressed?" I hissed, leaning close. Licking at the underside of his jaw. Tasting that forbidden sweetness one last time. "Is this not what you wanted, *Asher*?"

He bared his teeth, arms flexing as he held me against him. Trying to master the ki whipping and lashing between us. But his eyes wandered... going back to the fallen soldier turning blue where he lay in the springy loam. Not breathing, and not-quite dead.

"Poor Marco," I spat. "Surely he doesn't have much time left..." Savoring the taste of him, his ki and all that I'd refused, I let the Glaith bite my palm. Fed it everything that spilled over, keeping my bloody promise, no matter how much it hurt to do so. "Well... If he can be saved at all, of course."

At this, Asher's attention splintered. The warrior broke with a roar that hurt my ears but filled my tainted heart with glee. Thrusting me back, he turned to collect his dead. Sweeping a muscled forearm beneath lolling head, he breathed life into slack lips.

And then he did a thing he had no rights to. A thing meant only for the Goddess' chosen few—those named Trila-Glís, who could both store ki, and *use* it.

He took from the well of ki shared between us, took what I'd stolen to free black wings, and gave it *back* to Marco.

Gasping, I stuffed the Glaith back in my pocket, trying to cut him off from using my power. To thwart this lesser victory and make him feel the same loss I'd been forced to endure.

But the captain took no notice of my effort, for it was not *my* ki he used.

It was his own.

I stayed only long enough to see the soldier gasp awake, watched the color return to his lips before I fled to the shadows. Back from where I'd come. To the rebels. Running as fast as my legs could move, I didn't stop until I could go no further. Until the very ki in my blood ran dry and the temptation to seize the Glaith was on me once more.

There was only one place I could go. One being in all the world that could shelter and feed what I'd become. The great-grandmother oak. And even in the throes of ravenous madness, I knew.

I couldn't do this alone.

But I had been tethered by promises made to the dead and the taken. Leashed and enslaved without the ability to barter or negotiate.

Don't drop the Glaith. Keep the scientists free to fight another day. Don't allow yourself to be made a slave to a treacherous Elite with a pretty smile and tasty ki. And never, *ever* tell another about the dark Truth squirming and writhing inside me.

I thumbed the branded letters below my knuckle, scowling into the night. All four promises couldn't exist at once. I couldn't keep anyone safe *and* hide behind the Glaith, but neither could I drop it and expect anyone to survive the fallout—and that was to say nothing of the thousands of other refugees choking the wood or the ki-mad captain coming for my blood.

There would have to be compromise.

And it would have to be now.

I knelt at the grandmother's many feet, humbled.

Shaking and sweating, gasping for breath, I knew it wouldn't be long before Asher was after me again. Already, I could feel his fury rising. Oh, he'd saved his precious Marco, all right—but he'd never make the same mistake again. Wouldn't underestimate me *or* give me the advantage of surprise. I was sure of it.

Worse, he had an army of ki-wielders to my three Triloth and a scattering of semi-functional gadgets.

Expelling a brittle laugh, I pressed my forehead to that ancient wood.

No, I couldn't do this alone. "I need..." I swallowed, throat aching around shards of broken glass. I needed an *ally*. One who could accept what I'd become without judgment. An ally who'd take the corrupted ki festering in my heart and ask for more, allowing me to retain my freedom.

At my touch, the great-grandmother oak—whose trunk couldn't be ringed by a dozen outstretched hands —leapt in greeting. Answering my call. Ancient, she was connected to all things, and all things in this wood belonged to her.

The heartbeat of the forest, lacking a pulse.

It was enough to humble. Enough to bring tears to my eyes, and with a final shuddering breath, I thumbed the captain's brand on my right middle finger, then plunged my hand into my pocket. Withdrawing the first of my promises and the only one I intended to break. In defiance of past experience, the Glaith glittered in the grandmother's shadow.

Virgin Glaith no more. Filled with ki both Priestess and Elite, but ki all the same.

"Don't know what I'm doing," I whispered, inspecting the ore for obvious flaws. "But I can't... I need help." Swallowing back the urge to scream myself hoarse, I set the Glaith to the grandmother's thick skin. "I can't do this alone. We need sanctuary. We need"—I grimaced, pressing, trying to crush the Glaith into dust —"a sentinel."

While the grandmother didn't fight back, trying to pass stone through wood was a rather *strenuous* ask. Almost asking the impossible, really, except of course, I knew it wasn't. Knew it had been done several times before, and so I ground my teeth and forced everything I could spare into the Glaith. Risking everything for a whim, I broke my promise. To sacrifice the High Priestess' Glaith was to leave myself vulnerable to both the temptation to feast upon ki the others needed to live, and the seductive manipulations of one Caledonian Captain of Special Forces.

His monogram winked at me, taunting, back-lit by Glaith beginning to overheat beneath my palm. Showing clean through twisted skin as new sweat built atop the old.

The captain felt my effort, used the bond he'd left lurking behind my ribs to try to pull me back. To stop me.

It was his second mistake, for through him, I had enough to build the vehicle of our freedom.

With a sigh, the grandmother accepted my offer, taking the flames of blue, green, and purple into her mighty trunk. Dissolving the stone before my eyes, her new pulse fluttering through leaves and tiny, invisible root fibers.

She was *everywhere!* Her roots were spun throughout the entire forest, connected to everything.

Connecting me to *everything*. Lending a home to a rare and dangerous thing stained by moonlight and pitch.

I laughed, collapsing at the edge of the Grandmother's skirts.

And banished one Caledonian Captain of Special Forces from *my* lands.

That I had returned before anyone noticed my absence went without saying, for with the Grandmother at my back, I no longer suffered exhaustion. No longer hungered of felt the ache of muscles growing tired from endless marching. Any minor scrapes or bruises were swept away before the pain could be felt. Any emotional hurts fed into the soil beneath my bare feet, exchanged for the whispers of ancient, wild power.

And the blackest of urges—the ones that begged for me to take just a little more, to taste the pure ki of a *Priestess* and indulge the starving monster wearing my skin—became bearable.

Through the Grandmother, I saw everything. *Felt* everything.

And if the wood reflected that reciprocity with the black and silver petals of my Truth, none seemed to notice but me.

"Miss Tannovic?" Josh asked, startling me. Pulling

my attention away from the Grandmother. "Alright lass? I havena had a chance to ask since—"

I gagged, for there, dangling from a leather cord at his hip, hung three squirrels. Dead and broken. "I'm fine."

"Well, you see," he said, reaching for me with blood-stained fingers, "you keep sayin' that, but you're pale as death and I can see you shaking from here."

"Just tired." I dodged his touch. "That's all."

He scrubbed at the back of his neck. Confusion whipping at me through the air. "Right. I know. Come on then. Let's get a bit t'eat and drink."

My lip curled. "Not hungry."

He cleared his throat. "You have to eat, lass."

"I'm not hungry. But—" I backpedaled, cursing when my foot landed on a spherical green fruit with a sharp pit. "Thank you for your concern."

"Mila, what—" his gaze drifted down, eyes widening. "What happened t'your shoes?"

I kicked the strange fruit aside and glanced at my filthy, bare feet, spreading my toes in the dirt. "Took them off."

"Why would you do such a thing—"

"Blisters." I slipped my hand behind my back and tugged my sandals forward, showing him the cord from which they now hung.

"I suppose," he said with a tiny frown, then shook his head. "Come now, lass. I know the wee forest creatures aren't your first choice, but—"

"I'm *fine*," I snapped, and slipped into the shadows. Filling him with a sense of foreboding that warned him not to follow. It was nothing to disappear into a brush that parted for me alone. Nothing to let the forest swallow me whole and take me to a place of compromise. With every bare footfall, I bathed in the magnificent beauty of everlasting power thrumming around me, pouring my excess ki into the soil and flora through the soles of my feet. The forest took it all and asked for more, stretching greedy fingers toward me as I wandered, content to be nothing more than a conduit of this ancient being.

Conduit or not, however, the hollow space forming between my ribs was proof enough that I couldn't feast on the ki of the forest forever. Josh was right, Goddess take him. Whether I felt so mundane a hunger or not, it was clear that if I didn't find something I could stomach —and soon—I wouldn't be able to fight off a squirrel, let alone an army of Caledonian Elites led by one Captain Asher Rawlings wielding *my* pendant.

I'd need my strength for his next assault.

With a sigh, I sank to the forest floor and crossed my legs, back pressed against a tree as I watched the animals go about their daily business. Where I could scarcely take a step without blundering it in some way or another, the wildlife around me thrived. Eating some plants and avoiding others, the squirrels stored various nuts and berries in the hearts of the trees, fattening themselves on the bounty of the forest in preparation for the coming winter months.

A saucy red squirrel chattered above me, angling for a cluster of the same green fruit responsible for bruising my heel. I watched as it shimmied to the end of a branch, hung on with dexterous hind feet, and reached with its forepaws. Curiosity piqued, I touched the furry little acrobat with a delicate tendril of ki as it selected the fattest fruit—and knocked the other two out of the sky. They hit the earth before me with a thump, green husk exploding to reveal an ovular black pit.

Eyebrows pinched, I moved for closer inspection.

A walnut! A tiny, nutrient dense gift from the Grandmother herself. I peeled away the remainder of the husk, frowning at the dark-brown stains left by the juice in the peel. Mere vanity, however, was not enough to stop me from gleefully bashing the shell to smithereens between two rocks. I plucked the edible pieces from the broken shell, licking my fingers clean before I stooped, and tore a strip of fabric from the hem of my filthy shift. Collecting as many as I could carry.

"Are those walnuts?"

I jumped, whirling to face the intruder with flushed, guilty cheeks. "Goddess, Josh." I laughed, trying not to feel the concern that lanced through my heart. That it was *easy* for all but the captain to sneak up on me. To catch me unaware and apparently ignore my command for privacy. "You startled me."

"Sorry," he said, then took my stained, scarred fingers before I could think to lurch away. He made a sound at the back of his throat. "Walnut stain, lassy. Nothin' but scrubbing will get those stains off your hands, I'm afraid. My brothers an' I used to—"

A man's scream cut him off—rescuing me from enduring his attentions and resisting the urge to take a sip.

Josh and I shared a single wide-eyed glance, then took off toward the disturbance. It was Ancaster my senses told me well before we broke through the clearing to find him fallen and clutching at a twisted, broken ankle. His attention, however, was not focused upon himself, but the massive, snarling tan cat crouched by the mouth of a cave.

Aided by the Grandmother, my ki pulsed through the soil, through the roots beneath my feet, the lichen under great clawed paws, and into the beast herself.

Muscles coiled. Heart pounding inside her chest. Ferocious territorial rage whirling through her veins. Her attention snapped from intruder to intruder, trying to decide which she would aim for first. Planning which of us to disembowel with her claws. Salivating over the vulnerable spot just below the ear that would be the perfect place to sink her mighty teeth...

Josh threw his hand back without turning to look at me, fingers splayed over my belly. "Mila, get back, lass!"

I slapped his hand away and took a step.

She yowled, the warning vibrating between my ribs, but still I persisted, smiling when her attention settled upon my face alone.

Lips pulled back from canines as long as my forefinger, she snarled, muscles in her shoulders standing out against her fur.

Flashing my palms, I ignored Josh's hissed warning and took another step.

Pupils no more than tiny pinpricks, ears flat against her skull, she hissed again, spittle spraying between gleaming yellow teeth.

Belle's ice-pale face burst onto the scene, hovering at the edge of my peripheral, her whisper deafening in the stillness of the moment. "Goddess, Mila. What are you *doing?*"

I stepped past Ancaster and Josh.

The lion's tail—thicker than my forearm—lashed

back and forth, her voice caught somewhere between a snarl and a growl.

"No, Miss Tannovic, you mustn't—"

I snapped my fingers, pointing at the downed man without looking, then at Josh. "Take him and go."

A strangled protest died in his throat, but he moved to do as I said, sweeping his hands beneath the fallen man's armpits. Dragging him back.

"Keep going. She can jump farther than that," I said, loud enough to keep the lion's eyes fixed upon me. Wickedly amused.

"Mila—"

"Go. All of you. *Now*." This was my business.

"You canna—"

"Did I not tell you to leave?" I snarled, knees bent, ki snapping through my skin, balanced on the balls of my feet. Backed by the Grandmother's might and the lion's temper.

The cat lunged as I took another step, but it was a bluff. I could feel it. From the pads on her feet, I pulled, draining her volatile ki and offering it to the Grandmother in payment. Driving it away.

When she began to pace, whiskers twitching on open-mouthed pant, I eased off. Pupils blown out, jaws hanging wide, I watched the young beauty as she moved. All grace and power. The embodiment of lethal perfection.

"The others are gone now, pretty." I held out my hand, cooing. "It's just you and I now. I'm no threat to you, beautiful lady."

She coughed, but I heard the rumble of a purr vibrate at the back of her throat.

With another step forward, I reached for her, fingers

outstretched, ki wrapped around and through her. "Such a beautiful girl. See? Not a thing wrong, is there?"

A tiny mewl echoed from within her cave, followed by one, then three more.

"Ah," I whispered, heart melting. Letting mother's rage twist through my brain. "Your babies are safe, Mum. See?" I reached for her flat, black nose, palm outstretched. "I don't smell of a threat, do I?"

She groaned, ears flicking back and forth between her kittens concealed from sight, and my soothing, low voice.

"That's it, pretty lady. Just relax."

She stretched forward, the tip of her nose only a few inches away from the center of my palm. And then, hair still standing on end, she bumped me, sucking in several half-breaths. Tasting my scent.

The lion's ki blossomed in my mind. A link burning through me as I gasped. Ferocious. Savage. Protective. Patient.

A perfect huntress.

The underbrush crackled and popped as Josh came barreling back into the clearing. "What the fuck are you doin', Mila! Get back!"

In a split second, the lion's pupils narrowed to tiny dots, and acting on pure, unfiltered instinct, she took a swipe. I twisted, managing to dodge a killing blow, but did not escape unscathed. Four long, hooked claws raked down the right side of my ribs, leaving a trail of fire and ripped clothing in their wake.

In spite of the pain, I did not falter—I seized her ki and burrowed beneath her skin. Tying us together. Driving her back, I slipped past the instinct that demanded my immediate death and begged for calm.

"I-It's okay, Mum. It's okay. See to your babies, pretty girl. That's it. They need you. G-Go to them."

She hissed, long and low, pinpricks focused on Josh, but with one final push, disappeared into the dark with an irate flick of her tail.

I staggered back, hands pressed to the gore pouring over my hip.

"Gods, Mila. Have you lost your damned mind, lass?" He rushed to my side, reaching for me. "Are you alright? I've never seen anything half as reckless as *you* in that moment, girl." And then, features pinched tight with concern, Josh pressed his lips to mine.

The wrong lips.

"What is *wrong* with you?" I wrenched free of his hands with a snarl, staggering as a fresh wave of warmth slid down my hip. "Kissing me as if you aren't responsible for nearly getting me killed!"

"I—" His eyes bulged. "I almost got you killed? How about the great fucking mountain lion you decided to take as a wee, vicious pet?"

"Just—" I hissed, baring my teeth. "Just shut up for a minute."

With a curse, he dropped to a knee, swept his arm behind my legs, and hefted me off my feet. "Gods above, lass. Protecting you is takin' years off my life."

I thumbed the brand instead of snapping at him. Instead of sinking my teeth into the soft bit above his collarbone and bleeding his ki dry. He'd earned no less, the bloody idiot—

"Mila!" Belle pressed both hands to her lips. "Goddess, sister. Let me see."

"Great stinkin' beast took a piece of her. I'll see about setting a trap to catch th'savage—"

I bared my teeth. "You'll do no such thing!"

"I'll not have that beast attacking us when our backs are turned."

I pushed away from his chest, landing hard on the balls of my feet. "I said *no*, Josh. You'll not lay a hand on her or her young."

"Mila, it took a swipe at you, and if I hadna come along she would have done much more."

"This is *your* fault! I wasn't in any danger until *you* showed up. *You* startled her!" I grimaced, trying to staunch the flow of blood. "If you'd done as I said and stayed back, everything would—gah. Get away from me, you fool," I gasped, unable to mend rent flesh in front of the others. Forced to suffer the pain until I could deal with it in seclusion. "It hurts."

Belle rushed ahead of us, snatching the Dosmui Circlets from Ancaster as she went. "It's alright, Mila. I've got you."

Black stars glittered at the edge of my vision but my lips twitched. This pain was an easy price to pay for the link I now shared with the lion—a link bolstered by each passing beat of the Grandmother's new heart.

Such a magnificent creature. A perfect huntress.

Priestess ki surged through my veins, staunching the flow of blood from the lacerations now marking the right side of my torso, but my attention had begun to wander.

I was with the lion as she settled down with her kittens. Safe, warm, and content.

21

We'd made it.

The Canodill Pass loomed before us, the gaping maw of granite and shale the only accessible entrance into the Glaith mines. With protected vantage points, elevation, and access to the forest, it was the *perfect* place to defend—and that was without mention of Alicia's ki shield. For when the Caledonian forces made it through the Grandmother's distractions... they would come.

He'd come.

I wasn't fool enough to think I'd put him off forever.

But this next time, I'd be ready. All I had to do was win this inane argument with Josh.

"Mila, lass, *no.*"

"How can you say that, Josh? You really think they won't come knocking at Elora's door next? They're coming for the Glaith in those mines"—I flung my arm wide, toward the Canodill Pass and the mountain beyond—"and we can't let them get away with it. We *have* to fight."

"We're *not* letting them get away with anything, you stubborn wee thing." He ran a hand through his short brown hair, blowing out a frustrated breath. "We need t'gather the *right* resources. We canna just turn and fight an army of Elites as we are now! You've only just begun t'recover from the damage done by that infernal lion you love so much, lass. And I'd think *you,* of anyone, should know better than that. Did you not see what happened in the caves? The High Priestess is a Trila-Glís, and she couldna stand against that man."

Yes. *That* man.

Tracing the brand, I bared my teeth, pacing the threshold dividing forest and the rocky skirt of the mountain. Captain Rawlings, with his soft lips and insidious promises of protection and untold wonders. Pulling at me. Humming a beautiful, seductive song even through his banishment.

Tossing my hair over my shoulder, I put my feet to the loose shale, ignoring the sharp teeth nipping my soles as I stepped toward Josh once more.

Glaith. Abundant in the soil beneath my feet—the answer to everything, according to the High Priestess and her followers. But unrefined, virgin Glaith was *hungry.* Each step cutting me off from the Grandmother and her ever expanding network of power, from the lion and her kittens. And from the captain, too, though he was still there. Muted.

"Mila," Josh said, reaching for me as I paced, eyes gone soft. Pleading. "You canna truly believe you can take on a single Elite by yourself, let alone the whole army."

With a snarl, I batted his hand away, returning my feet to the rich loam and the network of life and power hidden from mundane eyes. "Do not presume to tell me what I can and cannot do, Master Trapper."

"What's *wrong* with you, lass?"

I scrubbed at the tension etched between my brows. What was wrong with me? I laughed, fists clenched. "Shall I forget what they did, then? Be a good girl and run from the big, scary Elites? Submit to your perfect logic and ignore what that putrid did to my father—"

"I don' know why you're mad at me, lass. I'm not th'enemy here."

"If you'll do nothing, you're worse than they are."

Again, he swept his hand through his hair. "Just relax, Mila. I don' understand why you see fit t'do this now, when we've finally made it to safety. Can we finish this insane conversation as soon as the scientists get finished installin' that shield?"

"Insane?" I stalked toward him, braving the rocky poison beneath my feet. Fury crackling at my restraint.

He rolled his eyes. "If you could see yourself—*bah*! Never mind. I'm asking you as a friend, Mila, t'wait until we're through the Canodill Pass and into the Glaith Mines. We can talk when we've got an impenetrable shield between us an' them, yeah?"

For a moment, I merely continued to scowl, breathing hard. "Fine."

"Right. *Fine*." He returned my icy glare. "I'll deal with you later."

A sharp, hysterical bark of laughter burst from my lips, and before I could say—or do—anything that would destroy our friendship forever, I stomped away. Belle and the other Priestesses caught my attention, their soft, pure ki a beacon to the fire whirling through my heart.

"Come sit with us, sister."

I flopped down on the ground beside their tight circle, rubbing at my temples. "The earth here is poison," I hissed, tugging my sandals off their cord and jamming my filthy feet through the thin leather straps.

"Poison?" Belle laughed. "Hardly. It's Glaith, sister. We're close to the mines, that's all. The soil is saturated with it," Belle said, turning her pale face into the sun. "I find it rather enjoyable, truthfully. It's peaceful without the burden of our gifts. Reminds me of the salt caves."

"It's poison," I said again, turning my scowl upon the mountain. "I hate it."

Belle chuckled, cracking one sparkling blue eye at me. "You'll get used to it. I'll teach you to meditate."

When she returned to her sunbathing, I sneered. What use had I of meditation when the forest whispered secrets only I could hear? Secrets only I could understand? Why should I submit, when the Grandmother offered power enough to squash my enemies, if only I'd reach out and take it? Why would I hide my ki in the Glaith when even Captain Rawlings—the impossible, Elite parasite glued to the back of my ribs—couldn't squash the power at my disposal?

I scowled at the misty peaks beyond the clouds, tempted to chew his brand from my flesh. What use had I of the mountain and the Glaith beneath it, if I had to sacrifice the darkness running wild through my veins? "How anything can survive in this barren void is utterly beyond me."

"Oh, I don't know," Belle said, cracked and peeling lips tilted toward a smile. "Life here is surprisingly resilient." She paused, squinting at the rocky terrain separating us from the scientists working on the shield.

"Look there. A bit of green. Vines, I think. And of course, we're here. Alive. Surviving."

I snorted. Was I to be pleased by a few withered vines with the call of the wild at my back?

Belle sighed, patting the pink, twisted flesh of my right hand. "Have you eaten today, Mila?"

Without meeting her eye, I lifted my stash of walnuts.

"We must preserve our strength if we hope to gather enough ki to power the shield," she continued, pulling her knees to her chest. "Goddess, if only we had the Trila-Glís..."

My eyes snapped to her face. "Always this obsession with the Trila-Glís."

"They're an integral part of our process, sister. Without their gifts"—she shook her head—"the Triloth are spread too thin. We need ki to make progress with the Glaith technology. Four Triloth aren't nearly enough. Even with Ancaster's gadgets, things like healing will have to be sacrificed for progress."

"Progress," I whispered, tearing my gaze away. "You'd trap the Trila-Glís in a prison of Glaith for progress? Enslave them?"

"I imagine the High Priestess and the Elect would very much prefer to be with us, at the moment, wouldn't you?"

I swallowed, hard, but said nothing.

After a moment, she cleared her throat. "I'm afraid, Mila. Afraid that without the Trila-Glís, we don't have the power to fight." She met my eye. "I'm terrified, sister, because logic dictates whoever possesses the Trila-Glís will win this war. We Priestesses seek peace, before all else. But the Trila-Glís"—she grimaced, something fierce glimmering beneath the delicate mask—"they are fire and wind. Our most powerful weapon is not only lost, but lies in the hands of our enemies. I would do *anything*, sacrifice *anyone*, to recover the Goddess' chosen."

"You need a weapon."

"This is war. And we are badly outclassed." She shrugged, picking at crusted dirt on her knee. "Shall I take a look at those claw marks while we're waiting? I won't be able to do much until we've got the shield going, of course, but I hate the thought of leaving you marked like that. Those scars will be terrible."

I shrugged, scoring my newest scars with my nails. Tracing their length with something close to reverence. "They're nothing. Save your energy."

"Even so." She stood, motioning for me to do the same.

Standing before her, I flicked the clasp of my belt, exposing my entire right side and pressing one hand over my breast to cover my nudity. Otherwise careless of who might see.

"Goddess, but you were lucky, Mila. That mountain lion very nearly disemboweled you."

I clenched my fist, nails biting my palm. "Wasn't her fault."

Belle nodded, her attention fixed on the four angry red slashes marking me from the bottom of my ribs to mid-thigh. "Repairing those scars shouldn't be an issue, but it may take all three of us to do it. Even with the Dosmui Circlets at our disposal." She traced the lowest slash, the contact flooding me with the banked flames of Priestess ki. So beautiful... Soothing...

"Don't." I jerked back from her touch, rearranging

my shift. "Don't waste your strength on me, Priestess. Better to make sure Ancaster doesn't walk with a limp." Heart pounding, I spun away, stalking the edge of the forest.

Goddess, what was wrong with me? This urge to drink my sisters dry... it... it was mania. Uncontrollable, when I wasn't with the Grandmother. When my ki was left without the exchange of poison for peace.

Tearing my sandals off, I slipped into the shadows, burying my feet into the earthy loam, connecting to the pulse of life once more. I only needed a moment, just a taste of the forest to center me before I'd return to them and pack my ki into a convenient little box. Ready for use as their weapon.

It only took a moment for the captain to realize I was almost beyond his reach. He uncoiled, his ki snaking through my system, kissing the edges of my senses. Promises whispering through my blood, if only I'd abandon this silly flight and go to him...

The lion's roar echoed in the distance.

I grinned, tossing the captain aside. "What are you doing, pretty lady? Stalking us?" I reached through the roots, blending with the sharp senses of an apex predator, wetting my lips. No mere male had ever ruled *her*. None would dare to set foot upon her territory unless she allowed it. Unless she marked the trees with her scent and drew them to her.

A low rumble rose at the back of my throat. Oh, yes. If the captain wanted to keep playing his little games, *he* would come to *me*. Let him set foot where he was not welcome if he wanted his prize so badly. Let him test his impossible Elite ki against the lion's fury.

Let them all come.

The lion purred, watching from the shadows, motionless. Observing the refugees as they scrambled to get the shield installed between the mighty pillars of the Canodill Pass.

Humans. So soft. Vulnerable, with their dull, fragile claws and blunt teeth. It would be nothing to wait for the perfect moment, to surge from the shadows and pin one beneath me. Nothing to bury my teeth in the soft bit beneath the chin and feast on their ki until it was all gone...

And the Priestesses, so pure. Pale and filthy. Silver-blonde hair matted with sweat, faces marked with days of hard travel and the strain of tragic loss. Their senses blinded by the Glaith beneath the mountain. Unaware of the danger lurking so close...

"Alrigh'," Josh hollered, swiping at the sweat glistening on his brow.

I staggered, torn from the lion's mind. But... it wasn't the lion's hands curved into claws, reaching for the Priestesses from the shadows. It wasn't the lion who hungered for their ki, whose mouth watered at the mere thought of tasting them...

"We're ready here," Josh continued. "If you could all move to the other side o'the gates, we'll get the Priestesses to close 'em in just a moment."

A dozen groans echoed around the clearing as the refugees gathered themselves and began filtering through the pass.

Belle's hand dipped into the shadows. "Ready, Mila?"

I cringed away from her touch. "The Glaith... It's... It's not safe—*you're* not safe—"

"I know you don't believe me," Belle said, stepping

toward me. "But the Glaith is our most powerful resource. That and our brains."

Her smile lit the darkness, drawing me out.

"Come, sister. Let me show you the power of the Goddess' chosen. I know you think it's a prison, but the mines will be our salvation. We're no good to anyone if we starve to death or die of exposure in the wilderness."

I slowed as the forest slipped away from me, bare feet painful on the loose shale, stopping but a few feet from the threshold of the gate.

"None of us are meant to live like this. Like savages in the woods—Mila?" she asked, frowning in question when I stopped abruptly. "What are you doing?"

I blinked, holding her eye for a moment before I glanced at the rest of our ragged band. Head clear of the darkness, senses void of ki. More than a dozen faces turned toward me, some heads tilted to the side, others wearing frowns that matched Belle's.

"Come now, lass," Josh said, hands on his hips. "We'll be with my people by nightfall. You canna do anything to help if you're on the wrong side of this shield. Besides—" he held out his hand, "—we need you to help close the gates. And you canna do that from there."

Couldn't I?

Thumbing the captain's brand, I stilled, considering the refugees.

The Triloth. As beautiful as they were limited. Belle had joined the others, gathered around a shimmering panel much the same as the one barring entry to the High Priestess' office. This close to the shield, I could see Belle's vines rimming the top of the cliffs, a splash of green against the stark rock-face. Thin and starved in this barren patch of land, clinging to the barest wisps of life. And beyond? Nothing. Nothing but cold, dead soil and Glaith.

"That's right, lass," Josh said, smiling down at me. "Come on, then. We've got a lot of ground t'cover before we're safe."

How long before the Glaith beneath the mountain was as my pendant had been—filled to bursting with ki? No longer able to hold me in check? How long before my dark Truth broke through its cage of bone and sinew and demanded retribution?

I thumbed the brand.

There was safety behind that shield, yes. Freedom to fight another day, and to keep the Glaith Mines beyond the reaches of the Empire.

Stepping clear of the Grandmother's shadow, I took Josh's hand. Sandaled feet kept me separate from the poisoned earth as he guided me toward a prison of Glaith and stone.

I paused just outside of the barrier. How long before my soul festered? Before the hunger for ki could no longer be contained?

Belle took at step toward me. "Mila?"

My head snapped toward her and she faltered, feet coming to a stop on the other side of the gate. Belle wanted a weapon to help her fight this war. But how long would it be before her pretty blue eyes dulled, taking on the same flat gray of her precious mountain?

The lion screamed in the distance.

I nodded.

There was no place for a rare and dangerous thing beneath the earth where dark wings would whither and rot.

Whirling, I shoved Josh through the gates and slammed my scarred palm into the rock face, dumping *everything* into the thin vines laced over stone. They pulsed with new life, thickening as I sent a silent command for them to spread. To reach for the shield's Glaith panel on the other side of the gate.

My knees sagged as the ki gushed from my body, but I persisted, scowling at the backward AR mocking my effort. Defying the captain's paltry effort to stop me, I ground my teeth and pressed harder, reaching for the Grandmother's limitless strength. When the vines reached their goal, wrapping around the Glaith panel, I gasped. Pulling through the vines, the Glaith took and took and *took,* trying to satisfy a greedy, limitless void.

Cold sweat sprang up on my brow as the life slipped away from me, but still, I did not break, giving the shield and the refugees as much as I possibly could. The *only* thing I could, for behind that shield, they'd release me from the promises I couldn't keep.

A moment later, a wall of glittering blue burst into being, spanning the mouth of the Canodill Pass, and in doing so, severed the vines and my connection to those behind it.

I gasped, tumbling forward, left knee striking the ground hard enough to split skin. The shocked, pale faces of the refugees shimmered before me, distorted through the shield. And as I took a moment to recover myself, I watched Belle's lips form a single, condemning word.

"Trila-Glís."

She couldn't have been more wrong.

INSATIABLE CORRUPTION

TRITAN EVOLUTION, BOOK II

FOREWORD

Make sure you sign up for Myra's Newsletter so you never miss sexy NSFW art, free things, exclusive deals, and loads of other cool shit you do not want to miss...

Sign up for Myra's Newsletter today!

To the favorite child (not me), whose every action is beloved.
Cherished.
Right down to his dusty, second-born farts.
This is my redemption tour.
(A scream for attention)

1

———

Slavers.

They passed beneath me, a group of two leading three. Hacking and slashing at the flora in their path, they dragged their wares through the snow, dressed in chain, rope, and little else. Heedless of the young and frail trying to keep pace. Their cargo was a rarity these days, but to see three at once, let alone the same group?

Something dark and sinister twisted in my gut, pleased the slavers were kind enough to make my job so easy. For of course, stealing their wares would be a blow to the Empire, or at the very least, to whichever pompous, festering Caledonian lord was wealthy enough to afford to keep *three* Tritans as pets.

As slaves.

The Caledonians really should have known better, after all this time. Any refugee who set foot on *my* territory didn't remain a slave for long.

Concealed by shadows, I watched, lip curled, as the leader called a stop for the day.

"Fuckin' impossible to make good time in this hell-hole. I can hardly tell if it's sundown or not."

"Ah, but this is the Forest of Sorrows, isn't it, Jasper? What else can be expected of a haunted wood?"

I grinned, baring teeth.

"Don't joke about that, you fool!" Jasper snarled, raising the back of his hand. "You'll bring the Menace down upon us, sure as hellfire."

The fool laughed, unperturbed. "Those are fairy tales perpetrated by this lot." He kicked one of the slaves in the ribs, making a length of silver hair shimmer and dance in the gloom. "*Honestly.* A vengeful spirit ferrying Tritans to safety? Bah! They're trying to get in your head, mate. That's all. We should just cut this whole wood down so they have no more little hidey holes to lurk in."

Cut down the Forest of Sorrows? Over my bloated corpse.

"Don't think I haven't tried to cut it down a dozen times. It just grows back! This wood is cursed by the Menace, and I've seen it," Jasper hissed, spraying the other with spittle as he dumped his pack on the ground. "Six and a half feet of muscle, ain't nothing. The Menace"—Jasper flung his arms wide—"he carries a flaming battle ax longer than your arm. Killed my first crew years back, he did."

"Oh? Then why'd he leave you alive?"

Jasper grinned and tugged a golden pendant free of his furs. "I have a wealthy benefactor and the divine favor of the serpent."

"As long as I get my cut from this lot of runaways," the fool said, "I don't care how superstitious you are."

"We have to be free of this place by midday

tomorrow to make the auction in Liyas, otherwise we're stuck with them until the middle of next month. Get a fire lit. You don't deserve it," he said, stooping too close to one of the downed Tritans—a child, "but you'll need the strength. We're pushing harder tomorrow."

The youngest slave groaned, but remained silent. Captured and defeated.

Not for long. Not on *my* soil.

A thick, furred tail descended from the branch above, flicking before my nose. I glanced up with a smile, scratching the beautiful tan appendage with sharp, curved nails. A twitch, and it was gone, though the subtle rumble of a purr vibrated through the air. Coiled and ready for the strike, great, black claws sunk deep into the bark beneath her feet, Kas watched.

And I with her.

Waiting for the perfect moment.

Jasper scooped the top layer of snow off a fallen log, setting it in a pot to boil. "Coffee's on. You'll take first watch."

If I were willing to risk flaunting my power, I could have drained their ki and strolled into camp with ease. But there was no finesse in doing things the easy way. No skill. Not anymore.

Of course, there was always the possibility that I went too far... That I took everything they had to give and couldn't stop—

I turned my face away from the vulnerable and weak, feeding my dark compulsion to the Grandmother and through her mighty roots, the forest itself.

No. There was something to be said for the simple things in life. To hunt with the skill and expertise of a mountain lion, to strike once, or not at all. Watching as the unsuspecting insects beneath us went about their business.

Unaware.

Neither of us moved until night fell, until Kas stretched her long, lithe body and moved forward on silent feet—my cue. I nodded, soothing her with my ki as I wound a length of twine about my fist and tucked a small bag of powder into the heart of my palm.

Red berries. Left to ripen on the vine for maximum potency. Poisonous to humans, as Ancaster had discovered all those many seasons ago. Capable of inducing debilitating vomiting and explosive diarrhea.

I grinned, stalking closer. Each footfall carefully planned, eyes and ki-sense locked on the villains below.

Coming to a stop above the fire pit, I covered my face with a hand-spun scarf to protect my lungs from the acidic white smoke that only came from burning green wood. Inexperienced Caledonian idiots—but the white cloud gave agreeable cover for my purpose, so I gave thanks.

In position, I sent Kas a pulse through the branches, inflaming her territorial fury as my ki rushed through her blood.

She yowled, the sound chilling, though I'd heard much worse from her over the seasons.

"What in the bloody hell?" the fool gasped, slopping coffee down the front of his fur coat.

Kas yipped, dragging her mighty claws down the tree trunk, her glare reflecting bright, demonic green in the light of the flames.

The fool stood, moving on hesitant feet toward the edge of the clearing, a whip clutched in his hand.

Poor, sad little man, frightened by monsters in the

dark. Grinning, I unwound the ball of twine, guiding the bag of powder to steep in the pot of camp coffee while Kas rumbled a low, threatening growl. Daring him to cross the threshold and enter the wood.

Stumbling back, the fool called for Jasper, seeking the perceived safety of the firelight, his attention fixed upon the demonic, bodiless eyes.

At my signal, Kas fell quiet, crouched in the shadows above as I reeled the red berries in, leaving behind nothing but a few innocuous drops of laced coffee as I went.

"J-Jasper! Wake up, mate! It's the fuckin' Menace!"

Clutching the likeness of the serpent with one hand, Jasper pulled his furs tighter. Face set and determined, though pale beneath his tan. "Get me a coffee, will you? It's going to be a long night."

I almost laughed at my dancing pets. Almost spoiled the fun, for there was nothing left to do but wait for morning.

2

———————

Dawn broke to the beautiful sounds of retching, and with a sneeze, Kas slipped into the shadows, drawn away by the scent of a potential mate. Leaving me to deal with the downed slavers and the trio of terrified escapees.

Tritans.

My people, once.

On silent feet, I edged into the camp, my every sense primed for the sound of the slaver's return from where they'd gone to purge in relative privacy. Ready, should I need to call upon the Grandmother to destroy these trespassers. Three sets of wide, pale eyes tracked my progress and I pressed a single scarred finger to my lips for silence, offering a toothy grin.

The woman squealed, pulling at the heavy irons binding her hand and foot, leaning away from my approach.

"Hush," I hissed, frowning down at her. "You'll ruin the game."

"Game?" the man asked, soothing the woman as best he could with hands bound to a tree.

I frowned at the woman and without thinking, sent a tendril toward her, tasting her ki.

Fear. She was terrified.

Head tilted, I knelt in the snow, creeping closer. "What did they do to frighten you so?"

Eyes bulging, she shook her head and scrambled back.

With a scowl, I glanced toward the slavers. "I wasn't planning to kill them, but if they've harmed you—"

"N-No," she gasped, glancing to the child who bore her likeness, then back to me. "No killing. We've seen enough death."

A puzzling mix of bravery and terror bubbled to the surface, her face hardening in spite of her vulnerability. A mother's ferocity, though it was in direct contrast with the motherhood instinct I'd come to know—Kas would have gutted the men for daring to touch her young. Would have spread their innards across the boundary of her territory as a warning to those who would dare challenge her.

Trembling, she reached for me. "J-Just—can you help us? Please?"

It was my turn to pull away, avoiding the touch of her blue-tinged skin. "Of course. But you must be silent," I added, shaking her off, rewarding her cooperation with another toothy grin that made her pale.

The man nodded, steeling himself. "Hurry."

Humming a tune under my breath as I worked, I tugged a tiny wooden box free of my satchel and flicked the latch. Inside lay a selection of seeds I'd collected in late autumn. Tiny warriors drafted and bred to do my bidding.

"What are you doing?" the man hissed, twisting in his bonds. "They'll be back at any moment. *Hurry*."

"No appreciation." I tisked, and then, eyebrows raised I showed him my palm. "See? Keys."

He hesitated, pale brows drawn together above sunken eyes as he inspected my offering.

I curled my fingers, beckoning for his bound hands.

"Goddess," he whispered, looking skyward, "why have you forsaken us? Why send us this wild thing? Why mock us in our time of need?"

"The Goddess is *dead*," I sang, going instead to the youngest among them, and dropping a maple seed in the locks at wrists and ankles. "She burned up with the Temple." Eyes fluttering closed, I woke the keys with a burst of silent power. "Be still," I told the child, waiting for the infant trees to outgrow their prisons.

When they did, the boy cried out, eyes wide as he watched my keys rend the iron from the inside, destroying delicate mechanisms as they burned through the energy I'd given them. The chains fell away, leaving the too-skinny youth to scramble to his feet, staring.

I pointed at the slaver's packs. "Clothes."

"But—"

Lips pulled back, I snapped my fingers. Impatient to send this group to the coast and return to my solitude. "Focus. You're ruining the fun."

"Y-Your teeth. They're—"

"Jake," the man whispered, holding out his wrists to me. "Get us some clothes, son."

Moving on to the last of them, the woman, I

hummed my tune, jerking my chin at a narrow game trail concealed beneath the underbrush. "Go. And don't fear the lion," I added, beaming at the boy before he disappeared into the dark. "She hasn't got the taste for man."

There were no arguments after that.

3

___

"I know what you are."

I stilled, lingering at the edge of the clearing that would lead this battered family to freedom from the Empire.

"It's a clever disguise, I'll give you that." The Tritan man flicked his fingers toward my face. "The clothes? The hair? You look nothing like us. And certainly nothing like what you *really* are. Except for the teeth. And the claws. Those are a rather obvious tell—"

The woman elbowed him. "But I'm sure none get close enough to see it, do they, dear?"

I flashed her a quick, toothy grin, balanced on the balls of my feet.

Her breath caught, but she continued. "I didn't think so. And how have you managed to dye your hair such a rich brown—I'm sorry, I didn't catch your name, dear."

For a moment, I held her eye, then tugged a hand-woven, fingerless glove off my scarred right palm. Letting the captain's accursed brand see sunlight for the first time in at least three winters. Maybe more. "Walnut husks. Stain anything and everything they touch," I said, showing her the evidence on my twisted skin.

"Brilliant!"

With a nod, I turned back to the trees, one hand on a branch.

"Wait—"

"I didn't think there were any of you left," the man said, taking a careful step closer. "At least none free of the Elites. Have you been living here since the Fall?"

In the distance, Kas yowled—screaming furious defiance at her potential suitor.

I tilted my head. That sounded like rejection. Poor boy.

"How? How have you done it?"

My lips parted, but nothing came out.

"Come with us. You don't have to live like this," he insisted. "Like a savage."

I bared my teeth, tossing him my most *savage* grin.

His pale skin blanched, but he pressed on, desperation making him taste of fouled things. "Please. We won't last long out here! If it's not those two, it will be others. You know it. Tritans aren't seen on the auction blocks too often, these days. Mostly Elorans, since the Empire took Liyas." He laughed then, wrapping his palm about a thin sapling, desperate excitement dancing over his skin and mine. "But with your power— Goddess, we could *fight* them! We could start a rebellion! Claim vengeance for the wrong done to our people—"

Entranced, I stepped closer. What would it be like to embrace this fever for war? To bathe in it and finally take what was owed? I took another step, watching the heartbeat flutter at his throat.

"Are you not Tritan, girl? Does the need for justice not sing in your blood?" He made a bitter, humorless sound, the dash of salt adding an intoxicating aroma to his heated, simple ki. "To find a Priestess free of the Empire? Likely the very last of your kind, I might add. You're a gift of the Goddess, girl. A divine weapon."

I recoiled.

Always, *always* sent by a dead Goddess to be a weapon for the mundane. To those delusional few who thought they could control the darkness that hungered for their life-blood...

Those who thought it would be satisfied with *just* Caledonian blood.

Always, always, *always.*

Bored, I discarded the man's cheap vintage, cleansing my palate with the forest's ambrosia.

Pale eyes gleaming, he seemed not to notice, extending his hand. Thinking my allegiance guaranteed. "Come with us. Fight for us. We need food and water. Please—"

"Food." I tugged a parcel free of my belt, then stubbed booted toe into the snow. "Water."

"This won't last! We can't survive much longer in this weather without proper clothing. You'd rescue us from slavers just to see us die by the elements?" He laughed again, flinging his hand toward the forest. "You should have left us with them if you won't help us now. At least then we'd be alive."

The child whimpered.

I turned to face the father, letting him experience the full-force of my modified canines and savage, filthy visage. "It's a two-day hike to the coast. Stay on the trail." I tapped the parcel I'd given him. "One piece each, three times a day. No fires. Look for the lion's claws," I said, dragging four nails across tree bark to show them what to look for. "Four claws mark a shelter hidden just off the trail. Eight mark food caches. There's sympathy for your cause at the coast. It's all been arranged."

"And then what? I have nothing. I can't afford passage—"

The woman tugged on his arm. "Come. She's done enough, my love. Let's not linger." She looked to me. "Thank you, Priestess. Thank you."

With a single nod, I turned on my heel, reaching for the safety of the trees.

"And what if we don't make it?" the man called. "What then?"

"You will."

"You can't know that!"

Kas howled, impatient and irate, but I turned back to face him, spreading my arms wide. "This is my forest. My home. I'll know if you need me. And I will come." With that, I fled, racing along my treetop highway with practiced ease, sprinting toward sanctuary. Their ki lingered on my senses, making my skin crawl with revulsion and hunger—but not so much as the slavers whose toxic presence was still within the borders of my territory.

I sent a pulse toward them, checking their condition and opening the only path that would lead them free of the forest.

I did not want them dead on my land, where their corpses would taint the soil and feed the trees, or... *worse.*

Besides... if I killed them all, who would perpetrate

the danger of entering the Forest of Sorrows and the Menace who lived within?

The Grandmother sang at my approach, for hers was a heart of Glaith. And through her mighty roots, the forest yearned to do my bidding. Growing and withering at my slightest touch. The great-grandmother oak was a fortress none had managed to penetrate.

Save one, though *he* had only infected my dreams and inspired waking nightmares.

Clearing a gap forty feet above the ground in a running leap, I landed on a branch thicker than any tree for a hundred miles. It was rare for weather of any sort to breach the dense foliage above, and the well-worn path beneath my feet was free of snow. In the cradle of the Grandmother's arms lay an especially dense patch of vines and leaves—thriving in spite of the cold season. A door, hidden in the very trunk of the tree.

Kas yipped, landing on the branch above me, her glorious tan fur rumpled at her shoulder in a distinct claw pattern that made the scars on my ribs tingle in sympathy.

"Didn't meet your standards, pretty?" I asked, showing her the flat of my palm when she crouched low, straining to nose-bump me from her lofty perch.

She huffed, laving my skin with the flat of her deceptively rough tongue, then straightened, turning her attention upon herself and groomed the other, lesser lion's marks flat. Erasing them.

I laughed. "Only the best for the queen, hmm?"

A deep purr vibrated through her.

"Well, I hope you left him alive, you savage thing. Poor boy couldn't help but be drawn to you, could he?"

Placing my palm on the bark beneath me, I asked the forest the questions Kas couldn't answer.

The other lion was running at full speed, heading for the edge of Kas' territory. It was early for breeding, but Kas had sent her two most recent daughters to find territories of their own. She was coming into heat and the young male had probably caught wind of her, hoping to sire the next generation of the queen's children.

But my lady was older and stronger than any lion in the forest—unnaturally so, thanks to her association with me. She could afford to be picky about her consorts, but it was making me twitchy.

And over the next few months, it would do nothing but get worse.

Tugging on her tail, I cracked my neck. "You'd better choose one soon, my love. You were a nightmare last time. And there's the captain to consider," I added, rubbing at a spot just above my breastbone. Picking at the brand twisting my right middle finger. *His* mark. "Always looking for a weakness."

Tail twitching free of my fingers, Kas' teeth flashed, great gray eyes finding my face for an instant before she returned to her preening.

With a snort, I left her to it, pulled the hatch aside, and crawled through the Mila-sized hole in the Grandmother's trunk. It wasn't a spacious apartment, but a perfect hideaway made for one. And with a sigh, I hung my satchel of tricks on a tiny branch by the door and knelt beside my compact, insulated stone fireplace. I dumped a handful of walnut shells on the ash, stretching tired muscles with a groan.

"Wake up," I whispered, tapping the stunted bushes

I kept to house my personal night-lights. Grinning when hundreds of glitterbugs rose, flying toward the ceiling, I watched them dance. Flashing lime-green and yellow, twinkling in a sleepy, complicated pattern.

It didn't take long for the brittle shells to catch a flame and I opened the air vents before smoke filled my bedroom, gazing at the wall before me. It was covered in countless carved marks organized in tidy groups of five and consumed almost every inch of available space. I reached as high as I could, and carved three more marks with my claws, adding to a sea of memories immortalized by notches in the living wood.

Start a rebellion? Leave the forest that had been stained black and silver by my Truth and become a pawn? A weapon?

I snorted. No. It wasn't safe. Not when the ki of every living thing sang to me, begging me to take what was mine by birthright, to feast and gorge until my bottomless hunger was sated...

Squeezing my eyes shut, I dumped the poison from my heart, letting the Grandmother take away the heinous impulse to feed on the weak—and came up against another intruder. One less welcome than even the slavers infesting my lands.

A Priestess.

4

____

It took two days to reach the northern border of my lands. Two days to find the clearing my unwelcome guest had chosen for our meeting place. A clearing so close to the Canodill Pass, and the glimmering blue shield housed between its mighty walls, that my eyes watered with the bite of burning ozone.

Being this close to the mountain and all its virgin Glaith threatened my access to the Grandmother, and should I be foolish enough leave my perch in the trees to set foot upon the soil, or worse, venture beyond the tree line?

It was a risk I wouldn't take for so inconsequential a reason as meeting *her*.

Even surrounded by an entire mountain of virgin Glaith, she did not have the advantage here.

Using Kas' ki to mask my own, I sent the lion to the opposite side of the clearing, watching from the shadows of my lofty perch. The silver-haired woman below followed Kas' stealthy movement without err, turning until her back was to me and the lion had hunkered down on a branch, out of sight.

I didn't need to see her eyes to know they'd gone glassy and blank, for she was a Priestess with access to Ancaster and Alicia's many inventions. On her brow, a golden diadem with a core of Glaith—enough to enhance a Triloth's pitiful senses, certainly.

"You're not as clever as you think you are, Mila. I can sense you," she said, talking to the lion.

I rolled my eyes. Yet her arrogance did not soothe, but merely drove me to further vigilance. This trick had been played on me too many times to count—and by a much better player than *she.* So with simmering irritation, I plunged my senses into the earth. Looking for her cohorts—and was not disappointed.

The forest whispered of unseen intruders skulking all around us in the dark.

Men. Soldiers ringing the clearing, ready to spring their little trap, their paltry ki disguised beneath the Glaith. Where their life-forces should have been, there was nothing but a fuzzy, gray hole.

Child's play, and for the insult, they would learn to kneel.

I sneered, turning my glare upon the deceptive woman in the clearing. Belle. The traitor who'd *dare.*

"Mila, please. Come down so we can talk."

Bracing against the need to taste her, my ki seeped through her with a touch so light, the Triloth didn't so much as flinch at the invasion. Oh, and the stories her blood had to share! "You're pregnant."

And then she did flinch, whirling at the sound of my voice and staring into the gloom to my left. "Y-Yes. My second."

"Josh's spawn, I presume," I said, lip peeled back from my teeth. "And it's"—I tisked—"mundane."

"It is my *child*, Mila." Her piercing blue eyes were not enough to penetrate the dark, but she tried, squinting into the trees. "And she—or he—will be loved regardless of—"

I chuckled, untangling my ki from Kas, giving the illusion that I stalked the branches at my leisure. Confusing the poor little Triloth down below. "You can't sense the gender?"

"No," she snapped, glaring at my phantom ki circling the clearing. "And neither can you. It's far too soon for that."

"Hmm. Is it?" I picked at the dirt under my claws, withdrawing from the Priestess ki before it became too... tempting.

Belle's brow pinched in frustration. "Do you know how long it's been? How long you've been in the forest?"

I snorted, tossing my essence into Kas once more, making the Triloth spin and dance for me. "Time. That's all your kind thinks of."

"'Your kind?' Are you really so..."

Raising my brows, I peered down at her. "So, what?"

"Lost. Are you really so removed from us that you think—" she took a breath. Exhaled. "Mila, it's been *five years*. We need you. Please. It's time to stop playing vigilante in the forest, sister."

"Sister?" I laughed, yanking my ki from Kas, letting it fly about the clearing without moving a muscle. "What kind of sister brings an army to a family gathering?"

She blanched. "What?"

"Did you think I would not notice them? Did you

think the Glaith would be enough to hide your little soldier pets from me? *Here*?"

Belle tore her gaze away from my phantom's progress, looking to the shadows on her left. Guilty.

"Tell them to fuck off, Belle."

"Wh-What—"

I clenched my fist then, forcing ki into the Glaith her soldiers used to hide from me, pushing it to the limit, then slithering through their flesh and bone. Making them kneel. "Can't you feel them, Belle? They're suffering. The Glaith. It burns them..."

Her hand went to her throat. Eyes rimmed in white. "Mila—You can't! They're soldiers of the rebellion. They're *good men*."

"Tell your good men to fuck off, or they die by the very Glaith you love so much." I grinned at her, though she didn't see it. "You recall the way I burned my hand, *sister*? Do you think you can heal all six of them the way you once healed me? Do you think you can reattach limbs before they water my land with blood?"

"You're not powerful enough to make that much Glaith explode," she snapped, glaring at Kas.

I shifted forward, one leg dangling over the edge of my perch. "And you're willing to take the chance that I'm bluffing?"

She didn't flinch.

"Mmm, I must say, Belle, I'm impressed. Motherhood has made you"—I licked my lips, letting my specter settle into Kas—"vicious."

Belle glared at the trees, following the illusion of my ki as it circled the clearing. But on some level, she knew. She knew I had no reason to bluff. Somewhere deep down, she feared what I'd become in the dark.

"Leave us!" she shouted, flinging her hands toward the mountain.

For a moment, nothing. And then, the leaves crackled with the retreat of men, and with their departure, my hold on their fragile lives.

"We need you, Mila," she whispered again, taking a step, sending a beseeching gaze into the dark. "We need the might of a Trila-Glís or we can't—"

"*I am not a weapon!*" I snarled, surging to my feet. Temper frayed.

Kas flew from her perch, bursting from the shadows into Belle's startled face, landing on padded feet before the pregnant Triloth. Her gleaming yellow teeth bared. Hackles raised, but otherwise motionless. Coiled.

Belle gasped, hands splayed over her belly. But she held her ground.

"I am no one's weapon, Priestess," I continued, calming with the effort to rein Kas in, though the lion refused to take her eyes off Belle's throat.

"I-I'm not asking you to be a weapon. I'm offering protection, Mila."

I laughed, settling back against the tree. This tired routine? Protection beneath the mountain was a death sentence to one such as me—I'd told her so a thousand times. And yet, every single time Belle ventured into the forest, it was the same bloody argument. The offer of protection nothing more than a promise to cut me off from the forest and all that went with it. A leash about my throat, strangling me, turning me into a starved attack dog desperate to do her bidding for but a taste of ki...

I laughed, sending a pulse through the wood, getting infinity in return.

Never. I'd never leave this.

Not willingly.

"How long before they figure it out?" she asked. "Before they send a real army to collect you, Mila?"

I lifted my shoulder. "I'm careful. And if he comes," I continued, rubbing at the brand sitting high on my knuckle, "I'll be ready."

"He?"

I stilled, turning my gaze upon her. Clever, as always. "I wouldn't recommend turning your back on a mountain lion, Belle. There's no telling how she might react."

Belle swallowed, hard, returning her eyes to Kas' beautiful, savage muzzle. "I know you won't let her touch me."

"Ha!" I barked, head tilted back. "Your trust is dangerously misplaced, Priestess. My lady does as she pleases."

"And yet," she replied, and for a moment, said nothing more. Perhaps waiting for me to argue, or simply pausing to gather her courage in the face of the lion. "I can help you," she pressed, tilting her ear toward my voice. "I can teach you to control your gifts, before you kill someone and become an Empath—"

"I have no need of your help, Priestess. The forest is enough. It alone sustains me."

"Look around you! *Look* at this place!" she shouted, flinging her arms wide. "Your precious forest is twisted with hatred and sorrow, Mila. I can feel it clawing at my soul." She took a breath, diadem glittering in the half-light. "You can do so much good for the rebellion. Without you, we can't take our prototypes to the next level."

"Good? Who do you think has kept the Empire at bay, all these years? Who has given you the freedom to play with your toys and build a family? You cannot fathom the Empire's power as you are, Priestess. Hidden away beneath the mountain. Denying the true potential of your gifts. Cut off from your senses." I stood, letting her see my shadow. "They'd have already taken the mountain, your prototypes, *and* the remaining Priestesses if it weren't for this twisted forest you hate so much." Her beautiful, soft Priestess ki tempted the darkness flickering inside me, and I grinned. "This forest has saved you more times than you can ever know."

"You're wrong," she spat, glaring at my shade. "You're not the righteous savior you think you are, and this haunted wood isn't the impenetrable fortress you believe it to be. They've taken Liyas, or had you not noticed, hidden away as you are?"

I bared my teeth. "One city in five years, and one that is outside of my territory. What have *you* done? Built prototypes and whelped mundane brats?" I laughed, sinking into the shadows. "I'm done with this conversation. Leave. You have what you came for."

Belle stepped after me and was stopped by Kas' low grumble. "What I came for? Mila! We need you to power the prototypes—"

"And I sent your good little soldiers away with enough ki in their Glaith to keep you busy until spring comes."

She glanced over her shoulder, at the men waiting for her at the edge of the wood. Assessing for herself with her crown of lies. "Make no mistake," she said at length. "I am prepared to escalate things. We cannot allow you to risk yourself like this. Not when our technology can turn the tides."

I clenched my fists, nails biting my palms as I resisted the wisp of Priestess ki heating with passionate conviction. "At the moment, the only thing keeping you from death is the brat in your belly," I clicked my tongue at Kas, blending with the forest. "Some things remain sacred, even to me," I said, letting the wind carry my voice. "At least for now."

5

———

Months passed without much to mark them. Except the dreams.

Dreams of ki, licking and petting every forgotten corner of my being. Dreams that seeped through my skin and settled deep within my bones. At once the breezy flames of Priestess *and* a granite wave of Elite strength. The perfect harmony of a rare and dangerous thing beseeching me to join him. To give up my fight after all this time.

Wouldn't it be nice? To give over to someone else? To let him carry the hopes of my people so I could rest... if only for a little while...

He would make it *so* good...

They were twisted lies of power and seduction that got progressively worse as the months passed and the flood of Eloran and Tritan refugees began to dwindle. Until they stopped altogether, and the wood was truly quiet for the first time since the fall of my people.

Leaving me nothing to do but think.

Of those I *hadn't* been able to save. The thousands

upon thousands of honest, hardworking people who'd been enslaved by a bigger power for nothing but the sake of power itself.

Of the Priestesses, of whom I'd not seen a *single* example in five long years.

There was nothing to comfort me but the burden of my failures.

That the captain was trying to wear me down wasn't lost on me, for he'd been at this for years. There were periods of draught, certainly. Even one time I thought I felt him close to death, only to pull from the pendant he'd stolen and restore himself.

But that could have been just another dream—a fabrication meant to confuse and mislead, to fuel my isolated paranoia.

I honestly couldn't sort the facts from the lies. Didn't even really bother to try.

And so it was that Kas' heated yowl jerked me from restless, tormented sleep thick with dreams of *him*.

Disoriented, I sent a pulse through the Grandmother before I'd done more than blink. What had roused Kas' ire? Another suitor who didn't meet her standards, perhaps? Or—

Impossible!

Jaw slackened, I turned sightless eyes toward the familiar ki, trying to blink the sleep away. To decide if it was real.

But it hadn't been a dream.

He was *here*! On my soil for the first time in working memory, pressing *my* pendant to the earth in blatant challenge as he'd done the very first time!

Captain Rawlings. All the way at the western border of my lands, the tease. Traveling north, on the last remaining road between Elora and what had once been my homeland. A road that skirted the farthest perimeter of my reach.

Cocky amusement whispered through my blood as he caressed the soil, burying his fingers and the pendant within the earth, the touch felt both through the forest and the raw nerves that had connected us since Tritan's fall. Drawing me in. Taunting me with the bottomless wealth of ki that wasn't his to wield.

Roused, the darkness surged to the fore, reaching for his power mixed with mine—but he pulled back, breaking contact with the forest before I got close enough to strike.

I laughed, baring modified canines and thumbed the brand.

Did he really think he could touch what was mine and be gone before I could retaliate? That I would allow him to play the same trick he'd played on an innocent girl whose heart had been broken by the murder of her only parent?

Foolish to assume I could not cross the width of the forest in time to catch him, *here,* where the rules were of *my* making, and there was nothing stopping me from using any advantage to tip the scales in my favor.

I had prepared for this meeting since the last, refusing to fail again.

Eyes drifting closed, I sank into the Grandmother, sending my ki further north, intending to leave a little present for the good captain.

Alien amusement skated along my senses as I worked, but this time, I didn't cast him out. Merely concealed what I was doing, setting off dozens of decoys to dazzle his pathetic Elite mind, for if the captain wanted to feel true power, who was I to deny him?

Laying my trap took longer than I'd hoped—I was dreadfully out of practice wielding ki for anything more strenuous than merely connecting with the forest. But when finished, I scrambled out of bed, determined.

This was no time for sloppy mistakes, no matter that I'd grown lazy and fat, content to wallow in self-pity while the forest blossomed with spring. Doing little more than suckling at the Grandmother's teats.

The captain was making a move at long last—and I'd be there to ensure he regretted it.

Snuffing the embers in my fireplace, I snagged my satchel and told the glitterbugs to sleep while I was away, then pushed through the door and scanned the Grandmother's dense foliage for Kas' tawny fur.

With a thump, she landed on the branch before me, forepaws first, ears flattened to her skull, teeth bared.

I held out my palm, cooing, "Easy, pretty," but she avoided my touch with a huff, glaring in the captain's direction. "Alright then," I said, with a toothy nod. "Lead on."

Following the flash of Kas' lithe behind through the trees, I moved as fast as my feet would carry me, leaping and ducking with ki-fed, unnatural focus. And when my muscles began to ache, I fueled them with more ki, not stopping until I was soaked through with sweat and the sun was high—but I was in position. Breath coming hard, I paused on my branch, staring at the empty road below me.

Where was he? Had my ki-sense really atrophied so badly that I'd miscalculated? Was the captain heading elsewhere and I'd been duped... again?

I sent a pulse through the wood, searching for my lost Elite, scouring the forest for hidden traps and things out of place. What I found set a smile to bloom across my lips.

"Not missing," I whispered, gazing at the empty road before me. "Just late."

With a jerk of my chin, I sent Kas to prowl the branches, ready to fill her with my specter should I need the diversion. Burying us *both* under the forest, I disguised us from eyes that could see deeper than mere shadows, then settled against the branch at my back.

The only thing left to do was wait, knowing *this time*, he would spring *my* trap.

It didn't take long.

"What in the bloody hell—" An ornate Tritan coach glided to a graceful halt, settling in the new grass speckling what had been a barren gravel road only hours prior. Staggering from the cockpit into sunlight, came none other than Jasper, my favorite bottom feeder. "Impossible! I was here just last week!"

"Those trees didn't grow in a week, mate," the pilot said, dangling one bronzed arm over the open window as he gazed up at the trees. "Maybe we missed a turn?"

Jasper shook his head, aiming trembling finger at me in the shadows. Purely accidental, surely. "No. No, this is the work of the Menace." He clutched at the serpent's likeness on a cord about his neck. "We shouldn't be here. Turn the coach around, Marco."

Ah, *yes*. Marco. I tipped forward, straining for a glimpse of the man whose life I'd taken in the palm of my hand and crushed to buy my freedom. The man whose death, however temporary, had freed the darkness within me.

I smiled with a certain sort of fondness. And, with a flick of my fingers, sent my vines to creep forward. Ready to give me another taste...

"What's going on?" asked a man whose face I could not see. "Why have we stopped?"

I froze. Blood going cold, then flashing fire-hot.

That voice!

General Tilcot.

His was a voice I'd recognize anywhere, for I had spent these last years hearing it beg for mercy in my dreams. I almost laughed! To be able to take my father's murderer? To feed him to the darkness after all this time? I'd have to keep the captain alive long enough to thank him for such a kind and thoughtful gift!

Dropping into a crouch, Kas stilled on a thick branch, baring gleaming yellow teeth, pupils tiny, unmoving pricks.

My every muscle flexed in preparation to call forth the might of the Grandmother and claim my vengeance.

Five years, according to Belle. I could finally add another mark to my wall—but this one would be drawn in blood.

"L-Look, sir. It's the trees. I swear on the serpent," Jasper stammered, pacing the new grass and the tiny, creeping vines. "I was here just last week and the road was clear. It's the Menace. I'm telling you, he's here. We have to go back."

General Tilcot laughed, pushing his door open and stepping down from the coach. "I'd like to meet your wood's menace, Jasper."

I rolled my shoulders. Cracked my neck.

The general patted a holster on his hip, gazing at the

trees. "Perhaps we'll send a hunting party to catch him after our dealings with the Elorans?"

Glee surged through my blood.

Oh, please do, General Tilcot! To feast on an Elite hunting party? I licked my lips. Perhaps the Divine lived after all?

Abandoning his post, Marco lit a cigarette. "Is there another way 'round, Jasper?"

"No, sir," Jasper said, pushing his hand through sweat-soaked hair that reeked of terror, even from my removed position.

But where was *my* Elite parasite? I crept closer, and when I couldn't see him through the coach windows, I did something I'd never had the nerve or inclination to do before. I reached for the link between us, plucking it with the most delicate finger of ki I could muster. "Come out to play, Captain Rawlings," I whispered, voice drowned by the men below me.

And there he was, obeying my command. Adjusting his jacket, he stepped into the light, a crooked smirk set upon his lips.

Kas' tail twitched.

Did he think he was safe? Did he think I couldn't reach him simply because he was not in the forest? Because he'd surrounded himself with the general and fancy weapons?

Poor, foolish man. It was *nothing* to expand the limit of my lands a few dozen feet beyond the road... *Nothing* to bring the seat of my power with me. Gleeful, I set my palms to the bark beneath me, senses snaking toward him through the grass. Spreading my ki thin enough to go unnoticed while Kas paced the tree line, waiting for my signal.

A cloud of white smoke surrounded Marco. "This weather reminds me of the evening breeze back home, doesn't it, Rawlings?"

"Not quite as warm, perhaps," the captain said, "but a nice change from all that snow in the west."

"Well?" the general asked, thumbs hooked into his belt. "Are we just going to stand here staring at trees, or are we going to get moving?"

"Sir," Jasper said, holding a door. "Please, you must get back into the coach. It's not safe. The Menace—"

"Oh, stuff your silly menace," Marco replied with a lazy flick of his wrist, ashing his smoke.

At that, the captain's lips bloomed in a full smile, pendant catching the afternoon light in a brilliant shower of those trademark purples, greens, and blues. Obsidian eyes scanning beyond the foliage. Searching.

For me.

My mouth watered. After five years in the captain's possession, my pendant was likely the only thing in existence capable of matching the Grandmother for power. By the dead Goddess, to swallow that forbidden Elite ki he'd teased me with for so long...

Fingers wrapped around the pendant, the captain's brow creased. Senses trickling into the dark.

Oh, but it was much too late for *that*. I let my specter fill Kas, giving her a nudge to send the lion pacing through the trees.

Inky gaze following along, he tracked the shadows concealing Kas. Blind to the ki building beneath his very feet.

"According to the maps," Marco said under his breath, moving to the captain's side, "we're not off course. You think Jasper might be right?"

The captain smiled, revealing straight, white teeth. "There's only one road to Liyas, Marco."

Marco snorted, elbowing the captain and stamping out his cigarette butt. "You know that's not what I meant, sir. Think it's this wood's menace?"

The captain's smile widened, but he said nothing more. Merely rolled the pendant between forefinger and thumb.

"Hmm." Joining them, General Tilcot squinted at the roadblock. "We may have to do a little gardening, boys."

Flexing my fingers, I gazed at my little puppets all lined up, as I gathered the strength to strike...

"There's only one way to be sure." The general snapped his fingers at the coach. "Priestess!"

My breath caught.

"Come along, girl," General Tilcot said, rapping his knuckles on the coach door.

The coach shifted, and as if in slow motion, a woman stepped into the clearing. Golden circlets encasing wrists and throat. Face fuller than I remembered, eyes downcast, she knelt in the dirt—on the vines—without being told to do so.

Gooseflesh erupted all over my skin.

Not just a Priestess.

The Priestess.

"Time to earn your keep," the general said. "Tell me, is Liyas through the trees, or have we gone off course?"

The High Priestess glanced at the gnarled tree trunks before her, brow furrowed. "My strength is not what it once was, my lord."

"It's a simple answer to a simple question," the

general said, stroking her gleaming silver-blonde hair as she waited at his feet.

But, *why?* If she lived, why wouldn't she fight? Why kneel? She should have been able to sense that there was more than enough Tritan power in this single, small clearing to destroy the Elites even if Captain Rawlings was among their number.

I glanced at my parasite, only to find a devious smirk painted on his lips, tracking Kas as she paced through the trees.

He was taunting me. Using *her* to taunt me. My gums ached with the effort *not* to scream, but, leaving the bulk of my power buried in Kas and the Grandmother, I sent a single tendril of ki toward the High Priestess. Cautious, should the flavor of Trila-Glís waken the darkness with temptation.

But my care was unwarranted, for the Divine glory of the Goddess' chosen Priestess was *gone!* A shaky breath rattled into my lungs, covered by the wind dancing through the trees. How in the name of the dead Goddess could all that power have simply disappeared?

Gold gleamed in the sunlight. Circling her wrists and throat, while her Elite counterparts remained unmarked. Had the general not threatened the High Priestess with a similar collar the day Tritan fell?

Glaith. It had to be! It *always* came back to the fucking Glaith!

Heedless of the captain's forbidden senses, I pressed harder, drawing on the Grandmother to help me break through.

What I found almost sent me flying from the trees, raging with the force of the wild ki at my back. Almost unleashed the darkness with my full blessing, for the most powerful of us, the Trila-Glís, was no longer pure.

The taint was not the Glaith—though she was ruined by that too—but the Elites. She stank of Elites! Worse was the man shimmering with stolen power, dazzling to even my senses, now that I could *see*.

General Tilcot was tied to a Trila-Glís, dressed in a cloak of unimaginable power.

"Goddess, *no*," I breathed, pressing my back to the bark, trying to ground myself, to pull away from the horror dawning in my mind. To deny it.

But the truth came unbidden, refusing to be ignored. In spite of my efforts to deny them, the Caledonians had made advances with the Glaith. They'd figured out how to leach power from the Goddess' chosen to augment their own mediocre strength, while I had busied myself with refugees.

Slaves. The Priestesses—*my people*—were slaves.

Claws buried into thick bark, I tried to reach the High Priestess in the only way I could.

Her head snapped up, beautiful blue eyes scanning the trees.

I sent her another pulse, fighting the Glaith wrapped about her throat and wrists. Fighting the terrible cold leaching at her strength.

And then she pushed back, gathering all she could, pitiful as it was. Stealing her strength from the Elite holding her leash. All to send me a warning.

Flee!

"What—" The general staggered, tanned skin paling as the High Priestess wielded her Goddess-given power in spite of his hold on her.

Hackles fluffed, Kas snarled at the top of her voice, making Jasper scream and dance. "It's the Menace!"

"What did you summon, woman?" the general asked, scowling down at her.

The High Priestess' chin dipped. "Nothing, my lord. I sensed a wild animal, too curious for its own good." She licked her lower lip, wetting the delicate pink skin. "It should know better than to bother with Elites of your magnificent status, sir."

My stomach heaved.

"It sounded like a cat of some sort," Marco said, peering into the trees, and he too drew a shining Elite weapon, as if the mundane soldier had any right to it. "Wildcats aren't usually so bold, but if the poor creature is sick or hungry, perhaps—"

"It isn't sick," the High Priestess snapped, holding Marco's gaze for the space of three heartbeats. "It is young and foolish. Entirely too confident for its own good. Nothing more."

I rolled my shoulders and cracked my neck. Limbering up. It had been a long time since I had been any of the things the High Priestess accused me of. A long time since she'd tried to force my compliance with tales of corruption and addiction.

And look at us now.

My knees were not the ones dimpled with pine needles and filth.

Mine was not the power sullied by the Empire.

Whisper soft, the vines caressed the exposed skin of the Trila-Glís. Tempting.

How many times had her stolen power been used to kill for the Empire? How many *more* lives would be lost if I did nothing about it?

Still smirking, the captain's senses whipped out, tugging at the link left behind my ribs, making the mark on my right middle finger itch and burn.

He thought he was winning, did he? With a flick of my wrist, I blended my energy with the tree beneath my feet and everything beyond, taking Kas' ki with me. Linking us to the network of life waiting for my command and seizing every animal within reach. I spread myself too thin as I worked to disguise us from the keen obsidian gaze of the only man who could expose me.

The forest stilled, waiting.

I could handle two Elites, even if *he* was one of them. Two Elites with the power of a Trila-Glís, however, was another matter. And one I could not allow to continue.

The darkness within flexed, stretching shadowed feathers toward the woman kneeling in the dirt. What would it be like to taste a Trila-Glís? To take her ki and turn it upon the Empire who dared to use it...

Mouth watering, I coiled about her ankles, winding deeper still. Pulling her ki through the vines—and choked on tainted flames. Gone, was the clean, refreshing breeze of memory. She was destroyed. An empty husk, dead in all but name.

With a gasp, the High Priestess pushed me back, throwing her power at my feet—and I lapped it up.

"Stop that at once," the general snarled, striking the High Priestess with the back of his hand, splitting the skin of her lower lip.

In turn, Kas howled at the abuse, pacing the length of her branch, murder gleaming in her beautiful gray eyes.

"I-I have done nothing, sir," the High Priestess stammered, pressing a trembling hand to split lip.

"Do you think I cannot see your lie?" the general said, wrapping a meaty hand in silver hair. Wrenching her head back. "You are mine. Your power is mine, Sasha."

No. It wasn't, for I alone supped at the dead Goddess' table. Drunk on her finest wine while the peasants argued beneath me.

"I-I tried only to frighten that wild thing off, sir. I could not bear to see the beast slain for its foolishness."

At this, the captain broke the ranks, taking a step toward the forest. A frown pinching the space between his brows as he searched for me. Trying to use our link to draw me out.

Behind him, the Trila-Glís wilted.

Only a little more...

Kas yowled at the very top of her lungs, hissing and spitting as she crouched, pale gray eyes fixed upon the captain's handsome, doomed face.

"We should get back in the coach," Jasper whispered, sweat beading along his hairline as he unwound a cruel braided whip. "You don't want to know what happens next."

Weapon trained over the captain's shoulder, Marco took aim at mere shadows. "Give the command, Captain."

Standing back, the general drew his weapon, lips pressed in a tight line. "Do you see anything, Rawlings?"

The captain didn't respond, instead taking another step. Breaching the sanctity of the wood.

Without my command, Kas reacted. Leaping from her perch, she landed heavy on her forepaws in the shadows. Shoulders rolling, she stalked toward the Elites, silent. Ears flat. Paws tucked beneath her bulk.

Heart in my throat, I broke from my task of keeping us hidden, trying to reel her in before it was too late. But she would not be distracted. After all, this was *her* territory.

"What is it?" the general asked, raising his weapon in her direction.

Unable to comprehend the danger, Kas rumbled deep in her chest—a final warning for those keen enough to listen.

"What are you waiting for?" Jasper asked, voice shaking. "Kill it! Kill it before it gets too close!"

The captain glanced over his shoulder, exposing his neck to the apex predator lurking in the gloom.

A fatal mistake—and one that would cost Kas *everything* if I couldn't stop her *now!*

With a curse, I sent a pulse through the Grandmother and burst into action. The forest exploded in a symphony of chaos as I sprinted, launching myself from the branch, heedless of the twenty-foot drop. I landed hard, knees buckling with the impact, but I rolled, beating Kas to the edge of the clearing by no more than half a foot.

She pulled up short, snarling in my face, her fury finding a new target in *me*, gleaming yellow canines a scant few inches from my throat.

Returning her snarl, I planted my hands on her beautiful, savage muzzle and shoved her back, wrapping my ki as deep inside her as I could get. Commanding her to leave! Flee, and not turn back for *anything!*

"Don't shoot!" the captain shouted at my back. "Don't shoot her!"

A flash of watery green sailed over my shoulder, striking the mighty trunk of the tree I'd been standing in. Showering us in bits of splintered wood.

"Shit, sorry!" Marco cursed.

Kas' pupils dilated as I pushed again, pouring my terror into her. When she reeled back at last, I tisked, jerking my thumb toward safety.

Fur puffed up, she spun, leaping fifteen feet in a single bound, nothing more than a specter to the untrained eye as she disappeared into the shadows.

General Tilcot's deep, booming voice broke the ensuing silence. "So, this deplorable creature is your wood's menace, is it Jasper? You've been had by a girl with a pet lion!"

In spite of my proximity to General Tilcot and the fallen Trila-Glís staring at me with bulging blue eyes, it was Captain Rawlings' inky gaze that snared my attention.

He took in every facet of my appearance—from the handmade boots and clothes, to the wild dark brown tangled mess my hair had become. His ki lurched in my chest, a foreign barb of power striking deep. Searching for me beneath the years of filth.

Amusement kissed the edge of my senses—and victory too—but there was... something *else*. Something I wouldn't have recognized but for my years tied to Kas.

It was hunger, yes. But this... it was *more*. And then my cheeks flushed with comprehension, and I snarled, trying to cut him off as I had all those years ago—but made no difference. Not to Captain Rawlings and the ki that was a match to my own. I could feel him just there, lurking. Waiting.

Claws itching with the urge to strike the gloat off his stupid face, I returned his smile—toothier, since we'd last met. He would regret challenging me. He'd regret *all* of it. For the captain had made a fatal error.

"Kill her, please," Jasper breathed, peeking out from behind the captain's shoulder, and before anyone could do the sensible thing and act on his request, I spun, retreating after Kas into the Grandmother's bosom. Hounded by victory's grin, I fled, though this time, it was not with terror nipping my flanks, but renewed purpose.

The Trila-Glís.

She was here. Chained, weak, and tainted by the Elites, but *here*. Bound for Liyas.

I sent a pulse through the forest as I sprinted.

A summoning beacon.

6

The Glaith.

It always came back to that tainted, hated ore. The earth beneath me was sick with it, poisoned, and threatening to cut me off from the Grandmother and all of her power should I let it touch my skin.

Looming misty gray in the distance, the mountain mocked me. It was packed with enough Glaith that it would take *decades* of exposure to ki-wielders for me to tolerate setting foot there. But some things were important enough to draw even me from the forest—important enough to prevent me from going after Kas, though I ached to mend the harm I'd caused in sending her away.

There was but a single reason, however, that *I* would summon Belle.

The High Priestess. Sick with Glaith, fed upon by Elites, but headed for Liyas.

I scowled, picking at the raised edge of the brand. *He'd* arranged this, of course. The High Priestess was bait, for why else would he draw me out? Why, after all this time, would he make a move using the most valuable Priestess alive if he wasn't certain of the outcome? He could *never* have me—not with the Grandmother at my back. We'd been in a bitter stalemate for five years, with no real victory on either side.

No. There was something else the captain wanted. Some part of his plot I couldn't yet see.

With a sigh, I hunkered down against a tree, reaching across the distance for Kas' beautiful, sullen ki. Concealed by elevation and shadows, I watched as two women shuffled into the clearing I'd chosen—a meeting place that straddled my territory and hers.

Where life met Glaith.

A heavily pregnant Belle waddled forward, one hand pressed beneath her belly button, the other pushing sweat-soaked hair back from her eyes, over her augmented diadem. At her back, none other than Alicia, lead scientist of the rebel forces, and creator of the shield. An auspicious day, indeed.

"Have you changed your mind about joining us, Mila?"

I didn't look at Belle, choosing instead to keep my eyes shut, beseeching Kas to forgive me even as I scanned the forest for Belle's armed guard. As ever, seeking them was not a challenge—but this time they had come prepared to do battle.

I tisked. "Really, Belle? Weapons? Are you no better than *them*?" I sighed, turning my attention back. Toward home. "How... disappointing."

She folded both hands atop her swollen belly. "I did tell you we are prepared to escalate this discussion."

Without Kas, I made no effort to conceal myself

from her dull, Triloth senses. I let my left leg dangle, swinging it as I braced my chin on the opposite knee. "You cannot take me, Belle. Not here. None of you can."

"Don't be arrogant. You're not untouchable, Mila. Our weapons are finally something worth bragging about. But they can *always* be better, sister."

Arrogant, was I? With a sigh, my eyes drifted closed —and I seized the ki of every man on my soil, draining them unconscious in an instant. Leaving Alicia and her weapon untouched. Careful not to taste lest I rouse the hunger lurking in the dark that had already been sorely tempted this week.

"Goddess, Mila—" she clenched her jaw, icy blue eyes trying to light the shadows as she glared at me. "They are *good* men—"

"Then stop sending your *good* men to hunt me, and maybe one day they can leave my lands the same way they enter it," I snapped, then took a breath. Marshalling my temper, I conjured a throne of vines and soft things for her to sit on. "The child. Can you sense the sex yet?" I asked, leg swinging.

For a moment, she did nothing but glare. And then, "It's a girl." She sat with a huff. "We're having another girl."

I nodded, making a sound at the back of my throat, letting the silence drag on. "Tell me, Belle," I rasped watching her. "Are you not curious?"

Belle blinked, frowning up at my shadow. A delicate wisp of augmented Triloth ki probed the dark. "You called," she said at length. "You *never* call."

Clever girl. Grinning now, I hummed, lips parting to share my good news.

"The truth is, Mila," she breathed, speaking over me

as she settled into her seat. "It doesn't matter *why* you called. Only that you did. I'm terrified for you. This place... It gets darker every time I come." She shivered, rubbing at the gooseflesh on her bare arms as she plucked a tainted leaf and worked it between forefinger and thumb. "It's time to abandon this foolishness. You are Trila-Glís! You can do so much *good* with your gifts."

"Trila-Glís?" Ire prickled, I stood, hands balled into fists. "*Good?*"

Belle swallowed, clutching at Alicia's hand as the gentle flames of a Triloth whispered to the darkest of Truths.

I laughed, reckless, leaping from my perch. Making no effort at grace, I landed with a thud, allowing her to set eyes upon me for the first time in five years. "You speak these words as if you understand them," I spat, stalking toward the pair, fury spiking through the soil, through the vines in her seat—vines that grew thorns in tune with my temper. "You speak of *good* as if you've seen its opposite. You whisper '*Trila-Glís*' like a prayer, as if you know what it's like to live with it twisting in your guts day and night. Calling out. Begging for terrible things."

Hand pressed to her throat, Belle gasped, white rimming her eyes. "Goddess above. Y-You should see yourself, Mila."

"Vanity? Ha!" I bared my teeth, grinning down at her as I approached, unable to stop myself from taking just a *little* taste... "What use have I of vanity? *You* see me, Belle. Tell me what you see. Give it a name, sweet sister."

Pupils blown out, she responded without hesitation, though her voice trembled. "D-Darkness."

"Hm." I set my hands on either side of her brier throne, almost nose to nose. Not touching. Denying the hunger. "What else? Say it."

"Empath." She swallowed, hiding her belly beneath crossed, protective arms. "I see an Empath unleashed."

"Oh?" My head tilted to the side as I glanced at the child ripening in her womb. "Not a High Priestess surrogate, then?"

A quick shake of her head.

"You're right, of course. You've named me truer than you know. 'Darkness'..." I straightened, spreading my arms. "I am the bedtime story the High Priestess used to scare you into completing your lessons. Do you really want me under the mountain with you? With your mundane, *helpless* children?"

She met my eye. Bottling her fear. "I can help you."

"You're wrong!" I snarled, whirling away, claws scoring my palms. "I am *not* Trila-Glís! I never was. You should be focusing on rescuing those who fit into your perfect little world—"

"Rescue the Trila-Glís?" She laughed, bold as ever. "And how do you expect me to do that, Empath? They're locked away in the heart of the Empire. No, like it or not," she continued, breaking a thorn before it pierced her tender skin, "you're my only option. My children will have a secure future."

I rolled my shoulders, reaching for the soothing majesty of the Grandmother. Trying to temper the so-named Darkness before it slipped its leash, I funneled my excess ki into the weapons of Belle's good, unconscious men, then said, "What if you *didn't* have to settle for me? What if you could free the High Priestess today? What then?"

Belle stilled. "If that were true, the Eloran forces would move the mountain itself to rescue her."

"Liyas," I said, scrubbing the heels of my palms into my eyes to dispel the growing headache. "I saw her myself, just yesterday. Enslaved and in the company of Elites, but headed for Liyas."

"Goddess, Belle. Do y'know what that means?" Alicia breathed, turning wide eyes upon the pregnant Priestess at her side.

"She's tainted," I warned, blinking at them for a second, then looking away. Tempting. Far too tempting. "I would have freed her myself, but—" I couldn't be trusted with ki like *that*, "—but the Caledonians have tainted her. Figured out some way to use her as if that power were their own. Fucking parasites. They're feeding on them." I laughed, utterly void of humor. "But having one of the Trila-Glís, even the way they are now, is better than..." I trailed off, flicking my claws toward myself.

Belle made a sound at the back of her throat, snapping her fingers. "The dirty Glaith! It *must* be their dirty Glaith—they mix it with iron, the fools. Goddess, if we could get our hands on some of that!" She laughed, giddy excitement dancing through the soil, straight into my skin. "This is *incredible* news."

I nodded, trembling, sweat soaking my hairline. "An alliance, then. Your forces shall have their weapon," I spat, cracking an eye to glare. "I'll work with you long enough to free the High Priestess, and then you will leave me in peace. Forever."

A righteous speech hovered on Belle's tongue—I could *feel* it, could feel her desire to break our pact even before it had been agreed upon. But she nodded, the gesture meaningless.

I smiled, baring teeth.

"Come," she said, standing. "The others will be so happy to see you."

I glanced at her outstretched hand. "You'd share your home with me, even now? Knowing what I am?"

Belle's lips twitched. "I do not believe you are the villain you claim to be." She shrugged. "At least not yet. I see you struggle to keep your distance, even as you work to give refugees sanctuary. To keep us all safe. It counts for something, Mila. Now," she said, smile blossoming on her lips when I snorted. "Come, sister—"

Unexpected ki lanced through my chest.

Ki I knew, for it was *mine*.

Twice in as many days, my pendant touched soil on my lands. A challenge so blatant, even Belle—with her augmented, inferior senses—felt it.

"Dear, Goddess," Belle breathed, pressing a slender hand to her ripe belly. "What—"

"What's your game, parasite?" I whispered, turning glassy eyes toward the sound of clattering stone. "It..." I cursed, taking a step. "He's beyond the forest. I can't sense anything! There's too much Glaith! I can't sense—"

"Mila you *mustn't*," Belle whispered, wrapping her fingers about my elbow. "I think there are men between us and the wall! Caledonians! You must be silent or we'll be found out. *You've* taken away my armed guard. We are helpless here."

"We're not helpless," Alicia said, drawing her weapon. A fine replica of the ones I'd had pointed at my face just yesterday, and the very reason I'd sent Kas away.

Jerking away from her touch—from the temptation —I spun to face Belle. "That pendant has enough stored ki that even *you* can sense it, Triloth, and is the only thing that has a chance of stopping me if it remains in their hands. This is a *gift*. A foolish mistake on his part, and one I shall capitalize on."

"That's absurd," Belle snapped, reaching for me.

"Is it? I've been trying to reclaim that pendant for the better part of five years. And now here it is, on the eve of rescuing your precious Trila-Glís."

Alicia stepped forward, green eyes glittering in the gloom. Weapon clutched in white knuckles. "Why? Why bother for a pendant when you've the power you claim to have?"

My eye twitched. "It belonged to a girl I used to know. A long time ago." Teeth bared, I turned toward the mountain, pulling as much energy as I could from the Grandmother in preparation for the lack once I stepped clear of the forest. "And today, it shall be mine."

"Whatever that power is, you cannot risk yourself to claim it," Belle said, trying to stand. "I won't allow it."

When I glanced over my shoulder, my smile was borne of the darkest Truth. "Don't worry, Priestess. This won't take long. And when I return, my hands will be soaked to the elbow in Caledonian blood."

"No!" she hissed, moving to stand in my way. "To kill as you are is to feed the Empath! You will lose yourself to the hunger. It will *never* be sated—"

I snorted, for of course, it was far too late for such a warning, no matter that Marco still lived. And she knew it.

"Save the bedtime stories for your brats," I drawled, and planting a hand on her chest, I guided her back, forcing her to reclaim the brier throne. "Why don't you stay here?" I purred, commanding the vines to hold her. To wrap about her wrists, ankles, and hips, pinning her in place. "You're no help to me in your condition."

"Mila," she hissed, pulling at her bonds. "You can't do this! Please. *Please* don't do this. We need your help to rescue the Trila-Glís! We had a deal!"

But I was already slipping into the shadows, racing for the limit of my territory.

7

Burning ozone seared my nostrils, making my eyes water with my proximity to the shield, but I pressed forward, trying to see through the brush. To find Captain Asher Rawlings and finally end this coy little war game. Or worse, to retreat in spite of the lure he knew I couldn't resist.

My pendant.

I thumbed the brand, tracing a ridge of twisted flesh on the back of my palm. To *finally* reclaim it... to drink from that cup of rare and dangerous ki, after all this time...

Willingly seduced by our mixed song, I crawled forward, belly pressed to the springy loam at the forest's edge, trying to catch a glimpse of the battalion the captain had sent to collect me. But there, idling between the brilliant blue shield and a field of jagged virgin Glaith, was a single coach. *The* coach he'd shared with that putrid general and what remained of the High Priestess, *but no others.*

Had my Elite really been so foolish as to have come alone?

Hardly bothering to contain my glee, I plunged my scarred fist into the soil. I stretched my senses in all directions, unwilling to be fooled by hidden soldiers or badly laid traps. Searching for any hint, any whisper, of something unnatural.

But there was no forbidden hint of the captain's ki. No soldiers lurking in the shadows, like the last time he'd played this trick. There was, in fact, nothing at all except the hum of my pendant.

Begging... Reaching...

"Mila—"

I jumped, choking back a snarl. "Bloody, buggering f—"

"Belle says you canna do this, lass," Alicia whispered, gasping as she knelt in the shadows on my left. "And I know you may not remember me, but—"

"Go back to your mistress, Alicia. Unless you'd like to find out why Belle's good men hate me so much."

"Aye, you can let that fiery temper win," the scientist said, her accented voice a harsh whisper. "Or you can use your brains and listen to those who want t'help. We're on the same side, lass."

Sneering, I turned my attention back to the apparently unguarded clearing.

"You canna risk yourself or the chance to rescue the High Priestess over a bauble," she continued, following my gaze. "The High Priestess—"

"Just"—frustrated, I growled, brows creased—"trust me. You need that pendant just as much as I need *him* not to have it."

I could feel her grin on the back of my neck. "Him?"

"All Elites are men."

"Aye," Alicia murmured, fingers pressed to her lips, eyes narrowed. "That they are, but somehow I donna think you were talkin' about just *any* man—"

With a curse, I seized her forearm, forcing her to *feel* my words. To understand, because I didn't have the time or necessary finesse to win this argument by conventional means. "The High Priestess you remember is tainted and broken. Even rescued, she may be nothing more than a trophy enslaved to General Tilcot. That bauble"—I jerked my chin toward the coach—"contains enough ki to keep your lot busy until the sun burns out, and it doesn't come with the inconvenient hunger that demands I drain the entire mountain just to feed the darkness. Understand?"

Sparkling green eyes glassy, pupils dilated, she nodded, as a drop of drool threatened to fall from slack lips.

"Right." I turned back to the clearing, releasing her from my influence. "Then if you don't mind—"

"This is a trap."

I rolled my eyes. "Yes, thank you. I *know* that. Why do you think I haven't charged in—"

"It's a trap, and *you* are the prey." She snapped her fingers, and before I could respond, said, "And if that's true, the cocksuckers won't be expectin' you to have backup."

"And how exactly do you propose to help?"

"Come now, lass," she breathed, grinning, patting a bulge tucked beneath the lapels of her jacket. "Think Belle brought me along for my pretty smile?"

"Belle is an idiot if she thought I wouldn't sense your little weapon. Worse, if she thought it could slow me down on *my* land."

"That's not your land, though," Alicia retorted, pointing.

"I—" She wasn't wrong, the brilliant little bitch. My advantage was *here,* with the Grandmother at my back. But if I couldn't step on that poisoned earth and retain my advantage, neither could the captain—who was *absent*, as if to prove my point.

"Out there," she continued, eyes still glassy, "you're just as vulnerable as the rest of us. Worse, as you donna have a plan worth speakin' of."

Glaring, I said, "I'm waiting for an opportune moment to strike. You think you can tip things in my favor with nothing but a mimic of their weaponry?"

She gave me a funny look. "Who, me? I'm just a poor, defenseless refugee"—she batted her big green eyes—"on the run from some *very* bad men. *Help me!*" she simpered, tears pooling on her waterline. "Please, help me!"

I snorted at her flimsy acting. "You're also Belle's lead scientist. Can't imagine it'll go over well if I get you captured or killed."

She slapped my shoulder, then stood. Something of a manic gleam sparkled in eyes that were a dark, forest green. Her pupils too big. "If your wee bauble is as valuable as you think, we've no other choice but to try. An' I can see there's no changin' your mind, so you've got my help, lass. Lucky for you," she said, "this is no mere mimic of their weaponry. *I* designed it to 'ave a little more... oopmh, if you will." She patted her hip. "I'll get you that opportune moment, on one condition. If there's killin' t'be done, you'll let *me* do it. Don't need a ki-mad Empath on the loose, and Belle assures me that if you taste death... well..."

"And in return?"

"Enough ki to last until the sun burns out."

8

Before I could speak another word or refute this reckless and ridiculous plan, Alicia winked, pushed through the trees, and stumbled into the glaring afternoon sun. Tripping and gasping, she headed directly for the coach. "Help!"

Acting the damsel, without a single thought in her head except the one's I'd planted in my haste and temper.

Grimacing, for I'd left myself no option but to pull as much ki as I could from the Grandmother, I readied the darkness to fly, not in vengeance, this time, but defense.

Laughing, a burly man hopped down from the coach. "Well, well! What's this now? A pretty Eloran bird?"

A man I knew. Jasper's partner. The fool I'd allowed to live so that he might spread the tale of the wood's menace. Which meant Jasper himself was likely the pilot, and so long as my senses could be trusted, my Elite was nowhere close enough to intervene. Fingers hooked into claws, I bared my teeth in a sinister smile, filling myself with ki. Almost there...

"Please, y'have to help me!"

He laughed, reaching for her. "'Course, lucky little bird. That wood is full of monsters who'd love to take a bite from a pretty thing like you."

Long repressed fury quaked through my frame—for all the refugees I hadn't saved, for the brutality I hadn't the power to squash, and the tragedy yet to come. It rattled my very bones. He had the nerve to speak of monsters, as if he didn't see one in the mirror?

But I would do him one better. I'd show him what a monster *really* was.

Fingers trailing through the saplings at the forest's edge, I stepped from the gloom, letting an Empath's great, dark wings consume my soul. Setting hooked claws to the brand on my knuckle, I strummed the link binding me to my parasite.

Taunting.

Come out to play, Captain Rawlings...

The slaver caught Alicia's wrist, yanking her to his chest. "Let's get you into somethin' a little more... comfortable."

"Wha—Get your hands off me!"

"Oh, I think I'll let my hands do a little more than wander, little bird."

Alicia hollered at the top of her lungs. No longer acting, as if the spell of my influence was wearing thin and only *just* realized the position she was in, Alicia tried to drive her knee into the seat of his groin. Trying to reach for the weapon hidden beneath her jacket that packed more oomph than the average Elite weapon.

A slap echoed through the clearing. "You'll do well

to remember your place, slut. Running only makes it worse. But fighting?" He grinned when she moved to strike him again, pinning both of her wrists with one hand. "Gets me hard. Go on. Be difficult." He reached for his belt. "I'm happy to remind you where you belong."

"N-No. Please, no."

For the tremor in her voice, Alicia didn't so much as glance over her shoulder. *Didn't betray me*, even as she quaked in the fool's hands. No, instead she worked to *turn* him in spite of the risk to her virtue, setting his back to the forest. *Giving me my moment, as promised.*

Perfection.

One hand on his buckle, the slaver abandoned her wrists in favor of wrapping his meaty fist in a length of honey-brown hair. Forcing her to her knees. "Open."

"Please... no..."

A Kas-like growl rumbled through my chest. *It would only take a moment... just one touch, and I'd consume this pest, drain him and leave the empty husk rotting in the spring winds. And without one impossible Elite to bring him back from death, there he'd remain until the elements turned him to stone.*

Shaking her head, Alicia turned away, even as her right hand drifted to her hip. To the firepower concealed there... "Please—"

"If you use your teeth, you'll lose them." He wrenched her head around, slapping her with the back of his hand. "Open."

"Get your hands off me, you great, stinkin' bastard!"

Now.

Stepping clear of the forest, I ignored the hungry pull of virgin Glaith beneath my feet and snatched a thin branch off the ground. It took but three strides to reach a full sprint and a further six before I was close enough to land a stripe on the back of the fool's thighs.

He howled, spinning toward the source of the pain with buckle undone—but I was ready.

I lashed out again, this time aiming for the sad lump of flesh bouncing between his thighs. But he managed to protect his manhood with cupped hands. "To the forest!" I hissed, flicking my free hand toward the woman bathed in the blue glow of the shield.

She scrambled to her feet, something wicked and reckless dancing behind her eyes as she pulled her weapon from its holster.

Pressing my advantage, I placed a lash on the fool's face, leaving a bloody stripe on his cheek, then snarled at Alicia. "Go, you stubborn woman! *Run!*"

"Fuck!" The fool swiped at the wound, fingers painted red. "I don't care how much the bounty is to bring you in alive, you little monster. You're going to pay for that!"

I grinned, baring modified canines. All I needed was one touch...

Bellowing, he lunged, fingers brushing my sleeve when I dodged left, flicking my wrist. Marking the underside of his jaw with another stripe.

"Bitch!"

Laughing, I danced around him with ki-fed grace. Waiting for my opening. Trying to keep his beady little eyes on *me*, even as Alicia took aim, her weapon glowing with cold, blue flames to match the shield.

"So that's how it is, huh?" the fool rasped, gaze flicking between me, Alicia, then back. "Think you two can take me down with a bit of stolen firepower?"

Alicia's sneered. "Let's find out—"

Moving faster than I would have thought possible, he silenced her with a single, well-aimed punch.

I was on him before she hit the ground. Leaping from the loose shale, I landed on his back, wrapping my legs about his waist as I clasped my hands together, bringing them down on the crown of his head with a mighty *thunk*.

He grunted, but found my knee with a meaty hand. Unseating me with a savage jerk, he used my momentum, spinning me. Crushing my back to his front, a muscular forearm encircled my throat, securing me against a wall of man more than twice my width. "I'm going to enjoy this entirely too much, Menace."

Settling my hands on his wiry forearm, a smile crept onto my lips. Oh, yes. So would I. To watch his dark, Caledonian eyes cloud as he stared into the Void? Ambrosia I hadn't tasted in far, *far* too long.

Not since Marco's life-force had given me freedom.

With a grunt, I tucked my chin and buried my teeth in the hairy, sweat-damp flesh, not stopping until I tasted the coppery tang of blood.

A string of colorful curses scalded my ears—but the slaver released me.

Twisting, I planted an elbow in his gut for added measure, then caught him about the throat, letting the tips of my claws sink deep. Letting the darkness surge to the fore. In spite of the Glaith beneath my feet, I buried myself inside him, latching onto his pitiful drops of ki.

Feasting.

"What—" His eyes went wide as I pulled, drinking him in. Watching as his face purpled, he wrapped his hand around my wrist, choking. "Evil... bitch..."

"Mmm, *yes.*" I grinned, flashing bloody, modified canines. "Can't deny it anymore, can I?" I asked, forcing him to his knees. "Not when it feels so *good...*"

In response, he made a funny sound, eyes bulging with the most *delicious* terror that whet an appetite long repressed.

Stolen ki swirled through me. Just a little more... Already his heart stuttered and spit, helpless as the darkness spread.

My eyes rolled back. Ecstasy pounding through my blood.

I didn't feel the whistle and crack of a whip, even when it snapped across my back, splitting my bark armor shirt and marking me from shoulder to hip. I was *lost*, drunk on ki, on the pure emotion swamping this man's very blood. So *good...*

"Get back, beast!" A fist slammed into my ribs, stealing my breath on the heels of a startled yelp. The sound of cracking bone was secondary to the deep, masculine voice that filled my ears. "Release him, or I skin you and use your worthless hide for a bath towel!"

Heavy boots crunched the loose shale behind me as I gasped, torn from my feast with a single, mighty pull. Landing hard on my knees in the shale, I blinked, disoriented. Power singing through my veins, yet I struggled to draw breath. "What—"

"Behold the might of the serpent, vile demon!"

For a moment, I nearly laughed, so absurd was the sentiment from a voice I recognized but couldn't place. And then something cold bit the back of my neck with a shattering, final *click* and mirth abandoned me all at once.

A terrible sound rushed into my lungs, something

akin to a gasp rattling over my teeth and into the seat of my belly. Frost spiked through my spinal cord, trapping a scream in my throat. Freezing it solid as the flow of ki reversed altogether, abandoning me in *seconds* in spite of the power running thick in my veins.

My breath bled from my chest in a wet, rattling hiss. Goddess, *no!* Not like this!

Wrenching, I forced frozen limbs into action, screeching. Staggering to a stand, I clawed at the back of my neck—heedless of rending my flesh into garish ribbons, if only I could break free! Nothing—*nothing*—I'd ever felt was a match to *this*. To the soul-sucking bottomless void peeling the muscles from my very bones. Stripping tendons bare, and leaving nerves exposed to frigid, burning wind, leaving sinew and bone charred black.

The faceless man laughed. "Kneel, Menace. Kneel at the feet of your master!"

When a booted foot swept my feet, I tripped. Knees splitting upon impact with the loose shale.

Screaming defiance, I lashed out, claws flashing. Blinded to everything but the vortex feeding upon my tainted soul.

The whip whistled, laying open my shoulder—and that time, I *did* feel it. Felt every bloody centimeter.

"Roll over, Menace. That's it," the man cooed, shoving me with the tip of his boot. His face too blurred by tears to identify, though some part of me knew who it was. "Be a good little forest demon for your master."

Breathing through a face full of dusty shale, I crawled, extending my scarred right hand toward the forest. If I could just get to the Grandmother... If I could just get to Belle and her good men...

But I couldn't sense her... couldn't sense Kas for the cold...

An elbow dropped across the back of my neck, followed by the weight of a full-grown man pinning me to the earth. "Don't you fucking move!" The fool. Recovered, in part. Wrenching my arms behind my back, heedless of the wounds splitting me open. Thick fingers tangled in my knotted tresses, yanking my head up and bowing my back. "Little bitch! Jasper, look at these teeth, mate. And her nails. Fuck. I'm bleeding. *Everywhere.*"

Goddess, *no*. Jasper? *Jasper* had done this to me? How?

Fancy leather boots stomped into my line of sight. "You'll have to get a shot when we get back to the city. There's no telling what nasty diseases the Menace has got, is there?"

Head spinning, I strained, trying to confirm his identity through the tears blurring my vision and the poison choking my ki—but all I saw was Alicia.

Swaying, left eye swollen shut, blood pouring from a crooked nose, she stood, weapon clutched in trembling fingers.

"Please," I gasped, crimson spittle spraying from my lips. "Kill them. Kill them both!"

Blue flames leapt at her command—but her aim left *everything* to be desired.

Going wide, she missed.

Jasper lunged, catching her elbow, he jerked her off her feet, spinning her in a wide circle.

Arms flapping, she did the only thing she could, and flung her weapon into the shield. For a single, blinding instant, both pieces of rebel technology married, joined in union against the Empire.

But it couldn't last.

Glowing bright enough to be seen through my lids, the shield won. An explosion of ki-laced plasma belched forth, tossing enemies and allies alike into blessed unconsciousness.

9

"Mila!" Desperate hands shook me back to life. "Come, lass. We have to move!"

I coughed.

Coughed again, trying to clear the ringing from my ears and the scent of ozone from my nose. Teetering between conscious and not. Too weak to fight off the cold feasting on my essence, draining me until there was nothing left to take. Leaving me pliable.

Mundane.

I felt him then, as I lay face down in the shale with Alicia, trying to peel my lids apart. Felt him as if his hands were heavy and rough upon my skin. As if he were actually *here*, and not leagues away.

The captain. Beyond shame, I tried to reach for that rare and dangerous ki before I was lost, just as I'd lost this private war between us.

Again.

With a twitch, he brushed my effort aside, denying me, though it wasn't a harsh blow. No. My parasite had the gall to kiss my tattered edges from some great distance, soothing the hurt and the cold. Giving me just enough ki to endure this cruelty. And though he wasn't present in body, I could *feel* his touch. Could almost feel his calloused hand push my hair back, petting me, while his rich ki throbbed with the proof of my failure.

Victory.

His victory.

I groaned, forcing my eyes open. Having narrowly missed incinerating us with plasma, the explosion had instead left a path of charred earth—a path that led straight and true to the Grandmother's edge. Ribs crackling protest, skin rent from shoulder to opposite hip, I planted scarred, branded palm to earth sick with virgin Glaith. Trying to follow the path laid down before me. Trying to drag myself to safety where I could recover from whatever sickness was stuck to the back of my neck.

"That's it, lass," Alicia whispered, wrapping her hands about my damaged middle. Trying to help me deny this loss for what it was—complete and utter defeat. Eclipsing humiliation, for I was nothing but the most reckless, arrogant fool! "Just a little further, and we'll get you back on your land. How's that sound?"

Like paradise. Only the Grandmother could chase this terrible frost from my bones and mend skin—all I had to do was reach her.

"Goddess, what've they got around your neck?"

"Hurts," I croaked. "Get it off."

"I think it's—"

"Ah, ah, ahh, I wouldn't do that," Jasper said, crunching shale signaling his approach. "She may be small, but she's a powerful demoness. It's only the mark of the serpent that keeps her docile."

"Get back!" Alicia pulled me to my feet, taking the majority of my weight. Head lolling against her shoulder. "Not another step!"

Jasper shrugged. "But you haven't gotten what you came for." Grinning through layers of grime and soot, he lifted his hand—and let my pendant dangle from his forefinger. It was dirty, as if it had indeed been buried in the forest's rich, dark earth. Unchanged for all these years in the captain's possession. And if Jasper was fool enough to risk my touching it...

I lifted scarred right hand, lips parted on a soundless plea.

Kas bellowed in the distance, crashing through the underbrush. Alerted to the danger, no doubt, by my absence from her soul.

"The fuck?" the fool asked, grunting awake.

"Lass, *run*," Alicia whispered, shoving me toward sanctuary. "I've got this."

Run? Without the wild rush of ki pounding through my veins? I could scarcely *breathe*!

Undeterred, Alicia bellowed. Throwing herself between me and the slavers, she charged toward them with madness glinting in her pretty green eyes.

Even injured and rattled by the explosion, she should have known she was outmatched. But I had infected her with my foolish fucking madness, stolen the rational part of her brilliant mind, and replaced it with seething rot.

Jasper caught her swinging fist, spun her, and passed her off to his fool partner—all before she'd finished screaming her misplaced rage.

"Quickly," Jasper said, stuffing my pendant into his pocket. "We've got to move before the Menace has a chance to call her hellcat forth. Knock the Eloran out if you have to," he added as Alicia snarled and struggled. "But don't damage her face more than you have already. We'll turn a decent profit off the pretty one. Fix her nose, if she'll let you."

"Get your hands off me, you sonofawhore—"

With an ominous *thunk* Alicia was rendered silent. Left to crumple in a graceless heap at the fool's feet.

I tried to run. Tried to fight the terrible cold leaching the strength from the back of my neck.

But I couldn't. Was utterly helpless to do *anything* but collapse into the jagged earth when Jasper closed the distance between us. With booted toe, he rolled me, setting his knee into the deepest part of the lashes bisecting my back. Laughing when he forced a wet, bubbling wheeze from my lungs.

Clapping the soot from his hands, the fool stood over me and confirmed my foolishness. "The captain was right."

"Oh?" Jerking my wrists together, Jasper grunted, binding my hands behind my back with leather cuffs. Tight enough to tear skin.

"The mark of the serpent does the trick on this one, though fuck me if I can explain it. Woulda bet money that all your superstitious nonsense was just that."

Fiddling with the bonds, Jasper wasn't satisfied until something cold and smooth touched the insides of both wrists. Stealing my breath, for it was more of the same nightmare fuel that had me about the throat.

I knew then.

This trap wasn't set for the Triloth under the mountain.

It was for *me*. It had *always* been for me. *He* couldn't touch me in the forest with the Grandmother at my back—so he'd pulled me out. Dangled the *one* thing he knew I'd never be able to resist. And I'd gone running, just as he'd wanted, not pausing to use my brain, though Alicia had tried to force me to see sense, before I'd turned her into a vessel of my temper. Before I'd filled her with false arrogance and sent her into my fight.

There'd be no aid from the Triloth hidden safe inside the mountain.

Nothing from Belle, heavy with pregnancy and bound to a brier throne by my own doing.

Not from her good men, unconscious in the brush where I'd left them.

Nothing from the rebels, with the shield standing strong between us, despite Alicia's misguided attempt to bring it down.

Not even Kas could save me now, though I knew she'd spare nothing in the effort.

There was nothing. Just... nothing.

Goddess take you with her into the Void, Captain Rawlings, you clever bastard.

Jasper's knee dug deeper into my spine as he cinched the bonds tighter, cutting off circulation. "There. Got the Menace all tied up." He chuckled, lifting me off the ground with one hand about my bound wrists, making my shoulders scream and the lashes weep.

"Can I get my licks in?" the fool asked, tracing the cuts I'd put on his face with a finger, his forearm sporting a perfect outline of my teeth. His throat tattooed by my claws.

Without waiting for an answer, thick grimy fingers pushed past my lips, running over my teeth.

With the meager strength I yet possessed, I snapped my jaws closed on his thumb. Tried to gnaw through solid bone.

"Nice try," the fool said, and jammed half of his fist into my mouth, putting so much pressure on my jaw that it was impossible to retaliate. He pulled me from Jasper's hands, whistling, low and long. "Would you look at this? I bet we could get twice what Rawlings is offering if we sell her to a freak show or something. Plus," he continued, withdrawing his hand, wiping my saliva on my cheek, "you've already got the first half of the bounty payment. Win-win."

Semi-lucid, I snorted.

Oh, what perfect irony! To go to all the trouble of planning my fall, only to be double-crossed at the end by this pair of greedy morons?

For a moment, Jasper was silent, watching me with eyes narrowed. "Rawlings isn't a man I want for an enemy."

The fool shook me, though I only noticed because my chin bounced off my chest. "Aw, come on, mate. Have you any idea what that traveling circus will pay for this little monster? Think of the crowds she'd draw..."

Yes, the crowds. As soon as I was freed from this terrible cold stuck to wrists and nape, the crowds would be *most* useful...

"Just get her to the coach. The rebels are stirring and I don't want to be here when that shield comes down." Laughing, Jasper turned his back on the Elorans and tugged a bit of leather from his belt. "Apparently they don't appreciate free pest control. We're doing them a service. Rebel filth."

Had reinforcements been drawn by the explosion? I couldn't lift my head to see for myself.

"Here, you take the Menace. I'll get the pretty one," the fool said, pushing me toward Jasper.

I staggered, only just managing to keep my feet.

Hand on my lacerated shoulder, Jasper steadied me. "Straighten that nose, will ya?" he said, then opened the coach doors, revealing the steel bars of a cabin altered for one reason—the transport of slaves. Standing aside as the battered Eloran woman was placed in the center of the cage, Jasper watched his partner jam a finger up each of Alicia's nostrils.

When he pulled it straight, her nose crunched and my stomach heaved—splattering Jasper's fancy, expensive boots with bile.

"Fuck! Check this beast for weapons before we get on the road," Jasper said, tossing me against the lip of the cage. "No more surprises."

Adventurous hands traced the length of my torso, sparing nothing for modesty. And had I the strength to do more than glare, I would have made the fool suffer for the invasion. As it was... his touch lingered on my breasts.

"I can confirm the mystery of her gender."

Jasper snorted, splashing his boots with water from a battered canteen. "Your magics are tied to this cursed wood, aren't they, my filthy little sprite?"

I sneered, trying to ignore the rasp of calloused hands.

"See, I have a theory," he said, chucking me under the chin and catching my tongue between my teeth.

"Once you've been separated from this forest, you'll be powerless. Oh, you don't need to confirm it. My benefactor agrees with me. Was the first to do so, as a matter of fact, after he saw what you're capable of on the road the other day. And who better to support me than one of the emperor's own magic wielders?" Jasper got close, his nose scant inches from mine. "He gave me these fetters, and told me *exactly* how to use them against you."

Of *course* he did, the manipulative dog! I should have *known* my Elite parasite would stoop so low without even bothering to show up himself. The coward couldn't even show up to set his own trap!

"He had them etched with symbol of the serpent, because one such as yourself can't stand against the power of the Divine."

The Divine? I barely avoided rolling my eyes.

"To be honest"—he shivered, thumbing the likeness of a serpent on a silver chain—"I'm not all that thrilled about the notion of an Elite coming into the possession of a powerful demon like this one. They're *all* cursed, if you ask me. The Blood. Downright unnatural."

The fool's hands ran over my hips. "Yeah? What you thinkin', then?"

"What if... what if she died?"

"Then we don't get paid," the fool returned, palming first my left, then right thigh.

"Ah, but you said it yourself. We've already got half of Rawlings' payment, which was more than the sum we received for gathering *ten* slaves last month. If we were to tell him she died when we took her from the forest..."

The fool's dark eyes lit with greed. "Then we could sell her to the circus *and* keep a generous business partner. He'd never know what happened to her. I can't imagine he wants her for more than an oddity. It wouldn't be a tragic loss..."

"The circus is too good for her," Jasper snapped, glaring down at me. "I'd rather see this wretch sold to the salt mines for all the trouble she's caused over the years."

"Yeah," the fool said, sliding his hands lower, to palm the globes of my ass, "but if you sell her to the mines you'll never recoup any coin."

Jasper grinned. "Circus it is." Dumping me into the cage, he slammed the door shut with an ear-splitting clang, sending a final glance at the glimmering blue shield and the chaos buzzing behind it, then boarded the coach. "There's an auction house not far from here," he said. "If we're going to double-cross Rawlings, we'd better make it there by nightfall."

Too late, Kas howled, her voice a haunting echo from the dense foliage. Screaming for me.

I twisted back in spite of the pain parting my flesh and the weakness weighing me down, trying to catch one last glimpse of the beautiful gray eyes I loved so much. She was close, yet entirely too far away.

But Jasper wouldn't have it. Reaching through the bars, he dug his fingers into the weeping wound bisecting the flesh of my back. "Ah, ah, ah. None of that."

Kas wailed, threatening to break the dam keeping my sobs contained.

10

A thump on my lacerated shoulder jerked me back to the land of waking nightmares.

A hand.

Alicia's hand—the hot, sticky pain of her touch existing in stark contrast to the genteel smile gracing her swollen lips. I pulled away—as much as my bonds would allow. Uttering a strangled groan.

"So," she said, taking in the bars of our cage, "we've been captured."

Given the fact that I was all but hogtied on the floor beside her, I held my silence, instead inspecting the landscape of bruises marring Alicia's face.

Although her nose was now straight, the site had swollen considerably, and beneath her eyes, half-moon circles of deep purple were *just* beginning to peek through the delicate skin. In a day or two, those bruises would be a spectacular testament to the violence needed to capture the Eloran scientist I'd corrupted with my touch. Bruises that spoke of both a defiant spirit *and* cloaked her beauty from the casual observer—a blessing considering where we were headed.

Groaning, I shifted. Searching for a comfortable position, despite the fact that my arms had gone numb and my shoulders ached from hours frozen in the same unnatural position. The sun now hung low on the horizon, but I'd been senseless as the lush, ki-fed greenery of my home had melted away. Replaced by a city blackened by war—and I recognized none of it.

Alicia scooted closer, pretty green eyes darting over the shattered landscape. And, pressing her lips to my ear, she whispered, "Looks like the outer reaches of Liyas. Won't be long now, lass. The auction house is—" she cleared her throat, squeezing bruised eyes shut. "It's going to be okay. This auction house supplies wealthy merchants, for the most part. But it's too far out for the soldiers on the front lines t'bother with. We'll have a few moments to speak freely when we get there."

But what—or *who*—would be waiting for us when we did? I took a breath, then plucked at the parasite buried in my chest.

Nothing.

No hint of wild, Elite ki. And if I couldn't sense him, surely it went both ways? Surely Jasper's moronic betrayal scheme had a *chance* to keep me free of the captain's clutches?

"It's dirty Glaith," Alicia whispered, forcing my head forward to inspect the collar wrapped around my throat. She tapped the stone affixed to the back of my neck. "Iron mixed with Glaith. Don't know what the Empire calls it, but we call it Raith, on account of what it does to the Triloth who touch it. Turns 'em into glassy-eyed ghosts, too weak to draw breath. We don't use it, as the

Triloth canna tolerate the effects long enough to determine if that filth has any purpose beyond a cruel restraint. But seein' as you're *not*... one of the Triloth... I have a theory—"

"Oy!" the fool shouted, pounding on the partition separating us from them. "Shut it, back there! I can hear you sluts whispering!"

"Bastard," she hissed, scowling at the back of his head.

But the coach was slowing, coming to a stop behind a battered brick building. Most of the windows were either broken or boarded up, the walls charred by fire. Regardless, the sounds of merriment spilled forth, hinting at a gathering of a great many people.

The auction house.

"Jasper!" a man called from a hastily constructed booth. "Good to see you, mate. What've you got for me today?"

"Only the best for your fine establishment, Caleb," Jasper said, deboarding the coach before it had come to a complete stop.

Caleb scratched the back of his head, leaning on an ornate walking cane as his eyes flicked over Alicia's bruises, and passed over me entirely. "Uh, well I wasn't expecting you for another fortnight. I'll... uh... I'll have to check the register to see if we've got time to fit these two in."

"A full roster, you say? That's unfortunate."

The fool joined Jasper, heaving a great, theatrical sigh. "I guess we'll have to move on..."

Jasper huffed then reached into his cloak, withdrawing a small sack. "Unfortunate indeed. And here we were, ready to make it worth your time for the late registration..." He bounced the sack, making it jingle.

Caleb's eyes gleamed. "You know, I seem to recall there being an opening toward the end of the auction," he said, reaching for the bribe. "And if you hurry, you can fill it right now. Wallace isn't aging well, you see. He makes mistakes with the roster all the time."

Jasper dropped the sack in Caleb's outstretched hand, grinning. "Good man! Through the back as usual?"

"Of course. If you'll give me a moment to inspect the wares. This auction house has a reputation to uphold. Can't be selling sub-par product—" he choked, face turning a blotchy red. "The fuck am I looking at?! Where did you find this... this *creature?*"

"Ah, yes." Jasper cleared his throat with a grimace. "This is the Wood's Menace who's been plaguing me and mine these last years. She smells like a dumpster and looks like a goblin, so we've decided to name her Hob. I'll be selling Hob more as an... oddity, in the unlikely event that there's a buyer among your fine patrons."

"*This* is the Wood's Menace? Ha! Hardly the six-foot monster wielding a battle axe, Jasper! She's just a little thing."

"Perhaps not," Jasper replied, cheeks pink. "But she's a powerful wood spirit. Took expensive talismans blessed with the serpent to bring her down."

The fool rapped his knuckles on the bars. "Say hello, Hob."

When I did nothing but glare, Jasper collected Caleb's ornate cane with a polite nod, then jabbed it through the bars, landing a strike in the center of my bruised or broken ribs.

I gasped, grimaced in pain, teeth flashing.

Caleb's head snapped back. "Bloody hellfire! You're not joking! Look at those teeth!"

"Yes," the fool said, holding up the arm I'd bitten, showing off the puncture marks I'd left peppering his skin. "And if you'd like to keep all of your digits, I wouldn't touch her."

"I'm afraid I can't let you sell *that* here," Caleb said, scratching at the back of his head. "She's hardly what the patrons will expect—"

Jasper grumbled, tugging a second bag of coin from his cloak.

"Ah, very good. On with you, then," Caleb replied, weighing the new purse in the flat of his hand. "Go get them registered. I'll keep an eye out while you're gone."

What exactly he was watching for, however, would remain a mystery, for as soon as Jasper and the fool disappeared down a narrow set of concrete stairs, Caleb turned his back on us. Dumping his coin on a small table, he began to count, starting over every time a patron shouted or cheered from within the auction house.

"Come," Alicia whispered. "Let's get you free o'the Raith, if we can. An' when you have the strength, you'll tell me every piece of the story I'm missin'. Canna make a plan if I don't know the players." She caught my gaze. "I'll need t'know who *'he'* is, lass. Oh, aye," she breathed, reaching for the cold thing chewing on my spinal cord, "I've put it together. You've had a run in with a man— likely a son o'the Empire, if your shifty behavior is any sort of accurate." With a shrug, she brushed a matted lock of hair off my shoulder. "But I'm not Belle, lass. You canna say *anything* I'll condemn you for. Us girls've got needs too, yeah? We're the only allies we've got. Understand?"

For a moment, I glared. But this clever green-eyed bitch wasn't wrong. More important, she was an element my Elite parasite couldn't have predicted. If Alicia could free me of this so-called Raith *and* disrupt the captain's plans?

Perhaps our purpose here wasn't entirely wasted after all.

Perhaps we could accomplish all we'd set out to do before I'd gone and ruined it. Save the Trila-Glís.

I tipped my head forward, allowing her nimble fingers to work at the poisoned leather collar ringing my throat.

"We havena much time. These things never last long, but when the auction is over, the men'll likely spend the rest of the night congratulatin' themselves on money well-spent. It's *our* job t'ensure they're so bloody drunk they can't find their own cocks, let alone think o'their new slaves."

"How—" I shook my head, straining to gather the strength to speak. "How do you know any of this?"

"Helped a few dozen girls and boys escape establishments like this one over the years." She winked, in spite of the bruising and swelling. "You're not the only one with a knack for helpin' refugees. Learned a few things over the last five years. It's the slavers you've got t'keep an eye on. Be meek in front of them. Look broken and terrified. Men like that love to see your fear. *Let* them. Play the part, lass."

Play the terrified slave in front of *Jasper*?

Alicia cursed, eyes narrowed as she worked at the collar. "Cocksuckers," she hissed, shaking her head. "It's got a lock. I'm sorry. I've nothing to pick it with."

My eyes fluttered closed, too drained to feel the disappointment. Too drained to feel anything, in fact, except for a detached sort of appreciation for all the captain's planning.

It was... impressive, how easily he'd manipulated me. The man hadn't set foot on the playing field, and had beaten me so thoroughly I didn't know where to begin planning my revenge.

Or even if I *could.*

"Come. Lean forward. Your hands are a bit blue. Probably cut off the circulation, by the look of those knots. Bloody idiots."

Grunting, I did as she bade, too stiff to do more than fall against her.

"Fuck," she hissed. "I... they're too tight. I canna— It's okay," she continued, guiding my shoulder to the floor. "You'll just have to scoot your bum over your hands."

It wasn't easy.

Straining the limits of my flexibility, I hunched into a tiny ball of broken skin and bones, trying to follow her instructions, though every corner of my being screamed for rest. To give it up as lost and let the Raith feast until there was nothing left.

"Here—" she gave me leverage, pulling on my knee as I strained.

I gasped, shoulders screaming with the stretch, ribs stiff and aching with the hours of inactivity. Nearly there... just a little more and I could slip my left foot between my wrists.

With a funny little *pop* from my thumb, I was halfway there. One hand throbbing with new pain, but free.

"Goddess, lass, did that hurt? 'M sorry."

I jerked my chin at my right knee, uttering a breathless, "Don't stop."

Alicia nodded, cheeks pink with effort as we worked.

Sweat dripped into my eyes—hers or mine, I wasn't sure—but I persisted until my second foot came free. Twisting my wrists in the too-tight bonds until my hands sat at the most comfortable angle I could manage. I ignored the ache when the leather tore my skin, breathing hard. Eyes squeezed shut. "This is my fault. All of it. I'm sor—"

"None of that, lass," Alicia said, bumping the back of her head against the bars. "We're not in the best way, but we're not quite fucked either."

With a snort, I cracked a smile, and said, "How so?"

Her eyes drifted shut. "Belle. If she'd move the mountain to rescue the High Priestess, already enslaved to the Empire, what d'you think she'll do to stop them from enslavin' a wee night beastie like *you?*"

I sneered. "She *is* determined to have me act the weapon."

"Aye," Alicia replied, her voice scarcely above a whisper. "But it's the sort o'determination we can count on, lass. They'll come for both of us. Lucky for me, these Empire pricks've no idea who I am, or what my unique qualifications are. Far as they're concerned, I'm just another unfortunate slave born on the wrong side o'this war. I intend to use that willful ignorance to do what we came here to do."

Raising my brow, I glanced at Caleb's back.

"We're not far from Liyas," she replied, a clever glimmer entering those pretty green eyes.

Not far from Liyas, and consequently, the High Priestess now stationed there. I nodded my understanding, and simply asked, "How?"

"If all goes well, someone'll purchase us, I'll find you in the crowd when the auction's over, then we'll escape together. Just follow my lead and *play the part.*"

"And if it goes badly?"

"You mean if '*he's*' there waitin' for you?"

I picked at the brand, grinding my teeth. "You have no idea what you're asking."

She grinned. "Clarification is generally why one asks a question, yeah?" When stony silence was my response, she sighed. "You canna destroy the Empire by yourself, girl. We've fundamental differences about how t'go about accomplishin' the same goal, it's true. But I canna help you if I don't know what we're up against, and I would very much like t'avoid using my feminine wiles t'purchase our escape."

Trust.

She was asking me to trust her with a secret I'd kept for the better half of a decade.

Trust for a woman who didn't see *me*, but my potential to be used as a weapon for her cause. Or worse, as nothing more than a power source for her weapons and gadgets. Trust for a woman who didn't believe I could bring the Empire to ruin without help.

I glanced at the leather straps cutting into my wrists, keeping the Raith flush with my skin. As time wore on, it got easier to breathe, as if the Raith *wasn't* the bottomless void I'd first thought, but could eventually be tempered by enough exposure to a rare and dangerous thing.

Eventually wasn't soon enough, and I *did* owe her something of a debt, didn't I?

"He's an Elite," I whispered, thumbing the brand. "And he knows exactly what I am."

11

"An Elite?" she asked, chewing at her lower lip. "Well, that's bloody inconvenient."

I swallowed. "That's putting it rather lightly. He's a little more than that, actually—"

The door to the auction house banged open as the slavers returned, taking the stairs three at a time.

"Balls," Alicia hissed, shifting. "Just-Just play the part. It'll be okay."

"My, my haven't we been busy?" Jasper purred, jangling a set of thick iron keys.

The fool eyed my raw and bleeding wrists, now sitting in my lap. "Is she secure?"

"Oh, quite safe," Jasper said, unlocking the cage door. "Hob is harmless while she wears the mark of the serpent, aren't you, Demon?"

I flashed a toothy smile, head a loose bobbling weight on my neck.

"Right. Well, come on out. And don't bother trying to escape. There's nowhere for you to go, but"—he locked eyes with me—"I'll enjoy beating the holy living hell out of whoever tries."

Graceful even dressed in bruises, Alicia stepped down from the cage, allowing the fool to place a large hand on the back of her neck as Jasper stepped between us.

Unblinking, I gathered my feet beneath me.

Eyes bright with excitement, Jasper entered the cage. "Come, Demon. That's it," he cooed, reaching for my bound wrists.

From my peripherals, Alicia mouthed, *Play the part.* Wide, green eyes beseeching in a cloak of abuse.

Didn't really have a choice, did I? Not with the Raith chewing at neck and wrists. Not with my back split open, and my ribs crackling protest at every breath. No, I'd have to do—

I didn't see the strike coming, but the backhand landed hard enough to put any notion of fight out of me —until he yanked my head back so hard my brain hit the inside of my skull. Dizzy and pressed close to his chest, I was without the leverage to act.

"Steady," Caleb said, aiming the end of his ornate cane at my throat.

I struggled, cringing away from the stick. But it was no use—Jasper fastened the hook at the end of his cane to my collar and dragged me from the cage. Thrown off balance by a savage tug, I stumbled, near to garroting myself at the end of a stick.

"Stop it!" Alicia screamed. "She's not doing anything!"

"Shut her up," Jasper snapped. "Easy, Hob. That's a good girl," he cooed, leading me toward the auction house. "Put on a show for the good men and women, hmm?"

And then I found I did *not* need ki *or* adrenaline to sustain me—not when the very sight of the man inspired enough rage to make my heart beat at the back of my throat. Not when Alicia had begged me to play the part, for of course, Jasper himself had named me *Demon*. Why, it would be unjust if I didn't live up to this newest moniker.

Running on fumes, I lunged, bellowing at the top of my lungs, broken ribs and lacerations be damned. Fingers hooked, claws flashing, I went for his eyes.

He stepped out of range, keeping me at the end of the stick as I turned my fury upon the collar, drawing blood in my effort to be rid of the Raith.

"That's it," Jasper hummed, utterly unconcerned as he tugged me toward the darkened stairwell. "This way."

I snarled, tripping on a concrete lip at the top of the stairs—the slaver braced the cane at his hip, stopping my fall and forcing me to stand on tip-toe if I wanted to continue breathing.

"Just down these stairs now, Hob. Come along. That's it... Good. *Get the door, man! The door!* Good girl." Cheeks flushed, he herded me, following me onto a small stage lit with by the dingy yellow glow of oil lamps.

The living heat in the overcrowded room slapped me with the sour scent of men drinking, but did not bank my demonic fire. I fought all the harder, raged— though my back was hot and sticky and my ribs screamed for relief.

Fight just a little *harder*... then the Raith could have it all...

Jasper shoved me forward, laughing when I stumbled, landing hard on my knees without the use of my hands to slow my fall.

"A fitting position for you, Hob," Jasper sneered, then seized a fistful of hair as an auction house employee fixed my collar to a large brass hook embedded in the wooden planks beneath me. "You see that man there?" he asked, guiding my chin, pressing his cheek to mine. "He runs the freak show. Keep it up, Demon. Your temper is good for business."

No. My 'temper' had blanketed the crowd in *silence*. A sea of faceless dark eyes stared back at me—seeing exactly what *I* wished them to see. A filthy demon dressed in chains and forced to kneel. Unbroken, in spite of the bruises and the blood.

Chin raised, I flashed a toothy grin, letting the hysteria bubble forth as the Raith took and took and took.

Oh, I had their attention—better yet, I had their disgust.

Jasper's golden serpent swung into my peripherals, and I shook with unhinged laughter that was swallowed by the press of bodies staring at the wood's menace. "A curse for you, Jasper," I rasped, voice a hoarse scratching as my throat tried to work around the Raith. "A promise for the slaver. I'm going to pull your intestines from your belly, inch by stinking inch. Only when your screams begin to annoy me, and your stench simmers in the midsummer heat will I give you death. I'll wrap your guts about your throat and hang you from the tallest tree so your corpse can't poison the earth." I leaned in, all teeth and madness even as my vision spun with fatigue, my voice for his ears only. "Salt mines or freak show, I'll have my chance at freedom, slaver. And I'll come for you. The serpent can't protect you. Not for long. Not from *me*." I licked his cheek then, cackling when he thrust me forward, his face pale. "But I mustn't be rude. Must give thanks where it's due. So, thank you, *Jasper*. Thank you."

I didn't need my ki to know how much he didn't want to ask it. But he couldn't help himself. "F-For what?"

But that, I would not answer. Better to let him stew with indecision. Better to let his tiny, superstitious mind fill the gaps, because the Raith was so *hungry...* and I was so... *cold...*

Trembling, Jasper stepped back, joining his partner at the edge of the stage.

The crowd roared, their fervor washing over me. Their uncomfortable murmurings all the accolades I needed for a flawless performance.

Play the part, indeed.

Alicia's face twisted, pretty green eyes glittering with tears. "Why would you provoke him, lass?"

"To play with his mind," I whispered, though I wasn't sure she could hear over the roar of the Raith.

A man with a deep, booming voice clapped his hands. "Attention, please! You may now inspect the wares if you are in possession of a buying card. Form an orderly line! Don't want to put undue stress on the merchandise."

Men and women of Caledonian descent flocked to

the stage. Each flashed a golden card marked with the twisty symbol of the serpent. They petted my fellow captives, inspecting teeth, hair, limbs, and skin for flaws. And like good little puppets, they cut a wide berth around me, tossing me disgusted sneers and upturned noses as they passed.

Alicia, on the other hand, was beginning to draw quite a crowd. In spite of the bruises.

"That fine bone structure! What is your lineage, girl?"

"I-I am Eloran, sir," she stammered, flushed beneath her stains of green and deep purple. Playing the part.

"Prettiest Eloran I've ever seen, to be certain. Now tell me, have you been trained in a pleasure house?"

She nodded, eyes dropping to the floor. Demure.

"Have you now? When?"

"T-Two years ago, sir."

"Ah. Very good news, indeed."

I bared my teeth, heart hurting for the brilliant woman I'd endangered. For everything she'd gone through, and everything she'd go through because I'd failed her. Because I'd *continue* to fail her once I was sent to the mines or sold to the freak show.

"Oy, Captain! Would you get a look at this one?"

I stilled, eyes dropping to the bronze ring on the floor between my knees.

Goddess, no.

Not so soon...

Surely there were dozens of captains employed by the Caledonian army? Hundreds, even. It couldn't be *him*.

"Come on, move along. You've had your chance with

the pretty one. Give the rest of us a look, will ya? I've been slaving away on the front lines all day, for pitiful pay and terrible working conditions under a tyrant. That's right. Move along. Dear old Marco needs the distraction more than anyone here."

A pair of black boots clomped into my peripherals. "Yes, Marco, you're quite hard done by, aren't you?"

Something inside me began to shake. Something deep I couldn't name. Something that had sweat beading on the back of my neck as acid churned in my stomach, clogging my throat with a thick clump.

"Would you like to come home with me, pretty girl?"

"I-I—" Alicia cleared her throat. "Of course I would, sir. But my friend—"

"You hear that, Captain?" Marco crowed. "You'd be doing the girl a disservice by allowing her to go to someone else. She *wants* to come with me."

"I'm quite sure that's not the case, soldier. It would be cruelty of the highest order to subject her to your charms. Beside, nothing she says in this festering pit can be taken as anything other than words spoken under extreme duress."

I clenched my fist, claws biting deep. Even through the Raith, I knew it. I could *feel* it.

Him.

Marco laughed, and I watched his shadow clap the captain on the shoulder. "You remember that day... oh, I don't know... three or four years ago? I think I'd just saved your life or something equally heroic"—from my peripherals, I saw him grin at Alicia—"you said—and this is a direct quote—'name anything your heart can think of, Marco, and it shall be yours.'"

"Is that what I said?"

"Sure is, old man. Your memory is going, but don't worry. You have me to remember these things for you."

"Old? I'm not—"

"Shall we start the bidding?" the auctioneer cried above the din, cutting the banter short.

But the scuffed boots didn't turn away.

The man bent at the knee, balanced on his haunches. Rough fingers brushed my chin and I jerked back as far as possible, eliciting a deep, raspy chuckle. And yet, I did what he wanted.

I looked. Couldn't help it.

He didn't say a word—didn't have to. It was all there, written on his face. Eyes darker than pitch. Left corner of his lips tilted toward the ceiling. Fingers finding purchase on the edge of my jaw.

He'd won.

Jasper appeared at his shoulder in a swirl of his fancy cloak. "C-Captain Rawlings, sir. I didn't expect to see you here."

Marco pulled a cigarette box from his pocket. "Well that was the whole point, wasn't it?"

Jasper coughed. "The—the point?"

Eyes drifting shut, I swallowed the clumpy hysteria. Of *course* it was.

"Did you really think, after going to all the trouble to find her, Captain Rawlings would allow you to cheat him? Should have known better, Jasper."

"It—it was an honest mistake—"

"Then why are we all here? Waiting for you to do exactly what you did?" Marco laughed, idly sparking his lighter. On and off, on and off. "You got greedy, slaver. Just like he knew you would. All it took was a lie about where we'd be waiting to collect the goods and you leapt at the chance to fuck him over."

"I-I—n-no—"

"Come now, Marco," the captain said, grinning, though he had yet to take his eyes off my face. "I couldn't possibly have planned such a complicated conspiracy. That would be... what's the word?"

Jasper stumbled back, clutching the image of the serpent. "I-impossible..."

Cupping his hands around a flame, Marco lit his smoke. "Nothing's impossible for an Elite, slaver. You should know that by now."

I almost smiled. There were *many* things impossible to the Elites. Just not *this* Elite.

Jasper's cheeks flushed a deep red, eyes bulging as they darted between the two, but he couldn't force a single coherent word past his lips.

"Captain, you remember what happened to the last one who tried to double-cross you?"

"Something to do with bleeding out in an alley, though I'm a little hazy on the details."

"Hazy on the"—Marco squawked, indignant—"Come on, sir. That was some of my best work!"

Jasper blanched.

"Now, if it's not too much trouble," the captain said, brushing the matted hair back from my face, "perhaps you could explain why you've got my merchandise listed as 'entertainment demon' in this dreary shit-hole?"

"It's... uh... a clerical error, sir." The slaver cleared his throat. "A simple accident. My deepest apologies. You see, my partner is new to all of this, and the bloody idiot added *all* of our stock to the registry, instead of just—"

"Hmm."

"O-Once an item has been registered with the auction house," Jasper continued, blotting the sweat trickling down the side of his face, "there's—there's really nothing I can do."

"Well," the captain said, inky eyes shining with something too dark for even *me* to name. "I'll simply have to be patient and make my bid like the others."

"Are you registered with the house, m-my lord?"

The captain smirked but didn't bother to answer the question.

"Very, ah, very good, sir. If you could take your seat, we'll get the auction under way."

For a moment, the captain continued to watch me, tracing the edge of my bottom lip with his thumb. "Very well," he said when I jerked away, with—of all things— a fractured whimper. "You may begin your little show. Oh, and Jasper?"

"S-Sir?"

"I'll be taking my pendant back."

"Of course, sir," the slaver stammered, digging around in his pocket. With little more than a flick of his wrist, he returned the length of silver chain that had been my undoing, and left it in the captain's possession once more. Only when they were beyond earshot, did the slaver whisper a shaken, "Unholy god," under his breath, clutching the mark of the serpent between slippery fingers.

The auctioneer banged his gavel. "This first Eloran treasure has the perfect temperament for a novice trainer..."

His voice faded to the background as I tried to quell the terror screaming inside my head. He'd found me! Goddess, of *course* he'd found me after the entrance I'd made, but then, he'd been *waiting* for me to arrive! And me, bound by the Raith, unable to do a damned thing about it.

Just as he'd planned.

Sweat trickled down the back of my rough-spun shirt, burning the whip lashes bisecting my skin. I dared not raise my eyes for I could *feel* him watching me, even without my ki.

"That him?" Alicia whispered, her voice barely reaching me over the din.

My chin dipped once.

"Fuck me *raw*," she hissed. "Chose a handsome villain, at least."

I shook my head, for I hadn't chosen any of this.

A scant few minutes later, the stage had been cleared of everyone but Alicia still standing on my left.

"This is our main event of the evening!" The crowd quieted as the auctioneer hauled me to my feet. "May I introduce Hob. I'm told this horrible little creature has been living in the forest for quite some time, causing all sorts of chaos for the good men who fill this fine estab-lishment with merchandise. But this delicate Eloran rose," he continued, stroking Alicia's battered face, "has befriended her. And yes, from what I've been told, there is indeed a female under all this filth." He poked me with the edge of his toe. "Though you can be certain I took Jasper here at his word. I wasn't brave enough to check for myself." He shuddered, smirking when the crowd erupted into peals of manly laughter.

"Either way, this beautiful girl cannot see Hob's

hideous exterior. But her charms are matched only by her stubborn will, gentlemen, so she is suitable only for those of you with experience. Wouldn't want to damage such a treasure, would we? On the other hand," he said, palming the back of my neck and giving me a little shake, "for those of you who enjoy a challenge or some sport, Hob is your girl. She certainly doesn't seem like much, and honestly I should be paying you to take her off my hands, but Hob comes with a nasty little bag of tricks!" He gave the collar a vicious tug, making me grimace—and bare my teeth.

The crowd gasped.

A man in the front leaned closer to the stage, eyes fixed upon my face. "You couldn't pay me to stick my dick in that mouth! Seems too risky for such important equipment."

"She'd be doing us all a favor, stopping you from reproducing!" shouted the man to his left, and the crowd erupted again.

"Shall we start the bidding for this beautiful Eloran rose at ten thousand?"

Alicia's eyes widened in surprise, and continued to do so as the price rose, climbing as high as thirty before a lazy drawl from the crowd rendered the room silent.

"I'll give you fifty."

"F-Fifty, sir?" the auctioneer stammered, flushing red beneath his tan. "That's *very* generous of you, sir. I hear fifty thousand, does anyone wish to better the captain's offer—"

"Ah, you seem to have misheard me. My offer is fifty. Full stop."

"Captain Rawlings, sir, that's not how this process

works. You see, the bidding is currently at thirty thousand—"

"That's odd," the captain said, parting the edges of his coat to reveal the glimmer of a silver handle snug in a holster on his hip. "I don't recall *hearing* thirty thousand. Do you, Marco?"

Boots propped up on the table, Marco grinned, blowing smoke rings at the ceiling. "No, sir! The only offer I heard was yours. You were very clear. All articulate n'shit."

"Ah, there you have it. Does anyone else recall hearing thirty thousand?" the captain asked, raising his voice above the silence. "How about you, Jasper?"

The slaver coughed. "Well, it's an unusually low price for a slave, but for one such as Hob's quality, I suppose I wouldn't mind parting with her for—"

"Fifty for *both*."

The auctioneer patted his shining forehead with a handkerchief. "I think I *must* have misheard—"

"Then allow me to be articulate. I'll give you fifty for *both* slaves due to their poor condition. Is there a counter offer?" Captain Rawlings stood, scanning the room with dark eyes, Elite weapon on full display as he surveyed his competition. "No one? Well," he continued, turning back to the stage, "I guess that means I win."

Marco snorted. "I don't think this Hob creature constitutes as much of a prize, sir. But a man wants what he wants."

"Do shut up, Marco. You got your pretty rose. I'm not paying you to voice every thought that floats through your mind."

Taking a puff, Marco grinned. "What you pay me is borderline criminal, sir. Silence is extra."

Jasper tried again, hands shaking. "F-Fifty is rather low, sir. I won't be able to cover my costs, you see, it—it took years to bring her in—"

The captain smiled, hand drifting again toward the butt of his weapon.

Jasper blanched, gesturing at the auctioneer with frantic fingers. "S-Sold!"

12

———

S *old.*

The word echoed inside my head, almost as loud as the constant, high pitched screaming and the bottomless sucking hunger of the Raith.

Sold.

Looping my pendant over his head, the captain tucked it beneath the collar of his shirt, and said, "Collect your rose, Marco. We're leaving."

"A flower? For me?" Marco ashed his smoke with a flick, heedless of where the waste fell. "Captain, I'm touched. You really *do* care."

"I trust this means you'll release me from your absurd life-debt?"

"Don't be ridiculous! Your life is worth far more than fifty measly coins. At least to me."

The captain snorted, hopping onto the stage and collecting the key ring from the auctioneer.

Sold. *Sold!* To Captain-fucking-Rawlings. Just as he'd planned. There'd be no escape with Alicia. No daring rescue of an enslaved Trila-Glís.

It was over.

Marco cleared his throat, jerking his chin at me. "You're sure? 'Bout her? 'Cause I can't help but notice she bears a striking resemblance to another girl," Marco said. "One who I was promised wouldn't kill me, which didn't end exactly the way you thought it might—"

"I said she *probably* wouldn't kill you," the captain said, and jangled the keys. "But you're still breathing, which I suppose means we're even in terms of life-debts, hmm?"

Marco recoiled, and said, "Ah, don't be hasty now. I said 'resemblance'. With those teeth, and the hair? Could be a different girl, I suppose. If this... *is* indeed a female, you've purchased..." The soldier stepped closer, and in a low tone, added, "But you're sure, Asher? Absolutely certain?"

With a nod, the captain knelt before me. "She's a prize beyond compare."

I didn't meet his eye. Couldn't.

Marco dropped his cigarette, crushing it into the wood beneath his heel. "And what does a man like you do with the prize he's coveted for so long? Personally, I'm curious as to what's beneath all this filth," he added, nose wrinkled as he reached to tug a length of my knotted, stained hair.

"I'm afraid a bath will have to wait," the captain said, running his thumb over the twisted scars on my right hand, his touch landing on the brand for the first time. Tracing his backward initials with quiet reverence, for of course, this was the first time he'd seen it.

And yet, his touch yielded nothing. No taste of powerful, forbidden ki. Nothing but the rasp of work-hardened skin and the terror pounding at the back of my throat when his lips curved in a soft smile.

"I've got something a little more... *permanent* in mind." And then he patted his breast pocket, inky eyes gleaming with smug victory.

The Raith feasted, dimming the lights as my heart fluttered. Permanent? What was in his pocket that could...

No.

Goddess, *no!*

I wheezed, jerking away from his touch.

Was I not *exactly* as he wanted me—on my knees? Bound and helpless before him, just like a...

Slave.

Like a slave.

Like the other Priestesses, bound in Caledonian gold. Tied to an Elite parasite.

Forever.

When the shaking started, it rattled the chain in the captain's hands, dusting frost into my lungs and chaos into my brain.

How? How could I have let this happen? How could I have been so bloody stupid? So rash and sightless?

The lock clicked open.

Meeting that inky gaze was all it took. I fell back, skinning my elbow.

He followed. Easily. Grinning. Extending his hand. "Come."

I shook my head, opening the whip lash as I inched away. Broken ribs chewing at my insides.

Pendant swinging forward against the inside of his shirt, the captain loomed over me with a smirk, hauling me to my feet with his hands on my waist. "You know, I never *did* get your name. I was able to narrow it down to Tannovic, but the records showed *two* Senators with that surname, believe it or not. I couldn't determine if they were both Senators at the same time, as the records were a bit... charred. Anyway, they *both* had daughters." He flicked a matted length of caramel brown over my shoulder. "So it's either Mila, or Grace. But somehow I don't think the latter quite fits..."

Fingers dug into the lash, parting the torn edges of my rough-spun shirt, but I did little more than grimace.

I had to get free! Had to get his hands off me before... before...

The room spun. Dark stars glittered in my periphery as I swayed, blinking up at him.

Ki! I needed ki!

Too desperate for pride, I reached for the parasitic link festering inside, trying to pull something from it— from *him*—to chase the oblivion away.

But the link remained lifeless to my touch. Cold.

The captain's gleeful smile faltered, hand coming away sticky with red. "Shit," he breathed, one hand steadying me as I wobbled, frowning at the other. "Are you injured?"

Blood. I could smell the coppery tang. But I huffed, trying to shake him off, though my lips tingled and the room tilted and bucked beneath my feet.

How in the name of the dead Goddess had this happened? How had I failed in such spectacular fashion?

"Miss Tannovic!"

In a detached sort of way, I watched his lips continue to move before everything went white and I hit the floor.

13

———

Astrong grip tightened around my ribs and the crooks of my knees, bringing me back midway through a hushed conversation.

"I can't do it if she's injured, Marco. I won't take the risk."

Cheek pressed to a muscular chest, I lay limp in his embrace. Rocking with every step. A masculine scent tickling my nose.

Sweet tobacco smoke wafted over me. "To the infirmary, then?"

The captain cursed, the sentiment rumbling through his chest and into mine. "No. No one can know I've got her. Not until it's done. It's too risky. If one of the others find out..."

"They won't."

Someone had freed me of the Raith—at least in part, for my wrists were no longer bound by leather *or* poison. It gave me a little extra room to breathe, without allowing me to touch the soul-deep well of ki that defined me. It wasn't enough, not with the same foul, ki-stealing substance encircling my throat, but it was something.

A start.

Without opening my eyes, I took stock of my limbs, checking for any new signs of damage.

Marco sighed. "To the bathhouse? We could clean her up a bit. See how bad her wounds are, and while we're there," he continued, his grin audible, "you and I could get all sudsy, pretty girl."

"If I must. And it's Alicia, sir."

"If you *must?*" Marco made a strangled sound. "Beautiful *and* she knows where to strike a man where it hurts! Captain, I think I'm in love."

"No." The captain's grip tightened further as he shifted me against his chest. "You're just an idiot, Marco. Now leave Alicia alone and focus, will you? The bathhouse isn't an option at the moment."

"Unwelcome eyes?"

The captain grunted, something heavy and unspoken in his tone when he said, "Of the worst sort, if you catch my meaning."

Where were we? I peered through the fan of my lashes, forcing every other muscle into limp stillness. Passing through an alley, by a massive gray building and an *open* door, belching thick, fragrant steam.

"Let's get her to my place. It's private and—"

To the captain's residence? Over my bloated corpse! I came to life with a shout, punching the underside of his stupid, defined jaw.

With a colorful curse, he dropped me.

"Alicia, with me!" I hissed, and rolled out of reach, sprinting the instant I found my feet in spite of the fire screaming in my ribs and back, arms pumping leverage into each stride.

Distance—I needed it to *flourish* between us.

Slamming into the door-frame took the breath from my lungs, but I pressed on, even when the damp heat of a bathhouse slapped me in the face.

"Oy!" Marco shouted, fingers wrapping around my bicep.

Snarling, I clawed his forearm from elbow to finger-tips, drawing blood.

He too, released me with a curse.

Climb! Kas would get to higher ground!

An ornate, spiral staircase snared my attention, and I veered off without warning as fingers brushed the edge of my shoulder yet again.

Another narrow escape—I grit my teeth and poured everything into my mad dash, strides long and sure, letting adrenaline fuel my flight whether Alicia was with me or not. And when I was close enough, I leapt, landing on the balls of my feet, maintaining balance in spite of the slick, polished banister.

I grinned, for I'd run the trees during an ice storm every winter since I'd claimed the forest as mine.

This was *easy*.

Pouring on the speed, I gained ground on the dark shadows closing in, legs and lungs burning with exertion. Freedom beckoned. All I needed now was a window or a door with a lock. Then I'd rid myself of these bonds, lock Alicia safely away, and unleash the darkness and all its unholy glory upon my enemies.

When it was done, and I was fattened by their life-blood, we'd find the Trila-Glís and be gone before nightfall. We'd return to Belle victorious, and I could have my solitude at long last.

Shouting echoed from all around me. Heavy, masculine steps from the stairs on my left, barked orders from the floor below.

Gasping, I claimed the second floor, launching myself from the banister with a war-cry Kas would have been proud of. Aches and pains all muted, nothing more than a dull roar.

A large man wearing naught but a towel appeared in front of me, blocking my path. "What's all the shouting?"

I skidded to a halt, sides heaving, jaw slack.

General Tilcot. Naked and vulnerable—and me, in no condition to claim the vengeance owed to me!

Kas would wait for the opportune moment. Strike once, or not at all.

Snarling, I whirled, searching for another exit.

The captain rounded the corner, palms up, blocking my retreat. "Nowhere to go, pet."

Teeth bared, I whirled again, ducking under the general's outstretched arm.

"Ho! You've got a wild one, Asher!"

Not yet, he didn't. The window! I lengthened my steps, slamming into the wall, desperate fingers trying to pry and claw my way to freedom.

It didn't budge.

The captain spoke from directly behind me, voice steady. "It's been sealed shut."

A wordless scream burst from my lips, and I slammed my fists into the window pane, trying to break it—but the ache in my bones told a tale of reinforced glass, and I spun one last time, facing my captors head on.

"Easy, now," the captain said, advancing.

Easy? I laughed in spite of the tears threatening to spill over my lashes. *Never.* I crouched low, feet spread, lips pulled back in a snarl indistinguishable from that of Kas herself.

"Would you get a look at those teeth!" the general shouted as Marco joined us in the narrow hall. "This isn't the same wild thing we saw in the woods the other day, is it? Jasper's menace?"

The captain grunted, but did not take his eyes from mine.

Marco reached the top-floor landing, breathing hard. "Shit. Like chasing a damned wildcat, this one. Did you see that fuckin' stunt on the banister? Fuck me running naked down the hallway! Never seen anything like—"

"*Marco.*"

Cornered. And if the captain got his way... No. There was *always* a way out. I just had to find it.

The captain took another step toward me. "Make this easy on yourself," he cooed, palms up.

My frantic gaze landed on the general. Nude beneath his towel.

"I know you're injured," the captain continued. "Let me have a look at those wounds and then—" He lunged.

I dove to the side, aiming for the general's spread legs, yanking the towel from his hips as I went between them, claws missing the soft inner thigh laced with arteries by no more than a hair.

"Got her!" Marco shouted, arms outstretched.

I threw the towel over his head, punching the fluffy

white fabric and the face behind it as hard as my momentum would allow.

Marco's yelp was but a brief instant of satisfaction before a wall of muscle barreled into me, a shoulder crushing my broken ribs.

A ragged yelp burst from my lips as we crashed into a steamy room with a shallow pool in the center.

No! This couldn't be the end! Writhing and kicking, I fought until my whole body shook with exertion and dewy panic-sweat coated my skin.

The captain simply weathered it, murmuring, "Easy, pet. Easy," under his breath, ignoring my teeth and claws as I tore his forearms to ribbons.

"Fuck you," I spat, and planted both feet on the nearest wall, drew knees to chest, then pushed with all my remaining strength.

"Shit—"

We toppled over the edge of the pool, splashing into the warm, soapy water in a tangled pile of limbs.

I surfaced, gasping, eyes burning with whatever fragrance perfumed the water, choking on it.

Warm forearms locked around my ribs, squeezing. Crushing the air out of me. "Enough," the captain snarled, giving me a shake.

I planted my elbow in his gut.

"Ommph. Just—*ugh*—just stop, will you?" he snapped, then wrapped a hand in my matted hair, plunging me beneath the surface once more.

It didn't take long—I was already comically short of breath. But Goddess be damned if I'd submit to *him*. No, better to drown here and now then allow Captain Rawlings to have his way with the darkness and all that went with it.

I opened my mouth on a great, fatalistic inhale.

He pulled me up, fitting me against his chest as I gagged and hacked, torturing my ribs. "Are you done?"

Blinking against the sting in my eyes, I grit my teeth. "Fuck—"

"Stop!" He slipped a bicep beneath my chin, gradually cutting off my air as he squeezed. Giving me no options, whatsoever. "You are outmatched, girl!"

Wait. Kas would wait. Bide her time.

I snarled, face flushed and pounding with the beat of my heart, but raised my hands.

Strike once, or not at all.

The captain's grip eased, though he did not release me. *Are you done?* he growled, lips moving against my ear.

I nodded.

"Say it."

Goddess take this man straight to the Void!

"Yes," I hissed, standing on tiptoe, most of my weight in his hands, if buoyed by the water.

"Good girl."

I buried my claws into my palms.

"Well," the general said, taking a hesitant step closer. "That was... something." Head tilted to the side, hands on his hips, he asked, "Why in the world would you spend good coin on such a creature, Rawlings?"

"Entertainment?" The captain laughed, swiping the water out of his eyes as he fit a loose hand around my throat. "She's a savage little monster. I thought it might be fun to toss her into the fighting pits and see what happens."

The general reached for my face, brows pinched as he inspected me.

He dared to touch me! My father's murderer! A terrible sound bubbled up from the back of my throat as I tried to twist away, teeth bared. And with a howl, I tried to pull myself up, out of the water, to strike at the general with the heel of my closest foot.

"Now, now," the captain murmured, sinking into the sudsy water, keeping me pressed to his front as he floated back. As far from Tilcot as the tight quarters would allow. Sitting against the far wall of the bathing pool, that smarmy prick positioned me between his thighs and dared to whisper, "Behave yourself, Miss Tannovic." And then, lips rasping against the shell of my left ear, he elaborated. "You wouldn't want the general to feel like he's entitled to manage your punishment, would you?"

I stilled. Goddess, *no.* Anything but *that.*

Color touched the general's cheeks as he stepped back, reaching for a fresh towel. "Right. Well. I think I've seen enough. Good luck with this one, Rawlings. It seems you're going to need it."

For a moment, we were alone, the captain and I. Back to front. An arm around my waist, the other buried in my hair as the sudsy water turned an ominous shade of pink, for *neither* of us had escaped unscathed. That the blood of two rare and dangerous things swirled and mixed in the steamy water was not lost on me, but that was far from the worst of it.

My mother's pendant was pressed to the base of my neck, mocking me with all its hidden potential as I floated there, ki-blind. On *his* lap. Silent but for the gentle swish of water and the ragged hitch in breathing. His or mine, I was no longer sure.

"The building is clear, sir," Marco said, rounding the

corner with a wide-eyed Alicia in tow. When he saw us, he whistled low, a wicked grin spreading across his face.

"Not a word, soldier," the captain snapped, hauling me back, toward a submerged stone bench. "Not one fucking word."

Dark eyes twinkling, Marco pursed his lips, palms raised—and I was happy to note the abrasion marking his right cheek. Imprinted with the fluffy, textured fabric of the towel and my fist.

Capturing my wrists, the captain hauled me to a stand then spun me to face him, inspecting my claws with raised brow. "An interesting modification. And certainly effective," he added, holding his savaged fore-arms aloft.

Blood trailed toward his elbow, soaking the fabric of his black dress-shirt.

"She's got a wicked right cross, too," Marco said, thumbing the imprint of the terrycloth and three bumps where my knuckles had landed. "Fucksakes, that was close. Basically ran straight into the general's arms."

"Yes. And let's get out of here before he returns," the captain said. "Take Alicia to my residence and get her settled in. I'll—"

Alicia came to the edge of the bathing pool, fingers pressed to her lips. "Sir. I—if I may. I'd... I'd like to help."

"Thank you, Alicia, but that won't be necess—"

"I know what she is," the scientist blurted, clenching her fists. Playing her part beautifully—of a traitor.

The captain stilled, fingers tight on my wrists.

"Jasper may be a damned, superstitious fool not t'see it, but *I'm* not stupid, sir. I was schooled in the Temple before the fall and I know a little of the Blood.

The teeth. The claws. The fact that an Elite warrior went to such great lengths to claim a wee forest demon, *and* made a spectacle o'punishin' a slaver the way you did?" Alicia swallowed, green eyes flicking to me for an instant, before dropping to the floor. "I'll admit I wasna fully conscious at the time"—she touched her bruised and swollen nose—"but I saw somethin' that needs explainin'. Something she did, out there at the edge of the wood. You almost had the slavers beat, didn't you, lass? If it hadna been for me, distractin' you, then..." Tears dusted her scowl, topping off a flawless performance—and one that distanced her from the rebels beneath the mountain, me, and all her powerful, deadly knowledge about Glaith technology.

Her technology.

"Clever and beautiful?" Marco said, looking Alicia up and down. "The perfect woman."

Marco didn't know the truth of his words.

But the captain was not so easily won. "There are some who would kill to keep that information secret, Alicia. In this very room."

She swallowed. "And I'm bettin' you're aware a woman like *her* will need more'n the attention of men. 'Specially now. Transitioning from what she was, to..." Alicia shrugged, trailing off. Avoiding my eye, the coward.

Long seconds passed with nothing said. With his hands on my skin and his eyes on Alicia. Warm water swirling around our hips, soaking through our clothes as he deliberated her fate.

"Not a word," the captain murmured at length, meeting—and holding—Alicia's gaze. "Keep this to yourself, and you'll be rewarded with your freedom as soon as I can manage it. You have my Blood-oath."

"Consider my lips sealed, sir," she whispered.

A bargain struck, and me, with no part in it.

"Traitor," I hissed glaring at her, and brought my knee up, aiming for the captain's groin.

He blocked me easily. "I had half a mind to give you a reprieve from the Eidolon, but because you *insist* on acting like a wild thing, you'll wear these manacles until I can make it official." He rummaged about in his pocket for a moment, then looped the leather bands containing the Raith around my wrists once more, catching me when I sagged against his chest. "There," he murmured, petting my sopping hair for a moment, pinning me with inky eyes. "That's better, isn't it, pet?"

In response, I flashed my teeth, unable to do much else but fret over three little words. *Make it official...*

His gaze stuck at my mouth, glimmering with something indecipherable before he stooped, setting his shoulder against my belly. Compressing my ribs, he hefted me from the water. "Let's go."

14

———

The journey to the captain's residence was at once short, and an experiment in ceaseless agony. Every step bounced my injuries against his shoulder, keeping me just lucid enough to dread whatever was to come next. Whatever would *make it official.*

Would it matter? With the Raith sipping at what remained of my ki, would there be anything for the captain to torture when we got to where we were going, or would he find he'd captured nothing more than a frozen, empty shell?

I missed the moment when the captain entered his home—the Raith was chewing holes in my time-line. I couldn't recall *how* we came to be sitting in a tiled bathroom, my head resting on his shoulder as he fiddled with something behind me. And neither could I decipher anything beyond the low rumble of his voice as he murmured to the others, working as he talked.

My mother's pendant was pressed between us, mocking me as it bruised my collarbone. Filled to bursting with years of rare and dangerous ki, yet utterly beyond my reach.

"Ready?" Marco asked, his voice distorted and far away.

"Yes," the captain said, gathering me against him, dragging my wrists above my head and fastening them to a bar fixed to the ceiling.

Body stretched taut, I cried out, eyes squeezed shut against the pain. "Mmph. D-Don't," I groaned, sagging in my new bonds, unable to fight any longer.

The captain ignored me, stepping back, inky gaze sweeping the length of my body.

"Is that blood?" Marco asked, frowning at the captain's hands, then looking to me.

The captain scowled, rubbing forefinger and thumb together as he inspected me. "Can't tell if it's hers or mine, at this point."

"Both, I'd imagine," Alicia whispered, twisting her hands. "The slaver... Jasper... she fought him."

Clearing his throat, the captain drew a wicked, curved blade, caught my eye, and said, "Right. Well. It's probably best if you don't move."

I summoned the fiercest glare I could muster. As if I had much choice in the matter, dangling helpless before him. Scarcely able to draw breath, let alone protest the destruction of my hand-crafted clothing, I was stripped bare. My armor against the elements, abrasions, and unwanted attention were cut away, discarded in a careless heap in the corner of a tiled shower stall. He didn't stop until I was all but nude before him, hanging in nothing but the strips of cloth wound about my breasts and between my legs.

"Oh, lass," Alicia gasped.

I craned my head around, inspecting the massive purple bruise spreading across my midsection. At the center, the outline of a fist was plainly visible, and below it, the bleeding edges of torn flesh.

"Fuck." The captain tossed his blade into the sink, pushing a crimson hand through his thick, dark hair. Circling me. *"Fuck!"*

"Wildcat must have caused a lot of trouble for the slavers to do *this.*"

"That's a *lash* from a *whip*, Marco," the captain retorted, gently prodding my wounds. "I'm going to kill that bastard very, *very*, slowly."

"Oh, Jasper's long gone, sir." Marco moved beyond my line of sight. "I'd bet he started running the instant the door closed behind us, the slippery little eel."

"I need the room," the captain said, voice clipped and tight. "Take Alicia to my closet and pick out something appropriate for both of them."

"Do I get to pick the underthings?" Marco asked, waggling his eyebrows.

Alicia ignored him. "The lass needs a Priestess, sir. I don't like the look o'her color."

"Don't you worry about that, pretty girl. Captain Rawlings has the wildcat all covered."

"But—"

Marco hustled her out, closing the door with a gentle snap as they went. Leaving me alone. With *him.*

For a moment, the captain watched the door, eyes glassy, hand on his—*my*—pendant. Following their retreat with his senses. Flaunting what he'd taken before he returned to me, nostrils pinched white. Lips a thin line.

"I felt this happen," he murmured at length,

matching four fingers against Kas' claws, following their path from my ribs to upper thigh. "Thought it was over then. That you'd die from whatever caused this. But you persevered. Thrived, even. Tell me, Miss Tannovic. Why did you keep the scars?"

"Don't—" I swallowed the pain of my familial name on his lips. "Don't c-call me that."

"Would you prefer... 'Mila'?"

I sneered, too tired to bother denying my given name.

"So," he said, hand lingering on my marked hip, eyes unreadable. "Here you are."

Pulling at my wrists, I held his eye. "Release me."

He smirked, stroking the ridges of my scars with his thumb. "You know I can't do that."

I said nothing.

"Have you any idea how valuable you are?" He shook his head, something akin to wonder spreading across his face, though without my ki, I was unable to know for certain. "An unbound Trila-Glís who *no one* is looking for? No one even knows to look because you shouldn't exist." He laughed, incredulous. "They even explain away your rather obvious modifications as magic. It's uncanny."

"Sounds familiar," I rasped, but in spite of my bravado, a cold pit opened in my belly. Made wider by the Raith.

He smirked, not denying it as he retrieved his blade from the sink. "Do you know how long it's been?"

Breathe. In. Out. The chance will come. Have patience.

Kas... she would be patient.

"Five years, Mila. Five years knowing where you

were, yet unable to do a damned thing about it." A smile creased his lips as he reached for my bound wrists, silver blade flashing in the dim light. "I didn't want to use the Eidolon on you, but I've got to give you credit." He paused, pendant peeking through the collar of his shirt as he worked the knife into the leather. "You're a resourceful little thing. A worthy adversary." The blade sliced through the leather on my right wrist. "No doubt about it."

With a flick, a little polished stone popped free of the bonds, clattering to the tiles beneath us. A flicker of ki hummed in my chest, gooseflesh prickling at my skin, and I blinked. He was freeing me from the Raith. From this... Eidolon, as he called it.

"I've been busy while you were playing forest demon with your pet lion."

I snorted. *No one* owned Kas. And when this bloody fool released me from these chains, he'd learn the same to be true about me.

He worked the second stone free. "I've got a surprise for you. Two, actually. Do you remember the day we met?"

Both arms unadorned by poison, the flickering hum bloomed, unfurling great, dark wings and stretching the muscles between my damaged ribs on a full, if agonizing breath.

"Of course you do," he said, slipping his hand into a pocket, withdrawing a tiny, iron key. "How could you forget the day Tritan fell?" The lock at my nape clicked open, and for a moment he paused, leaving the collar firm against my skin. When he stooped, his lips brushed mine with the weight of a falling leaf.

I bared my teeth, tasting his breath.

A crooked grin and he stepped back, letting the collar drop to the tiles.

Free! Ki whispered through me, a tiny spark licking at my tattered soul. At first a low hum, and then... The captain! Awareness of him pounded behind my ribs as he reclaimed the place he'd long since marked as his own.

So much *power*... just as I remembered.

And it would be *mine*, the fool!

Eyes glazed with renewed vigor, I stared at the floor, gathering myself.

How poetic, to make the only Elite Trila-Glís on the planet the catalyst for my victory. The fuel for my vengeance.

He hummed, brushing the hair back from my damp forehead, arrogant enough to let his fingers linger upon my skin. "Look at you, little Priestess! Going to show me everything you learned in the forest, hmm?" The rasp of calluses nipped my cheek and he tilted my head back, drowning me in an inky abyss.

And all the while, his potent, impossible ki rushed through my veins, restoring what I'd lost. What he'd taken from me.

Almost. Almost there...

He broke away, grinning at my squeak of protest when I tried to chase his hand. "I've waited a long time for this. For *you.* It hasn't been easy, going all these years without a Priestess of my own," he continued, unbuttoning his sleeves one at a time, rolling them back to reveal corded muscle and the mark of the Empire melted into the skin of his left wrist—a black stain I'd never noticed before. "There have been other Priestesses, of course. Dozens I might have claimed over the years. But none of them were *you.*"

My lips twitched as I watched him, unblinking. The pendant tugged at my periphery, but I didn't so much as glance at it. "Then come, Captain. Claim your prize."

"There she is," he drawled and returned to me, stopping but a hair's breadth from my chest, so close I could feel his heartbeat upon my skin. "You *are* a prize, you understand. Invaluable. Do you know what it's been like?" he murmured, tracing the air above my lower lip with his forefinger, his own lips parted. Breath sweet on my brow. "I've been trapped all these years. Forced to hide my true nature behind the Glaith in this pendant, or risk drawing the Empire's eye. Knowing the key to my freedom was out there, risking her precious fucking life every day, fighting a war that ended *years* ago."

So close... I just needed one touch of his bronzed skin, or better, my pendant. Just one moment more with his perfect, intoxicating power... and then I'd make him eat every word, laughing as I consumed him...

"It hurts, doesn't it?" he whispered, letting me strain to the limit of my bonds, maintaining the minuscule distance between us with a smirk. "Being so close to what you need, yet unable to take it. *Five* years I went without, Mila. But don't worry," he whispered, flicking a lock of sopping wet hair over my shoulder. "I won't make you wait that long. No, you can have everything you want, right now. Show me, little Priestess. Give me your best," he said, cupping my face in warm, rough hands at last.

My eyes rolled back, jaw slackening on a soundless scream.

So *fucking* beautiful.

By the dead Goddess, *this* was divinity. I could drown in it, drink from him for years and never find the bottom.

But of course... he had to die. I had to gorge myself to bursting and leave him crumpled at my feet. The darkness demanded nothing less.

My eyes snapped open, finding the captain's inky gaze without err, and I reached for him. Claws aching to find purchase at the base of his throat—but the restraints stopped me.

"Aww, is that it?" he whispered, pressing closer now, his forehead bumping mine. His ki pulsing through my skin. "Come on, Menace. This is your *moment!* Don't hold back now!"

Well of course not! Not when he asked with such civilized charm. But I hadn't enough purchase. I needed... *more.* More contact with his skin, more of his ki, just—*more.*

My gaze dropped to his lips, to that stupid, arrogant smirk. Goddess, what I wouldn't give to chew it clean off his face. I bared my teeth, lunging. Catching his bottom lip between the sharp points of my canines, I pulled him into me. Threatening to draw blood should he attempt to pull away. Drawing on his ki and his skin both. Tasting him. Drinking him in.

He allowed it, the idiot. Smirking, his lips moved against mine as he threaded his fingers through my wild, knotted tresses. Mistaking my actions, he tried to deepen the intimacy, pouring his need into me as he shifted forward, angling my head back. Blood thick with ki, my jaw slackened on a ragged breath. Such power... this was *everything.* Even the pain of my injuries was forgotten beneath the wave of Elite ki flooding my being.

With a chuckle, the captain pressed me back. Taking liberties, slipping his tongue past my lips. Tasting *me.*

No. I wrapped the chains around my wrists, hoisting myself up, level with his face in spite of the lingering agony lacing my torso. Pain was temporary. Once I'd consumed the captain, I'd mend the tears in my skin. Knit broken bones with his life-force, and go on a little hunt for one murderous general...

He hummed when the darkness blazed to life between us, not cringing away as I expected, but embracing it. Offering up ki laced with a heady flavor I'd never come across.

Skin aching with fever, I shivered, reaching to the limits of my restraints. Kissing him back if it meant I could have more. Goddess, whatever this was, I wanted *more.*

And I would have it.

Lips crinkling against mine, he abandoned my hair, hands sweeping down my semi-nakedness, careful of torn flesh though he palmed my bottom. Kneading the muscle. Facial stubble prickling against me as he inhaled. Breathing me in.

Vision sparkling, I didn't fight when he lifted me, when he draped my legs around lean hips. I didn't resist when his fingers tightened on the back of my thighs, or when his tongue plunged into my mouth. No, I hooked my heels, securing an anchor as I feasted. Restoring myself.

No mundane man, this. No shallow well of ki I could drain in an instant and be left starving.

My pendant. It hung between us, *just* out of reach,

singing with the promise of *more*. And he let me pull him in. Let me feed as he busied himself with my lips, and when I found his core, he whispered, "That's it, Mila. Take what you need."

So much power! Years of his impossible ki stored within my long lost Glaith. Ripe and unattended. I moaned, breaking the kiss as my head lolled. Goddess, with power like this...

The captain chuckled. "Feeling better, pet?"

My thighs flexed about his waist. "You will kneel—"

"Threats?" He hummed, eyes raking my partial nudity. "I expected so much... *more* from you, what with all your bluster over the years," he said, threading his fingers through my hair, bringing my glassy eyes back to his.

I didn't respond—couldn't. Was there no end to this man? Already, my skin was too tight and yet, he showed no signs of failure.

He leaned back, planting one hand between my breasts, fingers splayed. "You're a little ball of untamed fire, aren't you? All passion and fury, no real direction. Strength with no training."

I flashed my teeth, breath coming in shallow pants.

Too—too much! Without the Grandmother to share the weight... it was too much! I couldn't contain it! Not without exploding like so much Glaith—

He tisked, shaking his head. "Such potential." Palm heating against my skin, his ki spiked into my chest. Diving deep.

Jaws gaping on a soundless scream, my back arched, pressing my chest into his hand as every muscle flexed against the invasion.

"Breathe, Mila," he purred, shifting his hand from

my breastbone to trace my wounds. "Good girl. That's it." The seams of my lashed skin tingled beneath his palm.

"Impossible," I rasped, garbling the word, glassy eyes rolling back, fixed to the ceiling as he commanded torn flesh to mend.

A dark chuckle whispered over my collarbone. "Hardly."

"How?" How had he come into such effortless control? Such mastery of his forbidden power? To heal was a *Priestess* gift!

"A tale for another time, perhaps," he said, cupping my broken ribs, his touch gentle on the outline of another man's knuckles. Repairing the damage with the ease of a gifted healer. Touching every forgotten space within me as he went. An Elite. Using the gifts of the Goddess. *Healing.* "You've lived a hard life, Mila," he whispered, attention moving to the scars framing the right side of my torso. "But that's over now. Let me erase—"

"No!" I snarled, writhing, trying to plant my heel in his sternum, to wrestle control back. To cast him out lest he take the one thing that linked me to her.

My Night Queen. Kas.

The captain's head tilted to the side, his dark gaze lingering on my lips. "In the Empire, scars are considered unsightly. A sign of the lower class."

I said nothing, having already said too much.

"Interesting. A bit sentimental, are we? Very well. The scars are yours to keep, if you wish." He flashed a quick grin, set my feet on the tiles, then stepped back, tugging a little black bag from his breast pocket. "On to your second surprise, then."

My heart leapt, splashing bile across the back of my tongue.

"I bought these the day we met," he said, pulling the drawstring and dumping the contents into his palm. Three delicate golden circlets—two small, one large—and a fourth. Thicker. Masculine.

I recoiled, as much as I was able, for the pure Glaith buried within the gold sang a sinister song. Promising things I didn't want to think about, reminding me of broken Priestesses kneeling in the dirt.

"The technology is a little crude," he admitted, setting the fourth circlet on the edge of the sink, "but it serves the purpose we need." He flicked a tiny hinge with his thumbnail, letting one of the smaller manacles swing open.

With a whine, I leaned back, watching the pretty gold sparkle in the dim lighting.

"Five years," he whispered, closing the gap between us once more, grinning. "I'm going to get in *so* much trouble for this."

"Don't touch me—"

Ignoring my attempt to knee him in the balls, the captain thumbed my chin, ki whipping through me at his touch. Uncontested, he slipped the two smaller manacles around my bound wrists, clicking them shut.

I squealed, back arching, trying to keep the Glaith off my skin. "Get it off me!"

Dark eyes glittering, the captain waited for me to settle. "Here's how this works, little Priestess—"

"Release me!"

He cleared his throat. "To anyone else, this is nothing more than pretty, golden jewelry. But to you"—he smirked—"to *me*, it's something else altogether."

I followed his every movement, unblinking. Heart pounding. "Let me go, Captain Rawlings."

"Do you see this little glass vial?" he asked, tapping said object of interest with his forefinger. When my eyes didn't waver from his face, he jerked his damp sleeve back from his wrist and claimed his knife. "It's quite simple, really. These chains have a heart of Glaith, and to bind us, they require a blood exchange." He glanced at my glittering wrists. "I can feel it burning you, you know. Even without these chains—without a true bond —we have a connection. Your blood calls to mine, Mila."

"My blood screams for your death!"

"Such fire," he murmured, grinning as he pushed matted, wet hair back from my face.

Above my head, my claws sunk deep into bloodless palms. "You will not do this."

In response, he nicked one of the many claw marks I'd left on his forearm and filled the glass vial with a single swipe through the crimson smear. At my wrists and in his hands, the chains glowed white-hot for an instant, then returned to their original golden hue before I'd registered any discomfort. "I understand the bond is quite painful at first, and I'm sorry for that." He stroked the delicate column of my throat and I hissed, trying to twist away. To avoid the collar. Heedless of my wishes, however, it snapped shut with a gentle click. Cold and inert against my skin.

Threats of harm were useless here! Against him. An empty bluff he didn't bother to call. I was restrained, cut off from the Grandmother and my dark Truth while he remained strong. In possession of that stupid pendant I'd risked so much to reclaim. My gaze flicked around the room, seeking something—*anything*—I could use. But there was nothing. Nothing but a smirking, victorious captain admiring his work.

"Beautiful." He turned, retrieving the fourth, masculine cuff from the sink. The tiny vial already filled with a splash of crimson I could only presume was my blood. Certainly, enough had been spilled to satisfy his sick need. The exchange.

Something inside me quivered. Seething with fury. No pretty golden bracelets could possibly hold one such as me! To allow it would be an insult I simply would not abide. It disintegrated—whatever flimsy dam held the darkness in check withered at my command. Hungry. Reaching.

"Too late," he murmured with a sad little shrug, then fit the final manacle to his right wrist—opposite the matte-black mark of the Empire on the other.

Fire erupted where gold touched my skin and darkness be damned, I screamed until my voice gave out.

It burned! *Burned!*

Writhing, I tried to scrape the molten gold off my skin before it chewed through my bones. Before it left me a headless, handless corpse! Without the air left to gasp, I flailed, my every muscle seized against icy-hot intensity the likes of which I could scarcely grasp.

Freezing and burning, I felt it spill through my veins, trickling toward my heart. Oozing and rushing, contradicting my every sense until there was nothing at all but agony, and I would have *begged* for mercy—given whatever he wanted—had I been able to utter the words.

When the pain ceased, I sagged. Limp, dangling

from the ceiling, sweat tracing every inch of my flushed, bedazzled skin.

"Shh," he whispered, propping me up, taking the weight off my shoulders. "It's over now, pet. It's over."

Breath rattled through my lungs, only to be trapped until stale. For I was set before a magnificent pillar of strength—a source of ki now melded to mine in a way I'd never known possible. The sheer magnificence of the power radiating from the captain blinded me to all else, and I blinked, raising my head to watch him from lowered lashes. Awestruck.

Bound.

Forever.

To *him*.

I sobbed, trying to swallow past the lingering pain in my throat as he hushed me, brushing a sweaty forelock away from my eyes.

The sweet release of darkness beckoned, but before I succumbed, I met his eye. "I hate you."

15

When I woke, it was with a gasp. I was lying on a couch in a dark room, a blanket wrapped around bare shoulders. Feet tucked in.

"Ah, shit. You're awake sooner than I expected. How are you feeling?"

I flung the blanket off, a flash of gold catching my attention before I could whirl to face the monster who had done this to me.

My new manacles gleamed in the dim light.

A wordless cry burst from my lips as I tried to dig a claw beneath the warm gold—only to stare dumbstruck at my perfect, manicured fingernails.

"I had Alicia trim them while you were sleeping," he said. "Claws aren't appropriate for a slave of the Empire, you understand. I still haven't quite decided what to do with your teeth. But Alicia was able to brush most of the tangles out of your hair, and it shouldn't be but a few more washings before it returns to its natural color. The dress is Alicia's doing as well," he continued, matter-of-fact as if to assure me that he hadn't done something untoward while I'd been at the mercy of his whim. "Your underthings were... unsalvageable, so..."

Nostrils flared, I scowled at the manacles, not gracing him with an acknowledgment as I lifted the gold with a blunt claw. But there would be no chafing, no getting snagged on clothing, and no itching beneath these bracelets. It was fused with my skin. Almost pliable.

"They're quite permanent."

I spun to face the chatty bastard, but tripped on a length of black silk. Dizzy and off balance without ki filling my center, I staggered—only just managing to catch myself before I tumbled face-first into the carpet. With a snarl, I righted myself, fists raised, back pressed to the armrest of the couch.

He was naked from the waist up, hair damp and mussed, his lower half encased in black slacks. I swallowed, hating my beautiful, glittering skin *almost* as much as the captain's stupid, gloating face.

And then I reached for my ki, to destroy him once and for all.

"What—" A strange, choked sound burst from my lips. "What have you done?" I melted against the couch, weak and dizzy, hand wrapped around the base of my throat in an effort to stop the tremble of tears from spilling over. "There's nothing—" Desperate, I tried to fling my ki wide, trying to get around the captain. "I can't"—my hands flew to my temples, blunt fingernails grazing my scalp—"it's gone! *It's all gone!*" I cast unseeing eyes around the room, looking for it. Goddess, what magic would allow Glaith to steal everything from me? Everything but... "*You,*" I snarled, rising again on shaking limbs. "I can't feel anything—except for *you*."

"Yes, well." He cleared his throat. "We *are* bound. There are certain to be some, ah, minor adjustments."

Trembling, I pressed a hand to my heart, over the place where I could feel his ki draining mine, leaching my strength like he'd been trying to do for the better half of a decade. A new, stronger link living and breathing behind my ribs.

This one unbreakable.

I dropped low, one foot braced on the arm of the couch, the other tucked beneath me. And, hiking my skirts up, I swallowed against the anguish of so much loss, and said, "Undo it," in a voice thick and clotted with tears.

He shrugged, buttoning his trousers with a little hop. "Not possible, I'm afraid."

A whimper splintered on its way past my lips, a cry that fought with the snarl imprinted on my face.

"Breathe," he cooed, foolish enough to close the distance between us.

With a hysterical shriek, I launched myself from the couch with every spare ounce of strength I yet possessed.

"Holy shi—*oomph*—" He stumbled back, catching me about the waist with both hands as I wrapped my legs around his hips, leaving my hands free.

My grip settled on his throat, trying to crush the life out of him with sheer force of will. Tears spilling freely down my cheeks to land on his.

But the captain would not be taken so easily, and claimed my wrists in his larger hands, grinding my bones as he twisted them back, away from his airway. "As feisty as ever, my wild little Priestess."

I strained toward him, trying to sink my teeth into the soft flesh of his throat. "I'm *not* yours!"

"See, that's where you're wrong," he said, and with very little effort, thrust me back, laughing when I landed on the couch in a graceless heap of tangled skirts. "You've been mine since the day Tritan fell. We're a matched set, you and I." Collecting a leather strap off the back of a winged chair, he looped the belt around his waist, then tucked his sidearm into the holster at his hip. "And now? No one can claim otherwise, no matter how displeased they might be with the outcome."

Emotion wrapped a frigid fist around my windpipe, clenching hard enough to choke any witty rebuttal—but I swallowed it back.

Now was *not* the time for tears and weakness.

Kas would not simply lay down and die if *she* were crippled. No. There was always another way out. Even without my ki, even maimed and broken, I'd find a way.

I *had* to.

I glanced at the door without moving my head, swiping at the trail of wetness marking my cheeks.

He sidestepped, blocking my path. "Go ahead and try it, pet. Even if you could manage to get free, you can't hide from *me*, little girl. Not anymore. Never again."

Cornered, I did the only thing I could think of, the only thing I *could* do without my ki—I punched him in the solar plexus and dove past his hip.

With little more than a grunt, he caught me about the middle, wrapping one thick arm over my ribs, the other around my throat. "Come now, violence isn't the answer."

"You're a *soldier*," I snarled, squirming against his hold. "You deal in violence and death." I planted an elbow in his belly, using all my might in an attempt to gain the upper hand.

He hefted me off my feet and tossed me on a great bed with dark sheets. "Says the woman covered in scars who murdered my best friend."

Scrambling to get my feet beneath me, I backed away, not stopping until I found the headboard. "Yes," I replied, droll. "I'm sure Marco's death was excruciating for you, given how impressively spry he is today. For a dead man. And for the record"—I flexed my right hand, flaunting the twisted, branded skin I'd won at our first meeting—"I am *honored* to wear these marks."

A deep chuckle rumbled through the room as he approached the bed, blocking my path to the door. "That's sweet, Mila. I'm touched. Really," he murmured, touching the mirror image of the spot where I felt him in my chest. "I can't tell you how much it pleases *me* to know you're honored to wear my mark."

"That's not—" I plunged my branded fist into the bedsheets, cheeks searing hot. "Not what I meant."

He laughed, lunging for my arm, but I threw myself in the opposite direction. Strong fingers circled my ankle instead, yanking me back from the edge of the mattress. Before I could muster any real fight, his grip was tangled in my hair, bodyweight pinning me to the mattress, skirts riding high on my thighs.

"Get off—"

"Relax, Priestess."

"Fuck you!"

Long fingers traced the hollow at the base of my throat. Traced the collar.

A shiver raced through my blood as I tried to heft his bulk off me, twisting away from the weapon digging into my belly. But I had no leverage, pinned as I was, and tried to twist away, voice a breathy whisper. "Stop. *Stop.*"

Face flushed, his fingers tightened in my hair, words hot against my cheek. "Miss Tannovic—"

"You will *not* call me that!"

Chest heaving, he sat back on his haunches—perched on my hips—running a hand through dark hair. Adjusting his sidearm. "You're my *slave*. I'll call you whatever I want."

A tiny, fragile hiccup popped free of my lips before I could choke it down. And so, "Please, release me," held a note of piteous begging, instead of an enraged command. Mortified and holding back sobs, I clawed at the gold bonded with my skin, leaving ragged trails of red everywhere my touch landed. Choking back ragged screams.

He simply gathered my wrists and put his weight into them. Stilling my fight. "And where will you go? Will the forest recognize its mistress without her ki?"

With that, what little remained of my composure shattered, and I reached again for that which was no longer mine to wield.

"You belong to me now," he whispered, "and that belonging comes with my protection. You'll be cared for, Mila."

"I don't need your protection," I hissed through clenched teeth, blinking away those damnable tears. "I will not be used as a weapon by you or your men. I would rather die."

With a sigh, he rolled off me and gathered a black

button up shirt, shrugging into it and hiding his sidearm from sight. "You needn't worry on that account. I don't intend to share."

Hiding beneath billowing skirts, I righted myself, injecting my words with scorn. "Be still my heart."

Dark laughter rumbled through the room. "It's not your heart I desire, slave."

In spite of the tears, something slipped in my mind. A savage, toothy grin spread across my face and I tucked my feet beneath me once more. "You're welcome to try for more."

"Another time, perhaps, if you insist. But come along. There are some very important men on their way to meet you."

"They can wait all day."

For the space of a dozen breaths, we glared at each other. Dark eyes to light. Neither backing down.

"Don't spoil my good mood, Mila. You won't like the consequences."

"You're mistaking me for someone who cares." I laughed, head light and spinning. "You've taken every-thing from me."

His face twisted in the shadows. "More than you know."

"What more could there possibly be? What else could you do?"

But it was his turn to hold his silence.

I slipped off the bed, stalking past an ornate wooden desk, fists clenched. "It doesn't matter what pathetic little punishments you can dream up." A tremor rippled through my body, but I spread my arms wide. "I belong to no one. I am the darkness. You cannot hold me, *Captain.*"

Eyes gleaming, he said, "Have you forgotten, then? What *I* am?" He took a step closer. "I am your match, girl. In *everything*. Or rather"—the nasty little smile returned to the edges of his lips—"*was*. Now?" The captain traced the glitter of gold at his wrist. The match to my set, set and fused against his wrist. "You're a pretty pet on a leash. A symbol of power to be cared for. Cherished. Nothing more." Buttoning his sleeve, the captain took a breath, tugging my mother's pendant from his trouser pocket then slipped it over his head with mocking care. "You'll adjust. I will *help you* adjust. But until then... come. The general will be in my kitchen in ten minutes, and I don't trust you up here alone."

I stilled. "General Tilcot?"

He finished buttoning his shirt, eyebrow raised. "The very same."

The man who'd slaughtered my father and led the attack on my people was within striking distance, and I was permanently without the power to kill him? Was there no end to this humiliation?

I bared my teeth, quaking with a fury I'd never known. And yet... if the general was here, then his enslaved Trila-Glís wasn't far.

If it were possible to taste that darkest of Truths once more, *she'd* know how it could be done.

"Stop."

Startled, I glared at him.

"Whatever little plot you're cooking up can wait, Miss Tannovic. I promise you, now is not the time to test your new limits."

"Then unless you'd like to see the innards of that foul man, you will leave me here and hope I don't set the place ablaze in your absence."

The captain returned my scowl. "As much as I may like to take you up on that insane offer, I can't." He cleared his throat. "I may have bypassed a few of the proper channels to claim you. The general needs to be... appeased."

"Am I to smile prettily, then?" I bared modified canines, simpering. Playing Alicia's damnable part, and badly. "Would you have me get down on my knees? Praise his untouchable, Elite power? Would you have me stroke his cock—"

"Enough," the captain snapped, seizing my wrist and yanking me flush to his chest, pendant a hard dead lump between us. "Speak that way in front of him, and you'll be lucky if a public whipping is the only thing he gives you." He shook me. "Do you think I relish the notion of involving you?" He laughed, dark and cruel. "There isn't a rational bone in your entire fucking body. I expect the general will spend this conversation provoking you, just to see you react as you did last night in the baths! He'll start by insulting your people—"

"Every breath he draws is an insult to my people. Every breath *you* draw—"

The captain passed a hand over his face, pinching the bridge of his nose. "My *point*, Mila. If you'd like to continue breathing, I recommend you keep your mouth shut in front of my superiors. Do you understand me?" His voice dropped an octave. "I'm not above gagging you."

"Your threats are meaningless, parasite." I tossed my hair, ignoring the silky texture. The absence of tangles and burrs. "I have leverage."

"Oh? And how do you plan on using that leverage, you little lunatic?" He took a single, fluid step, herding me back. "Will you tell them you're a rogue Trila-Glís who's survived in the wood all this time, unmolested?"

I said nothing.

"Brilliant plan. Except, of course, for the fact that the Empire already possesses both of the confirmed Trila-Glís Priestesses recognized by your faith, and that *you*, Mila, cannot provide proof of your claim. Not now." He leaned forward, obsidian eyes glittering. "I own your power, and I will not allow you to jeopardize yourself by exposing us to the general *or* the Empire." He took another step. "But let's say for a moment that you can convince him Sasha and Carly aren't the only living Trila-Glís. That man"—the backs of my knees bumped a desk in the center of his room—"already owns the High Priestess. He's furious that I claimed you without permission, but what do you think will happen should he discover the truth of your power? He is bound to the most powerful of your kind, and holds unprecedented favor with the royal family. His power and resources are all but unlimited. How far do you think he'll go to double it? To be the first to possess *two* Trila-Glís?"

Heart pounding, I leaned back as far as possible, hating the breath warming the base of my throat. "Let him come for me. I will end his pitiful existence, no matter the cost."

"With *what*, Mila?" The captain claimed both of my wrists in one hand. "Your great physical strength?" Strong fingers circled my throat, subduing me with mocking ease. "Your saucy little mouth?" He cut off my airway with a gentle squeeze, silencing me, then kneed my thighs apart. "Without your power, you are *nothing*." His lips hovered too close, scant millimeters from... *more*. "You don't know how lucky you are to be *mine*."

Reaching for my ki, for whatever was left, I tried in vain to slaughter this impossible Elite and use his life-force for fuel—but the link between us pulsed. Filling *him* instead. "S-Stop," I rasped, forcing air past his fingers.

Releasing my throat, he pressed closer, scruffy day-old beard scratching my cheek, lips brushing my ear. "Do you think *he* will stop if you ask nicely? If you beg?"

Trembling against muscular frame, I couldn't find the words to refute him. Could only stand there in a mocking embrace, utterly defeated.

The captain's free hand skated the length of my back, callouses rasping at exposed flesh—a back absent the cruelty of a slaver's whip by *his* mercy. Healed by the last of the rare and dangerous things.

"He will see your fire, Miss Tannovic." The captain's touch settled on my lower back, blunt nails raising gooseflesh. "And if you are foolish enough to reveal yourself to him, General Tilcot will take what he wants and leave nothing behind." Inky black eyes darted to my lips for an instant, then returned to my face. "*I* would see you flourish."

Flourish? As a caged beast? I pushed at his bulk, swallowing an anguished howl.

But he buried his hands in my silky, unknotted tresses, pressing my lower back against the desk and forcing me to look at him. "I need your obedience in this."

Kas' fury rippled beneath my skin. Obedience? To him?

"Tilcot will enjoy killing you."

And without my ki, I was helpless to defend myself —all because of Captain-fucking-Rawlings and his insane obsession! "How well you've trapped me," I said at length. "A perfect cage. But..." I trailed off, tapping the pendant with the tip of a blunt claw. "But *your* power is not so easy to hide, is it? I wonder what will happen should the general find out what *you* are..." I met his eye. "I wonder what the general would do if he found out there is *already* an Elite wielding the power of two Trila-Glís."

For a moment, the captain did nothing but watch me with a narrow glare. "A bargain, then," he said, and smirked. "Make your demands, Menace."

"Release me—"

"Come on, Mila. You can do better than that."

I scowled, trying—and failing—to push him from my personal bubble, for at the moment, I *couldn't* do better than that. Not now, with a head full of impotent chaos and the echo of darkness smothered by his light.

"The High Priestess," I gasped at length. "I want a private meeting with the High Priestess."

He pulled back, just a little. "Do you, now?"

"No Elites. No soldiers. No filthy Caledonians breathing down my neck. Just me and the High Priestess —" I paused, racking my memory for her given name. "Sasha. That is the price of my silence."

"That's quite the ask," he drawled, kneading the back of my neck in an almost thoughtless manner. "But I'm afraid if you want a private meeting with the general's slave, it's going to cost more than your silence."

I stilled, hyper aware of where he was pressed against me. Of just how vulnerable I was without my power.

"I want your obedience," he whispered, shifting, thumbs tracing my cheek bones.

"And I want your head on a spike—"

"In front of the others, you will act the simple girl who lived in a forest," he said, pressing closer. Covering me from hip to chest with heat and the unspoken.

Hands braced on his wrists, I swallowed it down, conceding the point to my impossible Elite. Strike once, or not at all. "Get off me."

"Do you yield?"

My lip curled.

His nails scraped my scalp. "*Do you yield?*"

"Yess," I hissed, shoving at his too-firm chest. "I will do my best to leave your precious General Tilcot intact, and you will get me time with the High Priestess."

He grinned. "Deal. Now—"

"Get off me."

Nostrils flared, the captain ignored my attempt to separate us. "You will not speak unless spoken to."

"Ha!"

"You'll address me," he said, clasping a palm over my lips, "and anyone who speaks directly to you as 'Sir' or 'Mistress'."

I choked on helpless rage.

"Unless, of course, they are a slave, and then you may use one word sentences." He released my lips. "Do you understand?"

A shiver prickled at my skin, blood pounding in my ears. "Yes."

"Yes, what?"

I glanced at the spot pulsing beneath his jaw, hovering too close. Looming over me. His knee lodged between mine. To strike him now would result in injury to myself and offer nothing in the way of forward progress.

"Yes what, slave?" he drawled, inky pools gleaming above me. Lips twitching at the corner.

Oh, how the pain of retaliation would be worth it for the chance to bleed him dry! But I swallowed that too, and forced, "Yes, *sir*," through clenched teeth.

Stepping back, he smirked. Extending his hand. "Then you shall have your meeting, Miss Tannovic."

16

———

Scowling, I pushed off his desk, righting my skirts with far more force than was necessary. Noting, for the first time since waking, just how *much* skin was exposed by the silk draped around my body. Crossing once over my back, the fabric hung low, leaving me naked from hairline to hip, though it passed over my modest breasts before ending in an elegant twist around my neck.

Bloody impracticable rag. How was I to run with a skirt brushing the tops of my feet? How did one fight without the ability to take a wide, braced stance? I closed my eyes, dragging a breath into tight lungs.

The High Priestess. She'd know what to do. I just had to endure long enough to speak with her.

A calloused palm landed on my nape.

"Don't touch me," I snapped, bracing for the flood of ki that never came.

His smirk didn't falter. "It's what they'll expect, little Priestess."

I flexed my jaw, glancing again at the fleshy bit

where his pulse fluttered. Would I need leverage, or would I be able to climb him like a redwood? I picked at the gold marking my wrist.

"What murderous little thoughts are floating through your head, hmm?"

"I would like to bury my teeth—"

With a snort, the captain cut me off. "Sometimes it's better to say nothing, girl." He steered me from his room toward a narrow staircase. "Especially now. Lead him to think you're simple. That your brain has been addled by your time in the forest." The captain seized the pendant, glassy eyes staring through the bricks and mortar. "Give him no reason to think of you past this moment, and we may just come through this unscathed."

That the sentiment was almost *exactly* the same advice Alicia had given did not escape me. Had the little traitor been working with them all along? Conspiring to lure me from the Grandmother's embrace?

I couldn't help but think of the day we'd been captured. Had Alicia flown into danger without hesitation, not because of my insidious influence, but because she'd been paid to do so? Perhaps she'd been planting ideas in *my* head, leading me to be a docile thing with a pleasant temperament—and it had escaped my notice until it was too late?

Digging my blunted nails into the meat of my palm, I simmered, trying to find clarity through the layers of swampy, murky confusion and festering rage.

Alicia and the captain would have me play the part.

Kas would bide her time, strike when the moment was perfect.

And of course... Belle would have begged me to wait for reinforcements.

Something wicked danced in my chest. Something akin to *hope,* though I hadn't trusted that accursed trick of a foolish heart since I'd watched a deity burn. But Belle... Belle was the leader of the rebel army, and someone I could presume was free of corruption, no matter which side Alicia pledged her loyalty to.

That clever, vexing Triloth would move the mountain to claim a captured Trila-Glís, so her mundane brats might grow up knowing the comfort of a secure future.

My heart stopped racing as the captain guided me down a narrow hallway.

All was not lost, not yet. No, even bound to Captain Asher Rawlings. Even without my ki and all that defined me, I was not powerless. Not with me here, in the bedchamber of the enemy—not with Belle and her good men moving a mountain to us.

"Well, would you look at that," Marco crowed when we rounded the corner. Elbows braced on a granite kitchen counter, he continued, "The wildcat is all creepy smiles this morning. You really can charm them, can't you, old man?"

"Don't give me too much credit," the captain drawled. "I happen to know the reason for that smile is better left locked away inside her lovely, mad head."

I let the murderous thoughts play on my lips, grinning at Marco. "Unlike your master, I'm happy to share."

Marco straightened, palms raised, eyes wide.

The captain spun me, pinning me with an inky glare. "Come now. Failure so soon?" He tisked, jerking his chin over my shoulder. "Apologize to Marco for your rudeness, pet, or our bargain is off."

A tremor ran through me, but I closed my eyes, resisting the urge to reach for something that wasn't there. And then I turned, rigid, flashing Marco the widest smile I could muster. "My humblest apologies, *sir.*"

Sorry I cannot paint the walls with your blood and feast on your ki. Sorry I cannot wear your innards as a string of bile-soaked pearls, and winter inside your bloated stinking corpse.

Marco swallowed, throat working as his lips parted.

"Good morning, sir. I've got pork an' hash on for breakfast, and—*oh!*" Alicia cried, treacherous green eyes going wide as they flew over me. "Priestess! You alright, lass?" she asked, rushing to my side, her pretty face still marked with slaver's bruises.

I jerked back, bumping into the captain's hard frame, teeth bared.

She paled beneath the sickly yellow patch shadowing her left eye. "I-I only mean that your injuries were—they were gruesome, and—"

"Don't concern yourself with my well-being, traitor," I hissed, pressing deeper into the captain to avoid her touch.

Alicia's jaw dropped. "What—"

"Normally I'd enjoy watching two women get physical," Marco said, moving to stand at Alicia's back, hands on her shoulders, lips to her ear. "But let's not pick a fight with this one, pretty girl." He tugged Alicia behind him, whispering at full, theatrical volume. "You can never tell if the crazy ones are going to purr or bite. And you don't want to be wrong with the wildcat here."

The captain snorted, tucking my pendant under his shirt. Out of sight. Black gaze flicking over his shoulder before a tight, false smile graced his lips.

Eyes narrowed, I noted the tension in his shoulders. The hard edge to his lips. The white knuckles of the fist not tight on the back of my neck.

We had company. He could sense it coming.

Marco straightened, the humor falling off his face when he, too, noted the change in his master. "How many?"

"Just Tilcot."

"No guard?"

The captain shook his head, lips pressed in a thin, white line.

"Good. That's good," Marco said, arms crossed. "Means he's only here to scold you for being naughty."

"Scold him?" Alicia squeaked. "Is he—are we in trouble, then?"

"No, no, pretty girl," Marco soothed, petting the weapon at his hip. "Just a bit of broken protocol. Nothing important."

Ignoring the banter, I strained, listening for the heavy footfall of Elites. Straining for that which was not there.

The air pressure shifted, making the window panes chatter in their frames.

"I'll have a bowl of that hash, Alicia," the captain said, tracing my nape with his thumb. "And one for Mila."

My lip curled, but I did not acknowledge my parasite further, for my every available sense was fixed upon the kitchen door. On the *clomp clomp clomp* of boots in the hall. The whine of a squeaky hinge as it swung open to reveal the very man whose screams I'd serenaded myself with when the nightmares had been too much.

General Tilcot. A scowling tower of muscle surveying the room with stormy eyes, his gaze landing first on the captain before falling on me.

I ground my teeth, blunted claws pressing into my palms. Meeting the general's glare with my own, muscles coiled. Tight.

The captain's fingers tightened on my neck. A silent warning—and one I would abide.

For the Trila-Glís and the rebels.

For Kas.

Again, my eyes fluttered closed.

Play the part.

Taking a breath, I tucked a knotted length of caramel hair behind my ear, bowed my head, and said nothing. Did nothing. Painting a gory mosaic of death and destruction as I stared at the floorboards.

Alicia cleared her throat, drawing my eye and breaking the terse silence with a brittle smile. "Good mornin', sir," she said, scooping greasy muck into a bowl. "May I offer bit o'refreshments or—"

"Leave," the general barked.

Caught in the middle of her task, Alicia froze, mouth agape. Looking to her master for direction, color staining bruised cheekbones.

The captain nodded. "Thank you, Alicia."

Pressing her hand to her heart, Alicia fled, followed a moment later by Marco as General Tilcot filled the small kitchen.

Something wicked plucked at the general's lips as he approached, coming to a stop directly before me. "So."

The captain cleared his throat, palm clammy on the

back of my neck. "May I introduce my Priestess, Mila. She doesn't talk much, but—"

"Explain yourself, soldier."

"It was an accident—"

Head thrown back, the general laughed. "An accident, was it? You slipped, fell, and *oops,* bound a Priestess to yourself *without permission?* Do you have any idea how angry the curator is? This little trollop should be on her way to the capital, ready to take a bastard in her belly for the Empire. But she's *here,* bound to *you.*"

Forced pregnancy? My eyes flicked to the captain's profile as something sickly squirmed in my chest.

"I am prepared to answer for my mistake, sir," the captain said. "But it *was* an accident. I acted on a little too much whiskey and a hunch I got from Jasper's ramblings about forest demons and dark magics. Who could have expected the wood's menace was actually a Priestess?"

"Who indeed," the general drawled.

"When I saw her at auction," the captain continued, tucking a length of knotted brown hair over my shoulder, "I put the chains on her, thinking, 'wouldn't it be something if this little hellion was of the Blood?'"

The general sneered, eyes roaming my face. "My, *my.* How *convenient.*"

"Believe me, sir, I wasn't expecting—"

"To be clear," he said, and seized me by the throat, ignoring my startled yelp. "You saw this... *thing* on the auction block and all the pieces just fell into place, did they?"

"No—"

Teeth bared, I tried to wrench free, both hands on his wrists.

Goddess, burn these Elites and their fascination with my airway! I'd make him suffer the pain of all the refugees I'd freed before he begged for death on his knees like the parasite he was! Muscles coiled, I reached for my ki—but his touch gave me nothing. Not a spark, not a tingle.

Nothing.

The general grinned, fingers tight enough to leave marks and cut off my air. "She has the look, I suppose," he continued, eyes narrowing at my hair. "But her coloring is wrong. Her hair was darker yesterday, wasn't it? Dye, I suppose. And her temperament?" He laughed, batting my hands away when I took a swing at his stupid, smug face. "Tell me, Asher. What was it about Jasper's story that inspired this fortuitous little hunch of yours?"

"You were there, Harper," he spat. "Have you ever known fully grown trees to overtake a road in *days?* You've heard the stories over the years, just as I have. And you know better than most what a thorn that place has been for the Empire. The Forest of Sorrows, stained black after Tritan's fall? There had to be *something* causing it. Something *other.* Now with all due respect, *sir,*" the captain said, voice clipped. Tight. "Get your hands off my Priestess."

A nasty smirk creased the general's lips, but after a moment he thrust me back, gasping, into the captain's arms. "You're lying."

Choking on fresh air, I scowled, rubbing at my throat. Trembling fingers brushing my new collar.

"No Triloth Priestess has the power to do that, unless—"

I snarled, trying to recover my feet, murder in my

veins. He was right. I was no Triloth Priestess—he'd learn that just before I swallowed everything he was and—

"Unless," the captain said, dumping me on the floor in a disoriented heap, and stepped up to his superior, knuckles popping at his sides. "Unless she was working *with* the rebels. It's the *only* explanation that makes senses. The Empire already has both Trila-Glís," he continued, oh-so-reasonably, setting a clenched fist on the kitchen counter. "The only way they could compete with us, is if they have indeed made advancements with their technology. Advancements that would allow a simple Triloth to manipulate ki as if she were more than she is."

Jaw slack, I stared at the captain, my theories about Alicia's treachery growing solid roots in Caledonian soil.

The general crossed thick arms over a barrel chest. "I'm listening."

"It would mean you were right, *sir*. Capturing technology like that would turn the tide of this war overnight."

"And our little demon here can support these claims?"

"It doesn't matter what she says," the captain said, flicking a dismissive hand before my face. "That she exists—that she evaded the Empire for so long—is proof enough. You said it yourself. No Triloth could possibly have access to that much power."

The general sneered. "Then where is this technology?"

"My guess?" the captain asked, hooking his thumbs into his belt, finger a hair away from his sidearm. "Jasper. He was the one who brought her in. He'll be the one who has her personal effects, unless he was too stupid to gather them. But at the very least, he'll be able to point us in the right direction. Show us where she was captured."

I caught the outrage before it flew from my throat, fixing my gaze to the floor.

The High Priestess was worth my silence.

Belle and the rebels were worth my patience.

Vengeance was worth biting through my tongue to stop it wagging at will.

Deep breath in, deep breath out.

"Fine." The general rolled his eyes. "I'll accept your little theory and have the slaver brought in for questioning. I've a few... *extraction* techniques I've been looking forward to trying on some hapless traitor anyway."

The captain swallowed, only a little green around the edges. "Thank you, sir."

"Oh, it's not me you should be thanking," the general replied, straightening. "I argued for tossing your ass in a cell and having this little slut taken from you, but the curator wants to see what you can do with your new power. So the Golden Boy gets a free pass."

The captain shrugged. "Then thank the curator for me."

"You can thank him yourself. He'll be here in three days to interrogate your girl, but in the meantime," the general continued, "our little menace will report to the infirmary with the rest of the Priestesses so Sasha can have her power assessed, look her over for"—he sneered—"diseases, and give her a tour of the facility, if there's time. She doesn't get special treatment just because she's dimwitted."

A sharp bark of laughter burst from my lips.

Meeting with the High Priestess was *commonplace?* Expected, even? The captain was playing me better than I thought.

"Of course, sir," the captain said, drawing me off the floor, only to clap his hand over my mouth.

"I want her at HQ before first rotation ends. And do something about her temperament, hmm? Or I will." Evil spread over the general's face when I tried to buck the captain's touch. "I would hate to see her taken from you, should the curator decide you're unfit to rule a Priestess. Even one as undesirable as her."

"I find her temperament fitting for a man of ambition," the captain retorted, his voice easy, though his fingers too were leaving marks on my jaw.

The general snorted, pausing at the door. "Very well. You will report to HQ for first rotation. There's been some unusual stirrings on the frontlines and we may have to send the Special Forces out to investigate." He disappeared around the corner as quickly as he'd come, sending a brisk, "Good day, Captain Rawlings," over his shoulder.

Trembling, I was scarcely able to wait until the door had closed before I lifted my foot, trying to crush the captain's toes beneath my heel.

He grunted, hefting me off the ground with one arm wrapped around my torso. "Does it thrill you, Miss Tannovic? To test me so?"

I pried his palm away from my lips, wrenching his thumb back until he was forced to oblige me or suffer the irritation of a dislocated thumb. "You're a filthy liar—"

Chuckling, the captain tightened his grip, yanking his hand free from mine and burying it in my hair.

"Liar?" he purred, lips brushing my ear. "Whatever do you mean? I gave you exactly what you asked for, even though *you* broke our deal..."

Scowling as his heat began to infect me, I planted my feet against the kitchen counter and pushed, launching us back with a strangled war cry.

He hit the wall with a dull thud, expelling his breath against my ear in a great burst. "Well, that was stupid," he rasped, sinking to the floor and bringing me with him. Tangling his long legs with mine, he dragged my head back, forcing me to rest against his shoulder. Helpless and pinned. "You let your temper burn up all your leverage."

"You *knew*," I hissed, squirming between his thighs, pendant a cold and useless thing lodged between my shoulder blades. His sidearm bruising my hip. "A meeting with the High Priestess was mine whether you could arrange it or not."

"Perhaps," he said, stubble rasping against my cheek, imprinting a smirk on my skin.

Heart pounding at the back of my throat, I tried to wriggle free. "You got exactly what you wanted, free of charge."

"I usually do."

I snarled, planting an elbow in his ribs. "Enjoy it while it lasts, parasite."

He hummed against my ear. "Oh, I intend to."

17

As if summoned from nothing, Marco appeared at the captain's side, grinning down at us. "See? Just a gentle spankin'."

"Yes, well," the captain snorted, releasing me at last, though his inky gaze followed as I scrambled to my feet, putting the kitchen counter between us. "We're not quite free of trouble just yet."

Marco tugged a cigarette from behind his ear, twirling it between forefinger and thumb. "That's the only perk of working for you, sir. Always exciting."

"You're sure it's not the—"

"It's not the pay," Marco said, rolling his eyes. "It's knowing I get all your stuff when you die."

The captain rose from the floor, knees popping. "Then I guess it's a good thing I'm not trusting you to watch my back today, isn't it?" he asked, straightening his shirt collar.

I tossed a length of slick, caramel hair over my shoulder and said, "Perspective is a fascinating thing, isn't it?"

"You'll be escorting my new pet to the infirmary," the captain continued, lips tilted in a pleasant, obnoxious smile. "Feel free to gag her, should you be so inclined."

"Captain! *No.* Baby-sitting duty? For *her?* You recall what happened the last time, yes? I believe you said something along the lines of, 'Don't worry. She's just a terrified little girl. She's nothing but bluster, Marco. You'll be perfectly safe.'" The solder laughed, showing the whites of his palms as he took a step back. "And then, if you'll recall, *I died!* What did I do to deserve—"

"And now," the captain said, dark eyes finding mine, "she really is nothing but bluster. Isn't that right, pet?"

Scowling at the tiles, I couldn't gather the strength to speak. Knowing him to be right.

"You're perfectly safe this time, pup, and I need you there," the captain continued. "The general is punishing me with first rotation."

"Yeah, yeah, I heard," Marco said, flicking his wrist.

"Then give me your weapon, you big baby. You'll be my eyes for the morning."

Grumbling, Marco did as he was asked, handing over a battered, matte-black piece with an ornate handle. "You're a cruel, cruel man, Captain Rawlings."

"Stop pouting." The captain pressed both hands to the hilt, features drawn and tight. And then, for the first time since we'd been bound, ki surged to life within me —making my manacles burn anew.

I gasped, staring at my wrists, jaw slack.

The chains were *melting!* Filling my veins with molten gold, each beat of my heart fanning the flames, forcing them to spread. Building an inferno even as my ki abandoned me. Fed by my Elite symbiote, Marco's weapon lit the room, glowing with a searing intensity matched only by the agony spreading through my very blood.

Skin flushed with stolen ki, the captain laughed, ending my torment as quickly as it had begun. "My God, Mila, your power!"

Gasping, I wobbled, sweat tracing the length of my back. Soaking my hairline.

"Shiiiiit, Asher," Marco said, slapping his commanding officer on the back. "The wildcat packs a helluva punch! And I'm not talking literally, though"—he tapped his still-bruised cheek—"I can attest to that as well."

The captain tossed Marco his weapon with a careless buoyancy, watching me rub the lingering torment from wrists and throat. "Yes. She does."

"I've never seen a weapon charge so quickly. But her arms... and face..." The soldier trailed off, watching me from the corner of his eye. Shifting his weight from left to right.

"Do *not* leave her side," the captain stressed. "She's an unpredictable, reckless little lunatic, and I can't afford another near miss like the debacle in the baths. Tilcot is already far too interested."

"Captain," Marco said, holstering his weapon, "the infirmary is the most heavily guarded building in the north. Surely you don't need *me* there."

"It's not *her* safety I'm worried about," the captain drawled, rolling his shirt sleeves back to reveal not *one* manacle marking his wrists, but two. Black and gold. Right and left. "It's theirs."

"*Theirs?*" Marco squawked, setting his weight onto the kitchen counter. "Come on, mate. I know she's...

different, but she's just a little thing. You're not going to cause any trouble, are you little lady?"

"Course not," I whispered, and hauled myself to a full stand. "You've absolutely nothing to worry about." I flashed him a smile that went no further than my lips, trembling from the captain's latest assault. "I'm a perfect lady. Perfectly poised."

For a moment, Marco stared at me, cigarette dangling lax between his fingers. And then, "Reckless lunatic. Gotcha. She won't get out of my sight, sir."

He lit his smoke.

18

The infirmary.

A dank, single-story building tucked well back from the dangerous strip of the front lines, unassuming with its pockmarked gray walls and tiny blacked-out windows. And yet, it boasted the *one* thing I was both ill-prepared to deal with *and* needed desperately.

Priestesses.

The memory of their pure, white ki teased my deadened senses. Goddess, if I could just brush against that sweet power, even if it was tainted with the stink of Elite. Corrupted. Even if doing so tempted the darkness and drove me to a life of eternal solitude.

I ached for the torment, for the moment that it would be mine once more. But I did *nothing*, for the bond—that accursed, ravenous thing—writhed in my chest, tugging at what was left without his hand on my skin.

Scowling, I picked at the gold at my wrist, leaving the brand unmolested for the first time in five years, for

I had something else far, far *worse* to claw into bloody ribbons.

At least he wasn't *here*, irritating me with every breath, with every word that crossed his stupid lips. Every brain muddling, unwanted touch. At least I could *think* in his absence, because this *was* the most heavily guarded building I'd yet seen and if there was a way out, I needed every ounce of attention span I could get.

Elites dotted the perimeter of the room, dark eyes flicking over the rows of beds without ceasing, hands on their weapons. And down to the man, each was marked with a golden band encircling their left wrists.

They were bound Elites. Each augmented with the stolen might of a Priestess, just like the captain, and as a unit, they presented a formidable obstacle indeed. But... they were bound to *Triloth* Priestesses, for if General Tilcot had claimed the High Priestess, it would follow that a man of similar rank would have the remaining known Trila-Glís at his disposal.

And so far as I'd seen, such a man wouldn't sully himself with simple baby-sitting duty, regardless of how *many* silver-blonde heads were packed into this building. To *most*, the wall of Elites bloated with the power of the Goddess' chosen would be sufficient deterrent. But to a rare and dangerous thing on the cusp of reclaiming freedom?

Something wicked settled on my lips. How... *considerate*. To gather the Blood here, in one convenient place. Ripe for the taking.

My nose wrinkled, assailed by the coppery tang of spilled blood and a sour pinch of feces as we passed a man writhing on a narrow cot.

Marco's hand landed on my shoulder, guiding me away from the unfortunate, doomed soul.

"Don't," I hissed, trying—and failing—to jerk away from his touch. "Take me to the High Priestess."

"I'm working on it," Marco said, crushing his smoke beneath the heel of his boot. Watching me from the corner of his eye. "She's a busy woman and there's a lot of people here. Have to wait our turn."

A strangled shout came from somewhere out of sight, though few of the silver-blonde heads bothered to turn toward it. Most were occupied with the patients before them. Gentle, pale hands checked temperatures, set a twisted forearm, and three among them called for aid to manage more complicated patients.

My stomach lurched as understanding—horrible and undeniable—dawned. "They're...*helping* them."

"Of course they are," Marco said, brows climbing toward his hairline. "Your kind are healers. Women-magics, and whatnot."

Ah, yes. Arrogance. I swallowed the grin, picking at my collar. Women-magics, indeed. He'd be choking on it when I was finished here. "I'm no healer," I said at length, showing off my scarred right hand as evidence to my claim, "and I'll have no part in giving aid to the parasites who feed on Tritan Blood."

"They're not all soldiers, wildcat." He raised his arm to point. "That appears to be a pregnant woman struggling with childbirth, though by definition... I suppose it is a *literal* parasite."

I scoffed, scanning the crowd of silver-blonde heads for one woman. "Where is she?"

"Probably in her office. Over there," he said, jerking his chin toward the far side of the room.

I followed his gaze.

"Like I said, she's busy. We'll have to wait—"

Oh, I was quite through with waiting. Without hesitation, I pushed past an Elite not much taller than myself, making a direct line toward the High Priestess.

"Sonofabitch—Wildcat, stop. You can't just—"

"Can't I?" I sneered, spinning around a Priestess laden with a stack of fluffy white towels.

"Oy! Get back here!"

Ignoring him, I slipped through the crowd, letting his bulky size work to my advantage, not stopping until I was a scant few feet from a door marked, *Private*, complete with a stocky Elite standing guard.

He blocked my path. "Not so fast, girl."

"I have business with the High Priestess," I snapped, fists clenched at my sides.

The Elite crossed his arms, smirking down at me. "Is that so?"

"Sorry, Jackson," Marco said, catching up and seizing my arm. "Captain's new girl is a right wild little terror. Needs a leash."

"And a firm hand, by the look of it," Jackson said, smirking.

"Right, well. That hand is supposed to be mine, for the time being. Captain put me on babysitting duty, the sadistic prick."

Jackson snorted. "Got a runner, huh?"

"Apparently. And she's a vicious little bitc—oomph!"

I dropped an elbow in Marco's belly, this time successful in dislodging his hand—but paid for it, twofold. Jackson caught my wrist before I could strike again, yanking me off balance and pinning me to the wall, his forearm set against the back of my neck.

"What's all the commotion?" the High Priestess asked, standing in the doorway with hands pressed to lips. "Goddess, Jackson! Release her. This is Mila," she continued, tugging me to her side when the soldier did as she bade. "The new Priestess. She's here for an assessment, remember? General Tilcot sent her."

Jackson adjusted his shirt collar. "Someone needs to teach this new Priestess some manners."

"Yes, of course," the High Priestess replied, chin dipping. "Mila will behave, won't you, dear?"

I licked my lips, eyes tracking the length of Jackson's throat. "Of course."

The High Priestesses' fingers tightened on my elbow. "Marco, would you mind standing guard with Jackson? I'd like to have a private chat with Mila. See how she's coping with the change."

"She can throw a tantrum with the door open," Marco snapped, massaging his gut. "I have my orders, Sasha."

"I need *silence* to assess her abilities," the High Priestess pressed. "My power isn't what it once was, you understand."

For a moment, Marco continued to scowl. Then he rolled his eyes, muttering something about the agony of babysitting, and said, "This is the only way into your office?"

She nodded.

"Fine." He stepped aside, allowing us into the neat —if crowded—little space. A far cry from the opulent splendor that was the High Priestess' former office. But it was indeed *private.* "Just leave the door open, and we have a deal."

"Can we compromise with unlocked?" the High

Priestess asked, flashing him a beautiful smile. "The infirmary is never quiet for long."

My lips curled back. Who was this docile, submissive creature? Where was the High Priestess from memory? The fierce leader of women who lived and fought battles in my dreams?

Marco scowled at me. "Fine. Ten minutes."

"Ten minutes," the High Priestess repeated, shooing the men from the room.

The instant we were alone, I wedged a chair beneath the doorknob, though I did so quietly, so as not to rouse suspicion from the sentinels lurking out of sight.

"Mila!" she hissed, pulling me back. "What are you doing?"

I lifted my wrist, letting the gold play in the dim lighting. "Get these off me."

Making a sound at the back of her throat, she dislodged the chair. "Have a seat."

I took three steps away, three back, digging at my wrist.

She sighed. "I have to admit, I was hoping to never see you again."

"The manacles," I pressed. "How do I remove them, Your Grace?"

"It's just Sasha, now." A slender hand passed through her hair. "You can't take them off, Mila. Believe me. I've tried. The chains do not have a ki of their own and are, therefore, outside our limits as Priestesses."

Shaking my head to dispel the gathering frustrated tears, I thrust my wrist beneath her nose. "You're wrong. General Tilcot all but promised to separate me from my personal leech just this morning."

Her pale cheeks blanched. "He what?"

I jerked my chin at the door, scrubbing at the bond living in my chest, too agitated to control rattling nerves. "That imbecile soldier outside the door has a weapon full of *my* ki, Mistress. *Mine.*" A tremor raced through my blood. "The captain will *not* use me for his own gain. I will not allow it."

"Mila..." She paused, skirting the edge of her tiny desk, avoiding my gaze as she collected a clay pot from the shelf. "Please. Have a seat."

I scowled.

With a sigh, she placed the pot before me, giving it a neat quarter turn. "You don't understand what the general was threatening to do."

"No," I said, frowning at an artifact that had no business surviving the Fall of Tritan, yet there it sat. The Lotus Regula. Meant to be mine, in another life. "And I don't care. Neither will you when—"

"Enough," she hissed, and brought her palm down on the desk. "The only way to break a bond is to end the life of one of the bonded. The general was making a threat on Captain Rawlings' life. Or yours."

"I'm liking that vile serpent more and more. Not enough to spare him for murdering my father, of course. But..." I shrugged, trying to hear the hum of the Lotus' song—but that too, was lost to me. "The captain's death would solve a lot of my immediate problems. Should have done it years ago..."

Her mouth dropped open. "How can you—killing Asher isn't the answer! Mila, you *must* know what he is."

"What he is or isn't is irrelevant with our freedom at stake—"

"Freedom?"

"Keep your voice down," I hissed, glancing at the

door. "I'm offering you a chance to reclaim what is *yours*." Picking at my collar, at the skin around it, I leaned forward, seizing my chance when something dangerously close to hope glimmered in her beautiful blue eyes. "And if Captain Rawlings thinks he can stop me, he'll die for it. But don't worry," I drawled, showing teeth. "His will not be a frivolous death, for his ki shall fuel our victory."

"Goddess," she breathed, pinching the bridge of her nose. "You stupid, *stupid* girl. You've become exactly what I warned you against all those years ago. A full-fledged Empath."

"Oh, yes." I laughed, and pulled the Lotus from its nest of dirt and moss. I offered it my branded right hand, letting it feast, and though I hadn't the power to guide its growth or hear the song of my people, the Lotus flowered once more.

When last I'd touched it, the Lotus had exploded with the blooms of my Truth, issuing dozens of multi-colored florets kissed by darkness and silver moonlight. Now? A single, sad flower strained for life.

Pitch black, but for a twist of gold and silver running down the center of each petal.

"The darkness is my birthright," I whispered, setting the damning Truth back in its pot, then cracked my neck, watching her from beneath the fan of my lashes. "It shall be our *salvation*. The things I can do... the things I *will* do once I'm free of that fucking parasite... I'll teach you everything." Extending my hand, I let my blood-lust shine. "The darkness is not a thing to be feared, but embraced. They'll kneel at our feet and weep for the memory of mercy."

"They'll do no such thing, you deluded little fool."

She pulled the Lotus toward her, inspecting the tri-colored swirls with a critical, crinkled sneer. "You're going to get yourself killed. Probably take us all with you."

"But I won't die a slave," I said, fiddling with a trinket on her desk, eyes narrowed at my once-mentor.

"You're no good to anyone dead. With you and Asher bound—"

"No," I hissed, baring teeth, "I'm no good *here,* bound to the man who's hunted me for the better part of a decade. The man who pulls my ki from my veins at will." I scoffed, tearing at my wrist with dull claws, trying to crawl free of my skin. "He can *heal.* Did you know that?"

She swallowed, her throat working though no sound passed her lips.

"Do you understand the sort of power he now wields?" I took a step toward her, reaching for the darkness and missing. "He is not bound by the usual consequences," I said, hiking my skirt to reveal the ends of Kas' marks on my hip, heedless of baring myself before her. "I was never easy to kill, but now? What's to stop him from beating me senseless when he can be rid of the damage in minutes? He can keep me alive indefinitely. Make the torture *really* last, if he so chooses."

"He wouldn't," she whispered, tearing her eyes away from my scars. "Asher is a good man."

"You Priestesses and your good fucking men." I bared my teeth. "You're all the same. What would you have me do, Mistress? Hold the course? Tend to their sick and wounded as he goes out to create *more* on the battlefield? Killing with *my* power? How long shall I wait for a good man to lead the way when I have the power to build new paths from nothing?"

"The Goddess' plan is never clear—"

"Your Goddess is *dead*," I snarled. "I watched her fall beneath the boots of Caledonian soldiers as the city burned. I watched your Temple crumble to dust, and you've the gall to speak to me of the dead Goddess as if she's the one laying invisible clues in the rubble that remains? Waiting for her faithful to return?" I laughed, low and cruel. "Trust me. There's *nothing* left. Tritan's refugees came to *me*, Mistress. I sent them across the sea with the little I could spare. What have you done? Spread your legs for General-fucking-Tilcot and wait for a good man to save you?"

Her beautiful face paled further still. "How dare you"—she pulled a breath between her teeth—"you have no idea what I've been through."

I shrugged, belatedly trying to leash my unstable temper. "We all have our war stories." Taking a step toward her, I tried again, reaching for her hand. "We alone have the power to be free of those parasites. Help me. Help me gather the Priestesses and ready them to fight. Get these chains off me, High Priestess. Free the darkness in my soul and I will open the door for—"

"Goddess, don't you see? The Priestesses are no more. The Trila-Glís are no more," she said, her touch cool, absent the majesty she was born to wield. "With your capture, there are none of us free of the Empire. The Caledonians hold all the power, but with you and the young lord Rawlings bound"—she grinned—"everything has changed."

Something cold slid down my back. "What do you mean?"

"Two of the Goddess' chosen, bound as you are? Such a thing has never happened before," she said, reclaiming her seat and urging me to do the same. "The power that boy can wield is—"

"Not *his*," I said, stiff on my feet, resisting her and the secret glint whispering of something unknown. "Why... why are you championing him..." I trailed off, gooseflesh rising as the cold spread. "*You*," I whispered, taking a step back. "You taught him to heal. *You* gave him that power."

She sighed, opening a desk drawer and withdrawing an overlarge, iron ring. "I have been a slave of the Empire a long time, girl," she said, and donning the jewelry, the High Priestess stood, eyes fluttering closed as if euphoria cascaded through her blood.

It was a look I knew well. One that sent jealousy to pinch at the back of my throat.

Hands braced on her desk, the High Priestess continued, saying, "I've been a slave long enough to hear of the wood's menace, even in the capital." She sighed, straightening. "I've been here long enough to know *everything* has a price."

Swallowing the terror before it clotted at the back of my throat, I gave a voice instead. "What have you done?"

"I've always suspected you'd succumb to your weakness. Become an Empath." She rounded the desk, spinning the ring on her thumb. Her strides slow. Measured and sleek with a confidence she shouldn't have possessed. "I wasn't sure until I saw what's become of that forest. All the anguish, all the hurt and sadness of this war? You fed it to the earth. That forest is twisted with it. Dark, like the petals of your Flourishing." She stopped before me with a crooked smile. "It's a thing of pure, raw beauty."

Heart in my throat, I said nothing. Watching her twist that ring, my branded knuckle tingling with memories of fire and betrayal.

"But here I am. Left with the worst version of us. An Empath," she spat, venom dripping from her lips as she circled me. "While my true prodigy is wasted on an unexceptional Elite like Colonel Viridian."

I followed the soft footfalls without turning my head, committing that name to memory. "Do you think I've come to challenge your successor for a throne of ashes?"

"No." She smiled. I felt it on the back of my neck. "I can't remove your chains, and I wouldn't if I could." Coming to a stop directly before me, she added, "Not for you. To do so would be to condemn us all to death."

That ring.

The stone spit glittering flames that needed no introduction.

Glaith.

I understood, then. It was the price paid to learn the Goddess' teachings from a master. The captain had given it to her. I could feel it. Felt it in the twisted flesh of my right hand where once upon a time a different ring of iron and Glaith had glittered against my skin— and left behind nothing but scars. And I could feel the pull deep in my chest, behind my ribs, as the bond reached for the ki that had once fed it. Like recognizing like. *His* ki in the High Priestess' ring.

"They know you're here," I whispered, eying the Glaith as sweat trickled down my spine. Desperate enough to tell her everything, without reservation.

"Belle and the others? I told them. They're coming to rescue you. Us."

She paused, bejeweled hand curled. Hovering in the space between us. Poised on the cusp of a terrible decision. Eyes narrowed, she said simply, "When?"

"Today. Next summer. I don't know. But we have to be ready," I babbled, fighting the urge to flee as her ring glittered with ominous potential. "I need access to my power, Your Grace. Without it, I cannot help the rebels. Belle and her good men will die trying to buy your freedom. I—I need you. Are you with me, High Priestess?"

Lips quirked, she adjusted my dress, fingers hovering just over my skin without touching. "You're dangerous. The worst example of a Priestess and the exact reason our kind shouldn't go without training. Reckless and ki-drunk, you can barely focus on one thought before you're flitting off to the next." She laughed, toying with her ring. "It's the withdrawal. Painful, isn't it?"

I clenched my fists, swallowing the indignant fury, for her palm settled on my cheek. Her skin hot. Flushed with the only ki I could still feel.

His ki.

"An Empath bound to an Elite Trila-Glís?" She shook her head, tisking. "I should hamstring you and give Asher everything he needs for nothing more than the hope that he'll be better than the others of his ilk."

"Are you with me?" I asked again, voice a breathy wisp of terror, sweat beading on my brow.

By way of response, she set her palm flat on my breastbone, over the place where the bond thrived.

And then I felt it—ki, weak, tainted by the putrid stench of the general and the captain both, but ki all the same. It sparkled at the edge of my consciousness, a glimmer in the dark too fleeting to touch. A whisper in the Void speaking in tongues.

She pressed harder, forcing me to bend as she gathered the power trapped in the Glaith, wrapping it around the link between the captain and I. Insulating it. Insulating *me* from my Elite parasite and giving me a few, precious licks of independence before it was swallowed by the Void once more.

"There," she said with a gasp, wrenching away. "It's not much. Merely a concentration of your life-force, but it will allow you a little room to breathe. A buffer between you and him without unleashing an Empath."

A tiny sob followed my breath as I exhaled, trembling, for the High Priestess had given me more than a little room to breathe. She'd given me hope. Hope that it wasn't over, that I too, could wield the gifts of a dead goddess in spite of the Caledonians.

She'd given, when I knew she'd been tempted to take.

Standing before me was proof that it was still possible, though I'd need a crutch to access my dark birthright. And if I could not have my mother's pendant without the captain noticing the theft, that ring would make a fine substitute—made all the better for the poetic justice of events coming full-circle.

A pendant of Glaith in exchange for a ring.

The High Priestess brushed a drop of moisture from my cheek. A stray tear I hadn't felt or noticed. "He'll be able to break through it," she warned, sweeping sweat-damp hair back from her face and collapsing into her chair. "But you'll have a little of your former independence without risking you to your Empathy. Without risking either of you until—" she waved her hand, pulling the Lotus forward, and setting bejeweled fingers to its skin once more. "I have some research to do."

As I watched, she commanded the Lotus to retreat, sending my Truth into hibernation until only a wispy edge of green vine remained. No hint of anything inherently rare or dangerous by nature.

"If anyone should ask, your touch caused the Lotus to throw off runner vines. Nothing more, nothing less."

"Why?" I asked, unable to tear my eyes from that ring.

"General Tilcot is a paranoid man," she replied, shucking the ring and tossing it back into her drawer with a disgusted curl of her lip. "He'll want to see evidence of a Triloth of moderate potential, and that's what he'll get."

I nodded, not foolish enough to voice my interest in her Caledonian ring.

Folding trembling hands, she pursed her lips. "I've done things. Things that have compromised my standing with the Goddess. Things you wouldn't—*can't* understand. Not yet, but..." She lifted a delicate shoulder.

Picking at my collar with trembling fingers, I swallowed, hard. Played my part and bottled my temper. "You *survived*. There's no shame in that."

"We all have our war stories."

Rubbing my chest, over the insulated bond, I snorted.

For a moment, she said nothing, gazing at the surface of her desk. And then, "I've *always* been with you, girl. With Tritan. Always."

Inclining my head to the former Mistress of Milithia, I said simply, "Be ready."

A heavy fist hammered at the door. "Open the door. Time's up."

She met my eye, standing as the room was flooded with soldiers once more. "Isn't it just?"

19

———

Marco burst into the room, slipping around Jackson and seizing my arm. Without a word, he spun me toward the door, jaw flexing with what I assumed was unspoken anger.

"Where you off to in such a hurry?" Jackson asked, inspecting the Lotus Regula and its silent tale of a Triloth of moderate potential. "I thought the captain's girl was supposed to audit an infirmary shift?"

"She got the tour when we came in," Marco replied. "And Tilcot said he wants her at HQ before first rotation ends. Look, mate"—he clapped his left hand on Jackson's forearm— "General's already in a pissy mood on account of the captain claiming her without permission. I'm not about to catch any of that shit for bringing her over late. Besides, do you really want *her* tending to any of the wounded? Wildcat's more likely to laugh when someone begs for help, than work any Priestess magic."

"Depends on the patient," I purred, given that the inside of the Grandmother's ribs were etched with countless scores of refugees ferried to safety, and that I had never sworn an oath to give of myself without discretion.

Jackson reeled back, watching as I licked my modified canines with a leisurely sweep of my tongue. "Point taken. Off with you, then."

Hand to heart, Marco backed from the room, keeping a tight grip on my elbow as he steered me through narrow isles separating the cots. In fact, he didn't speak a word until we'd reached the exit and stood in the bright mid-morning sunlight outside.

"The fuck is wrong with you?" he hissed, voice a harsh whisper against my ear. "What happened to keeping a low profile, huh?"

"I have no such agreement with you, idiot."

He shook my arm, pressing close enough to fill my vision—but in spite of my newfound cocoon, his touch yielded nothing. "And if someone were to see your sprint through the infirmary as an assault on the general's Priestess? What then? Neither Captain Rawlings nor I can protect you if you insist upon—"

"Keep your pathetic protection," I snapped, trying to pry my arm free, teeth bared. "And get your hands off me."

"Oh, no, wildcat. I'm not taking any more chances with you today." And with fingers that shook, Marco flicked the clasp on his belt buckle.

Taking a step back, I eyed the strip of leather as he pulled it free from his pants. Uneasy. "What are you doing?"

"Preventing you from getting flighty on me again. And"—he gathered my hands, jerking me toward him and looping the leather around my wrists, cinching it tight—"I have no intention of being disciplined because of you." He tugged on the makeshift leash. "Now you can either walk or I can hogtie you, throw you over my shoulder, and drop you at the captain's feet. Which would you prefer?"

Lip curled, I twisted until gold was concealed by leather. "You know," I said, gesturing for him to lead on, "I get the distinct impression that you're not a fan of mine, Marco."

Marco nodded, setting a cigarette at the corner of his lips without lighting it, one hand tight on the end of my leash. "Wonder why that might be," he drawled. And then, under his breath, he said, "Don't know what he was thinkin', putting *me* on babysitting duty. 'Cause that went *so well* the last time."

"Yes, you poor thing. How vexing for you."

He snorted. "Don't you worry, wildcat. I'll have you back in the captain's care in no time. Safer this way, y'know? Better that the captain himself has his eye on you, eh?"

A laugh burst from my lips. Safer? With *him?* Sure. And Kas was a devout vegetarian. But I schooled my voice, and said, "Aren't the headquarters on the front lines?"

"Sure." With a shrug, he tugged the smoke free of his lips and began to roll it between forefinger and thumb.

"And I presume the front lines is where the rebels gather? Where the warfare is?"

"Yep. And they seem to have a real hard-on for punishment of late, too."

Despite bound wrists, I smiled. For who else but Belle would attack the Empire? Wasting no time and sparing no expense to reclaim the Trila-Glís and her treacherous lead scientist. With exaggerated patience, I pressed on, bobbing along beside Marco. "So, by your definition, safety is *closest* to the fighting?"

Grinning now, he patted the weapon at his hip, loaded with a blend of ki. "Safer for *me.*"

I flashed my modified canines, baring the sharpened points. "If you *really* want to be safe," I drawled, "you'll take me back to the forest before it's too late."

"Come now, wildcat. If I did that, who would get to enjoy all your creepy death threats?"

Thumbing the brand, I smothered an answering smile.

Was I not a rare and dangerous thing? A Trila-Glís the likes of which had never been seen, tainted by darkness and willing to do what my softer counterparts would not?

An Empath who had tasted death.

Was this pleasant idiot not leading me directly where I needed to be? Closest to Belle's good men and my mother's pendant?

Oh, yes. There was *always* another way out. I'd find it even if I had to carve it from the captain's chest with tooth and blunted nail.

He chucked me beneath the chin. "Don't worry about the rebels, wildcat. The captain will keep you safe and the front lines will hold against anything the rebels can come up with."

Not if I had *anything* to do with it. After all, the High Priestess could wield a ring imbued with Elite Ki. She had access to but a fraction of her *true* power, but power she had. In the right hands, a tool like that was not to be trifled with.

The tool *I* had in mind, however, contained enough

power to match even the Grandmother and had the added benefit of already being *mine*.

I turned my focus inward, brushing alongside the cocoon separating me from my parasite, tempted to flex my most powerful muscle before it atrophied and died. Before it became a ghost with no purpose but to moan about what I'd lost.

Instead, I took a breath, summoning the patience of an apex predator.

Ready to strike once, or not at all.

20

————

The walk to the headquarters building was brief, made shorter by the urgency lengthening my strides—with good men just out of sight, and me, bursting with a thing more deadly than even the darkness.

Information.

Even still, when the squat, gray building came into view, my skin was prickly with cold. It had nothing to do with the man lounging at the entrance, hip set against a railing. Arms crossed and inky eyes locked upon my face.

Nothing at all.

"Ah, Miss Tannovic," the captain said, smirking. "What naughty little tricks did Sasha teach you today, hmm?" The man stopped on the cusp of invading my personal space.

It was all I could do *not* to look for my mother's pendant. "Nothing that concerns you, parasite."

"There are a great many things that concern me, pet. Most every one of them has something to do with you."

Marco laughed. "Isn't *that* the truth?"

I smiled, head listing to the left as several dozen heavily armed soldiers trotted by, their footfalls speckling us with mud. Was my pendant there, tucked beneath his shirt? Warmed by his skin and ki both, just waiting for me to claim it?

"This one's a neat little bundle of crazy," Marco continued. "And look," he said, passing the belt binding my wrists to the captain. "A pretty bow, just for you."

Raising one brow, the captain took the makeshift lead. "Babysitting duty too much for you, soldier?"

"Hey," Marco said, cupping his hands to light a smoke. "She's 'ere, isn't she? Undamaged, as per your request." He exhaled, blowing smoke into my face. "But I'm warning you now, old man. I'm putting in for danger pay next week. How are things here?" he asked, flicking his lighter as someone out of sight cursed, shouting for another charge cell. "Rebels making a move?"

For a moment, the captain continued to watch me with narrowed, suspicious eyes. "It would seem they've made some advancements with their technology," he said at last, freeing me from Marco's belt, his fingers rough against my skin. Hot. "You can see their shields on the horizon, just there."

I flexed my wrists, picking at the gold even as I stood on tiptoe, peering over his shoulder. There, camped on the other side of a stretch of golden fields scarred black with the discharge of Elite weapons, were a dozen of Alicia's shields, twinkling blue. The scent of burning ozone teased my nose, and though I couldn't be certain it was from the rebel's shields and not the Elite weapons surrounding me, I grinned.

Belle wouldn't be pleased to see me, certainly, but I

knew exactly where the High Priestess was. And *that* was worth forgiving everything else.

"Clever bastards," Marco said, dropping a half-smoked cigarette into the mud when something in the distance exploded.

The ensuing shouts for reinforcements lifted the corner of my lips.

Frowning, the captain dragged me back, his sidearm pressing into my hip—and this time, I *didn't* pull away. "How was the infirmary? Any trouble?"

Marco snorted. "Of *course* there was trouble! And thanks to your little hell cat, I'm sure you'll hear *all* about it from Jackson first chance he gets."

Something poisonous lit the captain's eyes and his grip tightened. "Is that so?"

"You can save the pithy lecture for someone who cares," I purred.

"Oh?" the captain asked, eyebrows raised. "And why is that?"

"I think that's my cue," Marco said, taking several theatrical steps toward the squat headquarters building. "Good luck with... uh..." His eyes traveled over my face with a grimace. "Well. Good luck, sir."

Voice pitched low enough to go no further than his ears, I deigned to answer my parasite. Pressing close enough for his breath to warm my lips as I planted scarred right palm to his chest. "You cannot hold me," I drawled, letting him see what was bubbling beneath the surface. "Not for long. Even now, your grip loosens, Captain Rawlings. It's only a matter of time..." I trailed off, tracing the hard planes of muscle beneath black fabric. Fingers spreading, creeping... searching...

He trapped my wrist as my palm connected with my

prize. "You think the rebels are coming to save you?" he asked, lips brushing my ear. "Think you can help them break our line, hmm?" Tugging my hair over one shoulder, his next words traced the right side of my neck. "You think what Sasha did for you today is enough, my little lunatic? Do you actually believe she did anything without my knowing it? Without my..." he paused, stubble rasping at my jawline, "... *permission.*"

That something cold and wriggly from the High Priestess' office returned, bigger now. Slimy. "You're lying."

He smiled. Stepped back, though his hand lingered above my hip. Thumb tracing my lower back.

Trying to crush the icky cold thing, I let my fingers curl around the pendant, straining to pull strength from the lost family heirloom. "Is it really so hard to admit you're going to lose?"

"You'll have to let me know," he returned, glancing at my lips.

"Rawlings! What in the blazes are you doing out here?"

I whirled, jumping back from the captain with a pathetic little squeak, cheeks flaming with guilt.

General Tilcot stood in the doorway, glaring down at us, assuming much the same position as the captain had only minutes prior.

"Mila was just expressing her concern that the rebel scum are so close," the captain said, grip shifting to my shoulder, tight enough to bruise. "I thought it prudent to explain just how unfounded her fear is."

"Ah, Priestesses," the general said, and joined us in the muck. "Such soft creatures, aren't they? Meant to kneel to Elites, but unable to stomach the truth of *why* they were born with power. Except this one." His head tilted to the side as he inspected me. "She's... different."

"Different, sir?" The bond flooded with adrenaline, making my heart pound though I was not the one with sweating palms and white knuckles.

"Of course," the general replied, flicking a bit of dirt off his sleeve. "Living as she did, I'm sure her head is filled with all sorts of rebel propaganda. And if you're right, Rawlings," he continued, "then I'm sure she thinks whatever technology they've managed to slop together in those dank caves will be enough to break the Empire." He laughed, taking hold of my chin with fore-finger and thumb. "That, and she managed to tempt *you*, when so many others could not."

My muscles trembled, such was the force of will required to keep my jaws sealed around the vitriol burning the back of my throat.

"What was Sasha's assessment of the girl?"

"Triloth of moderate potential," the captain replied without pause, and that something cold spread to the bottom of my gut, for of course, Sasha hadn't spoken to him. Marco hadn't passed along any information in their short conversation, and unless the captain could be in two places at once, he couldn't have spoken to the High Priestess *and* been back in time to meet us here at headquarters.

Unless... the captain *did* have a deal with the High Priestess to keep my identity concealed. The teachings of the Goddess traded for pretty trinkets filled with scraps of power.

"Ah, well. That's unfortunate, but I suppose another Triloth added to the ranks is better than nothing. Come, Rawlings," the general said, beckoning with a crooked finger, turning away. "I'm eager to see what the Golden Boy can do with his new toy. Laying a few dead vermin at her feet should adjust our menace's opinion of the Empire's power, hmm?"

Dead? I bared my teeth, watching the phantom corpses of good men rotting in the general's eyes—and the dam burst. "You will *not* do harm with my power."

"I beg your pardon?" Half-turning, the general raised his brows.

The captain made to restrain me, but I slipped from his grasp. "I will not allow you to use my power to harm those people." Not when that harm was earmarked for the very man standing before me, reeking of death and foolish enough to show me his back.

Squaring his shoulders, the general's smug face lit from within. "And what, may I ask, will you do to stop us? You, a girl who wears the collar of the man who bought her at auction. A girl who owns *nothing*. *Is nothing but a power source with a warm hole.* Don't think I've forgotten the absurd circumstances of your capture, slut. And"—he sneered—"I'm sure the curator will agree with me. When the slaver has been brought in, your interrogation will begin as soon as I've finished with his."

"I—"

The captain clapped his palm over my lips. "My apologies for Mila's temper, sir. I can assure you, she'll be disciplined for her outburst. Enthusiastically."

"I seem to recall telling you to do something about her temperament once already, Rawlings."

"Yes, sir," the captain said, voice tight, pinning his front to my back. "She was at the infirmary all morning, and I haven't had the chance—"

"Did I ask for excuses?"

A tremor passed from the captain, into me. "No. You didn't. Sir."

"Well," the general said, hands spread wide, sending me a nasty glance, "then I guess her punishment falls... to me." He leaned in, filling my vision. "You think you can stop the captain from using you in any way he sees fit, using you like the tool you are? Now is your chance, slut. Impress me."

"Sir, I—" the captain cleared his throat, pendant lodged between my shoulder blades, sidearm bruising my kidney. "With all due respect, sir," he began, muzzling me. "I don't think Mila is quite ready for a demonstration of *that* magnitude."

With a shrug and careless flick of his wrist, the general turned, gesturing for us to follow. "I guess we'll see, won't we?"

For a few long seconds, the captain didn't budge. Didn't release me, or make further argument, merely tightened his grip on my skin. Only when the general was out of earshot, did he abandon my lips to cradle my throat in a grip that trembled with fury. "Are you completely insane?"

I laughed, deep and throaty, letting my head fall back against his shoulder. Enjoying the thrum of power set between my shoulders that I could only *just* feel.

"Move," he snarled, shoving me into the general's muddy footsteps.

Still grinning as we marched through a corridor between two uninspired concrete bunkers, my gaze fell upon the distant glimmer of rebel shields once more.

Six.

Six massive blue shields protecting good men.

Allies. My vessel to freedom, if only they could break the Caledonian line.

I picked at my collar, tearing skin.

Were I armed with more than my wit and temper, I'd salt the leeches clinging to this fallen Eloran city and fling the doors wide open, welcoming the true owners home.

As it was...

The earth trembled with a nearby explosion, making me jump, fists raised.

"Only a taste of what comes next," the general cooed, appearing before us and fixing me with a twisted smirk. He stepped into the bunker on our right, and when he reappeared, it was with an oblong chunk of chrome nestled in the palm of his hand. "Now. Rawlings, get out there and kill some rebels."

Jaw flexed and rigid, the captain nodded. "Yes, sir."

"Stop him if you can, slut," the general said, and dumped the egg-shaped thing into the captain's outstretched hands.

I gasped, eyes jerked down, to my wrists. Burning! My manacles were *burning,* just as they had in the kitchen! Veins pulsing with molten gold crawling up my arms.

Eyes cold and black, the general stopped, taking hold of my chin, tilting my face back and forth. "Interesting. A Triloth of moderate potential, you say?"

"Sasha said so, sir," the captain said, tucking the egg into his jacket pocket—and in doing so, separated his skin from the polished metal.

At once, the gold slid from my veins, leaving me sweaty and shaken, but without pain.

Glaith. Whatever the egg was, it *had* to contain the

Glaith. It *always* came back to that hated ore, didn't it? But... if the *captain* touching the Glaith affected *me*... could the same be true if our positions were reversed? What if I were to steal his sidearm and turn the general into ki-soup? Was it not powered by Glaith? Did filling Marco's weapon with *my* ki not turn my veins to gold?

"Apparently Mila was never formally trained at the Temple, sir. Perhaps a demonstration of this magnitude is—"

"A perfect learning opportunity," the general snapped, eyes tight though he released me, jerking his chin toward the battlefield. "Go."

Feeling a strange, woozy moment of camaraderie with the man I hated most, I grinned as the captain jumped to do as he was told. It was good to see his opinions ignored, good to watch him swallow the acidic retort I could feel bubbling beneath the surface.

He snapped his fingers. "Mila, come."

My grin slipped, and I picked at the gold embedded in my neck, forced to trot along behind the captain or remain with the general in his dank little bunker.

Emerging from between the utilitarian buildings, the captain led me to an unmanned turret flanked by a shallow ditch and yet another concrete wall—this one perched on the rim of a trench bordering the battle-scarred soil between us and the good men. Promising a measure of protection for the dozen or so filthy soldiers who hid in its shadow, though hardly an equal comparison to the glorious glimmer of rebel shields in the distance. Rebels whose faces I could see, even from this distance. Distorted by a shimmering wall of blue death, but there all the same.

"Marco," the captain hissed, hopping into the trench and tugging me down with him.

The soldier in question grunted in surprise, then spun to face us, lit cigarette dangling from slack lips. "Captain! What is *she* doing here? I know you're getting old, but senile, too?"

"I'm being *punished*," I sang, clawing at my wrist and fixing a toothy smile on Marco.

"Sit," the captain snapped, jerking me to his side in the muck. "Stay."

I stumbled, catching myself on his hip with a squeak. Teeth bared, I righted myself, palms tracing the edge of his sidearm beneath his jacket for a moment before I put some much-needed space between us.

My heart lurched.

Ki.

I could sense it, thanks to the High Priestess. A pale shadow of what I knew was there, but humming in the slumbering core of his weapon.

"She just can't help herself," the captain said, scowling at me. "Not when it comes to Tilcot. Just *has* to goad him."

"Fuck." Marco pushed a muddy hand through his hair, making it stick straight up. "Tilcot? What did she—"

Tugging the egg from his pocket, the captain said, "Later," under his breath, and tossed the bit of chromed Glaith to the soldier before my wrists could do more than tingle.

Marco paled beneath his tan. "Holy *shit*. Is this—is this ordnance for the SAG Turret?"

At Marco's exclamation, the other men in the trench stilled, hanging on the captain's next words.

"Sure is."

"Of all the bloody stupid wastes of—" Marco cursed, pinching the bridge of his nose. "We have the front lines under control! The rebels aren't doing anything that warrants a show of force like *this.*" He rolled the egg between his palms, puffing on his smoke as the other men murmured amongst themselves, scarcely bothering to conceal excited murmuring. "What exactly is your plan here?"

Inky eyes found mine. "Take a shot at the shields. See what happens."

"You *can't* be serious!" Marco flicked his cigarette, flinging a hand toward the hulking gray beast sitting sentinel on the battlefield. "Fucking Elites. You want to use this *precious,* limited ammunition to measure your cocks?"

The captain smirked, ignoring the men passing grins between them, dark eyes flicking to the turret, my parasite, and back. "If you're holding the tape, what does that make *you?*"

Marco clutched his heart, staggering as the gathered soldiers laughed. "Take it from a life-long veteran of this abuse, gentlemen," Marco announced, throwing up his hands in mock surrender. "Should an Elite come to you with hat in hand, *begging* for your expertise and protection, turn him down cold."

"Hat in hand, huh?" the captain asked, kneeling in the dirt behind the turret. Making minor adjustments.

I followed, eying the silver chain glimmering against his nape.

"Oh, he sells a pretty package. Spins visions of glory in battle," Marco began, painting a picture with his hands and voice. "Promising spoils of war, women, and luxury."

The captain rolled his eyes, lips twitching.

"The extra pay—if he ever bothers to cough it up—is bloody terrible," he continued, seizing my elbow and pulling me away from the captain's side and the pendant both.

I slapped at his fingers, splattering myself with mud.

"Any women he collects are either *his* or off limits. *And* he's given me the *luxury* of babysitting the lady wildcat here!" Giving me a little shake before he released me, Marco held the chrome egg aloft. "The only thing that makes it worth it, gentlemen," he continued, "is watching the occasional ki-fueled, dick-measuring explosion at close range."

"Alright, alright," the captain said, stroking the turret's flat gray flanks with a loving caress. "Just load it up, will you? There's not much I can do about your spending habits *or* terrible luck with women. Besides," he added under his breath, claiming the built-in stool behind the turret's shield, "we have an audience."

I glanced over my shoulder—at the giant of a man watching us from behind thick, tinted glass—and sneered. The general wanted a show, did he?

Marco's chin dipped once, though he said, "Now everyone *knows* you're lying, Captain," at full volume. "The ladies love dear old Marco." Setting the chrome egg into a tube at the turret's back end, he snapped it shut with an ear-splitting clang. "Back to it!" Marco shouted, swirling his finger in the air as the soldiers jumped to do his bidding. "Eyes forward. We need cover while the SAG charges."

"How close are they?" the captain asked, and I felt

his senses flare out around us, checking for himself with his forbidden, stolen ki-sense.

I picked at the collar, trying in vain to separate it from my skin, but did not fight him. Not yet. Rather, I watched Marco's lips, hanging on his next words.

Staring down the scope of his weapon, Marco shrugged. "A hundred yards. Maybe less?"

A hundred yards? That was *nothing!* I could cover that ground in *seconds*—all I needed was a single chance, a lapse in vigil and I'd flee. Even without safety of cover I could make that sprint, for the captain wouldn't destroy the one thing he needed most! All the better if I could tear my pendant from his neck and approach Belle's good men bearing gifts.

And once I was behind those shields...

Heart pounding, I let my eyes wander, tracing the path I'd take from this mud-pit the moment I could.

Marco jerked his thumb to a row of shattered buildings on the far left. "We've got two units waiting in the flanks in case they make another push."

Flicking the corner of his jacket out of the way, the captain took the handles, igniting the molten gold within my veins once more.

This pain was *irrelevant!* Goddess, it was all I could do to contain my glee, for there, peeking at me from the just beneath his shirt collar, was my *perfect* moment. What I'd been waiting for, all this time.

The pendant's silver chain glimmered up at me, forcing me to set my canines to the inside of my lip or spoil the surprise.

"You know," the captain mused, inky gaze passing over my veiny, alien skin before returning his attention to the glimmer of rebel blue. "The circumstances aren't quite what I had planned, but... this is going to be one hell of a demonstration."

"You got that right, sir. You are without peer."

The captain snorted. "You're not getting a raise, Marco."

"Tyrant."

Bracing his cheek against the hilt of his weapon, the captain shifted, bringing the turret to life once more, but this time, there were good men in his sights.

"Light 'em up, Captain," Marco said, shifting just enough to block my view of the captain's angular profile. And if I couldn't see *him,* he couldn't see *me.*

Now!

With a shout, I slipped my finger beneath the chain, and yanked—but it held fast. As if punishing me for losing it all those years ago, the chain did little more than threaten to garrote my parasite. Distorted his startled curse.

Planting my foot on his lower back, I pulled again, only to watch my pinned Elite seize the pendant in his large fist. Denying me with a choked growl.

"Wildcat, get *down,*" Marco hissed, wrapping a muddy fist about my ankle.

My foot lashed out, striking him in the solar plexus, even as I dove for the only option I had left. I yanked the ornate silver handle from the captain's holster and lunged for my escape route. Setting one foot on the ass-end of the turret, I hiked my skirts and rushed down the barrel. Leaping over the concrete barrier before anyone had the sense to stop me.

"Mila!"

And there they were. Belle's good men, no more than a few hundred paces away—less, if I sprinted flat-out. Shouts from *both* sides echoed through the stretch of ruined crops separating them, but the flurry of activity from behind the closest rebel shield lightened my tainted soul.

"*Mila!*"

I spun to the sound of his voice, weapon raised. Offering a parting gift for my impossible Elite.

After all, the general had wanted a show.

21

—————

I whirled, turning Caledonian firepower upon its owner, skin ablaze with Caledonian gold. "Call them off. Your men"—I flicked the weapon at the soldiers crouched behind the concrete, staring at me with mouths agape—"tell them to put their weapons down."

Behind me, the rebels shouted all at once, their voices melting into one, unintelligible dull roar—I waved them off, focused on the pale shock settling upon the captain's face. He was measuring the distance between us. Of that, I had no doubt. Knew he was trying to calculate how best to bring me to heel.

My lip curled.

Abandoning the turret, the captain stood, flashing the whites of his palms and revealing himself to the rebels across the field.

The searing pain at wrists and throat receded, though I didn't let him see my relief. No, I fixed a toothy grin upon my lips, memorizing every detail of this *perfect* moment.

Ignoring the surge of activity from behind the shields and the concrete barriers, the captain took a step and said, "You've made your point, Miss Tannovic—"

The rebels shouted, setting the air alight with an electric tingle of *promise*.

He stopped short, inky eyes flicking between my grin and the rebels. Cautious, barely containing the panic.

Oh, but the look on his face! If only I could bottle it, keep it for later when I was retelling the downfall of a forgotten Empire. "Not another step, Captain Rawlings." Gleeful, I brandished my stolen weapon, keeping it trained on the captain's chest. "I'm leaving," I purred, pausing for a moment to enjoy the ballad of chaos sung by the good men at my back. "Tell these parasites bloated with *Priestess* ki to drop their weapons, then bring them *all* to me."

For a moment, as his shock turned into something darker, he said nothing. Glaring with a tight-lipped fury that whipped at the bond, he pulled at me, at what remained of the darkness. Beseeching. Trying to manipulate me with tempting, drugging ki.

But I was quite finished with *that*. Burrowing behind the High Priestess' cocoon, I forced him out, though the effort made my head spin, stuffing my ears with fuzz. "Do it," I said, blinking away dark stars as the good men shouted. "Tell them to—"

"Don't move, you stupid, *stupid* girl!"

Incredulous, I laughed. "You're hardly in a position to—"

"Mila! *Get down!*"

A hollow thud hit the earth to my left, throwing me

to the ground in a shower of mud, the choking stench of ozone, and scorching hot rocks.

Shocked, I gasped. "What—"

Electric-blue plasma danced over my skin, singeing me with the unmistakable *zip* of ki. Bewildered, my eyes found the captain's, for it was not the first time he'd taken a shot at me—but his face had gone waxy with an emotion I couldn't name.

It looked like pure, unfiltered terror.

"Cover fire!" Marco bellowed, igniting the Caledonian forces. Dozens of shots sailed over my tangled body, setting the air ablaze and searing that trademark sickly green into the backs of my retinas. They pummeled the rebel shields with such enthusiasm as to give them no choice *but* to wait it out.

"Don't move!" the captain snarled, making his way toward me with Marco at his back, the latter sending wave after wave of Elite ki at the rebel shields.

Soaked in mud and filth, I scrambled for my stolen weapon, wrapping both hands around the grip. "Get back! Or you die where you stand!"

My threat did nothing to slow them, nothing to temper the fury etched upon the captain's face. "Go ahead, my fierce little lunatic," he purred, closing in. Lit by wave after wave of Caledonian firepower. "Shoot."

The bond crackled with dark flames, charring the back of my throat.

"You think I won't?" I rasped, hesitating only an *instant* before I cannibalized the High Priestess' cocoon, dumping what I could into the weapon as I lay there, flat on my back. Knees spread. Arms locked. Staring down the sights at the captain's handsome, furious face.

Obsidian eyes bore into mine. Utterly ignoring my

threat and the warfare exploding all around us, he simply raised his left wrist with a mocking sneer and tapped the matte-black manacle with his forefinger. "You are not Elite, little girl."

"Aren't I?" I whispered, and though my hands trembled and the air was thick with screams and ki, I smiled, cheeks flushed with fire—and squeezed the trigger with my remaining strength.

Nothing happened.

The captain's bark of laughter echoed through the empty place in my chest as he spread his arms, nearly upon me. "Passion and fury, Mila. No training. No knowledge."

"Quite a flare for the dramatic, hey, wildcat?" Marco asked, unlit cigarette dangling bent and broken from an unhinged grin.

Abandoning my attempt on his life, I scrambled to my feet, turning toward the last dregs of hope. Toward the glimmer of blue and the flurry of activity on the horizon. All I had to do was make it across the field of muck and scars, covered by Caledonian firepower, and I'd be free. Free to join the rebellion and fight another day.

I didn't need to bring them weapons! I *was* the weapon. Belle had said it herself, many times! Hiking skirts grown heavy with filth, I charged forward, slogging through the mud.

It was a foolish attempt.

Tackling me with his entire weight, the captain's shoulder struck me just below the ribs, driving us both into the mud

Gasping, I hadn't the sense to fight him before he was prying his sidearm from my stiff fingers with brutal force. At once, gold flooded my veins, the searing agony a promise of the devastation the captain could do with my power—*would* do, for I had failed.

"*Move!*" he snarled, jerking me to my feet and shoving me back, toward the trench filled with enemies.

"No—"

The tip of his weapon lit with blinding, furious green matched only by the terrible expression etched upon his face.

"*Go!*" Marco bellowed, unloading a volley of shots at the closest shield.

With a curse, the captain hauled me up. Tossing me over his shoulder, he spun, sprinting toward his countrymen.

Belle. Her good men. So close. "The Priestesses," I wheezed, forcing the words past the fragments of shattered hope, watching the shields shrink away. "They're here. We're *all* here."

"Move your ass, Asher!" Marco shouted, his attention split between forward and back, long-legged stride eating the ground between us and them. "Get her to cover, then get on that turret! We're already running low on charge cells."

If the captain got on that turret... Goddess. There'd be no good men left to fight another day.

The captain jumped, landing hard in the trench, dropping me with a careless thump at his feet. "Take her," he barked, hardly sparing me a glance as he lunged, taking position behind the turret.

Breath coming hard, Marco claimed my wrist, engulfing the deadly glitter spreading through my blood.

"*Please,*" I croaked, trying to crawl after the captain. "Don't."

Before I had gained more than an inch, I was face down in the dirt, Marco's knee planted between my shoulder blades. "Don't even think it, wildcat."

I choked, vision filled with the captain bent to his gruesome task. Forced to watch as he seized the turret's handle, and gathered our combined strength. Pouring it into the instrument of death as the gold in my veins spread.

And then he fired.

For a moment, the last scraps of the High Priestess' wall of ki held, protecting me as the captain's handsome profile light with a vibrant green.

Marco whistled, eyes reflecting the sheen of gold pumping through my veins. "My God..."

The link in my chest twitched. Lurched.

Beneath my cheek, the earth shuddered with explosive impact, and I bucked, trying to throw Marco's bulk off my back.

"Easy, wildcat. You wouldn't believe—"

The wall crumbled, consumed by the golden parasite with a new toy. White-hot flames encircled my throat and wrists, choking the screams before they could be heard as the captain pulled every spare ounce of ki from my body at will. My every muscle seized beneath Marco, any will to fight him drowned before the yawning mouth of the Void. So dark... so terribly, terribly *cold...*

"Wildcat!"

The crack of skin on skin echoed in my ears, stinging my cheek, but the Void beckoned... pulling me deeper... and *Goddess,* it would be easy to let go...

"Captain! *Asher!* Stop!" The pressure at my back eased. "The wildcat—she's—"

"Fuck. *Fuck!*"

I tuned them out, eyes fixed on nothing even as the Void retreated.

There was nothing left. No reason for any of it.

"Mila! Look at me, girl. That's it." The captain dragged me into his lap, supporting my head when I made no effort to do so myself. "Come back, Miss Tannovic."

I blinked. Why? What was the point? The Void was... peaceful in its absence. Such perfection in the dark... Such... *belonging* for a thing no longer rare and dangerous.

Just empty.

"Fucking hell, she's ice-cold. Cover me, Marco. Get back—all of you!"

"Sir," the soldier replied, and a moment later a shadow passed over my eyes, blocking the sun.

A warm hand pressed to my chest, fingers splayed between my breasts. Over the link fluttering between us.

His face swam into focus, dark brows drawn tight, jaw clenched.

My throat worked, though I could scarcely hear the sound of my voice uttering Belle's words. Unheeded and unheard. "Please, don't... They're... they're good men..."

"Return fire!"

The captain hunched, covering me as the earth shuddered anew, shielding me from a hail of dust and rock. "Fuck! Breathe, Miss Tannovic. *Breathe.*" And then, lips warming my cheeks, my Elite parasite began to feed me his ki.

I gasped, eyes going wide. The switch flipped, a

beacon to the slumbering, lethargic beast living within me. "Goddess, yes"—I groaned, eyes rolling back—"*more*. More, damn you."

The captain obliged, anchoring me to him as he replaced some of what he'd stolen. Feeding the darkness.

Cheeks flushed, I took it. The ki—so wild and pure—blazed through my every fiber, sending blessed, hated sensation back to my extremities.

Ki that wasn't mine.

He pulled me back with the ease of a master.

Expelling the cold.

LAVISH DESTRUCTION

TRITAN EVOLUTION, BOOK III

1

Head pounding, eyes puffy and swollen, I pried my lids apart, disorientated. A bed. I was tucked beneath heavy blankets in a dark room. Trembling, I pushed the comforter back, trying to distinguish between bedsheets and a mud-caked, crusty slave dress plastered to my skin.

"Ughh." Forcing my hand through layers of filth matting the hair to my scalp, I tried to stop the ceiling from spinning. "Water," I croaked. "Please..." But my inhuman rasp went unanswered, witnessed only by a still, dark room.

And I would have continued to lie there, trying to piece myself back together, if it weren't for the flashes of green lighting up the backside of my eyelids.

Memories, screaming to be heard.

I blinked, trying in vain to banish the phantoms.

The turret loaded with impossible power. Muddy fingers wrapped about a silver chain. A hundred yards separating me from Belle and her good men.

My finger on a trigger that wouldn't pull. The empty pulse of failure.

And behind it all?

Inky black eyes blazing with fury.

Captain Rawlings.

I gasped.

Goddess, this was his room.

His bed.

I rolled with a grunt, legs dangling, knuckles white on the edge of the mattress as I searched for familiar landmarks.

Two. There were two of everything.

Cursing, I squeezed my eyes shut in spite of the Elite ki dancing in the dark, forcing a breath into stiff lungs. I'd lost consciousness—that much was certain—but how long had I been out? And what had become of the good men trying to move a mountain? Had Alicia's shields held? Had they been able to escape the fallout of this most recent of my failures? Or were they...

Throat tight, I swallowed the raptor trying to claw its way free of my chest, and stood. Swaying.

No. They'd had technology they were proud of. They'd had a plan—a *good* one. This was a setback, nothing more. Their shields would have protected them from...

My chains tingled, a shadow of the pain I'd felt on the field. A hint of the magnificent power the captain had wielded with nauseating ease.

Goddess, Alicia had made her shields with *Triloth* ki at best. And even if Ancaster had ever managed to perfect his technology to allow the mundane to use ki as if they were of the Blood...

Could they withstand the combined might of two Trila-Glís?

Could... *anything?*

Vision blurred with the hot, watery ache of failure, I stilled. Trying to draw breath, to quiet the empty scream of the Void echoing inside my head.

How many good men now filled that Void because of... me?

Because someone had finally managed to weaponize the darkness of an Empath starving for ki?

From the floor below, the deep rumble of a man's voice penetrated my very skin, and though I couldn't make out his words, I *knew.*

There was only one man whose ki I still felt through this prison of Glaith. Only one for whom the bond in my chest surged and danced, tugging at the fragile, tattered remains of the High Priestess' cocoon.

Asher.

Teeth bared, I hauled myself toward the bathroom, swiping at the tears. Listing to the left, then right. I should have *known* he wouldn't be far away, should have known he wouldn't leave me to my own devices for long, the foul, Elite sonofa*whore!*

Clinging to the wall, I made the trek to the facilities, bladder full to bursting, head filled with poison.

The captain had taken too much.

In sheer selfish arrogance, I had allowed this game between us to consume everything I had been.

Finished with my business, I staggered to my feet, pausing a moment to let the black, twinkling stars recede from my vision. Sweat prickled along my hairline as I washed, glancing at the sealed bathroom window, stymied at every turn.

But he couldn't have thought of *everything*. There was *always* a way out. There had to be.

Letting a ragged breath escape my lips, I pinched the bridge of my nose.

Think.

He'd crippled me with the chains, turned my ki against my only allies, potentially corrupted the High Priestess for Goddess only knew what end, *and* pulled me back from the very cusp of death with a level of proficiency in the art of wielding ki to which I had never even thought to aspire.

Any way I turned, any path I chose, he'd been there before me. Already laid traps to tie me down and keep me pinned under thumb.

Seething, I picked at the gold on my left wrist, thumbing the little scabs.

I'd failed on the field because I'd been unable to admit I was no longer what I'd been. Headstrong and filled with impotent, arrogant rage, I'd relied on ki that wasn't mine. Tried to tap a well of strength I no longer owned.

And it had cost good men their lives.

It was time to employ a different tactic, for if I couldn't be the weapon, then I'd find one. If I couldn't find one, I'd make one. Ki did not define me.

Not anymore.

With a grimace, I left the bathroom, heading straight for the captain's desk on silent, albeit unsteady, feet. If there was a weapon *anywhere* in this room, reason dictated it would be there. I rushed toward it, leaving a trail of flaking mud behind me, thrusting pens, paper, and various other stationery utensils aside. At length, I came across a letter opener, rusted and forgotten at the back of the middle drawer. Hardly the weapon of a vengeful crusader, and far from glamorous, but it would do the job.

Wrapping the crusty length of my skirt around my left wrist to keep it clear of clumsy feet, I made for the door. Unlocked, of course, for what threat could I *possibly* be to the untouchable Captain Rawlings?

Stifling a hysterical bubble of laughter, I seized the banister, listening to the murmur of male voices out of sight. Clutching the opener, I took a step—and wobbled, vision hazy. Sinking to my bottom, I watched the world tilt off its axis, trying to tether myself to the ground before I floated away. Maybe I could close my eyes for just... just a few seconds...

No. I ground my teeth, shaking the cotton from my ears. *No.* I'd confront the captain *now*—tonight—one miserable step at a time, weakness be damned.

And if he killed me for it?

Teeth bared, I slid forward on my bottom, using the railing to pull myself to the next step.

Hands laden with a silver tray piled with soiled dishes, Alicia appeared at the bottom of the stairs, shimmering in two places at once.

I froze, squinting, trying to decide which image was the Eloran traitor and which was the hallucination.

Four pretty green eyes met mine, and she gasped, casting a quick glance over her shoulder. "What're you doing, lass?" she hissed, and, setting the tray on the floor, rushed up the stairs, skirts hiked to mid-shin.

Goddess, but she moved fast. I squeezed my eyes shut, swallowing back a wave of nausea.

"You should be in bed, you wee stubborn thing!"

"Don't." I bared my teeth, clinging to the banister, toes and lips tingling. "This does not concern *you*."

"Right," she said, hands on hips. "And what does '*this*' entail, exactly?"

Scowling at the left-most version of her, I struggled to stand.

"Sit down before y'fall down," she scoffed, but slipped her hands beneath my armpits, steadying me.

"No." Pushing at her, trying again for the stairs, I said, "He's going to answer for the things he's done."

"Are you out of your bloody mind?" she hissed, and plucked the opener from my fingers with startling ease. "Do y'really think you can take on an Elite warrior like Captain Rawlings with a wee bit o' rusted steel?"

"I don't expect *you* to understand, traitor."

She made a sound at the back of her throat. Something that was almost a laugh. "I havna betrayed you, but I understand the need to take it out on someone, if you must. Go ahead, Priestess." She released me, crossed her arms beneath her breasts, and cocked her head to the side. "Take a swing. Get it out o'your system."

With a huff, I raised a trembling hand, shoving my filthy hair back from my face. "He killed them!" I hissed. "*Your* people and mine. They were coming to rescue us, and he erased them. Using *my*—" I choked. "He killed them all using *my* ki. Now give me back my blade," I continued, knuckles white on the banister once more.

She tucked the opener into the folds of her skirt. "Get your wee ass back into bed before he realizes you're awake. The captain is white-lipped with fury, an' he's been into the drink. 'Tis good practice not t'antagonize a man twice your size, if he's tryin' t'lose himself in the cups—'specially if it's because o'*you*."

Teeth bared, I dropped low, assuming a wobbly fighting stance.

"Stop. *Stop*—" she seized my arm, tugging me off balance and using my unsteady momentum to force me back into the captain's bedroom. "You're weak as a kitten, girl. In no state to go attackin' one like the captain with nothin' more than misplaced fury." She shoved me toward his bed, closing the door behind us with a gentle click. "I took you for reckless, but I didna expect you'd be stupid as well."

Panting, I tried to face her, hands pressed to the captain's rumpled bedsheets.

"Now listen, an' listen well." She slapped the letter opener down on the captain's desk and crossed her arms. "You'll get nowhere but dead if you continue down this path."

I didn't blink.

"Fine." She spread her hands. "Assumin' you can get past me without falling down, you aim t'fight him. With what weapon?"

"You took it."

"Wrong. Try again."

"Perhaps you don't understand what's going on here, traitor." Fists clenched, I pulled a breath through my teeth. "I have *nothing*. Because of him. He's taken my ki. My freedom. And now whatever chance I had to regain that freedom lies dead in a mud-pit between here and there. If you won't help me, then—"

"They're not dead," she said, cutting me off. "No one died this mornin', though from what I understand, your wee stunt nearly put *you* in an early grave."

Deflated, head spinning, I clutched at the blankets. "Not dead?"

"Not even a captive was taken." She smoothed her skirts then stooped, gathering the stack of documents I'd flung to the floor. "You may have lost what the Goddess gave you," she said. "But you're *far* from powerless. *Look at me, lass.* I've been given ample chance t'escape no less than *three* times since the auction—"

"And yet, here you are. Working for the worst of them."

Her eyes fluttered closed. A breath hissing between clenched teeth. "And why do you suppose *that* is, hmm? Why do you think I stayed, when it would be easier and *safer* for me t'run?"

"What reason have you to leave? You've been promised freedom for your efforts. A comfortable life paid for by the Empire. The only rational solution is that you've been working for *them*. For years."

"I'm here for *you*, you abominably silly chit."

Brows pinched, I said nothing. Not quite daring to trust... fighting off the glimmer of hope.

She nodded, hip bumping the captain's desk. "I know how hard this'll be for you, what with your formative years spent with that great forest beastie. But you're *not* a lion. It's time to start thinking like a *woman*, Mila. Now, *what are you armed with?*"

I sat, perched on the edge of his bed, the slimy shock of realization oozing into my guts. "You want me to whore myself." I swallowed, hard. "To the captain."

She shrugged, reclaimed my letter opener and set the point into the surface of the desk. Spinning it. "Is it whoring to use the gifts the Goddess gave all women, then?"

Scowling and churlish, I said, "The Goddess is dead," but couldn't meet her eye.

"And yet, I still hear you using Her name under your breath when y'think no one is listenin'." Her pretty green eyes lit from within. "It's not whoring t'use what you got. An' if you seek to fight him, you haven't many other options."

"And they call *me* insane."

Lips tilting, she flashed her teeth. "There's nothin' quite so pliable as a man after he's slaked his lust. It's then you'll notice the perfect moment to strike."

I jerked, hearing Kas' wisdom spoken with her lips flooded me with some much-needed perspective. And yet... "Anything"—I cleared my throat—"anything is better than *that.*"

"Oh, I don' know," she purred, grinning now. "The captain isn't exactly hard to look at. You deserve a little pleasure too, girl."

Jaw working on a mouthful of desert air, my cheeks burned. "I think you're confusing pleasure and punishment."

"And I think the lines can get a wee bit blurry from time t'time. Besides," she continued, closing the distance between us, placing her hand on my shoulder, "the man is *expectin'* you t'be difficult. He's prepared for whatever mental thing you're plannin' to do next. Tell me, lassie, how's that been workin' out for you?"

I glanced at her hands, feeling nothing but a cool pressure. No hint of her life force through her skin on mine, and had to concede her point.

"Right," she said, and lifting a brow. "Play the part, Mila. Let him believe he's won. Bring him t'your side as I've done with Marco, and we'll be free of this place in no time. Together, and with any luck, the High Priestess herself in tow."

Together? Only hours ago, I'd been flying toward freedom, without a thought for Alicia's safety. But without my Truth, I couldn't differentiate between fact or fiction. Couldn't decide if her words were honest or designed. "I..." I shook my head. "I can't."

"Sure you can." She plucked a matted hank of hair off my shoulder, rubbing it between two fingers. "Just get you cleaned up a little, work to ease that temper, and he'll be putty in your wee dirty hands."

Face burning, I twisted away. "N-No—"

Shrugging, she pressed the letter opener into my branded hand, then moved to the head of the bed, pulling the blankets down. "Then stay the course if you seek oblivion, lass. Use that rusty blade. Won't take him long to tire of fightin' a losing battle. And when he does, I'm sure he can find somewhere to put you. Like a wee dark hole with no way out?"

I clutched the opener, watching the blood shift beneath the twisted skin of my right hand.

"Just make a decision an' see it through. But first you'll be wantin' to get your narrow behind back in bed. Won't be seducing any man lookin' like you just crawled from your grave. And certainly not that furious, piss-drunk captain."

Lip curled, I scowled at his bed. "I'm *not* sleeping there."

"On the couch then, lass." She pulled the heavy blanket off the mattress.

My stomach growled.

Glancing over her shoulder, Alicia shook out the

blanket, draping it over the couch. "Get some sleep, an' then we can think about getting you something to—"

I waved her off. "I'm fine. It's not the first time I've gone without food." Though it was the first time I'd done so without the wild rush of ki restoring my energy and dulling my appetite. I cleared my throat, trying to soften the edge of my tongue. "Alicia... I... I'm..."

"No thanks or apology needed, Priestess," she said, flashing a brilliant smile wreathed in bruises.

A raspy chuckle came from behind us, and he said, "I *must* be drunk if Mila is apologizing for something."

I jumped, spinning to face him, and hid my blade with the length of my forearm.

The captain.

2

———

"C-Captain Rawlings, sir," Alicia stammered, pressing a delicate hand to the base of her throat. "You about stopped my heart."

He grinned, swirling the contents of a crystal decanter as he lounged against the doorframe, inky gaze finding mine. Lazy, yet still sharp. And then, unbuttoning his shirt sleeves, he stalked toward us, dropping into his office chair with a huff.

"Ah," Alicia hummed, green eyes flicking to my face. "Will you be needing anythin' else, sir, or..."

He flicked the decanter in her direction, making the amber liquid slosh against the glass. "The night is yours, Alicia."

"Thank you, sir," she said, then glanced at me, raising a single brow.

I didn't react as she sashayed from the room, hips rolling, focusing instead on keeping myself upright as she abandoned me to one piss-drunk captain.

For a moment, the man was content to watch me, thumb tracing the lip of the decanter.

Shifting from foot to foot, I worried the scab marking the base of my throat, trying to draw his eyes away from my concealed weapon. "What?"

"You should be sleeping."

"Don't tell me what I should or should not be doing—"

"You almost *died*, Mila. I can feel how weak you are, even now. You need rest, and in the morning, we'll have a discussion about—"

"*You* did this!" I hissed, clutching at the bedpost with my free hand. "This is your fault, you twisted parasite."

Eyes narrowed, the captain said nothing, allowing me to fret under the weight of his gaze. "Come," he said at length, crooking a finger.

Fist clenched on my blade, my lips parted on a furious snarl—but I stopped short. Glancing at the soft spot beneath his jaw.

Play the part.

I moved toward him on stiff legs, lifting my skirt to mid-shin, mimicking Alicia's effortless grace. The effect was lessened, somewhat, by the mud spattering every inch of my exposed skin, but nevertheless, obsidian eyes went where I intended. The bond coming *alive* at my approach.

Perhaps Alicia hadn't entirely lost her mind.

Perhaps playing the whore could serve some greater purpose. I glanced at his chest... at the outline of the pendant.

Bare feet padding on the carpet, I stopped just out of reach. But how to slip past his defenses? How could I force him to let his guard down long enough for me to snatch the pendant and make this vile, unwanted partnership work for *me?*

"Good girl," he purred, smirking. "Now, if you're awake and finished with your tantrum, we may as well get to the business of your punishment—"

Throwing caution to the wind, I uttered a fragile whimper, falling forward, forcing my muscles to limpness. Miming the very weakness that he'd caused.

Cursing, he surged forward, catching me about the waist. "Shit. Are you—"

Grinning, I set the blade against the hollow of his throat, forearm brushing the pendant beneath his shirt. "Move and die."

Hands hot on my filthy skin, he stilled, though *nothing* but divine intervention could still his lips. "It seems I've underestimated you. Again."

I pressed my blade deeper into his flesh—only to feel the bond kick and pulse within my chest, setting my lungs ablaze with excitement.

The captain released me, flashing the whites of his palms. "Now what, my little lunatic?"

I jerked my chin at the office chair, pushing him back until he had resumed his seated position. "Now—" I cleared my throat, taking slow, careful steps until I was behind him, toying with the pressure against his jugular lest he forget which of us held this mundane power. "Now you hand over my mother's pendant and take me to the rebels, or I cut your throat and go there myself."

He swallowed, the bob of his throat nudging the blade. "I didn't realize you wished to die."

"In case you haven't noticed," I hissed, wrenching his head back with my free hand, exposing him further, "you're not in a position to make threats, *Asher.*"

"You mistake me," he rasped, scruffy cheek prickling my skin, bond prickling... everything else. "I'm merely concerned that your ultimatum will likely end in your death. And mine."

Adjusting my grip on his hair to disguise the tremor in my hands, I said nothing, eying the silver chain from which the pendant hung. Noting the band of raw, torn skin looping about his throat.

But how to get it without sacrificing my current advantage?

A dark chuckle filled the silence. "I'm a career soldier, Miss Tannovic, yet I've never been closer to death than I was today. With you, limp in my arms. So cold. Eyes glassy." His side of the bond caressed me, pulling me toward a state of serene calm.

I bared my teeth, letting the back of my knuckles graze his scalp, seeking whatever ki I could steal through the contact. "Your doing, not mine."

"A moment of unforgivable ignorance." He lifted his shoulder, agitating the air around us. Filling my nostrils with his scent. Thick with whiskey, and... *Asher.* "I was... unfamiliar with the finer points of owning a Priestess like yourself."

"You don't own me," I hissed, pressing hard enough to draw blood, watching it mix with a bead of sweat until the rosy drop disappeared into his scruffy beard.

"We are bound, Miss Tannovic," he said, voice a low hum. Enticing. "In every way. Long before I put the chains on you, I *felt* it"—he raised shaking hands, pointing at the space over his black heart, the mirror of the place where the bond lived in me—"right *here.* You nearly died on the field today, and you would have taken me with you. Almost did."

The silence that followed his claim swallowed me whole. But that meant... No. He couldn't possibly be stupid enough to tell me such a thing, to reveal such a weakness without there being hidden motive! For that would mean... the captain was *vulnerable* because of me.

"So," I whispered, teeth clicking beside his ear, "the most powerful Elite in the Empire has fallen." I grinned. "Gelded by his new toy."

"Ah," he breathed, far too relaxed for his precarious position. "But that's just it. It's not just *my* problem anymore, is it?"

"You assume I believe your little story," I drawled. "Or that I care enough about this life to be forced into protecting you. I don't. On both accounts." Lifting my shoulder, I watched his pulse. Watched a drop of crimson sparkle and dance beneath my blade. "I will use the pendant to break this ridiculous bond you've forced on me, and then I shall be free of you forever."

"And if you can't? If I'm right, and we are bound in *every* possible way? What then? Think about it," he pressed, breath warming my cheek as he turned his head a fraction of an inch. "There's never been a pairing like ours, Mila. Two Trila-Glís... one Priestess, the other Elite? The very notion of such a pairing exists only in the curator's wet dreams. What we are has never been done. There are bound to be side effects I didn't anticipate."

"Ah, but I'm no longer Trila-Glís, am I? You saw to that." I pressed the blade deeper, letting rage guide my hand to the killing blow.

In spite of it all, his lips curved. "Then call my bluff and let's find out, shall we?"

Teeth clenched, I inhaled the captain's essence, moving to strike.

But... What if he was... right? What if—

Faster than my eye could follow, the captain's raised hands were wrapped around my forearm, breaking my hold on his windpipe. Using my arm as leverage, he yanked me around with force enough to topple the decanter from the desk when my hip struck the polished wood. I hadn't the time or breath to yelp before he was on me, wrenching my blade arm behind my back and pinning me facedown to his desk.

"Drop it," he snarled, impossibly strong fingers prying the blade free.

"Oomph—No—"

He took my weapon, slammed it on the desk beside my face, then dropped the majority of his weight into me. Grinding the points of my hip bones into the hardwood with his pelvis. "A letter opener?" He laughed, breathless. "Sweet Emperor's *balls*, Mila, where did you even get this?"

"Get *off*." I tried to buck against him, only managing to press the round of my buttocks into his groin.

With his free hand, he swept my encrusted hair off the back of my neck, pulling it to the left and leaving my face clear. "Just how far do you think my patience is going to stretch, hm?" He hiked my right arm higher up my back, stealing my breath. "Do you have any idea what would happen to you if you belonged to *any* other Elite, Mila?"

"I-I don't care. You'd be dead if I"—I gasped, vision sparkling as my shoulder screamed—"if the choice was mine."

"Brave sentiment from a helpless little girl," he retorted, thumb tracing the hollow at the base of my throat. He lingered, weight pressing me to the desk, his heat fogging my brain.

"Y-You're drunk."

"Something about having a blade pressed to my throat has a rather sobering effect. Imagine that."

"Asher, please—"

"I don't recall giving you permission to say my name, little slave."

Teeth flashing, I strained against him, but opted to say nothing at all. Opted to *do* nothing. Goddess, so... *helpless*. Just as he said.

"Thought so," the captain purred, breath tickling my ear and raising gooseflesh down the length of my back. "Now, while I have your full attention, shall we discuss punishment for your behavior on the field this morning?"

"Is breathing the same air as your kind not punishment enough?"

He sucked his teeth, something akin to a growl rumbling deep in his chest. "You haven't the slightest clue what you're talking about, little girl. You are permitted to behave the way you do, publicly defying me at every turn, because I *allow* it," he hissed, pressing close, lips brushing my ear. "I asked for one thing in return—do not draw attention to yourself, and especially not the attention of General Tilcot." He kicked my feet apart. "Now let me make something abundantly clear. There is *nothing* General Tilcot enjoys more than breaking a willful slave—"

"He's welcome to try."

"And he will succeed!" he bellowed. "You've put yourself in his sights. Made it known there's something different about you, and told the entire world that I *cannot* control you!"

"You *can't*—"

A calloused palm silenced me. "Shut your fucking mouth before I have your tongue torn from your lovely, mad head." He shook me, bowing my back as he forced me to stand, trembling with a fury so vibrant I was swept away by it. "It's going to take everything I have to stop him from discovering what you are. What *we* are. Allow me to spell it out so it can sink into that thick skull of yours. If he is given cause, the general will take your punishment into his own hands, and the Law of Ownership doesn't apply if it comes into conflict with Chain of Command. A loophole he's rather fond of, but he won't stop with pinkening your ass, Mila. Oh, no," he breathed, releasing my lips in favor of palming my throat. "He'll make you chose the weapon he breaks you with. After you beg—"

I shook my head, gasping, unable to speak.

"And you *will* beg," he stressed, heart hammering between my shoulder blades. "He'll make me watch as he unbuckles his belt—"

"Stop." I squeezed my eyes shut. "Just... stop..."

"That's the thing, isn't it? There won't be a damned thing I'll be able to do to stop it. I'll have to watch him fuck you—"

"Asher," I wheezed, chest too tight to draw breath. "I get it—"

"No. You *don't*," he snarled, shifting his grip to the base of my skull and tangling his fingers in the matted, mud-caked caramel locks. "It will only be a matter of time before he realizes *why* you're different. He's bonded to the High fucking Priestess, after all... Intimate with the signs of a Trila-Glís. He will do everything in his power to keep you, after that."

Tears of pain dusted my lashes, but I persisted. "Then you lied."

He laughed, though the sound lacked any hint of mirth. "Fucksakes, Mila. This is more important than—"

"He can't keep me if I remain bound to you. So either you lied about the bond being unbreakable, or you're panicking over nothing."

"So knowledgeable, darling," he drawled, voice dripping sarcasm. "Go on, then. Tell me of all those we've lost since Tritan fell. Tell me what happened to the surviving member of a bound pair, either Priestess or Elite, since you already know it all. Tell me how the living party has gone on to bond again. Tell me what shred of evidence would lead Tilcot to think you won't be free for the taking after *my* death. I'm waiting."

I blinked. Then it was true, as far as he was concerned.

If the captain died, so would I.

He took my silence for acceptance, adding, "The general cannot know of this. Do you understand me?"

But I had been struck silent.

"Do you understand?" he snarled and spun me, leaving one fist buried in my wild mane while the other fell to my lower back.

"What I understand, is this," I rasped, voice deadly calm, in spite of the intoxicated Elite trembling with fury before me. "I don't take orders from you anymore. In exchange, I will protect your secret and, therefore, your life. Until such a time that you betray this truce."

"Just what in the fuck gave you the impression that this was a negotiation, little slave?"

"You've lost your leverage, Asher. Let your temper

burn it all up." I caught his eye, placing my scarred right hand on his chest, just above the pendant, and gave him a tiny push. Branded middle knuckle mocking my words before they even left my mouth. "And I'm no more your slave now than I was five years ago."

"I disagreed with that statement then, Mila," he said, distracted. Capturing my wrist, he ran his thumb over the meeting of gold and twisted flesh, then went on to find the backward letters married to my skin. He settled there. Fingers stroking. "What do you think my opinion on the matter is now, when here you are, wearing *my* mark?"

"What you think is inconsequential. I am not a slave." I pulled my hand free, flexing the shiny scar tissue in the half-light between us. "There is nothing you can do that will convince me otherwise."

"You have no idea what I can do."

I lifted a shoulder. "Such a sentiment may have intimidated me five years ago," I allowed. "The unknown is a terrifying prospect, and one that you wield to maximum effect. But I am no stranger to pain and fear, and I am not that innocent little girl who caught your attention the day Tritan fell. I haven't known her since General Tilcot shot my father in the back. So," I continued, meeting his gaze unblinking, "you can continue with your threats, but they won't have the desired results." I grinned. "*You* made me untouchable today. Oh, you can still strike me, if you wish," I said, cutting him off with a raised palm. "But the instant you do, I will not stop until every Caledonian on the planet knows your secret. Even if it guarantees my death. Even if you tear my tongue from my lovely, mad head."

He loomed over me, breath warming my cheeks with the spice of whiskey. "If you think this little power play of yours will protect you outside of this house, you don't understand what's going on here. If the curator ever found out what you are, let alone *me*... what we are together..." he shook his head, eyes icy, colorless chips of obsidian.

"Better not risk it then," I whispered, flashing him my most brilliant, toothy smile. "Now step back and get your hands off me."

To his credit, the captain returned my smirk.

And stepped back.

3

———

"I must say, you're quite the tactician, Miss Tannovic."

I shrugged, picking at the scab building on my wrist without meeting his eye. "My father was a politician."

"Then he taught you well. Come," the captain said, disappearing into his closet. "We're going to the baths."

"We're... what?" I asked, trying to match the speed with which he shifted topics.

"You're covered in filth from the front lines. And because you are now awake and hissing," he continued, emerging with a length of black silk draped over one shoulder, "I figured you might like to take a bath."

"You figured wrong," I replied, glancing at the door. "I'm not going back to that bathhouse." It held uncomfortable memories. To say the least.

"Guess it's a good thing I wasn't asking." He took my scarred right hand and filled it with more of the same black material. "Undergarments for the bath. Wouldn't want to offend your delicate sense of modesty."

Cheeks blazing, I clutched the fine cloth to my chest. "How gentlemanly of you."

"Naturally." With a slight incline of his head, he smirked, inky eyes twinkling. "You can put those on when we get to the bathhouse."

"Have you forgotten already?" I retreated, lip curled. "I don't take orders from you."

"It's a bath, not a grand inquisition," he drawled, tossing me a look. "A little soapy water isn't going to kill you"—his nose wrinkled—"but it'll damn sure do some good."

"Need I remind you of the shower, not ten paces from where we now stand?"

"After all these many years, I've come to understand one thing, Miss Tannovic." He stooped, meeting my eyes. "Nothing about you is harmless or innocent. Say I were to agree. To allow you to shower here, behind a locked door, as I would any other woman in my care." His fingers went to the tiny crimson smear beneath his jaw, where I had pressed a rusty blade. "There's the vanity mirror to consider," he said, ticking words off on his fingers. "The shaving razors. Various hygiene chemicals and several other items that could be used to maim, poison, blind, or otherwise injure me should you be so inclined." He laughed. "Hell, I wouldn't be surprised if you tried to bludgeon me with a bar of soap wrapped in a towel."

"Huh. Gravity weapon," I mused, fingers pressed to my lips to conceal a smirk. "Good idea."

"Exactly my point. So the answer is an emphatic, and instantaneous 'I think the fuck not'. We're going to the bathhouse where I can keep you in my sights. Within reach."

Baring teeth, I tilted my head to the side. "You'll have to sleep sometime, Captain…"

He set his palm on my upper back, steering me toward the door. "There are chains secured to the floor beneath my bed."

I squawked. "You're joking."

But to this, he didn't respond, marching me down the stairs with a savage grin of his own.

"Holy shit," Marco said as we approached the kitchen, taking a massive, guilty step back from a pink-cheeked Alicia. "And here I thought you'd gone to bed already, old man."

"If I did," the captain replied, pausing to bump his hip against the doorframe, "it's only because I've been doing it longer and better than you, pup."

Chortling, Marco conceded the point, asking, "Where you off to in such a hurry?"

"Bathhouse. Oh," the captain said, catching Alicia's eye. "Alicia, could you have the bedsheets changed while we're gone? They're soiled."

"Of course, sir." She grinned, waggling her brows at me. "It would be my *pleasure*."

"Ah," Marco said, tapping the side of his nose. "Better and *longer*, huh? Seems unlikely, given that you've been gone what? Ten minutes?"

Scowling, I picked at my collar, finding interest in the tops of my filthy feet. "I'm hungry."

The captain snorted. "And I suppose you think I should reward your most recent attempt on my life, hmm?"

"Attempt on your—" Marco choked on the words, eyes bulging. "Please tell me you're referring to this morning? I fuckin' *told you* to chain her up while she slept. But did you listen?"

"It's not a reward," I snapped as Alicia's smile slid from her face only to be replaced with a tight-lipped frown. "I'm not a dog."

"No, but by Caledonian law, you're still my slave. When you eat is *my* concern."

"Well, I may have lost count of how long I've been in this cesspit, oh wise and powerful master of everything beneath the stars, but you haven't fed me *anything* since I got here."

It was his turn to gape at me. "Fucksakes," he said at length, running a hand through his hair, making it stick up at odd angles. "I didn't realize—Fuck."

"A compromise," Alicia demurred, approaching with a graceful roll of her hips, holding a juicy, red apple aloft. "Something light until you return from the baths, all refreshed and... cleaned up." She caught my eye, squeezing just a *touch* too hard as she clasped my hands around the fruit.

I sneered, sinking my modified canines into the fruity red flesh without breaking eye contact. Oh, I'd play the part, alright. Just not the role the traitor had cast me in.

"Mm," Marco hummed, sliding his hands around Alicia's waist. "So thoughtful, pretty girl." He kissed the side of her neck, making her squeal, though still, she did not break from my scowl.

The captain flung the front door wide. "We're leaving now."

"Need back up?" Marco asked, dark eyes slanted in such a way that all but begged the captain to decline his offer. "I'm not entirely comfortable leaving you alone with your little terror."

"Anything that makes you uncomfortable is worth doing," I said through a mouthful.

The captain rolled his eyes. "We won't be long."

4

———

With anyone else, a stroll on a night such as this might have been enjoyable.

A warm evening breeze caressed my cheeks, dispelling the heat and the lingering fog clouding my thoughts. Mixed with the scent of a cooling city, the mouth-watering aroma of baking bread wafting through an open window, and the night itself, I almost forgot where I was.

And with whom.

I scowled at the glitterbugs lighting our path. Hating them for daring to twinkle in the dusk as we brushed by, for lending a romantic air to an evening that didn't come close to deserving it.

Aching with the weight of fresh memory, for I was unable to touch their tiny minds as they flickered about. Couldn't sense their ki, but was forced instead to scan the gnarled shrubs and elegant statues with my eyes alone.

Like a mundane fool.

Nothing.

Not so much as a hint of the Caledonians and slaves I knew were there. Just beyond my limited scope.

There was nothing but Asher, and his accursed bond.

Goddess, how? How was I supposed to live like this? Cut off? Ki-blind and at the mercy of *his* charity. Dependant on his infernal protection, whether I could stomach admitting it aloud or not. And the general... How was I to fight for the fallen? For the vengeance they were owed?

The streets were damp with dew, air heavy with a chill in the shadow of the setting sun. Struggling to keep up with his long-legged stride was costing me what little energy I had left, burning through the ki the captain had used to revive me on the battlefield. But he did not slow, for the bathhouse loomed before us, the sweeping, blocky pillars a testament to the Eloran architecture from which they'd been stolen. A representation of everything I'd lost, of everything the Caledonians had stolen and remade.

Cheeks warming with exertion, I gasped, tripping over my feet and muddy hem, forced to seize his elbow or fall. "Wait," I whispered, sweat beading upon my brow. "I... I can't... I need a moment."

Watching me with face void of expression, obsidian eyes gleaming in the dusk, he paused.

I swallowed the flapping wings at the back of my throat, eyes falling to the cobbled streets.

A rough palm settled on the back of my neck, making me flinch, coiled even as he worked a thumb into the corded tension at the base of my skull.

Shoulders hunched, my gaze flicked to his, confused —until he tugged the pendant free and his eyes lost their sharp edge. Sharing it, he allowed ki to pulse through me, demanding calm at every beat of my frantic heart.

"Better?"

Filling my lungs to capacity, I nodded, once, chasing it. Drifting closer to his heat, both inside and out. Goddess, if I could just—

He tucked the pendant beneath his shirt, cutting me off once more.

I stumbled forward, keening low at the back of my throat.

Something wicked flicked through the bond. Something akin to triumph. "Come along," he drawled, hand dropping from nape to lower back, nudging me through the heavy oaken door.

"Parasitic bastard."

Grinning, he mounted the steps, one hand hot on my skin, the other tight on the railing. "Got any more stunts for me today, Miss Tannovic?"

I tossed my filthy caramel hair over my shoulder. And though my eyes flicked around the darkened bathhouse and I picked at the scabs ringing my left wrist, I said, "I haven't a clue what you mean," and ignored his stupid little hum of amusement.

Steam clung to the tiles beyond the landing, chasing off the evening chill and inviting the memories of the last time I'd been in this very spot. When my ki was still my own.

Was it possible that only two days had passed? Or were there more than that lost to unconsciousness?

Baring my teeth to ward off the poisonous ache, I took the lead. Picked the same bathing pool we'd fallen into however many days prior, for I would not be ruled by ghosts. No, I'd wash the muck and grime away, and start tomorrow fresh.

The captain closed the door behind us with a gentle *snick*, unbuttoning his shirt.

"What are you doing?"

He paused in the middle of shrugging out of the garment, giving me a look. "Cooking dinner."

Hugging the underthings he'd given me, I stepped back, watching his pectorals flex and shift as each slow inch was bared. The pendant bounced, drawing my eye first to the familiar glint of Glaith, then... beyond. Bronzed skin. Corded, work-hardened muscle, tapering into a narrow waist. "Why"—I swallowed, glancing at the only exit—"why are *you* undressing?"

Inky eyes went to the bathing pool at my back, then returned to my face, shirt fluttering to the damp floor. "You *do* understand the point of this building, yes?"

"You're not serious?" I breathed, heels bumping the tiled pool wall. "I'm not getting into that water with *you*."

"Oh?" He flicked his belt buckle.

Sweat dampened my scalp. "Wait. *Wait.* Y-You can't —*I* can't." I shook my head, following his fingers as he shoved his slacks past his hips, letting them fall to the floor.

The buckle clinked against the tile. "What's the problem, Miss Tannovic? My little warrior Priestess isn't..." he trailed off, eyes sparkling as he stepped clear of his pants, that maddening hint of intoxication still clinging to his every movement. "She can't be..." Wearing nothing but the pendant and a tight pair of undershorts, he took slow, measured steps toward me. "She can't be... *afraid*... can she?"

My breath caught. Cornered. He had me cornered.

Again. With nowhere to go, I half sat, bottom resting on the lip of the bath as he closed the distance. Looming over me. Unable to speak for desert winds ravaging my throat, I clutched my undergarments close to my chest as if the flimsy fabric could offer a measure of protection.

"You know," he said, giving said pathetic shield a gentle, half-hearted tug, "seems a shame to put these on just to bathe in them. Perhaps I should order you to go without—"

"You—" My voice cracked and, cheeks searing hot, I cleared my throat, forcing, "You can try," through clenched teeth.

"Careful, Miss Tannovic." He smirked, head tilted to the side. "You tempt me."

Just days ago, such a warning would have been his death knell. Now? I heeded it. Going still.

"Good girl." Wickedness played on his lips. "Come on, then. Let's get your underthings on."

Planting my scarred right palm on his naked chest, just above the pendant, I shoved him back. The contact sent ki zipping through my forearm, but I ignored it through sheer force of will. "I'm quite sure I can dress myself, Captain Rawlings."

He shrugged, retreating the gracious distance of a single, tiny step. Arms crossed over muscular chest, he toyed with the pendant. Inky gaze caressing my flesh. Waiting.

"Do you mind?"

"Not at all."

"Look away," I hissed, trying to slide around him.

He blocked me. "And give you the chance to flee? I don't think so. Though, I'll admit, the prospect of hunting you down yet again does have a certain… twisted… appeal."

Flashing my teeth to hide the tremor rippling through my muscles, I set my attention to the little ball of silk, attempting to turn it into undergarments. He was enjoying this, my Elite parasite. I could feel his amusement thick in the air, whispering of dark thrills and sadistic pleasure through the bond.

Cursing, I dropped what must pass for Caledonian panties on the floor and stepped into the leg holes. Inching them over mud-spattered thighs beneath my dress was slow going, but there was nothing for it. Not if I wanted to preserve my dignity from those hated, obsidian eyes. "What do you expect me to do with *this?*" I thrust the remaining bit of fabric in his face, material *just* wide enough to cover my breasts.

"Wear it as a headband."

I blinked.

"Turn around," he said, and plucked the scrap from my fingers.

"I—"

"Don't argue just for the sake of it, Miss Tannovic." He smirked. "I could always make you go without—"

"And I could always have a little conversation with your precious general—"

"Relax," he drawled. "My offer is to *give* you modesty. Not remove it."

"Fine." I spun, crossing my arms over my chest. "But for the record, I don't think you know the meaning of that word."

"Semantics, darling."

I turned. "What now, you bloody stupid—"

He tugged the knot keeping my dress secured.

I yelped, scrambling to keep the silky fabric in place.

"Here. Over your head," he hummed, looping the length of fresh black silk around me. "Adjust it and I'll tie it off."

"You son of a *whore*," I snarled, given no choice but to do as he asked, tugging in an absurd attempt to stretch the narrow strip of fabric over my chest.

A dark chuckle kissed the back of my neck, but he continued with deft fingers, his touch clinical as he tightened the band, tying it off, as promised. "There. Perfectly modest."

I whirled, fists clenched and buried in a length of the soiled dress, trying not to see the pathetic way it flapped around my hands. "Modest by *whose* standards?"

"Mine. Now step out of that rag."

To do so would be to stand before him all but naked! I shifted my weight, knees bent, teeth bared.

"This isn't a fight you can win, Miss Tannovic. You're getting in that bath. This is your only chance to do so yourself."

"Fine. *Fine,*" I hissed, cowed by the idea of fighting him in this state of dress, allowing the ruined garment to fall. I didn't linger, didn't want to know if his gaze sampled my disfigured skin as I flung my leg over the rim of the bath. Neither would I think of the last time he'd seen me this exposed, or what his rough hands felt like tracing my modest curves.

No. None of that.

I stepped into the steaming water, breath catching as the ripples lapped at my waist, turning the skin below my bellybutton pink and soaking through my underthings. All before I'd even begun to adjust to the temperature.

Sparing nothing for courtesy, the captain splashed into the pool behind me, soaking my back and sending me bolting to the far side of the tiled bath with a squeal.

"Goddess—" I whirled to face him, retreating until my hamstrings bumped a submerged bench. "What is *wrong* with you?"

But he laughed, walking toward me, tall enough that his narrow hips remained above the water even where the pool was deepest. Each rolling step sent a surge toward me, sent the water higher up my ribcage as he approached.

Eying the pendant, I raised my hand, elbow locked, trying to force a demand for space past parched throat.

He didn't stop, but pressed forward until scarred fingers were splayed across his belly and his ki ignited beneath my palm.

Awareness pounded through my blood, restoring me. At once a refreshing breeze and a granite tomb I couldn't escape. I swallowed, vision going glassy as I took what he gave. My head tipped forward, toward the hard expanse of bronzed skin stretched out before me.

A sparse line of dark, curly hair caught my blurry gaze as it reached up from the tiny waves, crawling toward his belly button. Or—depending on vantage point—led down... toward that which was concealed beneath the hemline of his underpants.

Was it... as soft as it looked? I licked dry lips, head drifting to the side, hand drifting... lower. Bumping over ridges of muscle slick with dew.

His breath caught, flooding the bond with a heady ki that made my lips tingle with forgotten memories.

But... it was... a lie. A poison altering my perception. Making me forget. I scowled, tearing my attention from his belly, forcing my focus to match the inky gaze above me, then said, "Get your hand off me."

A single dark brow rose. And then, with that infuriating smirk, he raised both hands.

Cheeks blazing, I snatched my hand back, plunging it beneath the surface.

"Excuse me," he said, and stooped, one hand braced on the slick tiles beside my shoulder. Forcing me to take a seat or permit him to drape himself all over me.

"Wh-What are you doing?" I whispered, head bumping the lip of the pool, fingers tight on the bench beneath me.

He glanced at my lips, breath filling my lungs, and for a moment said nothing. Just hovered there. Pulse pounding at the base of his throat, pendant throwing a tri-shadowed rainbow over my collarbones and his. So close I could all but see the ki dancing on his skin, begging me to reach out and take it...

Knuckles popping beneath the surface of the water, I resisted, for Alicia was right, damn her. He *wanted* me to try again. Expected me to fight or fly. The bond was coiled tight. Hungry for the chase. Aching for my defiance.

Denying him, I pulled in a breath, trying for clarity. Trying *not* to see the pendant.

Goddess, I wanted it. *Needed* it. But how?

Play the part.

Could I? If it meant my freedom?

Yes. A thousand times, *yes*.

I squeezed my eyes shut, letting the bond infect me.

This... it was nothing. Just a physical act. Easy. Play

the part of a woman in heat and be free of him when he'd taken his pleasure, just as Alicia had said. It never took long when Kas chose a mate. Each season, the males would boast of their prowess, posture for their queen, and after a few grunts and yowls, it was over.

Nothing to it.

I swallowed, hard, eyes tracing the contour of a long, lean torso. Pausing on the waistband of his underpants. On the bulge lurking just beneath the surface. Distorted by the water. Flexing, I tilted my hips forward, trying to ease an uncomfortable ache tugging at my insides.

"You're filthy."

Something deep inside my chest recoiled, injecting my veins with sobering ice. And for a moment, as my heart rate tripled, shock pinned my tongue to the roof of my mouth. *"I'm* filthy?" I whispered, voice trembling. "This—this"—I gestured at myself, at the space between us, splashing him with my frustration—"this is *your* doing! How can you blame me for this when—"

He laughed, threw back his head and *laughed,* deep from his belly. "I was talking about the *mud,* Miss Tannovic." Reaching over my head, he retrieved a bar of soap, brandishing it before my nose.

Jaw slack, I could do nothing but stare. Gaping as he took a seat on my right with a low groan and began to work the soap into a purple tinted lather. "Come," he said, extending a sudsy hand.

I sneered, teeth bared, holding back the pathetic tremble of tears.

Lifting a broad shoulder, he shrugged, then passed the bar over his chest. "Suit yourself."

Tearing my gaze away, I cupped my hands, scrubbing at the brown stains until I glowed pink from the neck down and the water around me was clouded with filth. "There," I said, drawing my knees to my chest and wrapped my arms about myself. "Happy?"

He snorted, spreading the lather across his chest. "You haven't even touched the soap." Then he jerked his chin at the tangled nest atop my head, saying, "And it's pretty safe to say you missed a spot."

"I'm not putting my face into this water. Who knows what sort of diseases I could contract."

He rolled his eyes and set the bar on the ledge. "These tubs are fed by hot springs and replenish themselves several times a day. Any filth in this water is your own."

"*You* are here."

"Indeed I am," he returned, closing the distance between us.

"What—"

"Relax, Miss Tannovic," he breathed, twisting, taking my elbow in a rough palm. Tugging me closer. The surge of ki in his touch tightened the muscles in my lower back.

And though I remained stiff, I didn't fight, letting him pull me off the bench, weightless in the water as I glided toward him. Bracing on his heat-reddened chest—just above the pendant—my bottom brushed his knee. Prickly. But I didn't struggle when he set his second hand to my hip beneath the water. Breath frozen in my chest in spite of the sweat damp on my brow, I did nothing as he turned me.

What in the name of the dead Goddess was *wrong* with me? I should snatch the pendant now, while he was distracted! Allowing an apex predator to have my back was—

"Easy," he hummed, breath hot against my nape. His hands slid higher on my ribcage, fingers tight, framing the rapid, shallow breaths scarcely passing my lips. When he shifted again, settling me between spread, prickly legs, I was pinned. "Easy."

Hardly! Searching for cooler air, my head fell back. I couldn't do this! Couldn't breathe, not with his touch, and his ki, and—

Play the part.

Let him believe I wanted this. Let him take his pleasure, and when he'd slaked his lust? Strike. Claim the pendant and freedom both with one perfect strike.

Then it would be easy.

I felt him then. Swelling against my backside. The twitch and throb was at once foreign and utterly unmistakable. Separated from my skin by nothing more than thin strips of sodden fabric.

Cheeks ablaze, I set glassy eyes upon the ceiling, trying to will the pounding of my heart to go no further south than the pit of my stomach. Just a few minutes of unpleasantness and I would do exactly as Alicia said. I'd pay that price to have my freedom.

Just another war story to add to the list.

I'd forget it soon enough.

Forget him.

Rough palms compressed my ribcage in a tiny squeeze, then slid higher, blunt fingernails tracing the marks Kas has left upon my skin, now an angry red in the bath. Raising gooseflesh in their wake as they traveled up, ghosting over the insufficient bandeau wrapped about my chest. He found purchase in the hair at my nape and gathered the walnut-stained locks in both hands, tugging, guiding my head back as he wet the ends.

I shifted between his thighs, throat dry as his erection flexed against my spine, dragging an answering throb from the seat of my core—and I flinched. Arching my lower back to put a swell of heated water between us, useless claws finding his knees.

The powerful muscles beneath my palms provided a foundation almost as sure as the ki thick in my blood or the marble tiles beneath us, and instead of marking his skin, I clutched at him.

Trembling.

This was... *wrong.* To let this hated, manipulative beast touch me so. To let his perverted ki drug my senses was... it was... my only bloody option.

Play the part.

I forced a breath through clenched teeth as his fingers worked my hair, moving closer to the base of my skull.

This was *natural.*

A primitive instinct necessary to ensure the future of a species. Nothing more. Not a betrayal of my body or a sign of weakness.

This... this... *fire* burning in my belly was strength. Not brawn or Goddess-given power, but it was *mine.*

Breath ragged against my shoulder, he slid one hand forward, cradling my throat in his palm. Easing my head back until I stared at the ceiling once more. Back arched, hands tight on his skin. Elite ki fluttered alongside the tiny bird trapped in my chest.

Abandoning my throat to shield my eyes, the captain wet the crown of my head, scooping up slow handfuls of water with his free hand. Brushing away fouled water before it filled my ears. Petting my wild tresses into some semblance of order as he worked, he collected the soap, bringing it to a lather.

Sure fingers kneaded it into my scalp, filling the humid air with the nauseating floral scent, but I groaned, eyes fluttering closed.

Goddess, I *ached*.

His smile brushed my cheek. "Feel good?"

My eyes snapped open, lax muscles surging with tension once more.

"Easy," he breathed, cutting me off before I'd even begun, digging his thumbs into the stress knotting my shoulders.

"Mm..." I went limp, eyelids getting heavy. "Easy..." Let him take the lead as he'd taken everything else. My physical presence was the only requirement here.

Humming deep in his chest, he fit my head to the cradle of his shoulder, scooting his hips forward on the stone bench. He lined us up—back to front—sinking lower and maneuvering my soapy tresses into the water. Pendant pressed against my spine... but it was the pebbled nipples pricking my shoulders that dragged a ragged breath from the back of my throat.

And there, nestled between my cheeks, his erection jumped, beckoning to the slick heat gathering between my legs, clutching at nothing. Dragging a flinch from the shredded, rational part of my brain.

His hand snaked under one arm and over the other. Forearm laid between my breasts, he pulled me closer. Wrapped so tight his pulse hammered a rhythm against my skin, drowning out the pendant's song. Denying my urge to flee, he matched me. Forcing me to stay.

Clinging to his forearm with both hands, I whined,

heart pounding between my legs. Goddess, this was... madness. My blood was on fire, guts aching with tension...

Play. The. Part.

Make him believe.

And then he began to massage the bubbles away.

I flexed my calves, heels finding purchase on the edge of the submerged bench, knees breaking the surface as his fingers threaded through my hair. Untangling the knots and letting it float free in a cloud around us. My hair was returned to its natural, damning silver-blonde, absent the last of the dye that had protected me for so many years. Carried away by soap and strong fingers.

Belly flexing, he straightened before I could process the loss, keeping me in his lap. "That's better," he whispered, lips tracing my ear.

A shiver clawed at my lower back, making me tremble in his arms. "N-No—"

He plucked the bar of soap from the water and pressed it to my chest. Rubbing in tiny circles.

Black stars dotted my vision, my head fell back once more. "Goddess, what—what..." I shook my head, lips parted.

"Breathe, Miss Tannovic." Beard-scruff rasping against my cheek, he dislodged my grip on his forearm and swept my hair over my shoulder. Leaving a slash of chill between my breasts in his absence. An absence he filled with tiny circles and a bar of soap. Inner wrist teasing the swell of my right breast. "Breathe."

I gasped, aching inside and out.

"Good girl," he hummed against my neck, free hand dipping below the surface once more. Finding my hip and pulling me back. Against that hard ridge. He groaned, flexing, straining against my bottom.

"I—"

He slipped the soap beneath the bandeau, cupping my breast as he lathered the soap over a nipple pebbled in defiance of the temperature.

Some small, pathetic sound burst from my lips as he pinched the bud between the meat of his thumb and the bar, igniting my very blood with a belly-clenching surge of electricity.

"*Fuck,*" he grunted, picking up a tentative, rocking rhythm controlled by his hand on my hip. Grinding himself against me. Each tiny thrust edging his thickness closer to my core. Every pulse sending a wave of molten heat where it didn't belong.

Abandoning my nipple, he pushed the soap lower, guiding it over my belly. Fingers seeking the waistband of borrowed panties. Brushing the sparse hair at the top of my mound...

My eyes flew open on a gasp, unseeing. Flicking from one blurry, shadowed object to the next. "W-Wait," I whispered, "I don't—I—" The air was choking me, compressing my chest and filling my lungs with a thick, soupy mess. Drowning me in all things *Asher*.

"Hey—" the bond surged, wrapping the High Priestess' ragged cocoon with a wave of insulating calm.

A lie!

But without missing a beat, he retreated, tugging my hand off his thigh and filling it with the bar of soap. Wrapping his hand around mine, he guided me instead, directing the soap to my hemline, beneath the waistband.

"That's it," he whispered, taking my earlobe between his teeth. "Gentle."

"A-Asher—" The soap was little more than a tiny sliver, a thin pretense for what this *really* was. As he pressed my touch where he wanted to go, using my fingers to draw his stupid tiny circles against the knot of tension aching with painful pleasure. My back arched, bottom grinding against his erection, the blunt tips of his fingers overreaching mine. Diving deeper. Seeking the very spot where I ached most.

"Fucksakes, Mila." He groaned, spreading my folds as the heel of his palm forced my fingers to continue their infernal circles. "I can feel how badly you need this," he rasped, and growled, pressing his finger inside. Squeezing me. "Please let me do this. I want to feel you come on my—"

All at once, the air pressure in the room shifted, and I jumped, clenching on his fingertip as I stared at the door. Vision hazy, even through the steam.

"Well, well. Isn't this a surprise."

5

———————

"Sonofa—" the captain cursed, straightening. And although he did not release me, he pulled his fingers from my panties. Cupping my mound with his palm. Covering it.

Disoriented, I blinked. "Wh—"

"Startled you, did I?"

The captain cleared his throat. "Yes, I was—" his forearm tightened around my chest. "I was... distracted."

"Mhm. I noticed."

With the pendant pressed tight to my skin, I felt his senses whip out around us, tasting the man now standing witness to my *most* depraved moment.

The captain didn't stop there, even as my spine stiffened in delayed horror, letting his ki-sense flick out. Going further. Flooding the surrounding area for signs of others lurking unseen.

But he'd come alone.

General Tilcot.

Arms crossed over a naked barrel chest, the general

strode into the steamy room, wearing nothing but a plush white towel. Dark gaze pinned not to my face, but to that which was beneath the surface of the sudsy water.

Belatedly, I squealed, writhing in the captain's arms —but his grip only tightened.

"I see our little devil is as willful as ever," the general said, and dropped his towel without a shred of concern for the nudity staring me in the face. "Still unbroken."

"You can tell all that just by looking at her, can you?"

Back arched, I strained against the captain, neck extended to its fullest, head laid against his shoulder for leverage. "Please—I need—" Air! I needed air! Goddess, how had I allowed this to happen? How had the general —of all people—managed to sneak up on us? The captain should have sensed him coming from the city limits!

"Be still," he hissed, lips tracing the shell of my ear. He caught me behind the knees, slinging my legs to one side. Keeping his left arm tight about my waist while his free hand traced the outside of my hip. Indecently close to groping my bottom. Giving the appearance of a man at ease—but with the pendant trapped between his chest and the side of my breast, I could feel the lie as if it lived beneath my skin. "What do you want, Harper?"

"Come now. Don't be like that, boy," the general said, sinking into the bath with a low groan and evil smirk. "We're family."

My heart lurched. *Family?* I was bound to the blood of the man who'd murdered my father?

"Only when it suits you," the captain said, and, shifting me higher on his lap, set me astride his softening erection.

My black-clad breasts popped above the waterline, upper torso exposed to air far cooler than the water was hot, though the action drew an unwanted eye.

"Like right now," my parasite continued, collecting my hand. He set his teeth to my fingertips, nipping me, sucking my index finger past full lips. The very same digit that had been tracing those infernal circles only moments before. Ignoring my attempt to pull my hand free, the captain laughed, though it was a bitter, humorless sound. "You've interrupted what was sure to be an extremely enjoyable evening. What do you want?"

"Your slave cost me rebel blood today, Asher."

The captain shrugged. "And I told you she wasn't ready for such a display." Making a low sound at the back of his throat, the captain wrapped my fingers about the pendant then cupped my breast, flooding the bond with forced calm. Pinching my nipple between forefinger and thumb, his beard rasped the delicate skin beneath my collarbone, lips chasing a drop fleeing toward my cleavage. "I *did* tell you she hasn't been trained—"

"Explain something to me," the general mused, swirling his left index finger in a clump of purple bubbles. "How does a Triloth of moderate ability cause the Emperor's Golden Boy to lose control of the SAG Turret?"

"If I knew that was going to happen, do you think I'd have taken such a risk?" He scoffed, chuckling while the bond screamed in tightly controlled panic. Playing *his* part and letting me feel it. "She almost died on the field today, didn't you, pet?"

"Ah, yes," the general purred, eyes tracing every inch of my exposed skin. "Captain Rawlings. Golden Boy.

Youngest Elite to rise through the ranks in known history... rendered impotent by a slip of a girl we found living in the woods."

The captain stilled. Fingers stopped their wandering.

"Can't use her without killing her?" Tilcot grinned. "I haven't laughed so hard in *years*. So thank you for that, cousin."

"I'm not worried," the captain returned, voice absent the tremor rippling through him. "I've trained my share of slaves."

I stiffened, glancing at his profile. Had he now?

"How reassuring," the general drawled. "And what does *this* slave have to say on the matter, hmm?"

Beneath the water, fingers tightened upon my hip, near to bruising.

Play the part.

"I—I don't know, sir," I whispered, eyes falling to the water. Demure. "All I remember is... *pain.*"

"Is that so?" The general stretched his arms across the lip of the pool, chest rippling. "You've no recollection at all of charging into enemy fire just this morning, brandishing a stolen gun and babbling nonsense about the fall of the Empire?"

"I"—I blinked, lips parting—"I did *what?*"

"Mila's behavior has been corrected," the captain said, toying with the ends of my sopping, silver-blonde hair.

"Riiight. Well. While I have to admit I'm pleased to see you're finally making an effort to instill an ounce of discipline in the girl," the general said, "I'm afraid it's far too late to escape the consequences of her actions." Turning his palms toward the ceiling, he shrugged, though the contrite action did nothing to lessen the glee etched deep in the lines of his face.

"That so?"

"I might have fallen for more of your lies," he continued, teeth gleaming white across the pool, "had I not seen the way her skin reacts to the Glaith. Not even my Sasha—the most powerful of their lot—reacts so. Why is that, I wonder?"

Without breaking eye contact, I stilled. Watching him. No longer hearing the threats spilling from his vapid lips.

Why, indeed? Sitting before me, naked and unarmed, was the very man whose screams I'd been dreaming of since my father's death. Foolish enough to levy threats at a man far superior in all but rank, Tilcot was blinded by arrogance. Too stupid to heed instinct, to fear the unknown. Instead, he was drawn in by a golden glitter as if he could mine it from my veins.

The captain was *expecting* me to fight, his grip snaked all around, containing all the dangerous bits from lashing out. All... but *one*.

Alicia—Goddess take her—was right. Much as I'd like to deliver the killing blow myself, I didn't need to. Not now, bound to an impossibly rare and dangerous Elite, who fed on *my* ki.

A man who glutted himself on the darkest Truth.

A smile spread across my lips.

"Even now," the general said, "she carries herself like a little queen."

Naturally. I'd learned from the best, hadn't I? But he wouldn't have that same chance. Wouldn't learn from the lesson coming to him. I spread my fingers on the firm, muscular chest at my side, letting blunted claws catch at the edge of a flat nipple and delighted in the captain's sharp inhale.

I licked my lips, wrist brushing the pendant's hard edge. A delightful fool, my father's murderer. Stupid enough to challenge that which he did not, *could not*, understand. Almost... innocent in his thirst for a power he was not fit to wield.

"Tell me." The general returned my smirk. "What's it like? Fighting a war your people lost five years ago?"

Oh, he'd have his answer. Could draw his own conclusions along with his last, shuddering breaths.

Saying nothing, I caressed the pendant, scarred fingers finding the familiar carved edges of my mother's family crest. While my prey lounged, blinded by false confidence...

"Am I to believe you're going to take down the mighty Empire of Caledonia single-handedly, little slut?"

Growling low against my cheek, the captain clapped his hand over mine, trapping my fingers against his chest. "I would have thought you above provoking a slave just to prove yourself right," he said, squeezing hard enough to grind the small bones in my wrist. But that violence wasn't directed at *me*. I could see that now. My captain was fighting the urge to strike this feeble interloper down. Resisting the dark seduction twisting through his blood.

All I had to do was... feed the flames.

"Prove myself right? So you admit it. She intends to see the Empire fall."

"For fucksakes, Harper," the captain snapped. "The same could be said of *any* slave owned by *any* Empire. Especially at the beginning. Do you not recall how wild

Sasha was? How long it took to break her? It takes time to adjust—"

"Time is a precious thing, isn't it? Always running short. Perhaps," the general hummed, "she won't be yours to experiment with for much longer, hmm?"

The bond ignited between us, vibrating with a possessive, territorial rage the likes of which Kas herself would have been proud. But still, he fought. Refusing to embrace the darkness, he brushed my attempt aside. And, keeping me pressed close to his chest, the captain surged to his feet. "Either make the attempt, or fuck off. But until then," he breathed, storming past the lounging general, "I'm done with this conversation."

"Of course you are. It's not going your way. This has been your pattern since you were a child."

"See now, that's where you're wrong." The captain set me on my feet, dragging his pants over wet skin— and wetter underpants. "I'm leaving because I don't want your unborn child to grow up fatherless."

"A bold claim from a man no longer employed by the Empire. Oh," the general purred, watching from the pool, "did I forget to mention that?"

The flush abandoned the captain's cheeks in a single instant. Blanched white beneath bronzed skin. "What?"

"Your services are no longer needed, Golden Boy." The general grinned. "It is my greatest sorrow to inform you that, as of *this* moment, you've been relieved of duty until further notice. We simply haven't a use for an Elite who cannot master a Triloth of moderate potential. Your incompetence is a danger to the men. You understand. That much uncontrolled plasma spilling onto the field unchecked could have killed someone." Pausing, Tilcot took a breath. Seeming to enjoy the tension rippling between us. "Did I forget to mention we've got the slaver in custody? Jasper, I think his name was. He's singing *all about* the Wood's Menace. Only a matter of time before he pokes a few inconvenient holes through your stories, cousin. Your lies about how you came to be bound to her. And once the curator gets here," he continued, turning his attention to me, "who knows? Perhaps your duty to the Empire isn't the only thing you'll be relieved of."

I took a half step, teeth bared.

Saying nothing, the captain caught me around the middle, keeping me pinned to his side.

His skin sizzled, making my heart pound and heat bubble from deep within my chest. But he took a breath, wrestling his instinct to fight into obedience.

"It's really quite unfortunate," the general purred. "You've left yourself no room to argue should the curator declare you unfit to have a Priestess." He tisked. "Such a stickler for order, our curator. Perhaps I'll get our Menace with child once she's been freed of your mark," the general mused, eyes tracing the scars marking me from breast to hip. "As you should have done *before* binding her. There's always the chance that my bond with Sasha will interfere, of course," he allowed. "But I'm sure there's a long line of eager, unbound Elites willing to put a hybrid brat in her belly, however... unsightly the vessel."

As he wrapped me in a plush towel, I couldn't tell which of us was trembling harder—me or the captain. Bile fought with a scream to be the first to come pouring from my lips, both losing out to an unexpected, vicious curse. "Over my bloated, rotten corpse, you fucking—"

Clapping his hand over my mouth, the captain

tossed his shirt and the clean dress over his shoulder, kicking the soiled one into the corner.

"Ah, such fight in my girl," the general cooed. "I look forward to housebreaking her. Oh," he added, flicking wet, dismissive fingers at the captain, "before I forget. After the debacle on the field, Sasha and I had a little... *chat* this morning." He traced his bottom lip with the edge of his thumb. "She's agreed that her assessment of a Triloth of moderate potential may have been a touch... inaccurate. A second opinion is warranted. Just in case. I'll expect to see my girl at the infirmary first thing tomorrow, Golden Boy. I'll send Aiden and Reese to collect her."

The captain's chin dipped, muscles so tense, the acknowledgment was all but imperceptible.

"Pardon? I didn't quite hear you."

"Yes, sir," the captain said, forcing the words through his teeth. "She'll be there. I have nothing to hide."

"Mhm. Of *course* not. Run along now. Time's running out."

Without another word, the captain spun on his heel, the deep rumble of laughter chasing us from the room.

6

———

Grip hard enough to bruise, the captain propelled me from the general's presence, hand on my elbow. Ki bundled tight. Molten iron pumping through his veins and the bond, both.

Staggering, I hissed, "What is *wrong* with you—"

"Don't."

My teeth clicked shut, feet slapping at the smooth, damp tiles.

Taking an abrupt right turn, the captain all but flung a door off its hinges, shoving me into the cobbled streets and the evening chill.

Sopping wet hair plastered to my nape, I stumbled, clutching at the towel as gooseflesh erupted over every inch of exposed skin. "Easy, you colossal—"

He caught me, pressing close, lips tracing the shell of my ear. "Not. *Now*. Do you understand me?"

"If not now, then when?" I snapped, trying to thrust away from his naked chest. "The moment was perfect. His arrogance sat him before you, unarmed. Alone. We could have been done with this."

Wrapping his hand in my hair, he forced my brow to the gooseflesh prickling his chest. A mockery of an intimate embrace, for though it appeared to be tender, he snarled, *"Mila, shut your mouth,"* against my temple. Anticipating my bunched muscles for the coiled spring they were, he planted his left hand on my lower back and pressed our hips together. And then, allowing me a single precious drop, he guided my fingers to wrap about my mother's pendant.

The towel dropped, pooling in a ring at my feet.

Scarred and nimble fingers interlaced with those that were thick and hardened by work, the captain flooded me with enough ki to turn my limbs to jelly. Supporting my weight with a tight band about my lower back, he wrapped about my mind as we were coiled about the Glaith. Masterful, he sent my enslaved senses spinning around the darkened streets. *Showing* me what he couldn't speak aloud.

Watchers in the dark. A dozen unseen lurkers surrounded us. Waiting.

But, Goddess! Such power! Not even the sun burned so hot, so brilliant. He thrust the High Priestess' pathetic protection aside and opened the bond, showing me power enough to set dark wings aflutter.

I grinned, greeting the temptation, reaching for these poor, powerless fools with claws dipped in Elite ki. Tainted, yes, but it would *more* than suffice. None would live to regret issuing such a challenge. They were nothing before us.

Nothing.

"Enough," the captain whispered, breaking my grip on the pendant.

Gone. Any trace of ki left tingling on my skin evaporated with my next breath. Eaten by the accursed leech chomping at my ribs. Worse still, the darkness submitted to *his* command, sinking into obscurity without a fight.

Obedient.

Kept.

"We are surrounded by vipers," he whispered. "They must see *exactly* what they expect to see. Nothing more."

I gaped, trying to orient myself, reaching for what I couldn't have. "Destroy them," I returned, scarcely audible, my throat dry. "Pull the ki from their worthless, cowardly hides as you should have done to that putrid general—"

"*Stop.*" He glanced over his shoulder, wary of insubstantial ghosts. "You're going to get us killed. Do you understand that?"

"They are not a threat unless *you* allow it."

"Have you forgotten what happened on the frontlines?" he hissed, lips and scruff rough against my ear. "There are consequences, Mila. There is more to this game than slinging power at anyone who challenges me. We are bound, you silly—"

"Yes," I returned, voice a breathy rasp, "we *are* bound. You carry the power of *two* Trila-Glís *and* the darkness, yet you still think like an Elite—"

Clapping a palm over my lips, he made a sound at the back of his throat and flung his senses into the aether once more. Eyes glassy, even as they stared down at me. When he returned, it was with a snarl. "Keep you voice down, you stupid, brainless chit."

"Elites," I scoffed when he released my lips. "All the same. Dumping ki into your silly weapons. Wasting your greatest source of power for nothing but a bit of senseless destruction."

"Ah. I should indulge you, then? Feed your precious, so-called darkness even if it kills us? Even if your lack of training bleeds into me and we lose control? What then? Kill them all?"

I shivered, stooping to gather my towel, teeth chattering without that brilliant heat in my blood. "The dead c-cannot speak of what they've seen."

He chuckled, draping his shirt over my shoulders. "Can't they? The general is bound to the most powerful and experienced Trila-Glís in recorded history. His untimely death would be a declaration from beyond the veil, Miss Tannovic," he murmured, scarcely audible against my ear. "If the general dies, the entire weight of the Empire will fall on us, seeking the power that could best their most accomplished asset. And should they discover what we are," he continued, "Tilcot's threats will be but a pleasant memory."

"You are blinded by fear. Unfit to wield the power you stole."

He laughed outright then, fingers tightening on my nape. "This from a girl born with incredible gifts, but lacks the smarts to seek training. Too drunk on her own legend to even imagine she could fall." Thumb tracing the corner of my jaw, he smirked. "You've never spared a thought for the long term. Not a shred of discipline in your entire, reckless little body. Never planning anything unless it benefits *you*. All you had to do was join the last of the Priestesses beneath the mountain, and I might *never* have claimed you," he drawled. "Knew you wouldn't. Knew you couldn't help yourself."

"No," I hissed, slapping at his hand. "You wanted me

to run. You *all* wanted me to run. To fight another day. Fill weapons with ki, or *be* the weapon. Submit. But either way—*any* way—a slave." I glared at the cobbles. "Prey runs so the hunter might sharpen her claws."

He pressed the next words to my temple. Forcing them to strike deep. "And that's why it was so easy to take you when *I* was ready. So fucking easy to draw you out of that forest, little hunter. All I had to do was drop the bait, and you came running like the obedient pet you were always meant to be."

"Fuck yo—"

"Where are your claws now?" He thumbed the collar melted into my skin.

Scowling straight ahead, I clenched my fists, blunted nails biting my palms.

"You've always been mine, Mila." We turned a corner, cutting onto a gravel path running parallel to the street we'd used to make our way to the bathhouse. "It's what you were made for."

"Made?" I laughed through the ache. "By whom? A dead Goddess?" Fingers trailing through the bushes edging the path, I felt nothing of the network spanning unseen beneath the soil. "I'm to believe some unknown deity gave me power enough to make men kneel, just so I could be *your* slave?" Cold and empty, I shivered again. "Was I made so I could watch you squander what is *mine?*" My fingers convulsed, tearing leaves from branches, crushing the silent traitors in a bloodless fist. "So I could watch you flee from challengers who cannot hope to match you?"

He tisked, stepping back onto the cobbled streets and made a show of looking both ways. Seeing what no other eyes could. "This is not your precious Forest of

Sorrows. There are dangers you can't see. Your impulse to fight what you do not understand has cost you everything you hold dear. I will not allow you the same liberties here, with my life in your tiny, scarred hands." Trailing his fingertips over the edge of my shoulder, he propelled me from forested path to cobbled street. "Let's leave the tactical thinking to me, shall we?"

"Doing a fine job there, aren't you? Power enough to silence his threats, and yet"—I let the squashed leaves fall, palm stained with their scent—"we run."

"We have until sunrise to come up with a plan that isn't going to end in bloodshed," he replied, cutting across the street toward his residence.

"You are a coward, Captain Asher Rawlings."

"Says the woman content to hide away in her forest playing house with a lion while the world burns around her."

I sneered, trying to keep pace with his long-legged stride. "You're the one burning things."

He glanced at me, a single brow inching toward his hairline. "Ah, but it's *you* who burns for *me,* pet."

"Hardly."

"No?" he asked, slowing to match my pace, tracing the edge of his smirk with his right index finger. "That you continue to argue with that pretty little cunt still sweet and wet on my fingers is impressive."

"What?" Jaw slack, cold raced through my chest. "There is *not!*"

He sucked the digit into his mouth, eyes fluttering on a low groan. "Mmm. Divine. Want a taste?"

"N-No. There isn't—there wasn't—" A strangled denial bubbled in my throat, short-lived, dying deformed and broken on my lips. "There... there was soap," I whispered at length, picking at my wrist until the scabs oozed.

"Mhm. And everything was so hot and"—an evil smirk hovered on his lips as he jogged up the front steps —"wet. Look at you," he purred, extending his hand, the gatekeeper blocking my way to sanctuary, "you're *still* soaked through."

"You're a pig," I said, sneering at the offer of aid, flashing teeth. Shivering. Balanced on the balls of my feet. But I obeyed. Wrapped in his shirt and a wet towel, eager to embrace the warmth of his residence and find relief from prying, hidden ears, I obeyed—if only so I could give my fury a voice, free of hushed whispers and metaphors.

The door clicked shut behind me.

7
———

The captain had dragged both Alicia and Marco out of bed, sitting them at the kitchen counter while he paced. Shirtless. Dimples at his lower back flexing with each agitated step.

"What's this about?" Marco asked, pulling a tattered sweatshirt over his head.

Inky eyes met mine before the captain turned, beginning another lap. "House is surrounded," he said, thumbing the pendant and ignoring Marco's choked expletive. "They probably don't have orders to do more than watch, or they'd have taken us on the street."

"And you'd have let them!" I snarled, tugging at the knot binding my breasts, then pulled the sodden undergarment out from beneath my arm. "You'd have let them take us, still bragging of your smarts and bloody plans while that man does—" I gagged, eyes squeezed shut, bracing against the kitchen island. "While your *cousin* does unspeakable things to me, all in the name of gaining favor with the curator. Even now, he prepares to strike and you've backed us into a corner!"

Scrubbing at his bleary eyes, Marco asked, "Who's striking what now?"

Nostrils pinched white, the captain glared at me. Watching as I disposed of sodden panties in the same manner the bandeau had gone, letting them plop on the floor with a wet *splat!* "Harper. Said he'd send for Mila at first light, but we'd be foolish to take him at his word. He'll be here before sunrise. Probably sooner."

"That repulsive man should be a stain beneath your heel, incapable of independent thought, let alone making threats of such magnitude."

Slamming both palms on the granite counter-top, the captain cut me off. "That's what he wanted! Why do you think he came to me in the middle of the night, unarmed? Seemingly without a guard, yet promising to have me murdered? And worse, threatening to have you bred by any willing Elite before I'm cold in an unmarked grave?"

Alicia gasped, but it was Marco who said, "Bloody hell. Can't leave you alone for an instant, can I? You've been out of my sight for an hour. Maybe less."

But I returned my parasite's glare. "He said nothing of your death."

"Didn't he?" Speaking in a vicious whisper, the captain pushed off the counter. Stalking toward me. "He means to have you, Mila. There is but *one* way to break a bond between Priestess and Elite. If things were different, that would mean death for *one* of us. Need I remind you *why* that option is not available to *either* of us?"

It was Alicia's turn to gasp, pretty green eyes lit with understanding, even as they bulged from her lovely head.

Gaze gone darker than pitch, the captain stopped

before me. "That little show in the baths was a *test*," he breathed, plucking a wet hank of hair off my shoulder, giving the silver-blonde lock a tug. "A test you would have failed, had I not been there to muzzle you." Not touching me, he set both hands on the granite at my back, looming.

I stilled, breath shallow, unable to break from that inky fury—for it was nothing, if not a mirror of my own.

"If I had struck him, physically or otherwise, he would have had me stripped of everything I own in the name of high treason—"

"Which includes you, Lady Wildcat," Marco said, reaching for his smokes. "All perfectly legal. Uncontested n'shit."

The captain tilted his head toward the soldier, retribution glittering in eyes that didn't leave my face. "Harper sees your temper for the easy trigger it is. Knows just how to push to make you reveal your secrets, and that *cannot be allowed to happen.*"

"Cannot be allowed to happen? Asher! He *already knows!*" I hugged myself, shivering. Arms crossed over pebbled nipples. "Goddess, and all that innuendo about a 'Triloth of moderate potential'? He probably beat the truth out of the High Priestess before he followed us to the baths. And if he couldn't? If she was able to somehow stand against him? He'll be certain of it by morning."

"And what's happening in the morning?" Marco asked, speaking from the corner of his lips as he lit his smoke.

Pushing a hand through his hair, the captain took a breath—exhale leaving my lips damp.

"Go on." I slapped his chest with the back of my

hand. "Tell them. Tell them the general had a *'little chat'* with the High Priestess." I twisted, meeting Marco's eye over my shoulder when my parasite said nothing. "I'm to be tested again. But this time I'll have the honor of a private audience with the general himself."

"Shit."

I nodded. "I will not sit here and wait t-to be bred by any willing party." Teeth grit to cover the quiver in my lower lip, I shook my head.

Alicia's face twisted. "I'll not let that happen, lass."

Lips pulled back, I scoffed. "You can't do anything to stop it. The *only* one who can"—I swatted my parasite's chest again—"refuses to do anything, lest he endanger his precious cousin."

The captain laughed, incredulous. "Were you present in the baths, or were you lost in your own charmed little world? Blood means less than nothing to that man except when it can be used as a weakness. A pressure point." Clenching his fist so hard the knuckles popped, he admitted his failure. "Harper set a trap, and I was too distracted to notice it snapping shut. A mistake I won't make twice, but I *do* know that man—my *cousin* —cannot be defeated with strength alone."

"Because you're a coward—"

"Because it's not an option!" he roared, seizing my shoulders. Shaking me. "Did you forget I cannot use your ki without risking your life and *mine?*"

But his theatrics no longer held the power to subdue me, if they ever had at all. "Then what do you suggest we *do,* surrounded as we are. Trapped as we are."

"Well," Marco said, and exhaled, engulfing Alicia in a great white puff of smoke. "Sorry, beautiful." He swatted at the cloud, grimacing when she coughed. "We've got options—Oi!"

Alicia plucked the lit cigarette from Marco's lips. "It's a filthy habit," she snapped, tossing his smoke into the sink. "And you'll not be doing it in this house." In answer, the soldier could only stare, jaw unhinged. Prim, she nodded, turning back to the conversation. "You were sayin'?"

Marco cleared his throat, and began ticking options off on his fingers. His obedience the strongest argument I'd yet seen for Alicia's mandate to 'play the part'. "Murder. Call in political favors. Go out in a glorious last stand, fighting to the end. Or"—his nose wrinkled—"run. Flee tonight before the general comes to collect the Wildcat, and live out our pitiful lives in the wilderness, absent the luxury I've become accustomed to."

"There'll be no spilling blood unless it's our very last option," the captain countered, scrubbing at the back of his head. "Anyone who owes me a favor either doesn't have the rank to overrule a general, or is still in the Capital and too far away to help. I don't have to explain why I'm not interested in the 'last stand' option, *except* as a last stand."

I grinned. "Then we run. Leave this wretched place and go to the forest." A forest where none could survive if *I* didn't allow it...

The captain rolled his eyes. "Assuming we could get past the men watching this residence, to run would be to confirm Harper's suspicions. And there's nothing the Empire wouldn't do to recover the power of a Trila-Glís. *Nothing.* Tell me," he continued, cutting me off before I could counter his assessment. "Would you leave the other Priestesses to suffer in your stead? To bear the brunt of your punishment?"

For a moment, I merely gaped. And then a scowl crinkled my face. Ceding a point to the enemy.

Alicia snapped her fingers. "*We* have advantage."

"How's that now?" Marco asked, plucking a fresh smoke from the pack, though at Alicia's fierce glare, settled for twirling it between his fingers.

"The general thinks he's won. Plan already in place. Already counting the wee lassie among his winnings, isn't he? Thinks having Mila tested again will uncover her true nature and reveal the captain as a traitor, loyal only to himself. What we need is t'prove him wrong. Beat that inflated prick at his own game."

"And how do you suggest we do that?" I asked, eying the brilliant Eloran scientist.

"I was schooled in the Temple before the Fall," Alicia said, the evasive truth sliding off her tongue with a smile. "I know much o'Tritan lore. Could talk 'till your ears bleed, but more relevant, I saw my share o'Flourishings. It's how the Priestesses know who are Triloth and who will be their next Trila-Glís. It's not the general we've got t'fool," she continued, grinning now. "It's the Lotus Regula."

Gooseflesh prickled at my skin, but I didn't move. Didn't breathe, for fear that Alicia had given up too much and outed herself as one of Tritan's elusive rogue scientists. Unless, of course, they already *knew* of her past, and their lack of reaction was proof that she was the traitor I thought she was.

But the captain didn't appear to catch her slip, instead saying, "I'm listening."

"A Triloth o'moderate potential *before* the Fall

woulda had the ability to turn the Lotus green, and call thick, healthy vines into being. Now? Bound in Glaith? Who's t'say how the Lotus'll react to each Priestess?"

"I am," I replied, digging at a band of gold ringed with scabs, letting it catch the light and her eye, both. "*I'm* to say. I'm bound to *this* inflated prick, and I touched the Lotus yesterday. It bloomed."

"Yes," she said. "But were you wearin' the *Raith?*"

I recoiled, colliding with the captain's naked chest, teeth bared. "No."

"Raith? I'm not familiar with that term. What's—"

"*No.*" I shook my head, squirming when the captain tried to restrain me. "I won't do it."

"You've no other choice, lass. Raith's the only thing with even half a chance at foolin' the Lotus. Virgin Glaith canna compare. Your chains o'gold and Glaith canna compare. Neither can contain one such as *you* for long."

Jolting with apparent understanding, the captain's arms tightened around me. "Eidolon. You're talking about binding her with Eidolon. Alicia... that's... That's *brilliant.*"

"No," I said again, twisting and writhing. "It's insane. I could barely walk with that heinous filth touching my skin—and that was *before* you took everything from me, Asher. What do you think'll happen now, when I have nothing left to spare? If it doesn't kill me outright, it'll be obvious something is amiss."

"You needn't wear it for long, lass. Only long enough to fool the Lotus."

"She's right," the captain breathed. "I can tie the leather around your wrist, loosely, and when it's time, flip the stone so it touches your skin. We can only hope it'll be enough."

"Even if the Raith... your... Eidolon, was it? Even if *nothin'* happens when you touch the Lotus, it's better than makin' it bloom, lass."

Teeth bared, I scowled until I thought my brows might become one.

But Goddess take her, she was *right*. Again. Had my second Flourishing not produced a single, pathetic blossom, I might have had the capacity to argue. Were our lives not in immediate peril, perhaps I could have convinced the captain to run to the Grandmother. That the Lotus had even whispered my Truth was damning enough.

"General Tilcot can beat the High Priestess as hard and as often as he likes," Alicia continued. "Canna argue what *we* can prove, can he?"

"No," the captain purred, his smile brushing the back of my neck. "He certainly can't. Marco, fetch me the Eidolon. We might just get through this mess."

And then—as if the Goddess herself had grown weary of watching me bungle every facet of my life and had smashed a puzzle piece into my skull regardless of whether or not the edges fit—the solution popped into my brain. A backup plan, should the Eidolon fail, and all the better for the knowledge that Captain Asher Rawlings *wouldn't* approve.

Three booming knocks echoed from beyond the front door, and I jumped as if he could sense danger on top of everything else, wrenching free from his arms.

Meeting those hated obsidian eyes, I asked him to lie. "Do you trust me to do this?"

The captain laughed, breath spicy on my lips as he

denied me yet again. "I trust you want to continue breathing, if for no other reason than to cause me as much misery as possible."

For the first time since our meeting in another time, the bond vibrated with harmony.

8

———————

Having knotted the leather band containing a chip of Eidolon around my wrist, the captain stooped to inspect his effort. Ensuring the stone was separate from my twisted flesh.

I shivered, revulsion dancing on raw nerves. That the Raith was the only thing with even a *chance* of saving us was insult enough, for to embrace that heinous alloy was to shun Truth altogether. To be completely bereft of the one thing I wasn't sure I could live without.

Ki.

"It always comes back to the Glaith," I whispered, testing that these new bonds were loose enough.

The captain brushed the edge of my collarbone. "It'll work."

I didn't bother arguing. Couldn't muster the energy to ask him not to leave me defenseless and return my mother's pendant, for fear that the general would notice something out of place. No, we were well and truly cornered, dependent on the plan of a brilliant woman who was either critical ally, betrayer, or some morbid combination of both.

A heavy fist pounded on the front door, growing impatient. "In the name of the Empire, open this door!"

"Let them in, Marco," the captain said, pulling a rumpled dress-shirt over his head. Tucking the pendant away from unwelcome eyes as the soldier complied, revealing two burly men hovering on the porch. Faceless, until the light from the front hall spilled over them.

"Aiden. Reese," the captain said in greeting, hand tightening on my nape, tethering me to his side. "It's a little early for house calls, isn't it?"

"Here on official business, sir," the stocky one said, speaking through a mouthful of gravel. "We've been sent to escort the Priestess to the infirmary, and—"

"What a coincidence. We were just getting ready to make our way there." Pulling a shawl from a hook by the door, the captain draped it about my shoulders and guided my scarred, twice-bound hand to twist within the fabric. Hiding the Eidolon until the moment was perfect. "Thank you, but your assistance won't be necessary, Reese. I'm quite sure I know the way."

Smiling through his teeth, Reese shrugged. "With all due respect, sir, our orders are to escort the Priestess. Alone. You and your men are to remain here until General Tilcot has finished conducting his business at the infirmary."

Alicia didn't miss a beat. "Well isn't that a bit o'perfect timing?" Stepping between posturing, territorial men, she tossed her hair over her shoulder and laid a hand on Reese's forearm. "My first shift at the infirmary starts in a few minutes, an' I'd be a far sight more comfortable walking these dark streets with two strong, handsome men like yourselves." She shivered, clutching her throat. Ignoring Marco's tiny flinch. "Hate the thought of walking alone with so much fighting going on 'round us. Mind if I join you?"

"Of course, miss," the taller one, Aiden, said, moving aside, cheeks pink. "Happy to oblige."

I scowled at the clever little bitch. Was she taking it upon herself to act as my minder, or acting on the commands of the man who'd offered her freedom? Did it matter?

Reese held out his hand, the other resting on the hilt of his weapon. "Come along, Priestess."

Eyes lowered, I obeyed, giving up the heady flavor of the last rare and dangerous thing for the company of mundane soldiers.

"Mila—"

"Must abide by the rules of the game," I whispered, for there was nothing left to say. Not now, with the vipers standing so close. He could only watch through icy chips of obsidian, face drained of all color, unable to take the power from my tiny, scarred hands.

Not bothering to hide my smirk, I went to my escorts, ignoring the way the captain's fingers caught at the edge of my dress.

Pleased with just how *good* helplessness looked good on my Elite.

9

———————

In contrast with my first visit, the infirmary was quiet with the early hour. The victims and villains of war lying side-by-side, either slumbering by necessity or pharmaceutical intervention. Among them, a skeleton crew of silver-blonde heads floated between the cots. Pressing cool palms to foreheads. Pulling starchy white sheets over exposed shoulders, they tended with soft words and softer hands.

Bile scorched the back of my throat.

Teeth grit, I turned my attention away from the pale ghosts of my past, heading straight for the High Priestess' office—and was intercepted by a tall, statuesque woman whose silver-blonde hair had gone all but white.

"Ah, you must be the new Priestess," she said, and continued without confirmation, "I wasn't expecting you so early, dear, but there's always plenty to be done. Tell me, have you much experience in a professional setting?"

I blinked, backpedaling. "I—"

"A good mornin' to you, Matron," Alicia said, tapping her temple with two fingers, offering a polite and respectful bow. "I believe the lass is to have words with General Tilcot and the High Priestess, but I'm here. Ready to"—green eyes flashed, finding mine—"*play the part.*"

So that was her game, was it? The traitor had come to act as my conscience, as if the height of the stakes wasn't obvious enough?

Lip curled, I turned away, watching something painful glimmer in the Matron's watery blue eyes. Watched as she returned Alicia's gesture, and pressed two trembling fingers to her temple. "I... I see. Well," the elder Priestess said, clearing her throat, then eyed the soldiers flanking me, her gaze narrowed. "Well, alright then." She flicked a bony wrist. "Go on. I expect she'll be waiting for you, though I've yet to see the general. He's been delayed by some disturbances on the front lines, I believe."

I picked at my wrist, prying the lid off a scab for no other reason than to let the painful nip kill my eager grin.

Delayed at the front lines, was he? Something to be said for the small mercies, at least.

"Good day, Priestess," I murmured, and spun, leaving Alicia to her servant's work. Not stopping until my hand was on the doorknob and my toy soldiers had entered the cramped, dingy office before me.

Commanding me to stay by the door as they searched the dim interior.

The very picture of lady-like patience, I waited for them to complete their inspection, teetering on the edge of demanding they leave at once. But it was the slender figure sitting in the dark office who hastened their retreat without so much as spoken word or threatening scowl.

Something to be said for subtlety as well, it would seem. I'd have to ask the High Priestess how she did it without her ki—for curiosity's sake. Mustn't forget the very real consequences of failing in this cursed mission.

"Go ahead," the taller soldier said, forcing the words through clenched, ticking jaw. Aiden. His cheeks were pink. Brows drawn together over a thunderous glower that simply didn't match the situation.

Eyes narrowed, I frowned at him. He was... angry? Of the two soldiers sent by Tilcot, Aiden given the impression of being the one with mild manners.

When I saw the High Priestess' profile, I understood why.

"Thank you for the escort, gentlemen," I murmured, one hand on the door. Knuckles white.

Reese made a sound, wedging his foot between door and frame. A denial perched on his lips.

For a moment, I did nothing but maintain eye contact with Aiden, who surrendered with a tight, jerky nod, and pulled his partner back. Allowing me to plunge the High Priestess' meager office into darkness with a gentle snap.

It took a moment for my eyes to adjust, longer still for me to locate the crown of silver-blonde hair seated behind the cluttered desk.

I took a step, worrying the band of leather disguising poison. "Your Grace?" Sitting in the dark was ominous enough, but it wasn't until I saw what had her attention that something cold and slimy slithered through my guts.

There, displayed in a garish trophy case just to the left of her desk, reflecting whatever minimal lighting the gloomy office could offer—or emitting some sort of otherworldly glow from within—was a set of the very same golden chains that were melded with my wrists and throat.

Chains that hadn't been there the first time I'd entered this office.

I swallowed, hard, tugging at the leather band containing a shard of Eidolon, and tried again. "Your Grace?"

A deep, bone-weary sigh answered me, and she stood, flinging a black cloth over the case, as if disgusted by its presence. "Good morning, Mila," she said at length, turning her back on the symbol of our fallen culture. Instead, she stroked the pages of the ancient dusty tome topping her desk.

"Are you..." I trailed off. No. She wasn't alright. Even in this poor light, I could see the shadows. Bruises. The swelling. A dark line that bisected the bow of her lower lip. "I'm... sorry."

She waved me off, tracing her puffy left eye with ginger fingertips. "Not your fault."

"Isn't it?" I took a step, glancing at the clutter topping her desk. "He didn't strike you for entertainment."

"No. Not this time."

My teeth flashed in the dark, for if it had happened before, it would happen again. And, no, reckless personal endangerment aside, *that* wasn't my doing. *My* fists hadn't left those marks, and I wouldn't take responsibility for his actions. That guilt was Tilcot's to bear. To answer for. "Then I'm sorry for my part in this. And for your pain. That I couldn't stop it." I took another step, setting my hands to the edge of her desk. "Can... can you heal it?"

"Not without betraying that I *can*." A rueful smile plucked at her split lips and she opened the drawer, withdrawing the captain's ring. Setting it to glitter on the desk before her. "He likes to see his mark."

My guts roiled, serpents wriggling and squirming in earnest. "He'll like it less when those marks are on *his* skin."

A shrug.

Throat dry, I wet my lips. "He's coming for me. Tilcot. The things he promised to do..."

"I know."

Of *course* she knew—he'd already done those things to her, hadn't he? Practiced his technique, the evil bastard. "Your Grace... I..." I shook my head, unable to define exactly what I was.

She spun the ring of Glaith on its edge, watching it twist in lazy circles. "I don't think I can fix this, Mila. There'll be no hiding what you are. Not this time. The Lotus will speak the Truth." Metal danced on polished wood, lap after lap. "It's all been for nothing."

The Eidolon chewed at the back of my scarred wrist. "What if there was a chance?"

For a moment, as the ring wound down and came to a clattering halt, she said nothing. Did nothing but gaze across her desk, one eye half-lidded. And then, "You want the ring."

It was my turn to smirk. "I deserved that. Worse, because I *considered* stealing it from you only yesterday.

To deny it is beneath us both, because knowing it exists is almost all I can bear." Hand trembling, I allowed my thumb to trace the brand. "And you're right not to trust me. Right about *everything,* really." I laughed, at ease in the shadows. "I *am* tainted. Addicted to the darkness. An Empath who's tasted death. If it weren't for these accursed chains"—I lifted my left wrist to show off gold ringed by raw flesh—"I'd have surely killed you all by now."

She hummed, sliding the thick, ancient book shut with a careful, delicate touch. Packing it away in a box behind her desk. "If you're trying to convince me to let you have the ring, I can assure you—"

"I'm not here for that, Your Grace. Besides"—I smirked—"the Glaith is not the answer. At least not for *me.*"

The phantom of a similar conversation five years gone made her pause, lifting her brow. "Not for long, anyway."

"No. Not for long. Unless..." I set my wrist on the desk, letting the Eidolon catch what little light it could. "Unless I had access to a substance that could blind the Lotus and turn every Priestess who touched it into a living ghost. Absent their ki."

She jerked, clapping her palm atop the captain's ring. And then, leaning forward, she pressed her fore-finger to the exposed alloy hidden in leather, recoiling almost before I felt the pressure of her touch. "I... I should have thought... Raith. Goddess, Mila... that could actually work. How—"

"Alicia," I breathed. "She's out there right now, playing nursemaid with the Matron."

If possible, the High Priestess' face blanched further

still, making the shadows stand out against her translucent skin. "Alicia? She's been captured?"

I nodded, tight and short. "At first, I thought it was an unhappy coincidence. That it was *my* fault she was captured. Now? After seeing the way she navigates this culture?" I shrugged. "I'm not so sure. And it all makes a twisted sort of sense, given the Caledonian advances with the Glaith technology over the past five years. But without my ki? I'm not certain of anything, except that Alicia can thrive anywhere she lands."

"She is an impressive young woman. Does the captain know?"

To that, I couldn't say. Merely lifted a shoulder, still tracing the brand sitting high on my knuckle. "I hate him, you know? Asher. He's taken everything—" Pain tightened my throat, choking off my confession. "He's selfish and power-hungry, and sometimes I think nothing would make me happier than seeing *his* knees bruised in supplication. But..." A tiny, bitter laugh bubbled up, squashed before it could travel further than the space between us. "But I can trust that whoremonger. Much as I hate to admit it. He holds more power than the general can even conceive of, yet *I'm* the only one who knows the brunt of it."

"He's a good man."

I avoided the urge to sneer—but only just. "You *can't* trust me. Whatever good you saw in me all those years ago doesn't exist anymore, if it ever did." Teeth flashing, I tossed her a quick, savage grin born of my years running beside the queen of the forest. "If I have half a chance, I'll burn this place to the ground and drink from every man, woman, and child of Caledonian blood who comes bouncing from the flames. Innocent or not.

Elite or not. I won't stop until our people are free of these parasites, even if it means my death."

"Then—"

"But you *can* trust *him*," I pressed, giving voice to my darkest fear. "Asher will carve the darkness from my chest before he lets me have more than the table scraps he feeds me." Forcing a breath through my nose, I laughed. Shaky with the unburdening. "As much as I regret not tearing out his throat the day we met, the captain may be the only one capable of holding my leash. Maybe your dead Goddess sent him to do just that?" I grinned, quick and fleeting, then said, "I wonder how many will feel it if the general gets his way?"

"There will be casualties of untold proportions."

I nodded. "If..." My eyes dropped to the hands folded in my lap. One scarred, the other clenched. "If I fail here today, as I did on the field, can we afford the consequences?"

Saying nothing, she turned her attention back to the case housing the unused set of chains. When she turned back, there was ice in her gaze. And then she slipped the ring onto her middle finger, and said, "I will not allow that to happen."

My chin dipped, the hot burn of helplessness blurring my obscured vision. "I'm not ready to give up on our people. Not done fighting, even though the enemy has taken all of my weapons. But if I fail," I pressed, *needing* to lighten the weight compressing my lungs. "If even the Raith isn't enough to conceal what I am, promise me you won't condemn them to a life half-lived. Free them. Fill your ring with every ounce of ki you can, and free our people."

"I took vows," she said, pausing to adjust the ring.

"To protect my people. To do no harm. But most of all," she said, raising icy blue eyes to meet mine, "I vowed to make impossible choices. Today I am forced to choose which shade of black will suit the future best."

"Ah. You see, that's where you're wrong." Expelling a shaky breath, I laughed. "If the general wins, there will be no more impossible choices. No more chances to set things right."

Delicate brows came together, head tilting to the side.

"We're linked too deep, Asher and I. Probably my fault," I allowed, drawing tiny circles on the battered finish of her desk with blunt claws. "Or maybe it's simply because of what we are. Separately and together, I don't know."

"Unique," she said. "A gift from the Goddess."

"Perhaps." From the hall beyond her cramped office, came the rumble of deep male voices. Time running short. "But we cannot be separated, he and I. Even by death, and for that, I hate him most of all."

The High Priestess blinked, going very, *very* still. "What?"

"If the general tries to claim me for his own, as those chains would suggest he intends to do, Asher and I will both die."

Shaking her head, the High Priestess said, "No... that's... that's not possible..."

"I think it's sort of poetic, really. Most powerful ki-wielder who's ever lived, but can't use it without killing us both." I shrugged, picking at my hemline. "I don't know. It's probably best that something as rare and dangerous as the darkness isn't the prize for corruption and murder."

"Good morning, sir," said one of the soldiers standing guard, identity indistinguishable through the closed door.

But the man who responded needed no introduction. "A fine morning, indeed, soldier. Or... it *will* be. Inside, are they?"

"On the field yesterday, Asher fired a weapon," I whispered in a rush. "Took everything and not enough. I almost died, and he with me. Not enough of your barrier between us to stop it. Bond runs too deep." Fists clasped tight in my lap to stop the trembling, I choked on the next words. "With us gone, you *must* claim my mother's pendant. You'll have the power of *three* Trila-Glís. You'll be unmatched." My lips twitched, and fingers trembling, I prepared to loose the Eidolon and turn myself into a mundane ghost who dared to trust. "A-Are you with me, Your Grace?"

The doorknob twisted, light spilling into the room, making my eyes water. But still, I didn't break from her half-lidded, swollen gaze. Even when she stood, rounding the edge of her desk, head bowed to her master.

"Ah," the general said, his large frame blocking out all the light. "My girls. What a lovely sight."

A tremor washed over me, from the crown of my skull, to the very base of my spine. Waiting on an answer that might not come, if I'd placed my trust in the wrong woman.

"Oh," the general said, pausing, turning back to his men standing guard. "And gentlemen? We are not to be disturbed. Under *any* circumstances. Understood?"

The chorus of 'yes, sirs,' churned my stomach, but I

swallowed it down. Trapped in a tiny room with ghosts and dark feathers bound in chains.

Closing the door behind him with a sharp snap, the general spread his large hands and said, "Shall we begin?"

10

—————

The High Priestess clasped my shoulder, a flash of obsidian and silver glittering on her bejeweled finger as she met my eye.

"Why is it so dark in here?" the general barked. "Can't see a bloody thing. Sasha, go open the blinds and get some light in here, you lazy cow."

"Of course, sir," the High Priestess said, taking the long way around her desk. Concealing me from night-blind eyes as I upheld my promise and flipped the leather band. Allowing the Eidolon to sink jagged teeth deep into scarred flesh.

There was no time to brace for that bottomless hunger, no time to second guess or hesitate, for the general was almost upon me. And with him? Destruction or lies. Nothing between.

With my truest essence wrapped in a frigid cloak, I could only gasp as the flames of my ebon soul were doused without so much as a puff of smoke. Blinking against the wash of early morning sunlight pouring in from a tiny, forgotten window.

Disoriented, I was rendered completely and utterly mundane. Cut off from everything, including the parasitic leech who'd made a home in the hollow space where my heart used to flutter.

"Let's begin with a lesson in manners, hmm?" the general said, and came to a stop before me. "A slave stands when her better enters a room."

The obvious response hung heavy between us, but I stood, wobbling on legs made of overcooked noodles. "My apologies, sir," I murmured, head bowing against my will. "It... it's not easy to adjust to life here."

Finger curled, the general caught me beneath the chin. Tilting my gaze to meet his. And Goddess, how I wished the look in his eyes was unreadable. Wished I couldn't see the depravity for what it was... that the Eidolon could silence the *knowing* as it had silenced everything else, as it had spared me from *feeling* the sickness I could see writhing behind General Tilcot's murky eyes.

Clearing her throat, the High Priestess pulled the ancient, shriveled Lotus from its place on the shelf, and said, "The Flourishing, sir?" Letting the clay pot scrape against her desktop as she pushed it toward me.

The general hummed, neither releasing me nor breaking eye contact. Licking his lips. "I'm not in a hurry."

"I... I thought I had been summoned... to..." Blinking, I shook my head, fighting the wash of infectious apathy creeping up my arm, for in my haze, it appeared as if my veins weren't flush with molten gold as they had been on the field... but... stained with blackest pitch, inching closer to my heart. In one moment, spiders twisted and flicked beneath my skin, spinning webs of *nothing,* but an instant later? Perfectly twisted flesh the same pink and angry red I'd had since the Fall. "... thought I was here... to... to make the vines grow? Like... like they did last time."

The general exhaled, sour breath whispering over my cheeks. "Just the picture of innocence today, aren't you? Such a change from the demon in the baths of last night. Or the willful slave on the field, stealing an Elite weapon and igniting conflict with the Rebels. Conflict that is sure to be bloody, I might add." He thrust me back, setting the base of my spine against the cluttered desk. Fitting his hips against mine. "Did he coach you, hmm?"

The Eidolon clinked against the hardwood as I braced, fingers scrambling to find the desk's edge in my effort *not* to hurl my knee into his groin. "C-Coach me?"

"Did my dearest cousin tell you what it would be like when you belong to me? Did he tell you everything you need to do to help him keep you?"

I shook my head, glancing at the High Priestess' blotchy, white face. "I don't—"

"He'll say anything to avoid the inevitable, I imagine," he continued, stroking the hair back from my face. "Of course, I suppose I can't blame the man. Trials are such lengthy, bothersome things, aren't they?"

Ice splashed down my spine, potent enough to overpower the Eidolon, if only for a moment. "What?"

"Mhm. Yes, but don't fret. I have no use for such a colossal waste of time and resources." Pausing, he pressed his thumb to my lower lip, peeling it back to expose my teeth. Daring me to shorten the digit down to the first knuckle. "Though, now that I think of it, I suppose Asher may be more opposed to the *conse-*

quences of losing his Priestess than actually losing *you*. A rather homely, damaged little thing, aren't you?"

"M-My scars are—"

"And that boy *does* enjoy his luxuries." Tilcot smirked. "I expect you'll do just fine as a breeder. Especially," he continued, tangling his meaty hand in my silver-blonde mane, "if the sire is of high quality."

"Don't... don't touch me. Please. You don't..." Vision sparkling, I clutched at the general's forearm and tried again. "The captain said... by law you can't—"

"Ah, the *law*," Tilcot drawled, pressing his nose to my scalp. Inhaling. "So open to interpretation, isn't it? Laying hands on a bound Priestess is strictly forbidden, it's true. But"—he grinned, the heat of his over-large body covering me from the nose down—"who among us will tattle, hmm? I certainly won't say a thing. And my Sasha is such a well-trained, eager fuck-puppet, aren't you? It'll be our little secret."

"No..." I swallowed, fixating on the steady thrumming pulse at the base of his throat. Itching to tear the Eidolon from my wrist and *finally* be done with this pest. *"No."*

"Mm. Lucky for you, I don't need permission. Not from a slave." He grinned, collecting my scarred hand with a sneer of disgust. Seeming not to care for the humble band of leather that would either send me to the Void, or condemn me to a life of eternal slavery—he flipped my wrist, inspecting the binding.

"My Lord Tilcot," the High Priestess began, taking a step, face pale beneath the bruises. Palm raised as if to ward off a dangerous animal. But her hooded gaze was focused on... *me*. "The Flourishing. Please, we must—"

"Yes, yes," the general said, rolling his eyes. "Fine.

Let's get to your bloody Flourishing." He stepped back, allowing me to stumble free of the pinch between his hips and the desk, gasping.

Trembling, I met the High Priestess' battered gaze and wrapped my free hand around the Eidolon. Pressing it deeper into my wrist. Hoping it would be enough to choke the dark petals.

"Alright, dear. Just as before. Touch the Lotus, just there. And—"

A large, rough hand settled between my shoulder blades, pressing my chest toward the desk, hands braced on scuffed wood. "Don't mind me," the general cooed, and calloused fingers slid up my back, working at the knot holding my simple dress together. "I'm sure I'll find some way to amuse myself. Get on with your Flourishing."

"S-Sir," the High Priestess stammered. "She must not be interfered with. It—it could affect the outcome, as you are already bound to me."

He paused, abandoning the ties at my nape to grab at my hips. Pressing the growing bulge in his trousers to my backside. "You mean to say the girl could *appear* Trila-Glís, even if she isn't? The flower is that sensitive, is it?"

"Yes, sir," the High Priestess replied, voice stronger now. Confident. "Mila is Triloth, and as I am Trila-Glís, my power far outstrips hers. In fact," she said, "you may have already affected the outcome of this Flourishing. As I said yesterday, this ceremony was a rite of passage for our people. A week of quiet reflection in solitude, followed by cleansing of—"

Tangling his fist in my hair, the general wrenched

my head back. "Then I'll have to be sure to touch her a little... *deeper* to ensure it blooms, won't I?"

"It—my *lord*—"

I almost laughed. This wasn't about the Flourishing or my Truth, had nothing to do with the suspicion that I was more than I appeared to be, because Asher was right. General Tilcot meant to have *me*.

"Perception," I rasped. "The test. It doesn't matter. He doesn't care what I am," I continued, straining for breath. "Only that enough doubt is cast to justify killing the captain. The perception of wrongdoing."

"Now *that* is an outlandish accusation," the general hummed, and, bypassing all subtly, gathered the front of my dress and tore it down the middle, exposing my chest.

"General *Tilcot!* Unhand her at once!"

Filling a meaty palm with my right breast, the general chuckled, breath sticky against my cheek. "Well, well. It appears your attitude is catching, little slut," he murmured, toying with delicate flesh. "What is it about you that inspires such... disobedience?"

My eyes fluttered closed, for there, in the dark, I could pretend. There, I could put myself back in the forest, lost in the throes of a night terror. Anywhere was better than this, at the mercy of my father's murderer, allowing the Eidolon to chew a hole through me. Hoping it *would*. Hoping it would eat me up before it was too late.

"Get your hands off that girl," the High Priestess breathed, cold fury straightening her spine. "I'll not ask again."

"I'd very much like for you to stop me," he returned,

then pinched my nipple so hard I gasped, teeth bared. "I'm going to fuck this little slut, right here. Right now—" He fisted my hair, giving me a shake. "I can't breed her yet, of course, but there's plenty of time for that once she's free of Rawlings' influence. Do you think he'll feel it?" the general asked, ravaging the tip of my breast. "Do you think it'll be his last thought, knowing there was nothing he could do to stop it? That's right," he whispered when I jerked, hands scrambling for purchase, meeting the wide blue eyes across the room. "It's all been arranged. The Golden Boy will die a traitor's death. Today."

With a mighty snarl, the High Priestess lunged— and was struck down by a savage backhand. The blow landed with force enough to send her crashing into the pedestal, toppling the glass case containing the chains and the very last dregs of hope. The case shattered against the concrete wall as the High Priestess fell. Dazed but breathing, the rings of gold scattered about her crumpled form.

Unperturbed, the general's hand continued wandering. "Where was I? Ah, yes," he murmured, hiking my skirt up, inch, by painful inch.

"You're pathetic," I whispered, forcing myself upright, right hand planted on the desk. Eidolon drinking deep, I kept my eyes fixed on the crumpled form of the High Priestess—useless as she was. Unable to benefit from the deaths of two rare and dangerous things, or guard the last of the Goddess' chosen from becoming living wraiths.

Fully aroused by the violence, the general pressed himself against me, grinding my hip bones into the edge of the desk. Exposing me with the flick of his wrist, he flipped my skirt over my bottom, then jerked my scarred hand behind my back. Twisting until my shoulder screamed, rough fingers covered leather and gold. Putting too much strain on a knot that wasn't meant to last, the leather came undone.

Poised to fail on the edge of Truth.

"He did this to himself, you know. Rawlings. Taking you like he did? Without permission?" the general laughed, and stripped his salvation away, letting bracelet of leather and Eidolon fall. Clattering to the floor. "It was stupid. The actions of a traitor with something to hide."

Pinned beneath him, the general didn't notice what he'd done in freeing me. Missed the flex of my spine as the bond kicked my heart back to life, as Asher's strength poured through my every nerve.

The captain's scent filled my brain, his impossible ki flooding my veins with molten ore. His wrath almost came bursting from my lips when he tasted my distress, when he learned the cause. Territorial fires burning hot enough to make even Kas' claim on my soul crisp and char, he raged. Immolating the stench of the general's ki from my very blood, and in his blind frenzy, left the bond wide open.

"Please... don't..." I shook my head, trying to free my wrist as *feeling* rushed to fill my veins. To break the connection of skin on skin before the hunger woke and burned away all sense.

But... why? Why should I fight so hard against it when my bonded parasite was finally seeing sense? When bending knee to the beast could save us? Why should I fight to spare this man—this *murderer*—from a fate he was so desperate to court?

Snarling, I bared my teeth, eyes squeezed shut

against the flood of ki both foreign and intimate. "It's *wrong.*"

"Wrong and stupid," Tilcot agreed, blind to my struggle. "But it won't take much to convince the powers that be. Their perfect Golden Boy is unfit to have a Priestess of his own. Thought he was clever enough to keep you all to himself," he whispered, reaching between us to fumble with his belt. "But things have changed since the early days. There's no Priestesses left. None who aren't already ruined by the chains. You see, our greatest triumph was also our greatest blunder. The chains give us your power at the cost of fertility. The bound Priestesses are barren. Each and every one. Which means no hybrid soldiers for the Emperor to play with. The Golden Boy knew that, of course," he said, and the naked heat of swollen flesh came free against my thigh. "And if he'd been smart, he'd have left you unbound, put a brat in your belly, then used it to gain favor with the Empire. With such leverage, he might have traded you in for better standing. Better ranking. Might have been able to buy himself the rank of a general. Alas..."

"He's not a good man," I hissed, eyes squeezed shut, shoulder all but wrenched from the socket. "But he's better than some."

Setting his length between my thighs, the general laughed, beginning to thrust. Spearing through delicate tissue too dry to tolerate such unwanted action, his fingers tightened on my hip, and, breath picking up, he pressed his lips to my ear. "They might have let him keep you, then. After all, it'll be a few years until we can produce a new generation of Priestesses."

My eyes snapped open.

The tethers binding dark wings disintegrated at *my* command, for there, through a door left open, was the thing I coveted most.

"Dear Goddess, *no,*" the High Priestess whispered, waking to face a thing of nightmares. Struggling to stand before she'd fully opened her eyes or gathered her senses.

"Oh, you didn't know?" the general crooned, unaware of the thing he'd released. "I'd have thought that was rather obvious, by this point," he murmured, and stepped back, spinning me to face him. His erection bobbed between us, swollen and grotesque, straining toward reddened breasts. "I've chosen *you* to be the first of our Tritan breeding stock, little slut."

My hands, fingers curled into blunt claws, had found purchase on his wrists. Knuckles white, in spite of the great feathered beast unfurling behind my ribs.

Feasting.

"Harper—*don't!* Step away from her. You have to before—"

"A good slave thanks her Master when he gives her a gift," the general continued, then jerked my bottom to perch at the edge of the desk, reaching for the swollen bit of flesh dribbling between us.

"Mmm, yessss. *Thank you,*" I drawled, and with a slow roll of my neck, I met his murky gaze.

And smiled.

11

———————

I t started low in my throat, rising fast. Bubbling up with the speed of the repressed *finally* set free. Free of the one who held the leash. Beholden to nothing but the glow of power set in stone—*my* power mixed with *his.*

Coupled with ecstasy, it burst forth from the seat of the bond itself, taking flight.

Laughter, born of darkness.

"I tried," I rasped, head falling to the side, meeting wide blue eyes ringed in white. "I should be commended for the effort, at least. Not for what comes next, of course." I licked dry lips. "But I *did* try."

The general shook me. "What comes next will—"

"You want thanks?" I asked, letting my knees part, hooking my heels behind thick, muscled thighs. "Shall I call you 'Master' and plead for mercy? Is that what makes your cock hard?"

His head jerked back. Surprise etched into his skin.

"Shall I cry and beg? Or do you prefer your victims too weak to fight as you rut above them? Because if that's the case..." I shrugged, locking my ankles at his waist. Unconcerned with the sad lump pressing against my naked thigh. "You're going to regret barring your toy soldiers from this room. I know, because that was *my* mistake too. Once."

"Ah. Little slut thinks she's still got a chance at freedom, does she?" A nasty grin spread across his lips, replacing the shock. "Have you forgotten, then? Your kind was born to kneel to mine," he whispered, bearing down, wrapping his fingers around my throat.

But even as he began to squeeze, the grin remained fixed to my lips.

"Mila, no!" the High Priestess rasped, but it was far, *far* too late.

Too late to summon help or beg forgiveness, for through the bond, the pendant was *mine* once more.

My mother's Glaith spat shadowed flames of retribution, hanging from another's neck. Reaching through time and space to surrender my due. Liberated, I pressed branded palm to the general's chest. Pulling the ki out from under him even as he bore down, fingers flexing around my windpipe.

"I will break you into a thousand pieces," he snarled, sour spittle misting my cheeks and lips. "You'll be given to the men as a reward, fucked raw until you've been bred. The babe will be torn away before you've even seen its face. A gift to the Empire. A fucking commodity to be traded at will. Property from birth. It'll never stop. Not when you're ragged from birth. Not when you beg, and plead, and scream. *Never,*" he hissed, grip tightening.

Still, my smile did not slip. Even when my vision began to tunnel and my lungs screamed for relief. No. I merely concentrated on the thrumming pulse beating beneath my palm, willing the rhythm to break down. Become erratic. Claiming my prize, even as I reached for more. Hurling ki straight into his heart, then clawing it back. Watching as my veins began to pulse, as gold spread from the chains circling my wrists once more.

"You will never—" he coughed, sweat beading on his brow, blanching in spite of elevated blood pressure. "Never know anything else. Not until you've been used up and your cunt is stretched and sagging and only those being punished will bed you. Only then—" A bead of sweat dripped into his eye, making him wince, even as his grip slackened, just a little. "Only then will you be given to an Elite and bound again, as... as..."

I dragged a frayed breath in through my teeth, and with it, pulled his life-force through my palm. Exhaled, and sent ki surging into the frantic, fluttering muscle pounding away behind his ribs.

Breath in, ki out.

Ki in, breath out.

Again.

Taking everything.

Keeping nothing.

And he *burned,* dressed in flames fed by breath, tempered with sweat, and anchored by the stone sitting proud atop another's breast. A stone filled with power so brilliant, it could ignite the world with little more than a stray thought...

A perfect circle.

"What—What magic is this?"

"*Mine.*" Victory in sight, after all these years, I grinned. "All mine." I pressed him back, keeping my palm steady on his chest even as I slid off the desk.

Complete control with little more than a touch, even with the bond's nagging tug whispering of temperance and seduction. Begging for control.

"Im-Impossible. You... you *can't* be... Your *face*... it's... *how?*" Blinking sweat from muddy eyes, the general's fingers slid away from my throat, hands lax and useless at his sides. *"Trila-Glís"*

"Kneel," I purred, forcing him down with the toothiest of grins. Reveling in the thump of his knees on the tiles for I could *feel* it. All of it. Such sweet torment was *mine* once more! I felt the skin split, the glorious shock of pain lancing straight through me, radiating. Leaving sweat heavy upon my brow. And when I pressed forward, sending another surge of ki, I felt the muscles constrict and ripple through my own chest as the General gaped. Jaw working to swallow the terror clotting in his throat before he choked on it. But there was no stopping the spread, not when *his* veins began to fill with Caledonian gold. Radiating from my poisoned touch.

Faster than a lion's strike, gold lightning raced down his arm, curling in the palm of his hand for an instant before doubling back, feeding me. Letting me taste his agony as I swayed, drunk on power.

"Kneel," I said again, voice thick, head thrown back. Breasts standing high and proud, shamelessly exposed to the chill and both sets of wide, shocked eyes. I bared my teeth, pressing harder, pulling every available shred of ki to the fore, then forcing it into his heart. Relishing the purple tinge blooming on his cheeks... savoring the terror as I pulled everything back, drinking his agony even as it raced down *my* arm. "Kneel as you were born to do."

"Goddess." Staggering to her feet, the High Priestess reached for me with bejeweled hand. "Mila no! You're going to—"

"You will die at my feet, knowing what true power is," I whispered, wrapping my free hand around *his* throat, in spite of the borrowed agony curled in my palm.

Eyes bulging—etched with tiny golden capillaries—flicked toward the door and the reinforcements who had been ordered not to come.

"You will die at the hand of a slave, knowing it was *your* pathetic life-force that freed my people," I hissed, sweat dripping. "I will undo every nightmare you've unleashed in your wasted years, and you will be forgotten." I paused. Mustn't forget to savor the moment. To relish the sheen of sickness glistening on his cheeks and the terror thick on his tongue.

When he gaped for breath, I gave it all back. Filling him, drinking his agony even as it raced down *my* arm.

"Mila," the High Priestess whispered, edging toward her desk. "Stop. You have to stop."

"Never." Not when I was so close. Not when vengeance was *finally* within reach. Justice. For everything this monster had done. For the women he'd victimized.

For the High Priestess.

For my father.

Palm flat to heaving chest, I tore through every wall. Shredded every barrier keeping this beast from tumbling into the Void, opening myself to the chaotic beauty of his last moments, eyes rolling back.

The bond lurched, writhing in my chest. Fighting me for control. Trying to stop the pain infecting us *both*.

But it was too late, even for one such as *him.* For at that very moment our hearts fell into irregular sync.

Stumbling together, all three.

I exhaled, pushing the tidal wave into General Harper Tilcot's flailing heart, feeling it swell within my chest *and* the captain's. Watching the general exhale with us as his golden veins popped against flushed, blotchy skin. Pupils blown out as he stared at me in supplication, for he knew.

It was time.

One final draw, and he'd be mine…

"Enough!"

A rainbow of black stars exploded behind my eyes. Breaking my grip on my pendant as I was sent to the floor in a disoriented tangle of limbs, dirt, and shattered bits of clay.

I blinked, lungs pulled inside out and stuffed too full all at once. "What—" I pushed branded, trembling hand through my hair, fingers prodding a sticky, grit-filled wound at the back of my head.

But she wasn't finished. Palms cupping my cheeks, the High Priestess stooped, brushing her thumbs beneath my eyes. Stroking. Her brows tilted, as if to convey something beyond my fractured comprehension.

"Your—" I wheezed, clinging to her wrist to keep myself from drifting away. "Your Grace, what—"

And then, right hand slipping over my lips, she began to take.

Everything.

"You stupid, *stupid* girl," the High Priestess whispered, stepping through a door left open—*through the bond itself*—she commanded his ki and mine to go to the Mistress of Milithia.

Struck stupid as she filled her cursed ring with the power of *three*, I could do little more than gape at a woman unbent, even with the weight of betrayal hanging heavy around her slender shoulders. She pulled until there was nothing left to give, until the only scrap of ki left to my parasite was the pendant itself. She offered no explanation, even when she finished her macabre task and stood, whirling, leaving my side to go to... *his.*

General Tilcot.

The Glaith mocked me while she worked, glowing white-hot for a moment until she channeled all that glorious stolen power into the man who'd taken my childhood. Bent over the fallen, unconscious General with a dark shadow glittering atop her knuckles, she gave what I'd taken.

"Why?" I asked, drenched in cold sweat, quaking in the horrible, sucking absence of so much power denied. *Again.* "How *could* you?"

"You would have died with him, you silly chit," she snapped, voice a strained murmur, brow speckled with sweat as she worked to save the life of her abuser, his skin sallow. Absent that deadly golden hue. "You and Asher both."

"That's a price I would have paid, and one you had *no* right to take—"

"No right?" she asked, voice a vicious flicker. "You *are* your father's daughter, aren't you? An arrogant fool."

Swallowing the hurt, I pushed soaked hair back from my face. "Let him die," I hissed, trying to claw my way toward her. Crawling through dirt and glass, over rings of gold and the ancient, dormant Lotus passed through the ages from one High Priestess to the next. "He deserves so much more for all he's done. Please, *please* don't do this—"

"Do you think I haven't destroyed him a thousand times in my mind? Do you think it's easy to smile? To pretend I don't remember the Goddess' touch as I watch my Priestesses being abused, day and night?" she hissed, hands whipping over victim and torturer *both*. "No one currently breathing wants to watch this man fall more than I do, Mila. But my wants and needs are not my birthright. You must set your hatred aside and *think*. Harper Tilcot is *one* man. One whose ear *I* bend. Whose thoughts I guide and whose vicious impulses I temper, however possible. His death will be an inconvenience to the Empire, but his replacement? What will he be?"

An unknown brand of evil, *yes*, but... "I—I'm—You can't—"

"You, my reckless, wild girl, will *live*." She glanced up, shimmering blue eyes meeting mine for an instant before returning to her macabre work. "You will *both* live. Now go," she said, balanced on her haunches when the general drew a great, rattling breath. "Get out of here. They *cannot* suspect you, do you hear me? I can make this look like natural causes. At least until he wakes."

"And when he does?" I asked, staring at hands stained with blood and dirt, speckled with shards of glass and the shadows of Glaith. "What then?"

"Another war story for the book."

12

———————

I don't recall hearing the High Priestess calling for help she didn't need. Don't have a clear memory of her office-turned-crime-scene filling with soldiers, for I'd been left dangling on the edge between conscious and not. Head throbbing from blunt-force trauma, she'd left me with scarcely enough ki to keep my eyes open, let alone contend with darkness or do as she bade, and run.

But when one of the general's men stepped over me —kicking a golden circlet and ancient shriveled relic to the side—I cringed. Pressing my back to the furthest wall, I bumped the back of my head and the wound seeped in dirt and bits of shattered clay.

The other soldier, the softer one whose name had been purged from memory, stooped before me. His brow furrowed, lips moving, though they couldn't be heard over the ocean roaring and sloshing inside my head. Instead, deft fingers snatched the ends of my torn dress, concealing my chest and fresh bruises, both.

But I couldn't be bothered with modesty, not after

what the High Priestess had taken. Not now, while she wielded the power of *three*, and used it to save General *fucking* Tilcot.

My bleary gaze drifted to the fiend in question—and found him returning to wakefulness. Dark eyes glassy and rolling, yet open.

The realization sent adrenaline surging through my overwrought body, and I struggled to sit. Pulling from reserves I probably shouldn't, I pushed at Aiden's hands. Demanding space enough to breathe.

"...need supplies," the High Priestess barked, her voice tinny and distorted, peeking above the waves of absence. "Get whoever is available at this hour and help me lift him. Oh," she added, jerking her chin toward me, "and get her out of here, Aiden. The girl is in shock."

I shook my head, scrubbing glass-speckled hands over my cheek before I registered the pain.

"Goddess, *Mila*," Alicia breathed, appearing in the doorway. "Lass, what happened?" The green-eyed traitor extended a hand that shook, taking a step toward me. "I can escort the lady—"

"No," the High Priestess snapped, head jerking up at the sound of Alicia's lilting, accented voice. "I need competent hands *here*. Aiden will take her to Captain Rawlings. You will stay. Reese—get me a stretcher."

I didn't wait to see what glittered in her eyes. Didn't want to see her victory reflected on Alicia's pretty face, or see how deep their duplicity ran, so I allowed Aiden to help me stand, shucked his touch, then turned to flee.

The general's lips gaped, bewildered scowl spinning around the cramped room, until it landed on my face. For a moment, he seemed to chew on a sentiment lodged somewhere between hate and terror, lips moving around a single, damning yet unspoken word. *"Bitch."*

Before he could muster the strength to condemn me, I shouldered my way through the crowd of Elites and Priestesses alike. Stumbling. Shoving onlookers aside with palms full of glass, the torn edges of my dress flapped in the breeze, drawing shocked murmurs and helpful, cloying hands.

Chest too tight to draw breath or sustain my flight, I rejected them all, not stopping until I burst onto cobbled streets.

Bright morning sunlight seared my eyes, and I cried out, scarred fingers raised against the assault.

"Priestess!" the toy soldier called, catching up.

But I swatted at his touch, blind. Swinging. "Don't touch me, peasant. I'm *fine.*"

"I don't doubt it," he returned, and captured the torn fabric in one hand, my left wrist in the other. Moving my bleeding fingers to tangle in the ruined dress, he covered my breasts, and said, "Let's get you back to the captain, hey little Priestess?"

Even without the darkness thick in my veins, I knew that tone. Recognized that emotion for what it was.

Pity.

This Caledonian toy *pitied* me.

Lips tingling and numb, I scowled, glaring down a tunnel of narrowed vision. And why shouldn't he? What had I, but gooseflesh and shivers?

"Fine," I said, hardly aware of my feet on the cobbles. Unconcerned when all at once I became weightless and the entire world spun off its axis. "But... but I'll not be coddled."

A puff of breath whispered over my brow. "Of course

not, Priestess," he hummed, chest somehow, inexplicably, rumbling against my cheek. "I'd never dream of it."

WHEN MY FEET next touched solid ground, it was to a symphony of growled curses, spat in a voice I recognized at once. "What the *fuck*, Aiden?" Marco barked, engulfing me in a cloud of sweet tobacco. "You've had her for less than an hour! What—"

"There's been an... *incident* at the infirmary," the toy soldier returned, giving me a tiny push into Marco's hands.

Hugging the dress close to my chest, I peeled my lids open—one at a time—and met the shadowed glare of the captain's errand boy.

"Rebels?" Marco asked, though he didn't bother to look away from my face or shutter his condemnation.

"No," Aiden said, already halfway gone. "Looks like the general had some sort of fit. Broke a bunch of stuff when he... *fell*. Glass everywhere. See to your girl," he added. "I think she tried to crawl through it. Tried to... escape, if you catch my meaning."

Marco's fingers tightened on my elbows as the other man departed. Fingers too tight. "Have you lost your damned mind, Wildcat?"

Before he could chastise me further, I said the only word that could silence this idiot. "Assassins."

The hardened soldier broke through the man's righteous fury, eyes wide. "When?"

I wobbled, listing toward the door. "Don't have time for this."

Marco yanked me back, and snarled, *"When?"*

"Does it matter?" I asked, trying to wriggle free. "They surround us."

Nostrils pinched white, Marco tossed me over his shoulder, kicked the front door open, then closed. Stomping through the front hall, he followed the sounds of agonized retching, and the consequent echo of liquid chunks spattering the bottom of a bucket.

Upon entering the kitchen, my ankle struck the doorframe as he barreled through it, drawing a hiss from my lips, but little else. I welcomed the stab of pain for it pushed the hazy fog back, clearing my muddled thoughts in time to deal with a true opponent.

"Is there any question as to *why* you both look fresh from the grave?" Marco asked, setting me down across from my bonded Elite, whose back was pressed to the kitchen island. "What did you do, Lady Wildcat?"

Knees drawn up, the captain hugged a garbage pail, breathing hard through parted lips. The hollows beneath his eyes and sunken cheeks stood out against skin tinged a waxy green. Shirtfront unbuttoned, his uniform sagged open, revealing a chest flushed with the trauma of the previous hour. Absent the pendant, lest the High Priestess feed from that too. Disheveled.

For a moment, the captain did nothing but stare up at me. Pinning me still with that obsidian glare. And then, "She tried to kill the general."

He spat in the bucket.

Swallowing the sympathetic bile burning the back of my throat, I picked at the brand, eyes falling to the floor. "What would you have had me do, Asher?"

"Emperor's *balls*, Wildcat!" Marco threw back his head, and laughed. "Literally *anything* else," he said, flinging his arms wide, fingertips narrowly missing my face.

I yelped, legs buckling, knees striking the hardwood as my hands flew to protect my face. Cringing.

The captain frowned. "Marco—"

"Have you any idea of the danger you've put us in?" Scrubbing at his eyes with forefinger and thumb, Marco cursed, clipped and bitter.

"*Marco.* Enough." Setting the pail aside, the captain tipped forward, shuffling toward me on hands and knees. Settling beside me with a grunt, he stripped his shirt and draped it about my shoulders.

"Enough?" Marco asked, watching the captain's fingers trip over the buttons of a garment damp with sweat that stank of anxiety. Sparking his lighter. On and off. On and off. Left arm wrapped tight about his ribs. "*Enough?* Asher, she's fuckin' killed us all!"

Shaking, I glared at my ruined hands, letting the captain work. Only when I was decent, did his touch find purchase beneath my chin, thumb brushing the marks ringing my throat.

Fingerprints, presumably.

"The general would like me to become the centerpiece of his breeding program," I rasped, unable to meet that inky gaze that had gone inexplicably soft. Gentle. "But I suspect you already knew that. Knew bound Priestesses are barren and the chains are to blame. Just as you know what your cousin tried to do this morning, and that I *tried* to lay still beneath the man who murdered my father, listening to him brag of the assassins he's sent to kill you. But I didn't have a choice," I continued, cloaked in his scent. "*We* are out of choices because I failed. And now there is *nothing* we can do to stop him. He's awake. He knows enough to convict you of treason. And he's coming to collect."

Asher took my hands, careful of the glass. "It's not over—"

Edging toward hysterics, I snorted. "We couldn't beat him at his own game because he's not abiding by any of your precious rules, Asher. He wasn't interested in whether or not I could make the Lotus bloom, only in my potential for creating hybrid children for the Empire to play with. That's the sort of sickness that can only be cured with death, but you knew that, too. Because you were with me," I said, throat tight. "You gave me the power to end it and you were with me when I failed. When our freedom was *taken*, because you see, we have *no allies*. No brilliant green-eyed traitor offering insights we couldn't see, and no High Priestess working in secret to help you achieve your designs. Do you know who stopped me?" I asked, lifting scalding, blurry eyes to meet his at last. "Do you know who hit me with the Lotus the *instant* before I could send your cousin into the Void?"

My bondmate swallowed. "Sasha."

"Sasha," I whispered, cheeks wet. "She took it all. Took everything we needed to defend ourselves using the ring *you* gave her—" I pulled my bleeding right hand from his, driving my point home with the point of a branded finger. "She carries the power of *three*, and through her, Tilcot, though I don't know if he knows it. The pendant is the *only* option we have left, and we both know why that cannot work."

Asher claimed my hand once more, but Marco cleared his throat. "Care to explain for those of us whose lives depend on a little more clarity?"

When I answered him, it was with a voice absent inflection or passion. "I cannot touch my mother's pendant without succumbing to the darkness."

Marco frowned, spinning his lighter. "The darkness being?" The silence that followed was answer enough, and his eyes widened with horrified understanding. "Berserker," he whispered, stepping back. Hand wrapping about the butt of his weapon. "I do love a good 'I told you so', but... Bloody hell, mate. I fuckin' *told* you! Crazy ones are too much work. And this one, a bloody *Berserker* of all things."

"No," the captain murmured, picking glass from my palms. "Not a Berserker."

"An Empath," I whispered, not bothering to wince as he worked.

Asher's thumbnail caught at a bit of glass, sending it deeper before he worked it free. "Berserkers spend ki until they burn out. An Empath will take until there's nothing left."

"Whatever," Marco snapped. "She's unnatural. Cursed." He laughed, eyes wild and ringed with white. "You best believe I'm putting in for danger pay, old man —" he slapped the countertop, pointing with shaking finger. *"Double!"*

Asher shrugged. "If we live through the day, sure."

"I'm holding you to that," Marco snapped, and collected the pendant off the kitchen counter, holding it at arm's length as if it had the power to corrupt anyone but me. "You're not dying today, you understand me? We run. Let the wildcat take us to her forest and—"

"We're surrounded by Elites authorized to kill," Asher said, and tore a strip from the hem of my ruined dress and wrapped it about my left hand.

"Then we tell them what you are!" Marco pressed. "We go above Tilcot's head, and make the curator's wet dreams come true! It's not ideal, but at least you'll live another day! At least there's a chance you can be freed. That *I* can free you when the dust settles."

And then, from the street beyond, a bellowed challenge. "Asher Rawlings! Come out here and face me, traitor!"

A tiny, fatalistic smile tugged at the corner of my lips as the captain wrapped my second hand. Unhurried. "Time's up," I whispered, drying my cheeks with the makeshift bandage.

"Well then," Marco said, and tugged a cigarette from his pack. He paused to light it, in spite of Alicia's order not to do so in the house. "Looks like we get that last stand after all, old man." When he exhaled, blowing a cloud toward the ceiling, he thrust the pendant toward us, showering us in blue, green, and purple shadows.

Grimacing, the captain hauled me to my feet, leaning on me to keep himself upright. "Marco, go. You don't have to be a part of this."

"Asher!" the general screamed, voice thick with madness. "I know you're in there! Bring me your witch or I'll bury you both in rubble and take vengeance on your corpse!"

Marco drew his weapon, lit smoke dangling from a crooked smirk as he approached, then pressed the pendant into Asher's palm. "Give the man what he wants."

Rough fingers tangled with those that were scarred and bloody, and with little more than a nod, the captain looped his pendant over his head.

13

———

Peeking through the window at the street beyond, Marco cursed, and said, "Got half the bloody city gathering out there."

I swallowed. "And Sasha? Is she—"

"Yep. Looks like she took a trip to the fighting pits, but she's there. Oh, *fuck*," Marco gasped. "Tilcot just backhanded her! Doesn't look like she's conscious—oh, wait. Yep. She's still moving. Tough lady," he added, and passed his weapon back, into the captain's hands, without taking his eyes off the street.

Asher paused, holding the deadly thing by the hilt, his pendant with the other. Brow furrowed, bared chest heaving with indecision.

"Is that a good idea?" I asked, sweating and cold, remaining on my feet with willpower alone. "Whatever insulation Sasha built around the bond is gone. I destroyed what was left of it."

"You have ten seconds, traitor!" the general screamed, the declaration supported by the murmurings of a growing crowd.

"He's bluffing," Marco whispered. "I'll let you know when he draws and starts counting backward."

"Asher—" I tugged at the hem of my borrowed shirt. *"Don't.* It's bad enough that I can feel the pendant without Sasha's barrier. Don't you think—"

Taking a deep breath, he ignored me. And, pendant clenched, he filled Marco's weapon with scarcely enough ki to make my chains tingle. Ending it before my veins hummed with gold, then said, "That barrier was meant to protect *me* from *you,* Miss Tannovic."

Startled, I blinked, rubbing the rough spot where my chains met a ring of scabs.

"Couldn't take the risk that you'd infect me with your so-called darkness," he continued, and returned the charged weapon, watching Marco tuck it into the back of his pants. "So I took steps to minimize the danger. You have no idea the havoc a Berserker can unleash."

He met my eye. Light to dark. Both sides of the same exhausted whole united for an instant by unspoken understanding.

No, I hadn't any idea what a Berserker could do, and worse... *no one* knew what kind of horror would come from a ki-starved Empath *feeding* said Berserker. Darkness unleashed, I'd take without discrimination, fueling *him* until there was nothing left. If it were just the soldiers of the Empire in my path, I wouldn't hesitate to unleash that destruction.

As it was... I swallowed, hard, glancing at his pendant. "Asher... The Priestesses..."

His jaw flexed, and for a moment that inky gaze traced my face. And then, "You have enough for one shot, Marco."

The soldier whirled, cigarette dangling from parted lips.

"If this doesn't go our way, make it count and everything I own is yours, pup."

"Asher—"

"I drew up the appropriate documents five years ago," my bondmate said, left brow quirked. "It's all been arranged. All you have to do is claim the glory for stopping a Berserker on the rampage and take care of my mum."

"Fucksakes, old man! *No!* You can't ask me to—"

"There *is* no one else. You're the only one who will see it coming. Only one who even knows to look."

Marco cursed, pushing a hand through messy short hair. Cursed again, dragging a breath of smoke into his lungs. When he turned back to his vigil, it was with stiff spine and a tiny jerk of his head.

Up and down. Once.

I exhaled, not unaffected.

"Ah, shit," Marco growled, cracking his neck. "We've got crazy-hands aflutterin'. Time to go," he said, at the same time the general began his countdown.

"Shouldn't *you* be armed?" I hissed, allowing my bonded to capture my bandaged fingers once more.

Asher shook his head. "It'll provoke him. Make him think I don't consider him a threat. Ready?"

Ready? To walk into an impossible situation hoping for an impossible outcome? It went against every instinct I possessed—stolen from Kas or otherwise. But I wouldn't waste breath on such thoughts, merely sunk blunted claws into the back of his hand and reached for what was once my mother's pendant. Without touching the stone or tempting the darkness, I flipped it over his shoulder, letting it hang between his shoulder blades. Out of sight, yet within reach.

Wordless, we turned to face our doom, stepping through the front door behind Marco. Hands raised, all three.

General Tilcot.

Purple in the face, he paced, sidearm dangling from his right hand. Flanked by several Priestesses carrying various medical supplies—none of which were brave enough to approach—Tilcot's eyes were wild. Rimmed in red. Laughing when we emerged from the townhouse, he planted his boot into Sasha's belly as she lay fetal in the dirt before him. Brandishing his weapon before a mixed crowd of civilians, Elites, and Priestesses alike.

"Ah, at last. The Golden Boy deigns to grace us with his presence. And here I thought you were a coward as well as a traitor."

"Traitor? What's this about, Harper?" the captain asked, showing the madman the whites of his palms. "I thought I'd been relieved of duty?"

Frantic, my gaze darted around the street, bouncing over the gathered faces, searching for another way, even as I clutched at Asher's rough, raised fingers.

"Don't play stupid," the general spat, thrusting his weapon forward. "You owe the people an explanation about your girl."

Asher's laugh was a nervous, fragile thing, for all eyes were drawn to my face. "She's a bit wild, I'll admit that much. But with a little tempering, she'll be a fine example of a—"

"She tried to kill me!" the general shouted, seizing a

handful of Sasha's silver-blonde locks. Dragging her up to her knees. "Isn't that right, slut?"

But the Goddess' chosen didn't speak, merely raised her battered gaze to mine, both hands clutching the wrist of the man she'd betrayed everything to save. Wincing as he rattled her. It was the Glaith—sparkling in the sunlight on the back of her finger—that spoke volumes, though I hadn't the capacity to understand.

"That girl has an impossible power!" the general continued, throwing Sasha to the cobbles once more. "Unlike anything I've ever felt! And, brothers, I have a witness! The slaver who brought her in is ready to speak of all he saw in that forest! Now I ask you—is it right that *one* man claims her as personal property? Is that the Empire you swore allegiance to? I say *no!*" he shouted, trying to stoke the Elites into a seething mob with passion alone. "Hers is a bloodline that should have been added to the Imperial library and passed through the generations—creating obedient Priestesses each more powerful than the last! Sacrifice now, so that *all* Elites might know the strength that *one* man hoards!" He took a breath, pointing at Asher, sallow cheeks marked by deep crevasses that hadn't been there before he'd danced with darkness. "It shames me to discover my own kin behind this travesty! As such, Asher Rawlings, you are hereby stripped of rank and charged with high treason for the crime of knowingly binding a Priestess without permission and damaging property of the Empire!"

The gathered Elites shifted around us, attention flicking between wild-eyed general, shirtless captain, and *me*—an unsightly, damaged mess.

I almost smiled. Where the general painted a picture

of a hidden, Divine power, they saw a wild, broken thing with no fight left to speak of and only one thing left to give. No matter the general's pretty, rousing words, the Elites saw a creature spattered in blood and dirt, dressed in ragged layers of borrowed clothing. A girl who clung to her Elite, hardly able to stand, much less spawn *generations* of enslaved hybrid Priestesses.

They didn't see the curator's Golden Boy augmented by an unparalleled power, but a man who was too pale beneath his golden tan—and green beneath that. A man who leaned on his filthy, disheveled Priestess for support and faced judgment unarmed.

They couldn't see what had ignited the general's madness, caught no whiff of a power that could ruin them all. And if I took just a little more of his weight... allowed just a *little* of my fear show on my face... only a dead Goddess would ever know.

Allowing weakness to disguise chaos, I cowered in his shadow. Played the trembling victim with left hand planted on my bonded's lower back, pendant dangling just above my bleeding fingers. For if this was to be my ending, I wouldn't go without satisfying the vengeance that had driven me here.

Wouldn't meet my father without hands soaked in the blood of his murderer.

Marco melted back from the front step, putting distance between us and him. Taking a position that would save him from the fallout of a last stand.

"Have you nothing to say for yourself, cousin?" the general asked, throwing his hands wide. He didn't acknowledge the startled shouts from those who ducked, cringing back from the arcing path of an Elite with his finger on the trigger. No, standing in the center of a ring of onlookers, his lips parted to reveal a mad grin. "Or shall your silence be taken as admission of guilt?"

"Guilt?" Asher asked, having the gall to smirk. "That's a bit of a reach, even for you, *sir*. I'm merely trying to understand the nature of your accusation." Pulling me forward, he clamped both hands on my shoulders. "You think *my* Priestess is capable of making an attempt on *you*? I know she's a savage little warrior, but surely that doesn't equate to attempted murder?"

The mob began to murmur, soothed by rational words.

"I have to admit," Asher continued, tucking me close to his bared chest. Making me look as small and fragile as I felt. "I'm concerned for you, cousin. Radical, baseless claims aren't like you at all. Are you sure you're well? I heard you had an episode of some sort, just this morning."

Snarling over the crowd, the general took aim—though for the moment, it was absent that deadly glow of building ki. "She's Trila-Glís, you sniveling *dog!* And as such, I hereby claim her in the name of the Emperor!"

"Trila-Glís?" My bondmate laughed, then, pushing me behind him, though hardly clear of danger. "Only in my most selfish fantasies, I'm afraid. Did she not fail to make the Lotus bloom? *Twice,* at your insistence?"

At this, all those gathered stilled. All but *one* green-eyed impostor lurking beyond the circumference of our last stand. Edging toward the captain's house, Alicia's cheeks were stained with incriminating tears. Come to witness the rotten fruits of her labor, had she?

Trembling inside and out, I couldn't muster the

vitriol to sneer. Even when Sasha rose from the cobbles, standing at her master's back as if drawing a line between sides.

"Where is your evidence?" Asher asked, addressing his brothers. "Would you dispense a death sentence without trial? Where is the justice in that, cousin? I did not swear fealty to an Empire that would claim a Priestess at will and betray the sacrifice we make as soldiers! Where does it stop? What's to say *you* won't be next?" he asked, pointing at the closest Elite.

"You are not fit to keep her!" General Tilcot screamed, spittle leaving his manic grin wet and slimy. And then, before Asher's rational words could bolster support, a shower of brilliant green lit the faces of those gathered. Sleek metal glowing with the power of three.

I bared my teeth amidst the screams and shouts for reason, wrapped bandaged fingers around the pendant, and called the darkness to the fore. Asher didn't fight me, not even when my veins began to pulse with sluggish gold and Marco prepared to end it for good. Taking aim.

Asher stood, chest bared and unarmed, watching the general disgrace himself and flout Imperial law before an audience.

In life or death, condemned by his own hand, General Tilcot screamed, "Step away from the witch!" flinging drops of vibrant plasma with every syllable.

But it was Sasha—lips split, left eye swollen shut— who stood. Sasha whose right hand spit shadows, and whose veins flooded with gold. She, who threw back her head and laughed, wrapping her dainty, bejeweled fingers around her master's elbow. Silencing him with the slightest touch. "You want a witch?" she purred, ki swirling and whipping at her unbound hair.

Jaw slack, I could do nothing but stare. Struck stupid as the High Priestess was reborn. As she stripped away decades worth of protection and gave herself to the dark. "Goddess, *no.*"

Molten gold surged beneath her skin, bleeding into the general as he strained against her. Helpless, ki belched from the muzzle of his weapon. Not a torrent of misery, as it had been on the front lines, but the dribble of too much ki gathered in one place. Overflowing, it landed with a hiss, charring the cobbles with lime soot.

"You arrogant fool! *I am your witch!*" Sasha screamed, head thrown back. "I am the last of the Goddess' chosen! The last true Trila-Glís! Not this pathetic girl and her mundane Elite." Grinning, she batted the general's hand away when he clutched at her skirts. "I am the last of the line. There will never be another like me, with power like *this!*" Spine flexing at an impossible arch, she writhed as Elite ki pooled around the general, her voice coming from nowhere and everywhere at once. Glaith glittering as she worked to topple a monster. "For your crimes against my people," she said, and forced the big man to his knees, "you will burn."

Eyes bulging, the general began to smoke. Kneeling in an ever-widening pool of plasma, his mouth dropped open in a silent scream as clouds of green steam billowed around them. Thickening with each passing moment. Obscuring the High Priestess and the man she'd given everything to destroy.

"Take cover!" Marco bellowed, shocking the stunned

crowd of mixed slaves and soldiers into action. "Asher, get back! Take the wildcat and go! *GO! Get back!*"

But I slipped the captain's leash before he could utter a sound of protest, for I *knew*. I knew what she was going to do, because it had been *my* plan that had inspired her.

Running flat out, I leaped off the porch, ends of my dress snapping against my heels, kicking up swirling eddies of lime fog as I plunged into the cloud. Sidestepping the plasma, my eyes were not for the fallen general missing from the waist down, but the woman consumed in blackest flames.

Without thought, I lunged, tackling her free of the deadly plasma before it began to chew on her flesh and bones. Tumbling together on the cobblestones, I seized her right hand, trying to pry her Caledonian ring off her finger. Trying to break her connection to the parasite dragging her into the Void.

White-hot, it refused to part with her skin, degloving the finger as I tore it off the bone. Exposing gore-spattered muscle and tendons to air toxic with screams and death.

Choking on the gummy vapor, I retched, trying to peel the taste of charred general off the back of my tongue. Hands shaking, fingertips melting, I crumbled the blackened smoking flesh from the ring, and slipped it onto my middle finger.

Too late.

Though unimaginable power exploded behind my eyes, I was too late. Where the High Priestess had been, there was nothing but a bone-chilling vacuum. Absent everything but a tiny, flickering spark of life clinging to her shell.

"No!" I screamed, hurling everything I had into the abyss, trying to bring her back. To ignite what remained of the Goddess' chosen and force her to stay. Tethering her to life with vines of purest ki, I tied her to me.

Eyes gone almost white opened with a smile, and she cupped my cheek with her undamaged hand. "Precious, Mila. My wild rogue. There's so much you don't know. So much I wish I could—" she coughed, blood misting the dense air between us. Spattering my cheeks. "I trust you to know this isn't the answer for the rest. Free them... The Priestesses... from a life... half-lived..."

I shook my head, latching on to every shredded fragment of her being I could reach, fighting Death itself with the power of three.

"Stop." Brushing my efforts aside as if they were nothing, she smiled—and clipped my ethereal vines. Returning all the ki she'd collected to the ring, she said, "For Tritan," and exhaled her last.

"Your Grace..." I shook her, bones threatening to pop through my knuckles as her head lolled. "No! *No!*" Breaking apart from the inside out, I sobbed, latching on to her spirit as it faded away.

Chaos, all around me. Masculine voices ringing in my ears. "Get off her, you vile little witch!" Strong arms wrenched the corpse from my grip. Held a blade to the vulnerable pulse hammering away at the base of my throat, but I did not fight. If I could feed her just a *little* more...

"Miss Tannovic!" Bruising fingers gnawed at my bicep, tearing me between two unmovable forces. "She didn't do this, Reese! Unhand my Priestess, or so help me—" His voice faded, swallowed by the Void.

A heavy thud echoed in my ears, the sound of flesh

striking flesh, and I was thrown to the side. Limp beside the pool of stinking plasma that had eaten a monster. Watching as General Tilcot's murky, dark eyes popped, spewing their boiling innards as the last pieces of his skull slipped beneath the surface. Swallowed by plasma meant for me and *mine.*

"Mila!" A warm hand touched my cheek. The scent a familiar tickle at the back of my brain.

The captain. Asher. My bonded Elite. "You have to let her go," he whispered, cradling my face in his palm. "There's nothing you can do."

I whined, cold and dead in the middle.

"Let her go, Mila. She's taking you with her. Taking us both."

"I... I don't care..." And I didn't. The cold was spreading.

"Your fight isn't over," he murmured, ensnaring me with that inky, bottomless gaze. "Her death frees us. Don't take that from her."

Freed *us?* She'd taken *my* release! Left me holding the power of three and the fate of our people. Choking on cruel anguish, I cried out, wishing I could tear my chest open and expose my tainted soul to the light. Wishing I could join her, even as I let my spirit touch hers in a silent farewell.

When the last anchor broke, it was because *I* allowed it. Because I slipped my hand into my pocket and worked the ring off my finger, allowing her broken spirit to slip into the Void. It happened so quickly and irrevocably that for a moment, I wasn't sure if she'd ever really existed. "She's gone."

Asher brushed the hair back from my tear-stained face. "I know."

"All that power," I whispered, beginning to shake from somewhere deep within. Hardly aware of my own ingrained deception, I followed an instinct that demanded I keep this tiny piece of Milithia's chosen to myself. "Gone."

Humming, Asher didn't seem to notice. Didn't move to take his ring, in favor of running his thumb from cheek to ear. Whisking away my tears.

When he lifted me—sobbing into his heat, legs dangling over his forearm—none moved to block him, for he was right. Sasha *had* freed us. Obliterated all obstacles, suspicion, and threats aimed in our direction so that *we* might live. In their eyes, I was just another Triloth of moderate potential, grieving with all the rest.

And Asher was just another Elite trying to soothe an ache felt through the Blood, each and all.

Exonerated by her sacrifice.

None saw the shadows glittering on Asher's breast or moved to stop a rare and dangerous pair already half consumed by the Void.

None knew to look.

14

———

"Shit!" Marco hip-checked the front door open, cheeks flushed, hair matted with sweat. "I cannot *fucking* believe that just happened!"

Mindful of my head, Asher pushed by him and barged into the kitchen.

"He was going to kill us," I rasped, cheek lolling against him, pocket heavy with secret Glaith once more.

"Yes."

"She—She stopped him. I thought she was *his* but she wasn't," I babbled, reaching for the hard, prickly edge of his jaw. "Sasha saved us even though I said *terrible* things and accused her of—"

"Stop," Asher murmured, setting me on a stool. Balancing my weight between his left thigh and the island counter. "Sasha's death wasn't your doing, Miss Tannovic. Do you understand me?"

"I watched his eyeballs pop," I whispered, making concussive little *pop pop pop* sounds with my lips.

The front door slammed shut, separating us from the sounds of pandemonium echoing from the street beyond. "Are we alone?" Marco gasped, rounding the corner. And without waiting for a response, seized a pitcher of water left by the sink. He tipped his head back, throat working mechanically as water slopped all down his front.

Asher's knuckles went white around the pendant, ki surging through a bond without walls as his senses whirled around the premises. As one, we turned blank eyes toward the stairs and the ceiling beneath his bedroom. "Alicia." He dropped the pendant against his chest, letting it bounce. "Alicia's upstairs."

Swiping at damp lips, Marco took three gigantic steps toward the stairs, and hollered, "Woman! Get your fine ass down here!"

A yelp, followed by a thump of something heavy hitting the floor preceded Alicia's cry. "Thank the gods!" Quick footsteps pounded down the stairs, and in the next moment the green-eyed traitor stood before us. Cheeks pink and streaked with wet. "You're alright," she whispered, wringing dainty hands. "I canna believe it—you're alright!"

I bared my teeth, but it was Asher who voiced the suspicion writhing between us. "Alicia, what were you doing in my rooms?"

She blushed. "Hiding. The High Priestess—" she cleared her throat. "When General Tilcot woke, he wasna talkin' sense. Rantin' on about the wee lassie bein' a witch. Madder than anythin' I've ever seen. The High Priestess told me to hide, as I havena any power t'speak of and she expected him t'come for the two o'you. Said it would be best if I was outta the way."

"How'd you get in the house?" Marco asked, half-smoked cigarette dangling from his lips.

She shot him a funny look, and said, "Back door," as if it was the stupidest question she'd ever been asked.

And it might have been, considering her resume and just how accomplished a liar the brilliant Eloran was. She'd been prepared for questions—that much was obvious—but at the moment, I had neither the wit to catch her in an untruth, nor the energy to spare for the game. Not now, with my nerves frayed and my skin coated with a fine layer of soot whose origins I couldn't stomach.

"I need to bathe," I whispered, turning away. Peeling free from Asher's borrowed shirt, I flung it away. Keeping the edges of my ruined dress closed in spite of the bandages and lacerations marking my palms.

"Wait!" Alicia said, taking three halting steps toward us. "What happened out there? Last I saw was the general throwin' a fit."

Running bandaged hand down my skirts, I paused over the lump of warm iron topped with Glaith, and said, "Dead. They're both dead."

Alicia went white, grabbing for the edge of the table. "*No*. The High Priestess is... *dead?*"

"Went out in a blaze of glory fit for a queen," Marco said, tossing his spent smoke into the sink.

Claiming the seat on my left, Alicia turned liquid eyes on the captain's soldier. "She said... she hoped it wouldna come to that. But she wanted the two o'you t'be free of suspicion. Said she had a plan to take the blame for everything that's happened. T'shift it onto herself, so none would suspect there t'be truth in the general's words."

Marco snorted, cupping his hands around a fresh smoke, trembling hands making the flame of his lighter sparkle and dance. "Safe to say she accomplished that. Nearly shit myself when our little terror went and flung herself into the thick of it. Then again"—he blew a white cloud toward the ceiling in spite of Alicia's presence—"when Captain Nobility here followed in her footsteps. Almost killed you *myself* when you came outta that green smoke, Lady Wildcat limp as the Emperor's cock in your arms." He sent a hand through his hair. "Thought for *sure* I'd have to avenge you, old man. Tarnish my good name and perfect reputation. But Sasha beat me to it."

"She needed it t'be public," Alicia whispered, swiping at her eyes. "Had t'make sure no one could question who drove the general mad. I didna think she'd suffer any consequences at all, bein' bound to that prig of a general and Trila-Glís to boot. 'Specially not —" Her voice faltered as ugly sobs cut her off. Sounds that would be hard to fake, no matter my inherent suspicion. Sobs that made my eyes burn in sympathy.

Marco stripped off his jacket and slung it over Alicia's shoulders. "Tilcot's dead," he said. "But we're not quite out of the woods yet."

Nodding, Asher traced the hemline of my skirt. "There'll be a formal investigation."

"Right. And the curator himself'll be here in three days. Or is it two? I can't remember. Doesn't matter," Marco said, and clapped his hands. "Crack open a bottle of the good stuff, old man. I don't know how we did it, but I'm going to celebrate somehow living through the day before we get down to figuring out how to make it through tomorrow."

"It's barely noon," Asher replied, lips twitching. "But you're right. I think we've earned a little rest." Turning away, he left me to balance without him as he disappeared down the hallway.

Goddess, but rest sounded good. I wouldn't say no to a full-blown hibernation, such was the strength of the bone-weary itch scratching at the backs of my eyelids.

As soon as he was gone, however, Alicia threw herself at me, looping her arms around my neck. Bawling. Noisy and wet against my cheek, I recoiled, unable to evade and too weak to push her away.

Sniffling, she rambled nonsense in an accent so thick, I hadn't a *chance* of understanding let alone responding. I could do little more than submit, hands stiff at my side, inching toward Sasha's ring to lend me strength.

"Uh..." Marco backed away, features twisted with uncomfortable horror. "Do you need anything? Can I... get you a glass of water or... or something?"

"Please," she replied, then dissolved into incoherent tears anew.

"Asher!" Marco shouted, uneasy, retreating to the sink. "Hurry up, mate! And make mine a double!"

Lips brushing my ear, Alicia sobered in an instant, whispering, "There's a box under the captain's desk," in a voice absent the abject sorrow of only moments prior. "For your eyes only, with love from beyond the Veil."

I blinked, trying to keep up. "What—"

She hushed me, sobbing all the louder to keep Marco cowering by the sink, then said, "We're not quite free o'this place, lassie, but we *can* be. Do whatever it takes t'get that box, understand? You canna let her death be for nothing."

Returning with a heavy bottle of amber liquid and two glasses, Asher's countenance softened at the show of soggy femininity. "You knew Sasha well, did you?" he asked, and uncorked the bottle, splashing two finger's worth into each glass.

"N-No," Alicia hiccupped, releasing me with a sniffle and held my gaze. The duplicity between words and the unspoken straining my already limited capacity. "It's just so *sad!* She was a brilliant woman. Didna get t'work with her much, but she was always kind t'me when I did."

Clutching what must have been the world's most carefully poured glass of water, Marco risked patting her back, and forced an awkward, "There, there," around his cigarette.

Alicia claimed the whiskey glass meant for Marco and drained it in a single swallow. And then, wiping her lips with the back of her wrist, she claimed the bottle from Asher's hand, refilled her glass, and said, "To the Mistress of Milithia. Last o'her kind."

Asher raised his glass, tossed the contents back, then refilled it.

"And to freedom," Marco said, and got two mugs from the cupboard. He waited for Alicia to fill them before adding, "With Tilcot dead, you're free. You are without equal, old man."

Hiding his smirk behind the rim of his glass, Asher took a sip. Obsidian eyes glittering, he nudged the final mug toward me. "Drink, Miss Tannovic. The whiskey will settle your nerves."

I heard what he didn't say. Knew there was some deformed version of respect growing between us. A begrudging, fragile trust that would prefer starvation and neglect to existing, yes, yet there all the same. But as long as Caledonian gold burned through my veins into his, Marco wasn't wrong. Even with Sasha's ring filled to bursting and a mystery gift waiting to assault me with a whole new set of headaches, *none* could match my bonded Elite.

Eyes squeezed shut, I too seized the bottle.

I knew what it would take to distract a man like Asher. A man glued to the very fabric of my soul, who could sense deception before I'd even begun to lie. There was but *one* sure way to claim Sasha's gift. All it would cost was my dignity—and that got cheaper the longer I remained in this place.

With him.

Using both bandaged hands to keep the decanter steady, I whispered, "To Sasha," under my breath and threw my head back. Throat working to swallow great heaving mouthfuls of amber liquid, I couldn't be bothered to grimace.

Against my thigh, the ring warmed for just a moment, but I ignored the whispers that weren't there. Ignored the tingle heating my branded knuckle and didn't stop drinking until Asher pulled the bottle from my lacerated fingers.

"Hey," he breathed, crowding me against the counter. "Easy."

I snorted, smothering the derisive retort. Avoiding those inky black eyes, I embraced the caustic burn settling in the pit of my empty stomach, welcoming the return of false confidence I hadn't earned.

"You look tired, lassie," Alicia said, sweeping around the edge of the table. "Perhaps you should retire? I can turn down the bed. Get you dressed for sleep an' tucked away."

Thumbing the brand, I pulled a long, slow breath

through my teeth, modified canines pinching my lower lip. Licking at the pressure-cracks spidering throughout my torn psyche, I let my lungs stretch around held breath. Banished the trembly sadness taking root, and salted the wound with something... darker. Something familiar that sunk toothy maw to bone and drank from the marrow that spilled from the wounds.

Sasha hadn't bought my freedom—she'd taken it for herself. Left *me* holding the burden of her mantle and the fate of my people so she could greet her beloved dead Goddess as a fucking martyr. Worse, she'd stolen the retribution that had kept my fire burning all these long, lonely years. Barred me from *ever* being able to face my father for the shame of *constant* failure now utterly beyond my ability to atone for.

Her sacrifice had spared me a lifetime of horror, for *what?* To be enslaved to another Elite destined to grow sick with the lust for power? And this one I couldn't escape, even in death? How long before Asher followed in his cousin's footsteps? Before his mind twisted under the pressure and he was corrupted by what I'd become?

I exhaled. No. I couldn't rest. Not yet. Maybe not ever.

Asher touched my wrist and stepped as close as he could. Hip bumping my knees. Without speaking, he began to unwind the bandages wrapping my hands. Gentle. Intimate, yet ceding privacy, for he made no effort to catch my eye. Didn't try to soothe the tempest raging inside my skull or flood the bond with forced calm—though I knew he could feel my ire.

"Goddess, but some o'those are deep," Alicia breathed, making a funny sound at the back of her throat.

I lifted my shoulder, fixing my eye on the pendant sitting proud atop his breast. More a mark of uncontested dominance than *any* crown or scepter, for he was the only one equal to wielding it. And when he cradled my bloodied hands and commanded the ruined flesh to mend, I did not fight it as I once had. Might even have sensed it coming, if I could bother to untangle my thoughts from the heavy fog swirling and choking my vision.

"Freedom has never been my birthright." The words crossed my lips without intention. Without realizing my cheek was pressed to the heat radiating from my bond-mate's chest, or that my fingers idly traced the pendant as his threaded through my hair. Working at the snarls that suited me better than flowing silk.

I probably wouldn't have noticed *anything* but the steady thump of that black heart beneath my cheek, had the distant sounds of merry laughter not reached through the fog. Alicia and Marco had gone, left to do whatever it took to ensure Sasha's sacrifice wasn't for nothing.

The silence made my teeth ache. "I have nothing," I whispered, and spread my fingers. Palming his heartbeat. "Not even my thoughts are my own. Not really."

He stiffened when my manicured claws caught a pebbled nipple, but made no move to stop me. Didn't speak or contradict, merely worked his thumb at the base of my skull. Unwinding years of knotted tension, only to create it elsewhere.

Melting against his heat, twin rings of gold and scabs caught my eye—but I hadn't the energy to ask why he'd mend my palms and leave the rest. Didn't much care, not when he pinched my nape between forefinger and thumb and stepped closer, wrapping his free arm around my waist.

"I can't even hate Sasha for abandoning me without *your* knowing it," I whispered, voice scarcely audible. Forcing the words through a throat lined with broken glass. "And now there's no High Priestess to protect you from all the hideous, ugly bits no one else is supposed to see."

It was his turn to swallow too hard, but still, he didn't speak. Fingers drawing familiar, lazy circles, he flexed. Squeezing tight enough to keep me from falling apart.

"She taught you our ways. Gave you the education I lack, and maybe that's why you think my fight isn't over. That I have something left." Lids heavy, I blinked. Submitting to his lazy massage as I traced a circle of my own through the light smattering of hair on his chest. "But you haven't really looked. I'm not even really here."

His hand landed on my hip, just above the curve of my bottom, skating the edge of exposed skin at my lower back. "Where are you, little hunter?"

Heart thick, I swallowed it down before the silly thing crawled free of my throat and left me to die of humiliation. Leaving it to stew in darkness where it belonged.

Where *I* belonged.

Asher hummed, moving my hair to one side, the blunt tip of his finger catching at the edge of my shoulder. "Sasha knew," he said, and I felt him smile. Felt the melancholy seep through his skin into mine. "Knew what I am—even had a name for it when I didn't. She sensed the truth I'd been trying to hide since the moment I came into my power. And she knew it with little more than a touch." He traced the exposed skin beneath my ear—shoulder to jaw—then cupped my cheek. Thumb feathering over my lower lip. "She could have ruined me five years ago. Could have used her leverage knowing she was all but untouchable as a general's slave. But my death or imprisonment would have left a certain forest demon without a counterbalance to contend with darkness so powerful, it stained the forest black. So we formed an alliance."

I flinched, scalding hot tears spilling over my lashes.

"Back then, I was barely holding on to the Berserker," he continued, and eased the crease bunching tight between my brows. Breath spicy and whiskey-warm. "I was in the market that day searching for a jeweler who could replace the Glaith in my ring. A Tritan jeweler who'd worked the ore and whose silence could be bought with Empire gold. Instead, I found a scrap of a girl playing seductress, flaunting ki unlike anything I'd ever tasted. Risking everything for a worthless trinket." His lips crinkled—I saw it through watery lashes. Watched him lift his pendant and caress the ugly little stone with the pad of his thumb, exactly as I had done thousands of times before the Fall. "I slipped when I lost you. When you *escaped* into that cursed wood and worse," he laughed, breath filling my lungs, "when you refused to go with the other Priestesses into the mountain. Taunting me day and night with the possibility that you'd be taken by an Elite like my cousin, or that someone would *finally* put it together and realize there was another. An unclaimed Trila-Glís unknown to her own people, distorting the forest with her sorrow and grief—for what else could contend with that much power? What other being could command the very trees to swallow soldiers but leave the way open for refugees?"

I tried to twist away. To hide the salty burn streaking blotchy cheeks, but he caught my chin. Pressed his forehead to mine.

"Sasha taught me control," he whispered. "Freed me from dependence on 'dirty Glaith', and faced the Berserker time and again without flinching. I fed her my excess when I could. Practiced her techniques when I couldn't. All of it so I could tame a girl more wild than not. More lion than woman. Because, much as I wanted to storm that haunted wood and drag you from the trees, I knew my moment would come. Knew it was only a matter of time before you slipped too, and there was only *one* who could face you without flinching. Only one who could claim to match the infamous Wood's Menace and dare to bring her to heel."

A watery hiccup bubbled from my lips, and I twisted. Pressing my cheek to his chest. Wrapping my scarred fingers around the Glaith glimmering between us. Holding that power without touching it.

But my bonded wasn't finished. "Without your ki, you *should* be nothing." Jostling me, he captured both of my wrists in his left hand, fingers an iron shackle I didn't try to break, knowing it to be impossible. "You have no physical strength." His free hand circled my throat, tilting my head back. Inky eyes drilled clear through the back of my skull. "No training and no direction. Without your ki," he whispered, threatening my airway with a gentle, harmless squeeze, "your only resource is your saucy mouth and devious, reckless little mind. Plots spawned from a cornered animal *should be nothing* compared to an Elite Trila-Glís trained by both sides of the Blood."

I could only blink. Gooseflesh prickling every millimeter of my skin.

Lips hovering too close, he stalled at the threshold. "At times you make me so angry I can't decide whether I want to throttle you or bend you over my desk and spank the obedience directly into your skin." Something hot and heavy plucked at the bond—though it was impossible to discern its origin, so tangled were our minds. "But if I've learned *one* thing, Miss Tannovic, it's that you'll do exactly the opposite of what I expect and move mountains to defy me."

I couldn't swallow. The air was too dry.

"You are passion and fury embodied," he rasped, and released my throat, moving instead to seat his pendant in the cradle formed between my captured palms. Forcing me to feel the truth of his words. "Nothing can stamp out your fire. Not now," he pressed, cutting off my denial before it could crawl from the dark. "You have *me* to tend the flames when you need a break."

"I..." Nothing. No words came out as I stared at him, blinking stupidly.

Taking my silence as permission, Asher did just that. Slid through my veins, unencumbered, touching *everything*. Leaving power and health in his wake, yet allowing hard-won scars to remain untouched. Lingering beneath my skin as he restored what had been lost in trying to defy the Void itself. Tending my fire.

And Goddess, the scent of this man! My bondmate.

Mine.

Of their own accord, my knees fell apart. Allowing him to step between with a gruff curse whispering across his lips.

"Goddess, *Asher*—"

"You don't have to fight alone," he breathed, and freed my wrists. Cupping my face between work-hardened palms. "Give over to me. Let me ease your burden and in return, I will give you *everything*."

15

With those words, clarity ignited in my mind. Stilling fragmented, racing thoughts with the echos of a forgotten conversation. Echos that tugged at my brain stem and forced memory to the fore. And though tears continued to trace over-warm cheeks, their source had run dry.

Give over? Surrender the darkness for the promise of *everything* as if he had it to give? As if three bands of Caledonian gold had no consequence, and my submission would create balance?

I blinked through the fog but didn't sneer. Merely met his pitch-dark gaze and let him see his intention satisfied. Let him see the dark flames rekindle behind my eyes without hinting at the cause, for I would play the part until the perfect moment was revealed. Until I could strike *once* and deal a devastating blow.

Restoring balance, whatever the cost.

And when the space between us grew ripe with tension five years in the making, *I* was the one who closed the gap. Who claimed his lips and inhaled his ragged groan.

Warmth—both soft and gritty—washed over delicate skin as he pressed closer. Meeting my timid advance with an intensity I was unprepared to match. Taking liberties, his hands explored the length of my back. Passing over scars and unblemished skin without discrimination, radiating a heady greed unique to the last rare and dangerous thing.

Intoxicating, even for the lie.

Gasping, his hands dropped to my hips, fingers kneading, spreading my ass on the lip of the stool. Bunching the fabric of my torn dress with unspent strain, he notched narrow hips between my thighs and ground himself against my uncovered mound. Throbbing with need. Separated by nothing more than what remained of his restraint and the buckle binding his trousers.

I broke away, clinging to his pendant even as I strained for breath. Chest heaving, keeping the edges of my borrowed, ruined silk together with branded fingers while slick heat soaked the bulge straining *just* beyond my reach.

"Easy," he murmured, and placed a kiss on the frenetic pulse beneath my jaw. Pinched it between his teeth, as if willing it to slow. As if this inferno could be trusted as *natural* and not the true abomination it was. "Fucksakes, girl—" he licked me from collarbone to jaw. "The taste of you."

Squeezing him between my knees, I arched. "Gross. Wasn't"—my left hand dropped, scrambling for purchase on the countertop behind me—"wasn't there blood? And... and soot?"

"Don't care." He nipped my earlobe. Soothing it with his lips. Bathing the assault with his tongue, even as my hips bucked.

I grunted, eyes rolling back. Gooseflesh prickling in the wake of his touch. Too fast! This was happening—

Thrusting again, hissing as he strained against me, his right hand twisted in the hair at my nape, thickening my veins with the sheer weight of his desire.

"Can't"—my nails bit the back of his neck—"can't breathe." Can't think...

He abandoned my ear, drawing me to him with a hand on either side of my bottom. "Wrap your legs around me."

The command pulled my lips back in a snarl before I could register that he'd spoken.

Grinning, he met my challenge. Jerked me off the stool with a single, practiced tug that saw my dress ride up. Saw it race past decency only to collide with obscenity without signs of slowing. Not stopping until my thighs were balanced about his hips and my melting core kissed his bellybutton. Splayed around his middle, there was *nothing* between us. Nothing at all to disguise the slick mess he'd inspired between my legs. No denying just how well I could play this part.

With him.

The ring in my pocket swung out of sight and reach, and he adjusted my position, jostling the frayed edges of my dress. Revealing pebbled breasts to heated inspection.

I watched his pupils dilate, then. Watched that inky ring swallow what little color might have been in his eyes, and did nothing to stop his advance. I stared as he attacked my left nipple, shadowed beard scratching an itch I hadn't allowed to exist until *that* moment. Sucking and nibbling at my sanity.

Teeth bared, I shifted against his heat. Ground against *him* in an effort to ease the ache knotting my lower back and in doing so, wet that dark smattering of hair trailing down his belly... past his buckle and beyond.

"Fuck," he gasped against my nipple, refusing to free the tormented bud.

A distant *thump* and follow-up laughter reached our ears. Alicia and Marco, close enough to hear whatever disgraceful thing I was about to do. Interrupting us too late to stop whatever it took to maintain this lie, but enough to demand he, "Take me upstairs. *Now.*"

Smirking, he obeyed. Hands spreading the taut globes of my bottom, my dark captain left the kitchen in a swirl of wet kisses and breathy, desperate little sounds. Footsteps unfaltering, he took the stairs without breaking from my flushed skin. Each step bringing me closer to *the* moment and whatever lay on the other side.

Thighs wrapped tight, I tangled my fingers in his hair and let him feast. Let him fill me with fervor and drown the malice that had long lived between us, drunk on the naughty thrill of doing just that. Delighted by the strength keeping me aloft and the hands that wandered at will. Kneading and trembling.

When we made the landing, he growled, pressing me to the doorframe guarding his bedroom. Exertion pounded beneath his skin and through the bond as his breath came hot and ragged—laced with broken restraint. He abandoned my left thigh, pinning me to the wall with one foot on the floor, the other draped around his hip. Leaving me spread. Vulnerable as he ground his erection exactly where I ached the most.

And, haste battling greed for the right to strip me bare, he attacked the tie keeping my ruined dress secure, then stooped to plant a kiss to my sternum. The act somehow seemed more intimate than allowing him to suckle at my breast or wash my hair—or indeed, touch me at all.

Head braced against the doorframe, I gasped, helpless as the knot came free and black silk pooled between our hips. Habit saw me flinch, grabbing for the edges of silken protection before I was well and truly exposed. But it was ingrown deceit that drove me to catch the garment before it fell, concealing secret Glaith beneath the guise of trembling innocence.

My bonded was undeterred. Forcing hesitation to die so completion might live, he kissed me. Tongue plunging past my lips to flick over the points of modified canines, heedless of the danger. And then, sweeping his hands up my ribs—hips to armpits—he broke away. Pausing to douse me with a look that seared my flesh and tightened my nipples.

Brushing the sides of my breasts, he framed my bust in rough hands, making me shiver as I stood. Waiting. Allowing him to look, unimpeded.

"Exquisite," he growled, voice rough and gravely.

I held his gaze, marveling at the flush on his cheeks. At the glisten of swollen, parted lips.

Asher was the beautiful one. The one without scars or limits. Especially so, when he looked at me like *that*, with his ki hammering at every piece of me, filling me with a hunger not my own.

"Let go," he whispered, tugging at black silk. "I want to see you."

Something wicked unfolded in my chest. Something born of whiskey and madness, for unable to resist the urge, I said, "No," and didn't bother to mask the blatant challenge from an apex predator.

With a snarl, he lifted me, dress and all. Kicking the door shut, he carried me toward the bed.

I squealed when he tossed me, blushing to the roots of my hair as I scrambled to the far end of the mattress, clutching the Glaith in a ball of loose fabric even as I tried to conceal my nudity. Knowing it was foolish to keep my last secret so close, yet terrified to do what it took to buy his distraction.

Even with the whiskey, I lacked the confidence to meet him on a level that Kas could be proud of.

And yet, he watched me from the foot of the bed. Lips curving around a sinister smile, unbuckling his belt one-handed.

"I—" Inching back until my shoulder blades met the chill of the headboard, I shook my head. "A-Asher—"

His pants hit the floor. "Mila."

"You're not..." Entranced, I couldn't look away. Couldn't stop the perverted little shiver from racing through my blood, kicking at the bond in time with pumping fist gliding sure and easy over his erection. Couldn't help the blood that rushed to my core, or the flood of slick heat that followed. His unapologetic sexuality a drug to my sense of modesty. "You're not wearing any underwear."

He chuckled. "Very astute. Now come here."

That something wicked surfaced again, hushing the

uncertain voice searching for the nearest escape. I met his eyes. "No."

"Ah, yes," he drawled, and knelt on the bed. "Defiant as ever, my wild Priestess." Knees spread, one hand on his manhood, Asher licked his lips. "There's only one problem with your act, darling." He tapped the bronzed skin over his heart, bumping the pendant. "I can feel you." He stroked it, engorged head straining toward me, shining with need. "How much you want this."

"No."

Voice hoarse, he continued. "It's the fight, isn't it? The struggle. The idea that I'll pin you down and take what I want..." He smiled, slow and sexy. Watching me. "Oh, yes. Look at you. I'll bet anything I own that pretty little pussy is soaking wet, isn't it?"

Face burning, I shook my head, but that was not a bet I could make. And he knew it. As sure as looking at the evidence of just how much *he* wanted this too. "It's the bond. This is *your* fault."

"Oh, no," he drawled, then seized my ankle with his free hand. "You don't get to pretend this time." He pulled, not stopping until my bottom came into contact with his thighs, dress hiked indecently high about my hips. "Fuck," he grunted, draping each of my legs over his. Ignoring my insincere attempt to stop him with nostrils flared. Half-lidded gaze focused between my thighs, he sucked a breath between his teeth.

Clutching black silk and Glaith over my nipples, I waited for a verdict. Spread before him. Over him. Not sure if I'd see revulsion or desire shining in those inky depths—terrified of *both*.

"Move your hands," he murmured, rough palms

traveling from knee to thigh. Stopping only to draw those damned circles over my hip bones.

Again, I shook my head.

Asher grinned. All teeth and feral glee. "Mhm. Thought so." He lunged, wrestling my hands away from my breasts, and flung the ruined dress over his shoulder. Not recognizing the *ping* of metal and Glaith striking wood for the prize bared before him.

And it *was* a prize—or so the bond would have me believe. My submission, no matter the cause, was *his,* for I didn't fight him. Not really. Not even when he pinned my hands over my head and gave his weight.

"Feels good, doesn't it?" he whispered, naked flesh prickling mine, the weight of his arousal bumping the edge of my mound. "Feels *right.*"

My lips parted, but nothing came out.

"It's okay." He braced above me, weight pinning me to the mattress. "I don't need you to say it. Not yet." Shifting my wrists to one hand, he explored with the other, fingers bumping over every ridge of my stretched ribs... my breasts. He squeezed, snared by the image of my nipple flushing red between forefinger and thumb. "Fuck*sakes,* that's sexy."

And then his head dipped and he claimed the sensitive nub between his teeth. Nibbling.

Back arched, I tried to pull away *and* force him to take more all at once, vision blurred by the shock of sensation.

"You're wound so tight, Mila—" nimble fingers found that twin peak, pinching. "Aching for it. Like nothing I've ever felt..." He shivered. "Won't take much..."

I squeaked, pulling a smile from him when I tried to free my hands and writhed beneath him.

"I'd like nothing more than to taste you—" blunt tip kissed slick heat, winding the ache tighter. "To tie you down and make you come with my lips." Abandoning my nipple, he rose up, setting his teeth to capture my lower lip. "With my tongue." He sucked it between his teeth, then retreated. "But I have something else in mind."

My throat was dry. "W-What?"

Speaking so I felt the words move against my lips, he whispered, "I'm going to fuck you," then traced the length of my torso. Outlined Kas' claws with fingers that trembled, then went further still. Parting sodden, delicate flesh before dipping inside with a ragged exhale. "So *wet...*" Braced on right hand, he shook, setting something blunt and desperate to part my folds. Fist pumping out of sight.

I buried my face in the crook of my bent arm. Goddess... this was happening. With *him.*

"Hey," he whispered, kissing my elbow. "Come back."

"Just take—" I flexed beneath him, breath hitching as I shook my head. "Take what you came for."

He nudged forward just enough to remind me of his intent without taking the plunge. "You want me to fuck you without seeing to the mess I made?" A kiss at the corner of my lips. "Take my pleasure and leave you unsatisfied?" Another tiny, shallow thrust, teasing the ache ever higher. "Pretend I don't know what this needy little pussy needs, and ignore how much I want to feel you come apart on my cock?"

To my complete horror, fresh tears spilled over my

lashes, and no amount of willpower could force him to unsee that hated weakness. But I nodded anyway, pushing a warbling little, *"Yes,"* through the pain. "Please."

"Ah," he breathed, and brushed my hair back. "I'm afraid that's impossible, Miss Tannovic."

I scrubbed at the bubble boiling behind my heart, intending to crush the wild, terrified thing trying to punch through bone and sinew. To kill it before it escaped. "Why?"

"Because," he said, and captured my fingers, kissing the brand. "You're wild and beautiful and"—he fell forward, caging me beneath him, elbow at my ear, fingers scooping behind my neck—"and you're *mine.*"

A piece of my heart tore away, and I blinked, fighting desperate sobs before I even realized they were a possibility. Hating myself for needing this... with him.

He kneaded the base of my skull, and did the *one thing* that could keep from shattering beneath him. "Please?" he whispered, the plea laced with uncompromising honesty.

I could only nod. Giving the only way I could.

"Then touch me, Miss Tannovic."

Catching his lips between the sharp points of my teeth, I did just that. Threatening to break the skin, I reached for the man bonded to a black soul. A man who didn't recoil, but begged for more. Keening as he parted me, I found anchor on the bunching, quivering muscle heaving around his ribs. Nails scraping as he eased the ache and made it so much worse.

"Fuccck," he groaned, pressing forward at a glacial pace. Making me feel every cursed inch. "So... wet..."

Trembling, I breathed him in, caught and pinned

even when he pulled back. With right hand caging my nape, the other was free to slide over my hip. To find my knee and drape my calf over the round of his flexing bottom. Leaving the way open, unguarded as he redoubled his effort. Going deeper this time. Splashing us *both* with a fresh wave of goosebumps.

"God, you're tight," he gasped, shaking. Surrendering a kiss. Bumping something deep within my belly. "You're soaking my balls, Mila."

I hiccupped, grateful he couldn't see the mortification heating my cheeks. Pretending he couldn't sense it.

But he refused to let me hide, the arrogant prick. "I can't think of anything sexier," he grated, catching my hitched breath. Filling me to the brim... stretching until I was forced to accommodate the invasion. And when he stopped, it was because he could go no further.

"Touch me," he whispered again, and though he broke away with eyes squeezed shut, he remained buried to the root. Motionless. Waiting for me to adjust.

Cheeks wet—both above and below—I bared my teeth at this insolent man who would deny me the privacy he took at will. Hooked both legs around his hips, and caught a fist full of thick, dark hair. Trying to pull him inside. To consume everything he was and make it irrevocably *mine*.

As he had done to me, I ran my hands over his ribs, hungry for every silky, bronzed inch. My bondmate. Long lines of lean muscle—all mine. Forced to quiver and dance beneath the blunted edge of my claws, he shuddered, skin prickling as I raked his lower back.

The wicked thing within me reveled in commands issued and followed without pause. In his sharp inhale and the twisted, pained expression marring his face.

But still, he did not move.

Could he not *feel* this? This... dreadful tension twisting and churning my insides into a frothy mess?

Heels burrowing into muscle, I used him for leverage, grinding a tiny nub of pleasure into the dark curls matted and slick above his root.

"Sonofa—" he choked, bucking forward, pounding ecstasy through his tip, straight into the base of my spine. "Stop. *Stop.*"

"No."

"Mila—"

I dove into the bond like I'd never done before. Found the spot that screamed for *more* and smashed it with everything I had. Unleashed every dark impulse, every wicked, depraved thought I'd never intended to share, and showed this impossible Elite exactly what brand of evil he'd bound himself to. Showed him the basest Truth I knew.

"Mila... Fucksakes, go easy—I—" Deep inside, he jumped, making me clench around his base.

Starving, I hunched forward, kissing and nipping my way to his ear, both hands straining for the gloriously taut globes of his ass.

"Ugh, *fuck.* Mila," he rasped, pulling back, leaving me empty. Unfulfilled.

And that just wouldn't do. I sank my nails into the hard muscle beneath my palms. Taking my due.

"Mila—" he grunted, hips jerking forward, plunging into me as deep as my body would allow. The contact sent lightning to my brain and with a tiny moan, I arched my hips, chasing it.

But he pulled out with a breathless laugh. Leaving me empty and clenching on painful nothingness.

I hissed, eyes snapping up to find an answer in obsidian depths—and a dark grin that tightened fallow womb.

"Is this what you need?" he rasped, and plunged home.

"Please—" My breath caught as he began to work, picking up a torturous rhythm, making sure to grind his pelvis against my clit at the bottom of every powerful stroke.

He kissed me then, lips and tongue dancing on the dangerous point of modified canines as he dragged desperate little noises from my throat.

"Goddess," I whispered, breaking away from his lips. Gasping. Thrilled and mortified by the squelching slap of our hips meeting in this frenzy of bad decisions and ultimatums.

Settling back on his haunches, he wet his thumb between his lips, then moved those infernal circles to our joining.

Orbiting my clit with a slick digit.

But the angle struck something shallow that made me flinch, chanting *"No, no, no, no!"* Something that had me reaching for him with both hands.

"Shh," he soothed, and scooped me up. Settled me astride his lap in one fluid motion that saw hands damp with sweat run down my back, and offer support. "We're not quite ready for that."

And then he was rocking against me, slow, using his grip on my hips to guide. Back and forth, dragging my sensitive folds along the length of his shaft. Building the tension until my eyes rolled back. Until I wanted to beg him to stop, and destroy him if he obeyed.

As if he understood, my bonded picked up the pace,

positioning into me with a ferocity I couldn't hope to match. The only thing I could do was hold on, completely lost, drowning in a lust so tangible I could taste it. Drank deep of sin and divinity and knew ambrosia.

Couldn't take anymore. Couldn't stop. Wanted him to push me over the edge and forget *everything* for a few selfish minutes in forbidden arms. But... I *couldn't.* I couldn't forget. Not when—

"Please, Mila," he gasped, voice breaking with the exact shade of desperate piercing my sanity. "Stay with me. You're so close." Asher caught my nipple between his teeth, groaning, breathing me in. "Come for me. Come on my cock. I have to feel you—"

The deep rumble of his voice, strained and cracking, took everything from me. My every muscle flexed at his command, pleasure bursting through my system, rendering resistance moot. Goddess, even the natural instinct to draw breath was a distant memory, a hopeless second to the all-consuming ecstasy of *his* touch.

I tried to cry out, tried to give voice to the moment that shattered who I'd been, but the sound got stuck in my throat. Obliterated by wave after wave of ki crashing over my senses.

Buried as deep as he could go, he drove my hips back and forth, working me into a lather. "Ugh, fuck. I'm coming," he grated, voice a breathy, tight expletive.

I could feel his climax on my skin as clearly as I felt my own, could feel the pulse as he rocked against me. Filling me.

And in that moment, I knew the unique brand of our joint slavery, each forced to experience the release of the other until the line between pleasure and pain snapped. Confusing what was and wasn't.

Too much!

Stars blackened my vision—but still I rode. Milking him until his orgasm ran dry. Until I could take nothing more and his spend overflowed, splashing the sheets. Soaking his balls in earnest. Without thought, I sank my teeth into the hard muscle at his shoulder, hoping it would be enough to break me away. To keep me conscious astride his thighs so I could do what came next.

He flinched, but continued to rock against me, cock throbbing and empty yet still trying to seed a barren womb. Clutching my slick, quivering body against him. As if he felt the urge to crawl as deep as he could and incinerate everything that defined *self*.

But that brand of insanity couldn't last.

Face tucked against my throat, he pinched my pulse between his teeth once more, and said, "Fucking perfect, Mila," in a voice I scarcely recognized. "Perfect."

16

———

We stayed like that—me astride his thighs, cheek pressed to his shoulder as a thin trail of blood ran down his chest—for time undetermined. Twitching and breathing together, until my actions caught up to my thoughts. Uncomfortable both inside and out, I squirmed, making an embarrassing little *squelch* bubble out around our joining.

"And where do you think you're going?" he asked, kissing my collarbone. Grip tightening with the sort of territorial possession I'd only known from the queen of the wood.

"I'm... sticky."

He chuckled, easygoing and light. Punctuated by his cock kicking deep inside me—not as big as it had been moments before, but not quite exhausted either. "Sticky and disheveled and sexy," he purred, and grasped my thighs, pausing to kiss first left nipple, then right before proceeding to dump me on my back. Following me down without being evicted from my sticky, slippery walls. "And I'm not done with you yet." A gentle thrust before he licked my bottom lip. "Don't know if I'll ever be done."

"You *can't* be serious," I whispered, oversensitive and overworked. Halfway to limp, even as I set branded hand to his chest and felt that depraved tension begin to build anew.

He buried his face in my hair, inhaling. "'Fraid not. *This*"—he ground against the swollen bead throbbing at my apex—"is something I'm finding impossible to resist."

A whine crackled between my lips. "A-Asher, please—"

"Mmm." He caught my earlobe between his teeth, breath coming hot against my nape. "And there's my name on your lips."

I shivered, gasping when he ground his pelvis into my clit, when I felt him shiver in turn when my inner muscles flexed around his length. And when he kissed me, pinning me to sodden mattress as he played in the abundant mess gathered between my thighs, I was helpless to do *anything* but embrace it. Submit to base need, and lose myself.

"Feels so good," he groaned, eyes fluttering shut. Voice a splintered, broken thing born of desperate need. A thing that revived. That made me forget everything but surging hips and left resistance to sulk in an abandoned corner at the back of my mind. All but forgotten as he worked for another dazzling finish.

Honest work, in spite of tarnished origins, for when a bead of sweat trickled over his cheek, I watched. Entranced. Watched it get lost in the shadow of beard scruff before tracing the edge of his jaw.

Tangling my fingers at his nape, I pulled him down.

Caught the wandering bead on the flat of my tongue, and lingered. Reveling in the rasp of day-old beard and the salty blend of sex and taboo indulgence that exploded on my palate.

I hummed, savoring that sinful nectar and the perverse thrill it sent echoing through my nethers. Tasted like *more*.

And so it was that I was taken unaware by the inky gaze affixed to my face. Failed to note the look of complete shock scrawled across his handsome, hated features or that he'd gone still. Buried to the root.

Something incomprehensible came from his lips, and he kissed me, right hand sliding down to knead my hip as he redoubled his efforts. Fucking me into the mattress with reckless abandon, my captain was the first to tremble. The one who lost his grip on his precious control and slipped, striving for completion.

But I was *far* from immune. Seduced by the drive of thickening cock and sheer crushing weight of pressure building in his balls, I moved with him. Hips undulating, trying to draw him out and contain his release. To make it mine, along with everything else before he took it back and sent me spinning into bliss.

"I can't—" he gasped, hips jerking erratically, eyes squeezed shut. "Can't stop." And then, forehead falling to the sheets beside my cheek, lips scraping at my pulse, he lost it. "I'm gonna come. Oh, my fuck. Come with me, Mila. Please—"

Not quite there, but selfish enough to use any advantage I could, I sunk into the bond and let him take me. Drank from that unraveling, glittery spot pulsing within him and tipped my hips back. Letting him grind against my swollen bean as he started to break. As he twitched and jerked, gasping against my skin, sluicing through sopping wet, welcoming flesh. And when he stopped, buried to the hilt, it was enough.

Insides splashed with wave after wave of potent, euphoria-laced ki, I bucked. Milking him with clenching, greedy cunt. Heels locked and secured behind his thighs, I held him hostage as he filled me again. Kept him within me even after he had nothing left, and each contraction of *my* climax drew only empty shudders and hitching breath. Wringing him utterly dry.

Heart pounding into my chest, he remained. Even when the sensation became too much, and the head of his glans begged relief, he remained. Allowing me to finish, to use him up and find complete, twitching satisfaction.

And when he began to soften, easing the tension on my stretched walls, the slow retreat was... unwelcome. Shockingly so.

"That was—" he licked me from collarbone to jaw, withdrawing and shifting his weight to the mattress at my side, then shook his head. "I don't have the words to describe what that was."

Neither did I.

At least, none I was willing to speak aloud. Not to *him*, no matter the aftershocks, or the vulnerability taking root between us. The affinity.

Reverent, he cupped my far breast in a large palm. Dwarfing the modest swell, he passed his thumb over tender nipple, smirking against my temple when I flinched. He seemed to enjoy the involuntary shudder that bowed my spine and set my hands to his wrist. Planting a chaste kiss at the corner of my lips, he wound his left leg over and between mine. Pressing pubic hair matted with our mutual spend against my hip, he bathed me in warmth.

I don't know how long we lay there, wrapped in a cocoon of sticky heat and wandering fingers. Neither speaking for fear of shattering this quiet, stolen moment. But it was long enough for something horrid to find its way beneath my skin. An insidious nestling that curled around my lungs, and set poisoned barbs to anchor and burrow. Long enough for the whispers to creep in and infect me with a different sort of tension. One that tore down the untruths I'd built to sustain myself.

It would be so easy to stay here... with him. So easy to let him wrap me in luxury and forget the debt I owed but couldn't repay.

He twitched. Forearm compressing my ribs, hand convulsing around cupped breast. The sort of twitch that preceded exhausted sleep and spoke of slaked lust —*exactly* the sort that heralded the coming of *my* moment.

I swallowed, staring at the ceiling with dry, itchy eyes, and fought the urge to succumb. Instead, trying to wriggle free from his embrace.

He jerked, coming awake with a startled inhale and a half snore, tightening his grip and tucking me closer to his chest. "What—"

"I have to pee," I whispered, but couldn't meet his bleary gaze. Couldn't bear to see the drowsy contentment begging me to stay.

But he grunted, snuffling at my temple, then said, "Don't be long," and pulled his pendant forward. Over his head, and with a sluggish flick of his wrist, tossed it onto the bedside table.

I fled. Rushing from soiled sheets and satiated Elite lounging in a bed of lies, I fled. Past the heap of ruined silk hiding a secret of iron and Glaith. Pausing on the threshold of the bathroom to catch a glimpse of what would come next.

And there it was. Tucked under the desk, exactly as Alicia had said. A case with tarnished brass buckles, reeking of mystery.

I pushed the bathroom door closed with a gentle *snap* and left it where it was.

Before anything else, I used the facilities. Almost too scared to wipe and discover just *how* virile the Captain really was. But I tidied myself up at the sink, casting a longing eye toward the shower, yet knowing there wasn't time for such vanity. Not with so little between me and that case. No, what I needed now, was a plan.

Pushing a hand through my hair, I stilled, catching the overbright eye of a girl whose lips were swollen and too red. Whose hair was a wild mess of silvery blonde, framing cheeks stained with the unmistakable evidence of just how much it had cost to gain this moment of privacy, such as it was. A girl who looked *alive,* in spite of golden collar. Whose wildness was not born of Kas' teachings, but the attention of a man well-versed in the handling of a slave.

A *pleasure* slave.

I swallowed, *hard,* scowling at the girl who looked like she belonged.

Only a shade of the Wood's Menace glared back.

There was always another way. *Always.* When my world had crumbled all around me, had I not built a new one? Had I not found surrogate guardians in and Kas and the Grandmother, and *defended* them in spite of the High Priestess' decree that I was destined to become an Empath? It wasn't a killer without thought or remorse who'd sent refugees to safer lands. And neither was it a beast of mindless hunger who'd denied Belle's many ultimatums.

Impossible odds had never stopped me before, no matter that I'd been tamed and broken in.

Eyes drifting shut, I looked in. Looked to the bond to see what I might see.

What I found needed *visual* confirmation.

Hardly daring to believe my compromised senses, I pushed the bathroom door open. Just a crack. Just enough to see an arm slung over the captain's face. To get distracted by the rumpled bed clothes draped over lean muscle and partial nudity. But it was the rhythmic rise and fall of his taut belly and the unmistakable cadence of light *snoring* that showed me the way.

The captain was *sleeping*—just as Alicia had said he would.

I couldn't blame him. Not really. It *had* been a trying few days of near constant vigil. The poor, foolish man needed his rest.

Stalking toward my prize on silent feet, I denied the urge to grin for fear of disturbing him, and crept toward his desk. Moving only when his snoring could offer cover, I crouched. Naked. Palms and tiptoes pressed to the carpet, I inched closer.

One limb at a time, as Kas had taught me. Never taking my eyes off the most powerful ki-wielder who'd ever lived. Keeping my ki as compressed and far from the bond as I could manage in my corrupted state.

And when my fingers wrapped around the handle, claiming Sasha's case, I knew an instant of stark terror.

Felt it blend with the approach of that long-awaited moment and become something new. Something I'd never felt before and couldn't name.

Oblivious, the captain slumbered on, radiating a heavy and lethargic song that spoke of pure contentment.

Completion.

Stomping the urge to celebrate prematurely, I retreated once more, withdrawing into the bathroom with my prize clutched to my breasts. Hoping the weight of this enigma was some long forgotten Priestess weapon of apocalyptic might, I perched on my haunches and opened the case.

At first, as I inspected the four objects tucked within, I knew true dejection. Fell from the height of victory before I'd scaled the summit, and paid a price I could never reclaim—all for two relics used to laud a dead Goddess, and the very tools used to bring about Her fall and mine.

Sasha hadn't even the decency to leave a note, explaining her madness.

Tracing the symbol for Priestess with my forefinger, I swallowed back the rage. She'd spent years playing my puppet master, training the man who'd taken every-thing I had to give, only to mock me in my loneliest hour?

Why?

Just to laugh with her Goddess as they frolicked in the Void?

That was a brand of cruelty I had neither the experi-ence to deal with nor anticipate.

Crumpling, I sat back, setting my ass cheeks to the bathroom tiles, regardless of the chill. Scrubbing at eyes too drained to bother with tears—eyes that begged me to forget this insanity, crawl back into his bed, and embrace defeat with whatever shreds of dignity I possessed.

It wasn't until my vision sparkled with dark stars that I began to realize just how cruel a woman Sasha had truly been—all the more so for her genius, for it was then I realized one horrible, poetic truth.

There was *one* way through this that didn't involve me submitting to a life of slavery, but it would cost the sum value of the very thing I intended to reclaim. A price so steep, I'd never consider it if there was even a whisper of another way.

My independence.

Tattered heart singing with emotions too complex to unravel, I picked the scabs ringing my right wrist raw. Picked until it bled and the smear of crimson confirmed her choice to be the correct one.

As if *all of it* had been for this.

I sighed, feeling the weight of free will stripped away, leaving me lightheaded. Weightless, as dark feathers pulsed with hated, renewed purpose.

After all, I'd been promised *everything*—what more could I do than accept?

17

———————

It was clear, given the contents of this 'gift', that I wasn't the intended owner of three-fourths of the things bequeathed to me. Clear Sasha had meant me to be nothing more than a delivery agent of her most prized possessions. I cursed and began to unpack items I had no desire to touch, let alone accept guardianship over.

First, and largest among them, was the ancient text I'd first encountered the day Tritan fell. Marked simply with a silver etching of the Priestess symbol, Sasha had wrapped it in a fine, sheer linen. Protecting those elderly pages from desecration as best she could, and apart from removing it from the case, I didn't disturb those efforts. Just set the dusty old tome aside and moved on to sort the rest.

The next item, and last of the surviving Priestess relics, was none other than one withered Lotus Regula. Shriveled and absent its plain clay pot, I wrapped it in a dry washcloth from the sink and bundled it away. Careful to keep its desecrated flesh apart from mine, lest

I awaken it without the ability to return it to hibernation.

The third was far and above the most inherently repulsive of the lot, both for its ability to render the Blood fragile and mundane, and its history of ending an era by doing exactly that.

Sasha had returned the single, rounded ingot of Eidolon I'd lost in her office at the hands of the late General Tilcot. Arguably one of the pieces the Captain had used to sedate the Wood's Menace, and the very same I'd worn to disguise my Truth only hours before. That, too, was wrapped in a bit of cloth and set aside.

It was the fourth and final of her gifts that set my teeth on edge. The most loathsome of the bunch, and the only one I *had* to handle. An unused set of Tritan chains to match the ones already melted into my skin. Three delicate rings for a prospective slave, one thicker, masculine cuff for a would-be master. Sinister, even in their glittering beauty. Re-purposed with a prospect all the more heinous for my lack of participation in the matter.

Sasha hadn't moved against the captain for fear of obliterating the *one* being who could stand before an Empath without blinking. Who could bathe in darkness without suffering the consequences and balance the scales between the Blood. She'd trained him in the ways of the Goddess and had given him the gift of control. Freed him of Glaith dependency and shielded him from discovery.

But as I sat there—bare-assed and seething with fated impotence—I knew she hadn't done *any* of it for cruelty's sake.

Above all else, Sasha had meant to restore *balance*.

She'd paid with her life to get me the contents of this box, and no matter the urge to delay until time ran out, I gnashed my teeth and prepared as best I could. The largest of the golden circlets—the one meant to ring the throat of a slave—needed to taste the master's blood.

As he had done in the shower stall only days prior, I pressed the tiny glass vial embedded in the gold until it swung open. Sent it to drink from the deepest of the self-inflicted, scabby wounds ringing my wrist, then snapped it shut. Filled with a crimson smear, I watched the whole set glow white-hot for a single instant, knowing this was it.

There was nothing left, but the taking of my moment and the surrender of the only thing I'd never willingly give.

Grim, I stood, setting the bracelets atop the ones already permanently affixed to my skin. Warming the gold against my wrists, yet leaving the clasps unhinged. Ready. Hiding them where he wouldn't think to look until it was too late. I kept the largest two separate. Knowing the collar was too small to fit around his neck, and the master cuff couldn't be hidden in plain-sight. I'd have to improvise and hope the improvised positioning on his body wouldn't affect the outcome.

And if he could sense the subtle lure of Glaith within these chains through his sleep? Well... I'd just have to do something to distract him.

Whatever it took.

I didn't bother with a steadying breath. Didn't pause to fret about the possibility of failure, or what the consequences could be for victory. I simply opened the door and approached the sleeping Elite Trila-Glís, naked and unashamed.

Fated to restore balance.

He was as I'd left him. Right forearm slung over his eyes, left stretched toward the bedside table and his pendant. Glorious, spent, and far, *far* too trusting of the dark thing he'd chosen to share intimacy with. A thing without remorse for the prospect of *breaking* that fragile trust.

Silent, I claimed the foot of the bed. Crawled over rumpled sheets and long, splayed legs, careful of the golden circlet caught tight in either fist to stop them from clinking and clacking. My attention snared at the sight of that slumbering beast between his legs, waiting limp and placid against his thigh. Even shrunken, it made my sex clench with lewd memory, and fascinated, I watched it twitch.

Answering that most primal call.

I moved on. Up. Crawling over and above him, shoulders and hips rolling without the need for stealth. Not stopping until I hovered above his bellybutton with knees on either side of his lower ribs, I buried those golden circlets beneath the pillows, then settled back. One hand hidden beneath his armpit, the other braced on his chest. Feeling his ribs expand between my thighs. Skin hot and prickling against flesh that was swollen and still slick. His heart beat between my knees... Blood oozing from my bite high between shoulder and neck.

Connected to his slumbering ki, I moved as if my actions were not my own. Widened the hinge on the slave collar and fit it around the slimmest part of his left bicep. Leery of pinching his skin, but certain it wouldn't be enough to wake him, I secured the circlet filled with my blood.

I kissed him then, pressing my lips to his until he came alive. Until he groaned and shifted beneath me. When his left hand found my knee, I caught his fingers with those that had long been branded with his mark. It was nothing to flick the first bracelet forward. Nothing to set it above the matte-black mark of the Empire, and cover the soft *click* of it snapping shut with a breathy groan of my own.

"Come 'ere," he murmured, smile soft and pliant. Sleepy.

I shook my head, letting my hair fall forward in a silvery halo around our faces. Obscuring his view.

"Insatiable little witch," he breathed, and uncovered his eyes—though he couldn't seem to find the strength to actually open them. His forearm bumped my chin... scraping over the points of my nipples before he brushed my hair back. Cupped my cheek.

Lacing our fingers together against my skin, I deepened the kiss. Tongue slipping between his lips. Tasting.

He flexed, coming awake. Pressing stiffening length up, sending it between my cheeks to play in the creamy mess we'd made. "Tell me what you want," he rasped, left hand skating over my hip and down my back. Glittering out of sight. Coming to rest on the curve of my ass, while his fingers dove further still. Spreading me.

Again, I shook my head. But this time, the denial was mixed with something akin to fear. Vulnerability.

"'Sokay." He tilted my hips back and set himself between my lips. Pressing forward until the hypersensitive head slipped in, and though he wasn't fully hard, he rocked into my heat. "I'm too tired right now anyway. 'M afraid you wore me out, Miss Tannovic."

Well, *that* just wouldn't do. What was victory, even one so pale as this, without a witness?

Hungry, I shifted back, gathered the dark bedsheets around my hips—to hide the illicit flash of gold where it shouldn't be—and took him in. Not stopping until he reached as deep as he could.

His eyes popped open, wide and shocked in the gloomy half-lit bedroom.

Holding the dark glitter of his gaze, I kissed the palm of his as-of-yet unadorned hand, then shifted his grip to my breast. Telling him what I wanted the only way I could.

"Come here," he hissed, but pinched my nipple. Massaging and kneading. "Lie with me. Lemme fall asleep inside you."

I clenched around his girth. Denying him respite. Giving him one last moment of... *this* before I crushed it forever.

Nostrils flared, he grunted, straining deeper. Hardening within me against his will. Fingers tight on my hip, he spread his legs—just a little—making space for his sack to fall between his thighs and securing leverage in the twisted sheets. "God." He shuddered, guiding my hips. Rocking into me. "I want you. *Again.*"

I knew the feeling. Felt my pussy gush with renewed enthusiasm, thrilled by the notion that the most powerful ki-wielder alive was pliant between my thighs. That he trembled somewhere deep inside, already trying not to spill as I rode him. Unaware of what fate had chosen for him.

For... *us.*

Drunk, I fell forward, working his length at this new angle. Grinding my clit against his pubic bone, even as my fingers inched toward his undecorated wrist. Pushing that right hand above his head. Pinning it to the pillows, out of sight.

And when his head fell back, eyes squeezed shut with pained ecstasy, I struck. Licked the rough, salty skin below his jaw, and put the last of his golden bracelets in place, one-handed. Deftly nimble in spite of the tension rising in my core, or because of it—I couldn't begin to say.

"Fuck," he gasped, brow furrowed. Fingers clenching beneath dark sheets, hips flexing and bunching. Helpless to refuse.

Again, I sat back. Released his trapped wrist and cupped my swollen, reddened breasts, distracting that inky gaze with pinched, rosy nipples.

Something about having him like this—submissive as I rode him against his will—struck a chord. Set those dark wings to beat at their cage of bone and Glaith as I rushed to claim what was *mine.*

Fingers curved into claws, I denied myself *nothing.* Surrendered to this madness one last time and followed purest instinct, and in doing so, won skill far beyond my limited experience.

"God, *yes.* Fuck me, Mila," he rasped, sweat beaded on his brow, eyes chips of obsidian glass. Wrapping his hands around my waist, he meant only to feel me as I did just that, as I milked him for all I was worth and dragged the spend straight from his balls—but a golden flash caught his bewildered gaze. Made him blink. Confused. "What—"

But it was really *much* too late.

Grinning my toothiest grin, I wrapped branded fingers around his throat and claimed the master cuff with the other. Pulled it from beneath the pillow and sent that tiny glass vial to drink from the wound on his shoulder.

"Hear this, Captain Asher Rawlings of His Majesty's Imperial Army," I said, and squeezed his airway all the tighter, feeling his control begin to splinter when my blunted claws scored that delicate skin. "I decline your offer of suffering and servitude."

He choked. "What—"

I released him, and said, "I am *not* a slave." And before he could recognize the danger, I snapped the crimson vial shut and locked the master cuff about my left bicep.

The sudden, blinding agony bowed his spine and mine. Sent him rocketing into my pussy even as his awareness shuttered, blinking on the edge of bliss and *fundamental* change. Helpless as the molten gold seared his flesh, and his cock began to spurt, kicking me into climax with him. Bathing the entrance of my womb even as he tried to claw at the pain pumping through his very blood.

When it was done, he wilted beneath me—utterly spent. Succumbing as I had, to the gift of senseless darkness after a trauma so profound, it existed outside mortal comprehension. Altering us both in a manner that had never been done before.

And so it was that I was the first to experience the wild power surging in a bond unlike anything I'd ever felt. Unlike anything *anyone* had ever felt.

A perfect circle, *finally* complete.

Laughter began to bubble from deep within me.

Soul-deep mirth that couldn't be tarnished by the unknown power of a bond that now ran *both* ways, or the knowing that I'd all but guaranteed the sort of wrath another more cautious person might spend a lifetime trying to avoid.

I laughed without care or restraint, for there, between my soiled thighs, the master wore the glittering mark of the slave.

I stood, spattering his belly with pearly drops of our third joining, absent any remorse or weakness for the sheer power pounding through my veins.

And what power I had!

Anything lost had returned with a vengeance easily thrice the brilliance I could have ever hoped to attain. Left me connected me to any tiny spark of living ki within a hundred meters or more. Every breath sending awareness through the breeze and beyond.

But all of it—every infinitesimal, mundane detail now humming for attention beneath my skin—was overshadowed by the man lying supine on the bed beneath me. A man who matched me in terms of power, yet still outweighed me in both physical strength and sheer military cunning.

And I couldn't give up my newfound advantage so easily, now could I?

Humming a jaunty little tune, I hopped off the bed and strolled into his closet. Found sparse shelves lined with military uniforms, pressed shirts ranging in color from white to black, shoes, boots, a small backpack, a few simple items of jewelry, and of course, several spare slave dresses—but *nothing* suitable for hard travel.

With a sneer, I yanked open drawers at random, and found socks, underpants, leather belts, and a dozen pairs of stretchy winter leggings—lacking in utility purposes, perhaps, but they were far preferable to that bloody infernal rag my dear captain had made me wear.

Stepping into a pair of leggings, I yanked a black t-shirt over my head, seized two leather belts, and returned to the senseless man waiting on my mercy.

Or lack thereof.

Grinning, I allowed myself the luxury of his naked form. Eyed all that bronzed skin stained with my scent and *my* mark, then gathered his wrists. Bound them together above his head, and hid his new gold beneath leather.

Then, with the first belt cinched tight enough to restrain without endangering circulation, I secured him to the headboard with the second. Putting the buckle as far from his dexterous fingers as I could.

It wouldn't keep him—nothing short of a tomb made entirely of Eidolon could keep either of us now—but it was a start.

Flush and growing bored of waiting, I sat on his chest, knees braced beneath his outstretched armpits. And when I pressed my scarred palm to his cheek, it was with intention. My ki rushed through him, leaping and giddy, unrestrained for the first time since the fall of Tritan, filling that perfect, unwanted mate with vigor. With the wild rush of victory and claimed vengeance, tempered by profound, eternal loss. Loss of coveted solitude, for we were bound in *every* conceivable manner. Forever.

He sighed, coming back.

I felt the instant he became aware. Felt fury ignite behind flickering eyelids, as if it had been born in *my* gut. As if the injustice of having another buried deep and glued to every secret intimate hidden piece was *mine* to suffer all over again. But I didn't lash out. Didn't strike him or take payment from his flesh.

I waited.

Obsidian eyes snapped open, blinking around the most hateful glare I'd ever seen.

"Hi," I said, and grinned from my lofty perch.

He bucked, muscles heaving and bunching as he tried to use his hands. As he tried to reach for me and subdue the uncivilized darkling sitting astride his chest. "Mila, what the *fuck?*" he snarled, attempting to wrench himself free with nothing more than strength.

I waited him out, riding his temper as he strained, bowing back to inspect his new jewelry. One circle on each wrist, and a third looped around his bicep—to make no mention of those that had already existed.

I found patience in the tingly shock that replaced the wrath, then said, "Pretty, right?"

Inky, seething fury snapped at my edges. As his eyes returned to me and began to roam.

Tapping my latest gold band with a blunted claw, I guided his eye to my bicep where the master's circlet to match his now sat. "You like? It's not my first choice of body modification, mind you"—I ran my tongue over my elongated canines—"but there's no arguing with the results."

Tentative, he reached for me without touch, taking a terrified sip of what now lay between us.

"Can you feel me, Asher?" I leaned forward, didn't stop until our breath mixed. "How 'bout now?" I asked, and commanded my claws to grow anew. Watched them sprout from my fingertips and lengthen between us, as if I really *was* part lion and they'd merely been retracted. Waiting for me to extend them and mark my territory.

A strangled, confused sound burst from his lips.

"I asked you a question, slave," I whispered, running my scarred fingers through his hair, scratching at his scalp with pointed claws. "I expect an answer."

Still, he didn't speak. Seemed he couldn't.

I tisked. "Come now, pet. You should be *thanking* me! I gave you more power than you've ever had. Sharing it seems a small price to pay, given the results. It's all pretty unjust, if you ask me. Hardly seems right that you get to benefit from all my hard work and sacrifice, but —" I shrugged, planting my palms on the swells of his flushed pectorals. Dimpling his skin beneath my claws.

He stared back with stony eyes. "Are you having fun?" he asked in a voice that shook.

"Can you blame me? I owe you a rather lot, wouldn't you say?"

"Then take what you came for," he hissed, proving I wasn't the only one spiteful enough to throw the other's words around. "I can assure you, Miss Tannovic, you won't get a better chance than this."

My head tilted to the side as I considered him. "And what do you think I've yet to claim? I've already had every piece of you and found the experience... wanting." I laughed. "See, I *can't* take what I came here for because she's dead. But I suppose that means my task is at least *partially* complete, as the Empire doesn't have her power anymore either..."

A ghost of his usual cocky smirk curved the corner of his lips. "Release me, *right now*, and I'll spare you the bulk of the consequences your little stunt has earned. You and I are going to have a conversation."

The smile slipped from my lips and I patted his cheek. "No. Not just yet, I'm afraid. See"—I slid off his chest, mindful of his legs and the potential to get tangled up between those powerful thighs—"I have a little surprise for you."

"Well?" he drawled, but a bead of anxiety trickled down the side of his face. Betraying the truly delicious frisson of uncertain, aimless emotion that flew somewhere next to hate. "Get on with your theatrics or untie me, Menace."

Setting my feet to the floor, I stood, stretched my arms above my head and luxuriated in the *pop* and *crack* of my spine straightening without the weight of slavery beating me down. "I imagine you've some notion of coming after me," I said, and flicked a hank of silver-blonde hair off my shoulder. Stooped to gather my ruined, discarded dress and the secret weight contained within. "But given our lengthy history, I feel obligated to warn you against such an... *unwise* path." I met that inky gaze, twisting black silk between my deadly fingers, then paused at his bedside table. Hooking my forefinger beneath a loop of silver chain, I lifted his pendant, watching the Glaith sparkle and dance in a shaft of noon sun. "It's dangerous out there... in the wild."

Regarding me with fierce, dark eyes, he said nothing. Following along as I let the pendant swing, his fury was eclipsed by a flighty sense of... what was that delicate nectar teasing my palate? Ah, *yess.* Panic. The poor, helpless man.

I let the pendant drop. Let it clatter to the wood, forgotten, then began to unwind a fistful of dark silk. "You remember that day, don't you? The day we met? The day Tritan fell, and you burned my world down around me?" Another layer slipped away, and in my palm, Glaith and iron began to hum. "I still carry the scars from that day, Asher. They remind me of my greatest failure. That I was blinded by *you* and didn't see —" my throat constricted around ancient pains, and I choked. Swallowed it down and freed my ring at last.

He sucked in a breath, nostrils pinched white. Peppering the bond with the stink of fear.

"It's fitting, isn't it?" I asked, iron held between forefinger and thumb. Rolling it, yet avoiding the Glaith as I let it kiss the light. "That we find ourselves right back here. At the beginning." This new ring was different than the one I'd traded an entire city for. Slimmer. Feminine and dainty, while retaining the air of bold Caledonian artistry.

I met his eye, held his gaze and let him see my Truth, then slid Sasha's ring into place.

It settled over the ridge of old scars and branded initials, concealing them as if it was always meant to sit just there. On my middle finger.

As if... As if it had been *made* for *me*.

Startled, I met his scowl. Incredulous, for he *couldn't* have been so arrogant as to craft this new ring in the hopes that it would one day be mine. Couldn't have predicted his plans might lead to me wearing his ring, after all that had passed between us.

But he *had*. I could see it in the blush that pinkened his cheeks.

"Sentimental fool!" Nipples puckered with the power of three, I threw my head back and laughed, for the fit was perfect. Absolutely meant to sit atop my knuckle.

Shaking my head, I took a moment to admire the

hated glimmer of blues, greens, and purples that *belonged*, then reached for his bindings. Reached for the belts keeping him restrained, and married both buckles in bejeweled fist.

I commanded the ring to overheat just enough to turn the metal soft, then squashed it. Ignoring the pain and the stench of burning flesh and leather as the buckles twisted together—rendered forever useless as I bought myself some time. He'd have to be cut free, or tear the headboard clear off the wall.

"Thanks for the good times, Asher, but I'm off." I smothered the embers smoldering on his pillow, then banished the blisters forming on my scarred palm with a stray thought. "People to free. Empires to destroy. You know how it is."

"By all means," he replied. Civil. Tight and restrained, yet *seething* in his new place at the back of my mind. "Oh, and Mila?"

Out of habit, I turned to face him. "Yes?"

"Enjoy it while it lasts, darling. I assure you, we'll be seeing each other soon."

I blew him a kiss. "Try not to starve to death while I'm gone."

18

I stood at the crest of a modest hill, overlooking a place where I didn't belong, whose dirty secrets and defeated titans were contained by the last rays of a setting sun. A city stolen and held by serpents drunk on bottomless greed. A place mired in painful memory second only to the twisted wood at my back.

I stood on a path never walked but wasn't alone. Flush with power that wasn't *completely* mine by right, yet could never be taken from me again. With a woman whose allegiance I wouldn't bet on, and a parasite I could trust to be exactly himself, for the bond couldn't lie.

Not anymore.

Not to *either* of us.

Alicia cleared her throat. "I still canna believe you did that, lass." She laughed, brilliant green eyes twinkling above cheeks flushed with passion and adrenaline, both. "Just walked into that room and"—she clapped her hands—"*poof!* Told Marco to sleep, mid-thrust. Will say," she added, one slender brow raised, "you could've waited for a girl to finish, but I canna complain overmuch." She cupped her hands around her mouth, and took a deep breath. "Fuck the Empire!" she bellowed, voice echoing without strength enough to carry. "Fuck it long and hard and dry!"

I snorted. Traced my ring of Glaith and iron with pointed claw, then shielded my eyes against the rising wind.

"Oh," she said, and reached into her pack of stolen supplies. "Nicked this for you. I know you might not be able t'use it, but"—she handed me Asher's sidearm—"worth a try. Worth studyin' their inferior technology, if nothin' else."

At my touch, the sleek metal hesitated. Denying my unwarranted claim to ownership and rejecting my ki as it had on the frontlines.

But I would not be refused.

Never again.

Not with the power of three at my disposal and *certainly* not with a perfect bond linking me to its former owner. It was nothing to slip inside, to race through our shared wealth of ki and dig until I found the source of Elite destruction tied to his wrist.

Blinding, violet light burst from my curled fist. Trembling, but obedient. Ready and waiting for my command no matter the strength of his hatred howling at the back of my mind. Neither the vibrant green of my bonded, furious Elite, nor the electric blue of Alicia's shields—the blue that had been my mark, once.

This was something... in-between.

Something new.

I banished the ki with a thought.

"Goddess..." Alicia whistled. "Spare the fool who thinks t'cross the Lady Wildcat."

Lips crinkled around a confident smirk, I tossed her the weapon.

"By my count," she said, catching it one-handed and tucking it away in her pack, "we can be at the Canodill Pass in two weeks. Less, if we just so 'appened to be fortunate enough t'pass through that haunted wood without angerin' its Mistress..."

I didn't react past clenched jaw. Didn't turn away from what had been the Eloran city of Liyas, or acknowledge that she'd spoken. Wasn't sure I was... ready, in spite of all my power.

"What d'you say, lass? Shall we go home?"

I *did* turn, then. Avoided her eye and looked to the place I'd once called home. A place I'd stained black around the edges, twisting it to suit the lies I told myself. Until the Grandmother had been so corrupted I couldn't untangle ugly truth from the myths.

From my own fucking delusional legends of grandeur and destiny.

Alicia touched my elbow, then withdrew. "Mila?"

What right did I have to lay claim to something as pure as the Grandmother?

"Come now, lass. Call that glorious beasty you love so much, and let's go before Marco wakes up and cuts the captain free."

Swallowing the painful lump, I clenched my fists. Sunk *her* claws into my palms and shook my head. "She won't recognize me. Not now."

"You're not so changed," Alicia said, forcing me to look into those sparkling green depths. "A little quieter, perhaps. A touch of wisdom 'round the eyes, but not so different that she'll forget the scent o'your love, yeah?"

Brow creased, I frowned, but conceded her point. Knelt in the soft loam and pressed my palms to the earth, tugging at the Grandmother's skirt.

Hesitant.

And so I was unprepared for the rush of ancient ki that leapt in joyous greeting. Rejoicing and embracing my return with a thousand *thousand* tiny outstretched hands. A tattered sob burst from my aching throat when, in the distance, a lion roared.

"See? Not forgotten. And long as you can stop her from killin' me, I'd say we press on."

Standing, I nodded, letting my tears salt the earth with a plea for forgiveness—and felt something... flicker at the furthest edge of my awareness. Something powerful and wild and not quite sentient. A whisperer in the aether gone the instant I tried to look right at it, seeming to be in two places at once, and nowhere at all.

I whirled, gooseflesh erupting on my skin and *his*, for in the next moment the whisperer vanished. Chased away by the tsunami of wrath that flooded the bond, heralding the onset of a new hunt in a new game.

Baring pointed canines, I grinned. Queen of things both savage and wild, knowing he could feel my unspoken challenge as surely as I knew he was free.

Come out to play, Captain Rawlings...

Howling winds of passion and fury were answer enough, and I turned my back on that city of silver slaves. Knowing I'd be back.

After all... *nothing*—not even the sun itself—could stop the night things from taking wing.

Thank you for reading *Tritan Evolution*.

Now it's time to give *The Last Tritan* a read and see which Tritan series you like best! Flip the page for a full chapter preview of *Flame to Frost, The Last Tritan Book I* and see where it all began...

Grab your copy of Flame to Frost today!

If you like *free things, sneak peaks, giveaways, and super secret news about future projects*, then boiii is there a place for you! Tis called The Daniverse, and you can join by clicking the link or searching for "The Daniverse, by Myra Danvers" on Facebook.

FREE BOOK! Download Swallowed by Darkness now!

"Thrilling, addictive, a bit horrible, but oh so entertaining and funny—truly unique—I loved it!" ~Goodreads reviewer

FLAME TO FROST

Grab your copy of Flame to Frost today!

AUTHOR'S NOTE: Want more Tritan? Well I've got some good news! The ORIGINAL version of The Last Tritan, (an underground, chart-topping cult classic) is now available to purchase for the first time. Same characters, different world, alternate universe. Now you can see what took the internet by storm back in the early days, when Myra Danvers was still just a figment of my wildest dreams... *The Last Tritan* was meant to be read as separate story, and is not related to *Tritan Evolution* aside from the obvious connections. <3

I was eighteen when the capital city of Tritan fell.

With the element of surprise on their side, the fight was relatively bloodless and over within a week. They crushed our communication network, and it was days before we even knew who our attackers were. Once we saw the black-and-gold banners of Caledonia, however, our self-defense attempts were virtually nonexistent—they were known for being ruthless in battle. It was assumed the Caledonians had attacked Tritan for her abundant resources. And it was true—to an extent.

With the government disabled, mass panic quickly followed. Families trying desperately to escape the tattered carcass of Tritan fled to the northern country of Elora, but only found doors slammed shut in their faces. The Elorans were terrified of incurring the wrath of Caledonia.

They were right to fear.

Our enemy had more than a reputation for blood lust—their elite soldiers could channel energy into the weapons they carried. Specially modified guns that fired blasts of pure energy hot enough to burn through anything it encountered made for deadly warriors, unmatched in any known arena.

The true horror of our invasion had yet to be revealed. Renowned for our genteel natures, slight statures, light hair, and fair complexions, our people were valued for our contributions to medical sciences and bountiful food production. For our peacekeepers and healers.

And for our priestesses.

Tritan women who could feel the energy of every organic thing around them. Who could manipulate life by reshaping it as something new—trees, plants, animals—*anything* that held a spark of living energy. Priestesses were famous healers, using their abilities to detect and diagnose ailments in their patients. But the most powerful could direct that energy to heal any injury.

As medics, they might have been invaluable on the battlefield. Might have given our scattered forces a whisper of hope against Caledonia's elite warriors.

But the temple was the first to fall.

The true target of Caledonia's attack, for, by some cruel stroke of fate, the Caledonians could enslave the priestesses in chains of glittering gold. Bound to one of these elite warriors, Tritan's cherished holy women were nothing more than conduits to the world's living energy. Taken by the conquerors who came to enslave, to use until there was nothing left but an empty husk. Tritan burned, and from her smoldering corpse, the enemy rose in a cloud of ash.

Invincible.

Limitless power at their disposal.

There was no chance of a rebellion after that.

But it wouldn't be a story worth telling if it ended there. I escaped the city before the fighting reached us because my father used his position as a senator to get me to safety. Just as he'd done years before, when my modest talents as a potential priestess had begun to manifest. Forbidding me from honing my craft—from wasting my life in selfless worship—was a biased decision that eventually saved my life. Unfortunately, he couldn't secure the same for himself and my mother.

It was the last time I saw them.

Some of Tritan's refugees managed to find a temporary haven in the vast forest separating Tritan and Elora. Not rebels—just desperate people trying to avoid the nets of those hunting them. I was among those small clusters of terrified people, and though I never met another priestess, it became obvious the Caledonians wanted even the ordinary citizens of Tritan. Our unusual coloring made us highly sought after in the slaving markets across the world.

It wasn't long before slavers invaded the woods. Before they attacked.

Drawn in by the ignorance of those who knew nothing of survival in the forest and even less of the stealth needed to escape unnoticed.

Late one evening, I awoke to the scent of meat roasting over a fire. Serenaded by the merry sounds of popping and crackling flames. One of the men had brought down some type of fowl and had started a fire to cook it. The smell of roasted bird soon woke the remaining sleepers, and although we knew better, it was a temptation none could resist.

There was only enough for each of us to have a few mouthfuls of the succulent meat, but as the hot juices dripped off our fingers, I was sure it was worth it—until the slavers crashed through the brush, weapons drawn. The camp sounds, which moments before had been contented eating, became screams of terror as everyone scrambled for safety.

It was my first good look at the dreaded Caledonians.

Where Tritans were slight and fair, the Caledonians were the opposite. Dark hair and eyes with considerably larger, heavily muscled frames.

I had but a moment to make this observation before my impending enslavement became apparent. I was a Tritan priestess, albeit an untrained one, and I couldn't allow myself to fall into the clutches of an elite warrior to be used against my people in such a perverse way.

To my everlasting shame, I took the opportunity the chaos offered and slipped away. I knew I wouldn't have long before the slavers finished subduing my country-men, so I took to the trees. The largest branches were thick enough to jump from one to the other, effectively allowing me to distance myself from any incriminating trails.

Safe in a delicate network of branches, where no bulky Caledonian might follow.

I had a head start, and I wouldn't waste it. After I had almost fallen to my death, I slept the rest of that first night huddled inside a hollow log. I awoke the next morning with bugs crawling all over my skin, tangled in my hair. As it turned out, sleeping in a rotting log was far from the cleanest place I could have chosen.

Pushing aside my revulsion, I brushed away as many insects as I could while listening for any sounds that could be out of place in the silence of the forest. Thankfully, I could hear nothing, so I carefully crawled from my hiding place into the brisk chill of early morning.

I quickly realized I faced more problems than evading capture. If I didn't find a reliable food source, I would likely starve to death before the long winter months. Heavy rainfall was a daily occurrence, so water was not an issue. Being raised with the privilege of being a politician's daughter, I had never lacked fresh meat and vegetables, though I was certainly feeling it now. As far as I knew, starving to death wasn't even the worst of my problems. If I didn't have access to fresh fruit with vitamin C, I could develop scurvy or other issues.

With no option but to deal with one thing at a time, I fashioned a snare for trapping a small animal. I had seen plenty of squirrels and rabbits as I made my plans. I just needed to catch one.

It was three days before I managed to trap anything. By then, I was weak with hunger and spent most of my time sleeping. With a detached certainty, I knew I didn't have much time before I wouldn't be able to drag my tired body to safety if the slavers found me. But to my immense satisfaction, I had a plump rabbit caught in my snare within a few hours of those dreadful thoughts.

All I had to do was kill the fluffy little thing. Placing the blade of my knife at the soft throat, I braced for the kill.

I should have closed my eyes.

Shouldn't have looked into the inky black depths of an innocent creature's terrified gaze. Of their own accord, my fingers began stroking soft brown fur, soothing it. Its little heart beat so fast against my palm that I began to worry it would die from fright in my hands, when I ought to have been eager for its death.

And with a whispered apology, my grip loosened, and I let it go.

I'd showed mercy to an animal that would have made my existence much easier. But when I'd gazed into those beautiful dark eyes and saw the absolute terror I had recently had a taste of, I felt a certain kinship with the captured rabbit.

And I'd failed to push the blade through its soft fur to take its life.

I still faced imminent starvation, and now I was without the strength to check my remaining snares. The chance to change my mind had passed with a breath of mercy.

I collapsed onto the forest floor, staring up at the thick foliage and squirrels as they raced along their treetop highways.

This was the end.

But as I lay there, I noticed the tree above had large green fruits hanging from its branches. Though I didn't recognize them, malnutrition had a funny way of making one keen to try anything. Glancing around, I realized there were several of the fruits scattered across the forest floor. The squirrels certainly seemed to enjoy them, so I hoisted myself off the ground and reached for one. After all, I was beyond the point of caring if I died from eating a poisonous plant.

I bit into the green husk and promptly retched—the flavor and texture made it clear the thing was not for eating. Hurling the offensive fruit against the nearest tree in disgust, I watched with detachment as the green husk exploded, leaving behind an ovular black pit. Frowning, I crawled over to the palm-sized pit for a closer inspection.

"A walnut," I whispered, excitement lending me the energy to find two rocks. Knowing it was edible, I bashed the walnut into smithereens in my enthusiasm. Gleefully picking the pieces out of the shell, I stuffed the 'meat' into my mouth, knowing walnuts were jam-packed with nutrients, proteins, fat, and vitamins and would keep well during the winter months.

At the very least, I knew they would keep me alive.

I spent most of the day collecting walnuts and throwing them against trees to remove the husks. Touching them with my bare hands produced a dark brown stain that no amount of washing could remove. But what did I care about dirty hands when I now had a food source? One that would keep well without spoiling, that I could store for months and eat well even in the winter.

It was time to find shelter.

I decided to take inspiration from the wildlife that thrived, where I could barely take a step without blundering it in some way or another. So, I sat and watched the squirrels and rabbits for the better part of a day, hardly daring to move for fear of disturbing them from their regular habits. I observed as they ate some plants and avoided others, stored food for the coming winter, and fattened themselves on the forest's bounty.

Most importantly, I watched as the squirrels darted in and out of their homes, hidden in the very hearts of the trees. My face cracked in the first genuine smile I'd had since the horror of the invasion.

I had a plan.

Grab your copy of Flame to Frost today!

ALSO BY MYRA DANVERS

Swallowed by Darkness ~ **FREE**

- Grab your free copy of Swallowed by Darkness now!

The Last Tritan

- Flame to Frost, The Last Tritan, Book I
- Frost to Dust, The Last Tritan, Book II
- Dust to Smoke, The Last Tritan, Book III

Tritan Evolution

- Ravenous Innocence, Tritan Evolution, Book I.
- Insatiable Corruption, Tritan Evolution, Book II
- Lavish Destruction, Tritan Evolution, Book III

The Feral Court

- Renegade, the Feral Court, Book I
- Giaus, The Feral Court, Book II
- Sickle, The Feral Court, Book III

Atom and Evil

- Delirium, Atom and Evil, Book I

MYRA DANVERS

USA Today Bestselling author, Myra Danvers, is best known for her compelling mix of unique science fiction and dark fantasy worlds that feature feisty heroines, antihero men, and of course, proper villains. Though you may not always know who is who until the final pages...

facebook.com/MyraDanvers

instagram.com/myradanvers

bookbub.com/profile/myra-danvers

goodreads.com/Myra_Danvers